HEAD OF STATE

It took Hamid-Jones an hour of patient work on the DNA of the Emir's prize stallion which he had been given from the Clonemaster's precious hoard, and he was just about to set the computer when he became aware of a growing hum of voices outside his cubicle.

Rashid poked his head inside the door. "Why are you still hanging around? We're being let out early."

"What are you talking about?" Hamid-Jones asked.

"A holiday's been declared. Three whole days starting at sunset."

"Why? What's it for?"

"Haven't you heard? The Emir is having himself beheaded again."

By Donald Moffitt
Published by Ballantine Books:

THE GENESIS QUEST
THE JUPITER THEFT
SECOND GENESIS

The Mechanical Sky
Book One: CRESCENT IN THE SKY
Book Two: A GATHERING OF STARS*

*Forthcoming

CRESCENT IN THE SKY

Book One of
The Mechanical Sky

Donald Moffitt

A Del Rey Book
BALLANTINE BOOKS • NEW YORK

"We have pried into the sky, but found it filled with strong guards and meteors."

THE KORAN, SURA 72: *The Djinn*

CHAPTER 1

The call to prayer sounded from his wrist monitor, and Abdul Hamid-Jones reluctantly pressed the hold button on the haft of his micromanipulator remote and set it down carefully on the laboratory bench. With a martyr's sigh, he consulted the glowing 3-D arrow that seemed to be floating somewhere within his wrist on the little holographic display.

It was a little complicated this afternoon. Mecca was located somewhere underfoot, through the entire bulk of Mars, with an ambiguous east-west orientation, and moreover, since that face of the Earth happened to be turned away at the moment, it was upside-down in Hamid-Jones's frame of reference.

He cast a last despairing glance at the magnified events unfolding on the big bench-mounted screen. The restriction enzymes had done their work, but DNA was leaking all over the place, and if he didn't do something about annealing the loose ends immediately, the carefully prepared plasmid chimera waiting in the wings would be spoiled. He was almost tempted to skip the afternoon devotion, but the door to his cubicle was open, and the overseer, Yezid the Prod—a man of limited understanding—had been on the prowl all day.

The insect buzz of the muezzin's voice grew more insistent at his wrist. *"Allahu akbar, Allahu akbar!"* it repeated for the last time; *"La ilaha illa Allah!"* With a muttered "All right," Hamid-Jones drew the monofilm prayer rug out of his shirt pocket and unfolded it to full size. He flexed his wrist a couple of times, making sure that the arrow held steady, then hastily made his silent declaration of intention—though somewhat guiltily limiting himself to the minimum number of *rak'a*s.

1

"Allahu akbar," he responded with not a moment to spare and sank to his knees in the light Martian gravity, prostrating himself in the direction that, according to the astronomical computer's tiny brain, most nearly approximated that of Mecca.

Halfway through his specified *rak'a*s, he felt a shadow fall across his back. He knew without looking that it was Yezid and was awfully glad that he had not given in to the impulse to evade his religious duties. Yezid had been more foul-tempered than usual of late. Only a few days ago he had had an unfortunate Callistan slave flogged for a minor infraction of department regulations. Not that Hamid-Jones himself was in danger of such treatment; Yezid would hardly dare to touch an assistant to the Clonemaster of the Royal Stables. But it would be deucedly embarrassing to be hauled in front of a religious court and scolded, and it might hinder his advancement.

The shadow went away. Hamid-Jones finished his prayers and scrambled to his feet. He left the rug where it was; his first thought was for the bright twisting shapes of the gene assembly displayed above the lab bench.

. He gave a groan. It was ruined. Even from the pseudoimage with its computer-assigned colors, he could see that it was a hopeless tangle. The passenger gene had come unstuck and attached itself to a section of an inverted repeat sequence on the wrong strand of the heteroduplex he had created that morning.

He shuddered to think of the consequences if a clone with a hidden defect ever were allowed to come to foal. He was working with genetic material from the Emir's prize stallion. The Emir tended to take a personal interest in the offspring of his beloved al-Janah, the Winged One.

Knowing that it was hopeless, he punched up the magnification and called for a schema to confirm the bad news. The computer obliged with a color-coded abstraction that showed the sequencing of base pairs on the offending palindrome as a series of little plugs and sockets. The replication fork was busily zipping itself up to the end of the molecule—a repeat structure gone wild.

Hamid-Jones flushed it all away. He was going to have to do it all over again, from scratch. Wearily he began assembling the components of another plasmid from the DNA fragments he had in storage.

"Ya Abdul, why so serious?" a voice said from the door. "Coming to tea?"

Hamid-Jones looked around. It was Rashid, from the protein

assembly section. Like himself, Rashid was descended from *mawali*, or "client" forebears, and it showed in Rashid's sandy hair and boiled complexion. Hamid-Jones, on the other hand, might almost have passed for a pure-blooded ethnic Arab—with his hawklike visage, deeper coloring, and fierce dark eyes—but he was painfully aware of his origins. Like it or not, he was an Anglo-Arab—forever to be known in the social scheme of things as an *'arab al masta ariba*, "one who becomes an Arab." He was not as low on the social scale as the ubiquitous *dhimmi*, or unbelievers—who nevertheless enjoyed perfect tolerance as long as they paid the *jizza*, or head tax, of the unconverted—but he would never achieve the status of a true Arab of tribal descent, an *'arab al' ariba*. He would always have to work harder to get ahead.

"No, I'll skip tea today," he told Rashid somewhat brusquely. "I want to finish this."

He bent over the workbench again, a rather ordinary young man in cheap shirt and trousers, with a headcloth that was carelessly askew. Hamid-Jones's six feet two inches would have been considered tall on Earth, but he had already completed half his growth when his parents had emigrated to the Martian Emirate, and as a consequence he was a head shorter than most of his Marsborn co-workers, and had heavier bones and musculature. Strength, he had often had cause to notice, was not as important in the world as height; it was eye level that counted. There was still a trace of the British Protectorate in his Arabic accent—another factor setting him apart.

Rashid did not go away, as Hamid-Jones had hoped. He lingered in the doorway, his eyes straying alertly to the screen. "Let it go, whatever it is," he said. "It can't be that important."

Hamid-Jones reached up and switched to a muon-scope view in uninformative shades of gray. He went on working without replying. After a moment, Rashid tried again.

"Who's it for?" he asked slyly. "Not a falcon or saluki for someone in the palace, is it? That would be a terrific plum."

"It's a horse," Hamid-Jones said unwillingly.

"Ah, a horse. Very nice." Rashid's oily gaze shifted to the sealed cryocontainer that Hamid-Jones had neglected to stow out of sight.

"I'm giving it a third lung, like that mutation that cropped up in the Horse Guard stables."

Rashid pounced immediately. "Ah . . . but you're working with sequestered material, I see. That means . . ."

Hamid-Jones clammed up. "You'd better get going if you don't want to miss the tea break."

"As you like," Rashid said with a shrug. *"Ma'al salaama."* He left, the envy plain in his eyes.

Hamid-Jones set doggedly to work once more. Rashid would be spreading gossip in the canteen, but there was nothing he could do about it. The assignment *was* a plum, and he had no intention of shirking it. The Clonemaster, the esteemed Hassan bin Fahd al-Hejjaj, was grooming him for higher things—there was no doubt about it. There had been other tests before this one.

It was a great opportunity, but not without its perils. One of Hamid-Jones's predecessors in the job had come to the Emir's personal attention—unfavorably—and the story was still told in whispers of how he had been fed alive to the Royal Aviary. Of course the circumstances were hardly comparable; the unfortunate cloning assistant had been guilty not of mere failure, but of stealing sequestered genetic material and selling it to members of the minor aristocracy anxious to improve the breeding of their hunting dogs. But salukis—the Noble Ones—were a royal prerogative. They could never be sold, only exchanged or given as gifts—and that went for their DNA, too. Still, stealing genetic material of treasured animals was a time-honored custom, and it was usually the servants who were caught. Even in the time of the Prophet more than two millennia before, enterprising desert sheiks had schemed to purloin the semen of prize stallions and race it across the sands to waiting mares. That was how the Arabian breed had spread. Nowadays it was done by contraband nucleotides.

It took Hamid-Jones an hour of patient work to put together another plasmid carrying the passenger gene and to tease out an undamaged six-foot strand of the Winged One's DNA from the precious hoard the Clonemaster had entrusted him with. An enucleated egg had already been summoned from the files and was on standby. Now he was ready to prepare the cleavage sites.

He was just about to set the computer to do a search of base pair sequences on the long molecule when he became aware of a growing hum of voices in the main dome outside his cubicle. Doors slammed. There was a gregarious babble, almost like a Thursday night. A chattering group hurried past his door, and he could distinguish calls of *"Allah isalmak"* and "Take care." It sounded as if the laboratory was emptying out, but it was still a couple of hours till quitting time.

Rashid poked his head inside the door with a big grin. Beyond him, Hamid-Jones could see two of his friends, Ja'far and Feisel, looking flushed and excited.

"Why are you still hanging around?" Rashid demanded. "We're being let off early."

"Huh? What are you talking about?"

"A holiday's been declared," Feisel supplied, leaning in past Rashid's shoulder. "Three whole days, starting at sunset. There'll be public feasts and everything. Old Yezid Bent-Stick came round himself to pass the word. *Yallah*, come on, the place is closed."

"But we've just celebrated *Iid al-Fitr*. And the Feast of the Sacrifice is still two months off."

"It's a new holiday, I tell you," Feisel said impatiently. "It's been declared by the Vizier at the orders of the Emir himself."

Hamid-Jones scratched his head. "Why? What's it for?"

"Haven't you heard? The Emir is having himself beheaded again."

The passageways were crowded with people milling about looking for something to do or hurrying home early to make holiday preparations. A few scruffy vendors and street entertainers were already circulating to get a head start on the pleasure-seeking throngs that could be expected later as the celebrations gathered steam; Hamid-Jones at one point had to squeeze past a clot of idlers who had collected around a juggling act, completely blocking the intersection of the Tharsis North and Gazelle Lane tunnels. There was not a tricab to be had when he emerged from the transit tube, and he was resigned to walking the rest of the way home.

He had tried to stay on at the darkened lab until he could finish the annealing job and get the altered nucleus safely into the egg, but Yezid had come around with his jangling key ring and kicked him out. Now another clone had been spoiled, and Hamid-Jones was going to have to screw up enough courage to ask the Clonemaster for more specimens from the Winged One after the three-day holiday was over.

He dodged past some workmen who were stringing colored lights across the main concourse and ducked into the maze of narrow, winding tunnels that led to the Old City, the *Medina al-Kadima*. Here the warrens of closetlike shops that lined the walls had been hacked out of the rock of Mars itself, and generations of owners had been adding illegally to their property by excavating the long alcoves inch by inch at the rear; sections of tunnel had been known to collapse when the burrowers went too far and met fellow moles from parallel lanes.

"*Balak, balak,* watch where you're going, fellow!" a voice shouted close behind him, and he jumped aside to let a beeping scooter past. Its rider was a plump, complacent man in flowing robes, with baskets piled up high behind him—a merchant laying in stock to take advantage of the unexpected fête, Hamid-Jones supposed. The man's robes brushed Hamid-Jones's leg as he squeezed past, and the scooter continued threading its dignified way through the thickening traffic, its wheels masked by the merchant's skirts, so that he seemed like a floating apparition in white.

The *suq* was already gay with colored streamers that the shopkeepers had draped from the upper arcades, and Hamid-Jones could sense movement behind the lacy shutters where hidden eyes followed the excitement down below. One of the shopkeepers saw him standing there and came out of his boxlike stall to accost him.

"*Ya sidi,* don't you want to wear your finest for the holiday?" he said, staring accusingly at Hamid-Jones's cheap plastic sandals. "*Yallah,* let me show you a pair of shoes in real leather."

Hamid-Jones shook him off and continued. Other tradesmen clamored at him from their stalls, for the most part automatically after assessing him as a poor prospect, and turned to importune the better-dressed uptunnel slummers and unwary tourists from the starships docked at Phobos.

A man with alcohol on his breath bumped into him and reeled away after mumbling an apology. An early celebrant with the bad judgment to be drunk in public. Hamid-Jones hurried to be out of the idiot's vicinity as quickly as possible. It was best not to be around such people. Sooner or later they were picked up by the religious police. Even the rug merchant toward whom the man now lurched was not eager to have anything to do with him and melted into the depths of his cubicle.

Another twenty minutes' walking took Hamid-Jones to his own tunnel, the Street of the Well, with its cleft ceiling and rough-hewn rear escarpment. The well was only a centuries-old memory, but the Emir's pipelines brought untaxed water to the district, and even the meanest streets in the capital city were plugged into the power grid.

He reached the blank stone face of his lodgings and rattled

the gate until the porter came to let him in. "*Ya* Ibrahim, you're getting slow," he said, smiling.

"People going in and out at any hour they choose," the old man grumbled. "What's the world coming to?" He was a dour, creaking person with one milky eye where an autocloned replacement, after some accident in his youth, had failed to take. Hamid-Jones had often urged him to have it done over again and had even offered to take him to the Palace employee clinic where he could help him finagle a discount, but the old man would only sigh, "*Inch'allah*, it is the will of God." Hamid-Jones knew that he was afraid of the procedure.

The gate swung shut behind them, and Ibrahim shuffled off to his cubbyhole in the wall where his equally ancient wife no doubt was preparing his holiday supper.

Hamid-Jones skirted the rocky wall of the courtyard toward the back stairs that led to his own room, hoping to avoid a protracted encounter with the small coterie of lodgers who liked to sit out here at this hour for tea and interminable conversation. Mr. Faqoosh the mullah, in particular, liked to lecture him at length about the wicked ways of today's youth.

But they saw him, and he was trapped. "*Ya* Abdul, come join us!" Mr. Najib called out genially. Mr. Najib was the manager of a prayer-rug factory with a good source of income from rake-offs on government contracts; a portly, self-important man who liked to lord it over the others.

"*Bikul surur*, with great pleasure," Hamid-Jones replied, and trudged resignedly across the yard to the circle of old chairs and sofas that had been arranged cosily to make a sort of *diwaniyyah*—an open-air social hall—in the angle of the wall.

He sat down on one of the sprung couches next to Mr. Fahti, an inoffensive little man who was employed as a *farash*, the person who made the coffee, in some government bureau—and saw too late that he had placed himself opposite the mullah.

He looked around. It was a larger group than usual this evening, when people would be dying to discuss the meaning of today's surprising turn of events. Hamid-Jones saw Mr. Kareem, a desk clerk at the Tharsis-Savoy, who usually kept aloof, and shabby, furtive Mr. Daud, who lived in one room with a rarely glimpsed wife and a swarm of noisy brats whom he kept hidden behind a curtain.

"*Messakum, ya* Abdul. *Allah bil khair.*" The greetings began, and he had to go through them one by one and respond in kind until everybody had had a chance at him. Then it was his turn; he inquired ritually about the health of each of them until the circle was completed a second time.

"Have some tea, *ya* Abdul," Mr. Najib coaxed him, and the landlord's servant, Saleh, was at his elbow, pouring it for him out of an imitation Wedgwood pot that Hamid-Jones recognized as being from the landlord's second-best service, trotted out for special occasions. The landlord was laying out the refreshments this evening, too—trays of hard candies, melon seeds, and sweet cakes. Hamid-Jones was impressed. The servant passed him a tray of sweet cakes. Hamid-Jones accepted one reluctantly; the landlord, al-Hajji Arif ibn Zayd, a stingy buzzard who had long since forgotten whatever virtues he had acquired on the pilgrimage to Mecca that had given him the right to his honorific, usually found a way to make one pay for his sporadic acts of "hospitality."

He bit into the cake. It was a *kolaicha*, made with cardamom seed, just as if it were the Small Holiday itself that was being celebrated.

The discussion that had been going on before his arrival resumed in full swing. "I don't understand why the Emir decided to have himself beheaded all of a sudden," Mr. Najib said with a frown. "His current body can't be more than fifty years old."

"That's right." Little Mr. Fahti nodded. "I remember when the last transposition of heads took place. It was exactly thirty years ago—the Year of the Prophet 2451. I remember it well because that was the year the Christians—may God forgive their impiety—celebrated the beginning of the year 3000 in *their* calendar. They made a great fuss over it. Some of their more fanatic sects even claimed their messiah would reappear to usher in the Third Millennium and overturn the order of things. They stopped paying their head tax, can you imagine? There would be no taxes in heaven, they said. But the Emir—may God preserve him—was merciful. He gave them time to come to their senses, and then when it became plain that there would be no Second Coming, made an example of the leaders who had led them astray. The cages were on display for a month, if you remember, until people began to complain about the smell. Then he collected double the *jizza* for that year, to the enrichment of the treasury. Such is his wisdom."

"The Emir is too lenient with unbelievers," the mullah growled. "The old Emir would have done away with all of them, *jizza* or no *jizza*."

"Yes, yes," Mr. Najib said, impatient at the digression, "it was thirty years ago exactly." He turned indulgently to Hamid-Jones to include him in the conversation. "You would not remember, of course, *ya* Abdul; it was before you were born."

"That is true, *ya sidi*," Hamid-Jones acknowledged. It was all that was required of him for the moment.

"The cloning prosthesis was a youth of twenty," Mr. Najib continued. "It's still a good, strong body—good for another ten or fifteen years, conservatively speaking."

Mr. Fahti's head bobbed up and down in agreement. "It's another twenty years before it's due to show the first signs of the degenerative disorder that always afflicts the Emir at that age, and afflicted his father before him, may God rest his memory."

"Twenty years at *least*," Mr. Najib said firmly. "Changing bodies is not a thing to be undertaken lightly. The Emir's previous grafts have always been delayed until his body was well past sixty—not that any of us are old enough to remember *those* occasions personally. And then, from the tales of my father and grandfather, the event was scheduled at least two years in advance, so that the public celebrations could be properly planned and the utmost profit taken." His ample jowls quivered. "The loss to the economy will be severe, and that is what I find particularly hard to understand. The Emir has always been considerate of the interests of businessmen. This sudden rush to decapitate seems precipitous . . . even impulsive." He added hastily, "Though I'm sure the Emir's advisors must have had good reasons for urging this abrupt course of action on him at this time."

"It's politics," Mr. Kareem said.

Mr. Najib blinked at the interruption. "I beg your pardon?"

"It's all to do with the politics of the Caliphate Congress." The dapper desk clerk crossed an indolent leg to show off a foot shod in English leather and looked round the dowdy circle with a condescending smile. "It's obvious to anyone with an understanding of these matters."

"And why is that?" Mr. Najib asked politely.

"He wants to complete the hajj before the pan-Islamic summit next year," Mr. Kareem said, as if he were amused by the subject. "He simply wants to get his decapitation over with. The pilgrimage season is only two months away, and he'll need time to recover."

"But the Emir has already completed the hajj—and more than once, may God reward him for his devotion," Mr. Fahti pointed out.

"Aha, but only his head has performed the hajj. His current body has not been thus sanctified; the last time he visited Mecca, he was wearing a *different* body. And some nitpicking mullah would be sure to point that out at the conference."

"By heaven, he's right!" burst out one of the regulars, a bearded retiree named Khaled, who was obscurely related to the landlord. "When you think of it that way, the Emir is a hajji only from the neck up."

Kareem gave a self-satisfied nod. "Exactly. You can imagine the ammunition that would give the Emir's rivals for the Caliphate—especially the Sultan of Alpha Centauri. His lobbyists would be working overtime to sway the delegates. No, my friends, the Emir is a very smart politician. He's simply moving decisively to remove any possible shadow from the legitimacy of his candidacy."

Mr. Fahti looked stricken. "The Emir at least is part hajji. But the Sultan is not a hajji at all, and never will be, may God destroy him for his evil machinations!"

Mr. Faqoosh, the mullah, scowled under heavy black brows. "The Centaurans are spawn of the devil, perish their hands and perish they themselves," he rumbled. "They will be dragged screaming to the great fire whose fuel is men."

"I've met many Centaurans, and I can assure you that they are not devils," Kareem said with a laugh. "They're like any other star dwellers who stop off at the Savoy on their way to Earth, and a fair number of them have come to this system to make the pilgrimage to Mecca."

"Assuming it is so that the Emir plans to perform the hajj once more for political reasons," Mr. Najib said, looking down his nose at the upstart desk clerk, "why is it necessary for him to change bodies? He could just as well do it with his current prosthesis."

"An impression of vigor is very important in politics," Kareem said promptly. "A new, young body will be an asset in his campaigning. Besides, if he waited too long to make the change, there's always the possibility that he might be caught short at an inconvenient time."

It was too much for the mullah. "It is forbidden to alter the creations of Allah!" he erupted. "If sculpture is enjoined by the Prophet, how much greater an abomination is it to sculpt living flesh? Six-legged camels! Horses with toes! Turbofalcons and three-headed hunting dogs! The production of novelties for the idle rich! And now the idolaters have not shrunk from dabbling in man himself!''

He sat back, breathing hard and dribbling a little at the corner of the mouth. Faqoosh was a dear, seedy old thing, and everyone tried to help him out with the odd donation, but there was no denying that his views were antediluvian; he was one of those extreme fundamentalists who held that Mars was flat, space travel a hoax perpetrated on the pilgrims, and that Mecca was actually on the other side of the Tharsis Range and could be reached on foot. He had no regular connection with a mosque and eked out a bare living by presiding at *kraya*s and filling in at weddings and sacrifices.

Some of the other lodgers looked away in delicate embarrassment. Hamid-Jones carefully studied his fingernails. Poor, secretive Mr. Daud cringed in his chair, terrified at being caught in company where the Emir and his self-cloning program were criticized even by implication.

Mr. Najib moved smoothly to deflect the conversation back toward politics. He dispensed a smile to Hamid-Jones and said, ''Well, here is the young man who ought to know about the ins and outs of such things. Tell us, *ya* Abdul, the announcement from the Palace caught all of us by surprise, but you must have been in on the preparations. What's the inside story? *Is* the Emir renewing himself because of the hajj?''

''I'm only a junior cloning assistant and not privy to matters of state,'' Hamid-Jones protested. He saw the mullah glaring at him and gulped before going on. ''My work is in the stables— mostly things like propagating mounts for the Horse Guard. The Emir insists on them being uniform, and he changes their look frequently. Earlier this year, for example, we got out a rush order for one hundred duplicates of a hoofed albino that had caught his fancy. Of course we often craft a special order for some high palace official, like when the Vizier wanted a peacock that could sing and we provided a flock of peacock-nightingale chimerae for his garden, but mostly it's just dull, ordinary work.'' He did not mention the special job the Clonemaster had entrusted him with.

Mr. Najib raised a heavy eyelid. ''You're not involved in the cloning of spare parts for . . . important functionaries, then?'' Everybody knew he was being too discreet to refer to the Emir directly.

''Oh, no,'' Hamid-Jones demurred. ''Medical cloning is the province of the Palace Clonemaster.''

"New hearts for overweight eunuchs," Kareem said irreverently. "Livers and lungs for faithful courtiers. The occasional royal brain cell."

"No," Hamid-Jones said shortly, refusing to rise to the bait. It was common knowledge that the Emir kept himself on this side of senility through periodic cortical transplants. His head was close to two hundred years old and showed it, and one day it would finally give out, despite the succession of youthful bodies.

The hotel clerk persisted with bright malice. "And you're not involved in any of the Emir's pet projects, like the research program for genetically altering women for submissiveness and nonsentience?"

That, too, was common knowledge. It was one of the Emir's more unpleasant ideas. The first, unfortunate project managers had tried to point out the immense difficulty of stabilizing sex-linked characteristics and limiting them to genes on the X chromosome, and the fact that a change in human heredity such as the one contemplated by the Emir would end up affecting the entire population, both male and female. Computer simulations had borne them out. But the Emir was simply unable to grasp the notion and had executed the bearers of the bad tidings for willful disobedience. The subsequent project managers had been hacks who strung the Emir along and brought him hopeful tidbits from time to time. Mullahs like Mr. Faqoosh didn't last long around the Emir either; those who opposed such tampering with the clay of Allah had been done away with and replaced by tame religious authorities who were adept at finding theological justification in the Koran for the Emir's wishes.

"We don't work with human genetic material in our department," Hamid-Jones said stiffly. "Of course on great state occasions, like the decapitation ceremony tomorrow, my chief, the Clonemaster of the Royal Stables, the noble Hassan bin Fahd al-Hejjaj, will be present as a matter of professional courtesy. But I myself have never been within the inner palace precincts."

"Come, come, Abdul, you are too modest," Mr. Najib said insincerely.

It was the taciturn Dr. Daud, unexpectedly, who got the conversation back on track a second time, to everyone's relief. "Issayid Fahti is right," he ventured timidly. "The Emir doesn't need to make another hajj. The Sultan of Alpha Centauri is his only serious rival for the Caliphate, and the Sultan will never make the hajj. He doesn't dare to leave his kingdom for the length of time it would take.''

He gathered his frowsy robes about him and shrunk within himself again.

The others nodded agreement. ''Alpha Centauri is the closest of all the kingdoms that lie beyond the sun,'' Mr. Najib said, taking up the theme, ''but the round trip still takes ten years, even at speeds close to that of light. Any ruler would be stupid to leave his affairs unattended for that length of time. One cannot rule by radio, especially when the radio message takes almost as long as the physical journey. Why, the Centauran Sultanate could be overthrown by an usurper and the event not even *known* for four years!''

''Yes, and how much truer that is for the furthest kingdoms, like Beta Hydri,'' Mr. Fahti put in. ''Intrigues at home would run wild. Time may shrink for the traveler—Allah be praised for his miracles—but whole new dynasties could spring up while a ruler absented himself. That is why those who hold power in their hands—may God forgive them for their neglect of His injunctions—are precisely the ones who never visit our sun to perform the hajj, save for a few sainted exceptions, like the sovereign of Tau Ceti—may God ease his way to Paradise—who renounced his throne and came to Mecca as a simple pilgrim in the winter of his years.''

''And that is why Islam is at peace, brothers,'' the gray-bearded pensioner, Khaled, said sagely. ''Allah has arranged the laws of nature so that there is no way for an ambitious ruler to run an interstellar empire.''

''No way to wield *temporal* power, I grant you,'' Kareem said, carefully picking a piece of lint off the sleeve of his al-Sevilerow jacket. ''Not with a four-year communication lag even for the Sultan of Alpha Centauri. Even if he were to govern through the most trusted of satraps, he'd find it impossible to react to events. And if a satrap got too big for his britches, how could he be replaced? Poisoned through a spy at court? The exercise would take eight years from informer to assassin.'' He flashed an irritating smile. ''No, the Sultan knows that empire in the usual sense is impossible. But if the Caliphate were to be revived—ah, that's another matter entirely.''

''Whoever became Caliph would be the undisputed spiritual leader of all Islam,'' Mr. Fahti said as sternly as his mild nature would allow him to. ''He would exercise the moral authority passed on by the hand of the Prophet himself.''

Kareem favored him with a condescending stare. "Not only moral authority, my friend. We may take a lesson from the Christians. Through all the long centuries of darkness, the kings ruled Europe, but the Pope ruled the kings. And Rome remained the real center of wealth and power."

Mr. Faqoosh stirred and muttered a little at the mention of Christians, but there was no outburst from him, for which Hamid-Jones was grateful. The Joneses had always been as good Moslems as anyone else, but Hamid-Jones had received his share of thoughtless snubs as a child and had never entirely outgrown the old sensitivity.

"Alpha Centauri would become the center of things—the glittering capital of the Islamic universe, as Baghdad was in the days of the Abbasid caliphs," Kareem went on expansively. "It would draw in the wealth of the stars. And power goes with wealth, as is well known."

"This is all nonsense," Mr. Najib said, finally losing his patience. "The Sultan cannot campaign effectively for the Caliphate from afar. The Emir is a shoo-in."

Mr. Najib's gray-bearded relative cleared his throat and said with all due deference, "There are those who favor King Bandar al-Saud of Greater Arabia. As custodian of Mecca, he has a natural claim."

"The king is a mere tour director and hotel keeper, living off the alms of pilgrims," Mr. Najib said scornfully. "No, my friends, Earth is too fragmented to agree on one of its own. It's the Emir or nobody."

"I don't agree," Kareem persisted, either too stupid or too arrogant to know that he had been rebuked by the older man. "The Sultan of Alpha Centauri has his adherents here. His credentials for donning the robe of the Prophet are impressive, despite the fact that he's never performed the hajj. Not only is he a member of Mohammed's tribe, the Quraish, and a certified *chereef*, as the Sunnis require, but it is being put about that he is a descendant of Ali, the fourth Caliph, which makes him acceptable to the Shi'ites. Moreover, he has the Twelvers wrapped around his little finger. There are those among his followers who believe him to be the reappeared twelfth imam, the Expected Mahdi—the Rightly Guided One himself—and I must admit that he encourages this belief with a certain amount of mumbo jumbo."

Mr. Faqoosh almost choked on his tea. "Blasphemy!" he sputtered.

"Now, now, *sidi*," Mr. Najib soothed him. "Don't upset yourself. No one here believes that. He is only repeating what is said by foreigners. We need not take it seriously."

"The Mahdi was raised up by Allah and hidden somewhere between heaven and earth!" the mullah ranted. "On the day when the sun will be folded up—when the skies will split and the stars scatter—he will return to show us the way! There have been false Mahdis before, and they will roast in hell!"

"Yes indeed," Kareem said languidly. "There are always fanatics, like the mad mullah, Mohammed Ahmed, who gave the British such a hard time at Khartoum, or that lot who actually seized the Great Mosque in Mecca a thousand years ago, and had to be flushed out by the Saudi army. *Their* Mahdi, as I recall, turned out to be some lunatic university student with mystic pretensions."

Mr. Faqoosh was actually foaming at the mouth. Hamid-Jones watched, fascinated, as a bubble grew at the mullah's scraggly fringe of beard and burst.

"The Sultan is certainly wicked to encourage such claims," Mr. Najib interposed hastily. "But he is an arrant mischief-maker. On the one hand he claims the bond of Islamic brotherhood and sends the Emir gifts of Centauran novelties. On the other hand, his agents secretly channel funds to terrorist groups like the followers of the Pretender, al-Sharq, whose forebears were ousted by the Emir's father, but who persists in claiming that *he* is the true Emir!"

"He also provides funds for the Christian Jihad, or so I have heard," Mr. Fahti said. "Anything to stir up trouble."

"It was the Christian fedayeen who claimed responsibility for the rash of recent bombings of the oxygen pipelines," Khaled, the retiree, said with a sober nod. "A troublesome and contentious people."

"So did the pan-Sufist *mujahidin* and the Wahhabi Revivalists and the Popular Front for the Liberation of Israel and a half-dozen other splinter groups with various causes." Mr. Najib sighed. "It's impossible to know *who* was responsible. We live in difficult times."

With the conversation safely back on a secular plane, Mr. Faqoosh subsided. Everybody relaxed.

"Islam has been headless for too long," Khaled agreed. "The *Nadha*—the Great Resurgence—has lasted for a thousand years now, and in all that time there has been no Caliph. But now, by

the grace of God—and if the Caliphate Congress does its work—
we will have one, and it will be our own Emir!''

There was a pause while everyone digested this, and then Mr.
Fahti, his eyes shining, said, ''Think of it! A Caliphate Congress
has not been convened since the Christians' twentieth century,
when the Ottoman empire finally disintegrated and the Turk,
Mustafa Kemal—may God roast him—abolished the Caliphate
and tried to Westernize his country in imitation of the British
and the Germans. A golden age is coming, my friends!''

''Yes, that was the start of it, though no one realized it at the
time,'' Mr. Najib agreed. ''The Christians had their two thousand years, and then it was our turn again. Allah saw fit to give
us most of the world's precious oil—and the resources to invest
massively in space—just as the westerners lost their steam.''

''We have a thousand years to go, it seems,'' Kareem said
with a thin smile.

''The universe is Allah's,'' Mr. Najib said comfortably. ''The
next thousand years is just the beginning.''

''Ah, here comes our landlord,'' Kareem said, getting to his
feet. ''You'll excuse me if I don't stay. I have a previous en-
gagement.''

''A godless young man.'' Mr. Najib frowned when Kareem
had gone. ''Typical of the new generation.''

He smiled belatedly to show that he did not intend to include
Hamid-Jones in his condemnation, and Mr. Fahti picked up the
cue.

''Yes, that Kareem pup will talk out of turn someday in front
of the wrong people, and then the *shurtayeen* will come in the
night to take him away—may God have pity on him then. But
not all of today's youth are so thoughtless. Our Abdul is a fine
young man who knows how to show respect to his elders, and
if his attendance at Friday mosque is not as regular as it might
be, he is not given to mocking the order of things to show his
cleverness.''

He smiled a yellow-toothed benediction at the blushing
Hamid-Jones.

''Quite,'' Mr. Najib said with a broad wink to the others,
''though I think our young friend's mind may be too much on
the ladies. Those nighttime excursions. That preoccupied look.
Too much mooning about on street corners, staring up at harem
windows, perhaps? We all ought to know, eh? We're not too old
to remember what it is like. Take my advice, *ya* Abdul—you

should marry and settle down, and then you would not be so nervous.''

Hamid-Jones writhed in embarrassment. The others regarded him benignly.

"Let me make an appointment for you with a friend of my cousin," Khaled offered. "The family is trying to arrange a marriage for a very fine girl who is already sixteen and becoming overripe. The girl has nice eyes, and is the daughter of a *chereef*. You should snap her up before someone else does."

Even Mr. Faqoosh joined the nods of approval and murmured grudgingly, "The sacred Koran tells us, 'Blessed are the believers who control their sexual desires except with their wives and slave girls, which is blameless, but whoever goes beyond that is a transgressor.' "

"Perhaps you prefer your horses, *ya* Abdul," Mr. Najib teased. "The Prophet also has said, 'After woman came the horse, for the enjoyment and happiness of man.' "

The others laughed. Hamid-Jones smiled weakly.

"It is some particular girl, is it, *ya* Abdul?" Mr. Fahti probed kindly. "Nothing can come of pining. You should make a straightforward offer to her kinsmen."

Hamid-Jones was saved from having to reply by the arrival of the landlord, who planted himself in their midst, looked them over sourly, and said in Terran style, "*Ayamak sa'ida, ya jamas. Happy holiday.*"

The others inclined their heads and returned the greeting. "Good evening, *ya* hajji Araf ibn Zayd." "*Salaam aleikum.*" "*Messakum, Allah bil khair.*"

Mr. Najib became noticeably less expansive; he could not compete with ibn Zayd's status as a hajji, though he had been telling people for years that he had long had the passage money to Earth put aside and that he intended to make the pilgrimage as soon as the rug factory could spare him.

Ibn Zayd rocked on his heels for a moment, sucking on a tooth. He was a sallow, liverish individual, narrow as a slat except for a hard round belly that made a bulge under a crimson cummerbund. Finally he mustered a grimace that passed for a smile and said, "On this happy occasion, I would be honored if you gentlemen would be my guests at a repast to celebrate *al-Id al-Rass*, the Feast of the Head, which the Emir has proclaimed."

To punctuate his words, his servant, Saleh, bustled up and began clearing away the plates of refreshments.

"We would be delighted, hajji," Mr. Fahti said. Mr. Najib quickly put on an ingratiating smile and echoed, "Yes, of course, hajji." Mr. Daud, with a furtive glance at the quarters where he kept his wife secreted, accepted with alacrity, and the others followed suit.

"And you, *ya* Abdul?" the landlord said, looking down his nose at Hamid-Jones.

"Thank you, hajji, no," Hamid-Jones stammered. "I'm not hungry. I stopped for a bite at the *suq* on my way home."

The landlord studied him with pursed lips, saying nothing. Hamid-Jones was sure that ibn Zayd knew about the strictly illegal alcohol burner he kept in his nonhousekeeping room, on which he cooked an occasional frugal bachelor meal to save money, and was only waiting for the opportune moment to charge him for it.

Mr. Fahti came to his rescue. "Our young friend has no appetite. He is in love."

He had to endure another small round of gentle teasing after that. "*Ya* Abdul, you should eat to keep up your strength," Mr. Najib winked.

"I can have the slave girl bring you up some tea and falafel later," ibn Zayd said, unsmiling. "No charge."

"Please don't bother, hajji," Hamid-Jones said hastily. He made his escape, feeling the eyes of Mr. Fahti and the others on him as he crossed the rocky courtyard and climbed the outside stairs to his room.

CHAPTER 2

The sun slammed Hamid-Jones across the eyes, and he awoke with a start. A glance at the window showed him that he had forgotten to close the curtains the night before, and a preliminary buzzing at his wrist told him that he had also neglected to turn off his communicator. With a groan, he turned over and tried to squeeze his eyes shut.

"Prayer is better than sleep," the little voice exhorted, as if reading his thoughts. He punched savagely at the button, and the muezzin's miniature face disappeared from the tiny holo display, to be replaced by an image of the time. He squinted at it blearily. Something was wrong; dawn should have been at least another hour away.

Then he remembered; it was Decapitation Day. It must have been arranged for the sun to rise early this morning, in order to give an extra measure of time for all the festive activities.

He padded barefoot to the window. People were already moving about in the Street of the Well, which was just visible over the lowest part of the courtyard wall. He raised his eyes to the overhanging tent of rock and, yes, there indeed was the street's piece of sun, piped down from the surface and blazing pinkly from the big overhead mirrors. The engineers would have had to readjust the tilt of one of the orbital mirrors—even alter its orbit—but of course no expense could be spared where the Emir was concerned.

The overhead mirrors had been washed sometime during the night, and the multiplied images of the golfball sun were hard and bright, free of the film of dust that ordinarily gave the Street of the Well such a dingy appearance by daylight.

He looked down into the courtyard and saw Mr. Faqoosh in his tatty robes leading a small band of the faithful in the morning prayer. Sandals and shoes were lined up in a neat row and prayer rugs were already spread out. Hamid-Jones stepped back from the window so that the mullah would not see him.

The muezzin's call made a noise like a trapped wasp. Hamid-Jones started to turn it off, then the sound of the response from the worshippers in the courtyard weakened his resolve. He performed his ablutions in one minute flat, jammed his keffia down over his head, checked the current location of Mecca in the miniaturized *zij*—incidentally discovering that Mr. Faqoosh and his flock were facing the wrong way—and was down on his knees, his forehead touching the bare floor, in time to catch up.

Finished, he scowled at his communicator, and this time he did turn it off. By Allah, today was a day off, and he was going to enjoy the morning, at least, without anyone bothering him!

He cast a glance at his bed, but he was too wide-awake now to go back to it. He fixed himself a breakfast of tea, bread, and leftover *fool* from one of the fast-food places in the *suq*, reheated on the little alcohol stove, and sat down to eat.

He found after a few bites that he wasn't very hungry. He pushed the plate aside. Mr. Fahti had been uncomfortably close to the mark the previous night. Perhaps love did affect the appetite.

Or perhaps it was only a sense of hopelessness that was robbing him of the pleasure of the day. He cursed himself for an idiot. Nothing could come of foolish yearnings; Mr. Fahti had been right there, too.

He moped around half the morning, hearing the crowds in the street grow steadily noisier and the sound of hired musicians drifting in from adjoining courtyards where various private celebrations were in progress. There was nothing on television except respectful commentators droning on about the day's preparations, mullahs preaching, shots of crowded mosques, and long shots of the Martian surface looking toward the candy minarets of the New Palace, where the big event was going to take place. Below, from the kitchen and dining hall, he could hear the clatter of utensils and the scurrying feet of servants as tonight's feast was readied. Hamid-Jones grimaced. He had better leave the house or he'd be invited to that one, too. The prospect of having to endure the stultifying company of the other lodgers for endless hours of ritual conversation, and then being charged for it by the landlord, did not appeal to him at all.

He rummaged through his closet for a seldom-worn djellaba—everyone outside would be dressed in their finest, and he did not want to be conspicuous—and sat down on the bed to put on a suitable pair of shoes. From outside came the sound of footsteps on the stone staircase, accompanied by scuffling and laughter. A moment later they were knocking on his door.

"*Ya* Abdul, open up!"

It was no good pretending he wasn't home; the television was still on. He turned down the sound and opened the door. Ja'far and Feisel tumbled inside, still horsing around.

"Still here? Feisel thought we might catch you. We thought we'd stop by and pick you up. What are you waiting for?" Ja'far's eyes fell on the djellaba, Hamid-Jones's Friday best, laid out on the bed. "We're just on our way to collect Rashid, and then we're going to the Upper Promenade. That's where the best entertainments are—they're having a regular *fechta*, with acrobats, stick fighters, skits, and there'll be a feast laid on by the Vizier. Pigeon pie, stuffed lamb for everybody—no expense spared!"

"And afterward," Feisel put in as he and Ja'far winked and nudged each other, "we may even visit a house of women that Rashid's heard about. He swears he's already been twice, but I think he's still working up his nerve."

"Uh . . . thanks, but I thought I'd just stay home and watch it on television."

"What?" Ja'far's tone was incredulous. "Don't be a stick-in-the-mud. That's the trouble with you, *ya* Abdul. All work, no fun. Loosen up! What's life for?"

"Besides," Feisel pointed out, "there'll be big screens set up at all the public feasts—the mosques, too. So you won't miss anything."

"Ugh, who wants to see it anyway?" Ja'far said, making a face.

"Well, how about it?" Feisel demanded.

"I can't," Hamid-Jones said. "Go on without me. Have a good time. *Insharih!*" He saw Feisel's eyes resting on the good djellaba and lied: "I promised to be at the feast here, and then I've got to go to the mosques with the mullah who lives downstairs."

"Oh, come on, Feisel," Ja'far snapped. "Can't you see he's got something better planned?"

"Honestly," Hamid-Jones said. "*Bisarafi.*"

"Sure," Feisel said with a wink. "*Ya sitan.* Don't get yourself in trouble."

Ja'far took Feisel by the arm and led him to the door. Hand on the latch, he turned and said to Hamid-Jones, "If you change your mind, meet us at Sultana's Paradise on the fourth level later."

Feisel rolled his eyes, and the two of them left, giggling.

Hamid-Jones watched from the window as they crossed the courtyard, threading their way through the folding tables that the landlord had set up there. Rice was boiling in a great cauldron, and two bedraggled sheep, bleating piteously, were tied up in a corner, waiting to be sacrificed. Two sheep didn't seem like much for the size of the expected company indicated by the tables, but you could always trust the skinflint of a landlord to extract the maximum profit from any situation, even a festive occasion like *al-Id al-Rass*.

He waited until he was sure that Ja'far and Feisel were safely gone, then put on the djellaba, chose his best braided headrope to hold his keffia in place, and slipped out through the courtyard without encountering anybody. His heart pounding with excitement, he pushed his way on foot through the thick crowds toward the tube station that would take him to the Bab al-Dahub, the Golden Gate quarter, where he would find the only thing that mattered in the universe.

The Street of the Peacock was one of the Bab al-Dahub's better neighborhoods, a coveted address for medium-level officials and aspiring individuals with private wealth, though there was still a lot of old money there to give the place its cachet.

Hamid-Jones loitered against a wall, trying to be inconspicuous. When he thought he saw a porter across the way scrutinizing him, he sauntered to the corner and came back to take up his post again a few feet further on. The traffic flow was not as heavy here as in the Street of the Well, and the people were better dressed. Once he saw some gaudily costumed street players attempt to put on a skit, but a policeman came along to break it up and send them on their way. The actor playing the Emir, looking headless in his padded costume with its framework to build up the shoulders, attracted stares as he strode away with the oversize papier-mâché head tucked under his arm. No soliciting allowed, evidently, though the police did not molest a stilt-walker who moved along without stopping, collecting alms on the go by thrusting a tin cup at the end of an extensible arm under the noses of startled passersby.

He raised his eyes for the hundredth time to the small upper window set high in the blank wall across the street. This time he was rewarded by a glimpse of movement and color behind the carved wooden screen. Then it was gone, and he was left to continue his fruitless vigil again.

This is madness, he thought miserably. It is unmitigated folly. If he were caught staring up at the women's quarters, making a nuisance of himself like this, there was no way he could possibly explain himself. Everything he had worked for could go down the drain in five minutes.

What made it all the more reprehensible was the fact that he had been inside as an invited guest a score of times. For this was the house of the Clonemaster, his lord and patron, Hassan bin Fahd al-Hejjaj.

And within was the Clonemaster's treasure, his daughter Lalla bint Hassan al-Hejjaj, whose doting father—so a careless servant had once let slip—called her *al-Baroohelwa*, the Little Sugarplum.

He gave a guilty start as a passerby accidentally jostled him. "*Muta assif,*" the man apologized. Hamid-Jones managed a lame smile and an "*Afwan.*"

He was almost ready to give it up then, but he kept his eyes on the grille, hoping. The chief eunuch in the Clonemaster's house—as Hamid-Jones had reason to know—was lenient; he was not one to shoo away a woman who overstepped the harem rules a little and amused herself by looking at the activities in the street. And perhaps that very woman, whose flash of movement he had seen, was on her way right now to announce to Lalla with breathless giggles that her admirer, the young man who worked for her father, was waiting outside for a glimpse of her.

He knew that Lalla was aware of him. He knew that, like other male guests, he had been thoroughly and minutely inspected and gossiped about by the women of the household from behind the carved screens of the upper arcade of the women's quarters. And, like any red-blooded swain, Hamid-Jones had fantasized about what was happening on the other side of the latticework.

He imagined Lalla, the Little Sugarplum, watching him, responding to the small, surreptitious signals that Arab suitors resorted to in such circumstances—the dropped rose, the line of poetry with double meaning deftly inserted into the all-male conversation, the fleeting glance and gesture when his host's attention was elsewhere. The rustles and giggles he heard at those times came from Lalla, he had convinced himself.

And then his longing was rewarded. One night as the guests were departing and everybody was engrossed in the elaborate rituals of leave-taking, Hamid-Jones happened to be the last on the way out. At that moment, Lalla had passed fleetingly behind an unscreened gap, as if she were not aware that anyone was still there. Either the timing had been exquisite, or the eunuchs in the Clonemaster's household were unbelievably lax. Lalla had let her veil drop, as if by accident, granting Hamid-Jones a brief, delicious look at her face. She had done it on purpose, he was sure.

Since that transcendent moment, Hamid-Jones had lived in a fever of anticipation. The next step—after some definitive sign from her—would be an exchange of messages. Junior eunuchs could often be bribed—at both ends—to carry messages. Eunuchs loved intrigue.

It was not inconceivable, Hamid-Jones told himself fiercely. It happened all the time. He stared up at the window, willing Lalla to appear.

Just as suddenly, he felt deflated. Why was he deceiving himself? There was not a chance in the world for him. Such proxy flirtations were winked at—even encouraged—when the swain was suitable and a marriage arrangement was deemed desirable. But Hamid-Jones was a nobody, a mongrel—whose prospects moreover were hostage to the Clonemaster himself. If he were discovered in this impudence, the Clonemaster would be severe—promising protégé or no. At the very least, it would mean the end of his career.

Besides, he had come every night for a week and hung around as long as he dared, and Lalla had never appeared at the little window. She was laughing at him, he told himself with savage self-contempt.

Or still worse, he had been mistaken; she was not even aware of his existence.

As he prepared to slink off, the geometry of the grille above was suddenly altered by various opacities. An eye appeared within a star, a pair of lips could be seen between carved blossoms, and then a little pink finger poked itself out of a loop of vine and wiggled at him.

Hamid-Jones stopped dead in his tracks, his heart bursting.

Two perfumed gentlemen strolling hand in hand almost collided with him, then, raising groomed eyebrows at his lack of apology, moved around him.

While Hamid-Jones continued to gape, the suggested form behind the wooden lacework moved to position itself so that two dark, liquid eyes stared down at him at once through the spaces in the carving. The red lips smiled at him for a second or two of extraordinary license before a veil dropped to hide them.

He regained his wits and stepped back out of the flow of traffic. For a sweet eternity, he and Lalla exchanged burning glances, and Hamid-Jones placed a hand on his heart, heedless of who might see him.

But his happiness was not yet complete. The little finger withdrew, to be replaced by a thumb and forefinger pinching a white square between them. She waved the square to make sure he'd noticed it, then released it to flutter down to the street below.

Before he could react, there was a shadowed movement behind Lalla's screened form, and Lalla hastily disappeared. Hamid-Jones found himself staring up at a baleful ebony eye, above which was a pearly shimmer that might have been a eunuch's turban.

His paralysis lasted only a moment. In a flash he darted across the street to scramble under the feet of passersby for Lalla's token. Before he stuffed it inside his djellaba, he had time to see that it was a folded note in classical script; and nestling within— his heart almost stopped—a tiny framed hologram of Lalla's plump face.

The deep inset of the grille shielded him from observation from directly above, but very shortly, he was sure, someone would emerge from the gatekeeper's door behind him. Had he been recognized in that brief moment? He shrugged; there was no help for it if he had been. He hunched his neck down inside his djellaba and prepared to blend with the holiday traffic streaming by.

And then, to his horror, he saw the Clonemaster striding purposefully down the street, heading directly toward him.

Hamid-Jones stood transfixed. It was no good trying to flee; the Clonemaster's impatient eyes had locked with his.

There was no denying that Hassan bin Fahd al-Hejjaj was an imposing, forbidding sight as he bore down on him. The thick, cursive features, framed by an elegantly curled gray beard, were set in a stern, imperious expression. He was cloaked in the splendor of fine brocades and wore the chain of office around his neck. Hamid-Jones broke into a cold sweat, all too aware of the damning presence of the note and holo portrait hidden under his djellaba.

At that moment the gate behind him opened and he was trapped between the Clonemaster and the gatekeeper. He gulped and prepared to meet his doom.

"What are you doing, skulking about outside?" the Clonemaster demanded sternly. Hamid-Jones opened his mouth but found he had nothing to say. The Clonemaster continued, "Why didn't you ring the bell and wait inside? I've been looking everywhere for you!"

Dazed, Hamid-Jones allowed himself to be led inside. The servants brought him a glass of iced tamarind, and he sat down while the Clonemaster bustled off into the interior. He remembered then that his communicator was turned off, and he switched it on again surreptitiously. He looked up and saw the chief eunuch, a puffy, gray-complexioned man named Murad, standing in a doorway and gazing speculatively at him.

The Clonemaster returned. "No time to go home and change," he said, frowning at Hamid-Jones's Friday-best djellaba. "Never mind, I'll loan you a cloak. Finished with your drink? They're bringing my dune buggy around now."

"But what . . . where . . ." Hamid-Jones stammered.

The severe features of the Clonemaster softened in a smile of genuine pleasure. "It's a great honor for you, my boy," he said. "Oh, I went to bat for you, of course, but it was your own competence as a cloning technician that earned you the privilege."

"I don't understand, *sidi*," Hamid-Jones faltered.

"Haven't you played back the messages I left you? You're coming with me to the New Palace. You're allowed to be present as a witness to the Emir's beheading."

CHAPTER 3

Before he had time to digest the change in his fortunes, Hamid-Jones found himself climbing into the silk-upholstered interior of the Clonemaster's desert car, to sit among the overstuffed cushions next to the Clonemaster himself. A servant closed and sealed the door and stepped back while the kneeling vehicle rose on the jointed struts that gave independent suspension to its six fat tires.

"*Yallah*, my son," the Clonemaster said, leaning forward to speak to the driver, and the buggy began to roll down the Street of the Peacock toward the broad avenue that led to the outside airlock, the Bab al-Dahub.

Hamid-Jones settled back to enjoy the ride. The driver was using his horn liberally to send pedestrians scurrying out of the way. Beside the driver, sitting rigidly, was a hard-looking desert tribesman who had been taken into the Clonemaster's household to serve as a bodyguard; he wore the Clonemaster's family crest pinned to his headrope and carried a wicked-looking automatic weapon, a flat, stubby microdart spitter. Perched on a jumpseat facing Hamid-Jones was another servant, a crickety, skull-capped footman who was busy attaching ivory-tipped tubes to the gold-plated spigots on the refreshment console.

The Clonemaster waved aside the mouthpiece that was offered to him but graciously urged it on Hamid-Jones. Hamid-Jones, after a first refusal, took a cautious sip and found that it was an apricot sherbet with a bare trace of fermentation up to the allowable limits; truly, he thought, the Clonemaster did himself well.

"Well, my boy," the Clonemaster said to put him at his ease,

27

"how does it feel to have your name inscribed on the palace's guest list?"

"*Ya rayis*, I don't know what to say . . . I'm very grateful. Thank you for sponsoring me."

"Nonsense!" the Clonemaster said heartily. "You've earned it. I'm very pleased with the work you've been doing on the Winged One's genome."

"Thank you, *ya rayis*." It did not seem to be the moment to tell the Clonemaster that he had spoiled two clones in a row.

"This is only the beginning, my boy. Keep up the good work. There are great things in store for you."

Hamid-Jones's heart was thumping. "I never dared to dream that I could ever be connected—even this remotely—with . . . uh . . ." He stumbled for a euphemism. ". . . the medical cloning program."

The Clonemaster's lips tightened imperceptibly. "Don't allow yourself to be overly impressed by those palace functionaries, *ya* Abdul. I can tell you, without in any way denigrating our esteemed colleagues, that our little department at the Royal Stables need not take a backseat in competence or technical expertise. In fact, there are times when—" He broke off abruptly. "Our part in this is small. As one of the expert witnesses, you'll be required to professionally attest to the success and the bona fide nature of the graft, and add your signature to the *qadi*'s scroll. You understand that this is a formality?"

"Yes, *sidi*."

"Good."

The Clonemaster stared ruminatively out the curtained window of the sand car. Hamid-Jones looked past the driver's shoulder at the boulevard of the gate. The multilane traffic was narrowing to one lane as they approached the Bab and consequently was thickening and slowing down. The driver leaned on his horn in vain; others were doing the same, and the din was terrific, even in the sealed interior of the buggy. Hamid-Jones could see other balloon-tired limousines, expensive Rolls *al-arabiya*s and *khad al-lakh*s, stuck in the flow like flies in honey; presumably they belonged to sheiks and other notables on their way to the New Palace. The dome of the Bab was opening out overhead, and Hamid-Jones craned his neck to take in the dimensions of the enormous artificial chasm that contained this mighty artery of commerce. The old habitations, added to since the earliest days of the settlement of Mars, leaned dizzily overhead, story after story, many with holiday banners dangling from their balconies. At street level, a jumble of shops, warehouses, cheap hotels, coffeehouses, and commercial arcades riddled the native rock, like holes in an aged cheddar infested with cheese mites.

The Bab al-Dahub itself loomed ahead, two enormous airlocks able to take the largest and tallest vehicles, and a row of small *bab*s meant for people and animals.

The Clonemaster's driver drew abreast of one of the gatekeepers' booths to pay the toll, but notwithstanding the fact that there was still room in the lock for another vehicle or two, was told that the sand car would have to wait until the next cycle. With considerable presence of mind, the driver managed to bribe the man five dinars before the inner gate slammed down, thus avoiding a delay of at least fifteen or twenty minutes. The timing was perfect. The bribe should have been at least ten dinars, but by feigning stupidity until the last possible moment, the driver forced the gatekeeper to weigh the chances of getting a larger bribe from the loudly honking sheik in the sand car behind— who seemed about to take his business to the next booth over— against the possibility of losing a profit entirely on this cycle of the lock.

"Good luck to you, brother," the man said sourly as he let them through.

"Inch'allah, ya akhi," the driver said innocently. He squeezed the sand car into the lock and, when the gate closed behind them, turned in his seat to flash a triumphant grin at the Clonemaster and Hamid-Jones.

They were through the lock sooner than Hamid-Jones expected; during the rush hour the third gate was often kept open and the second cycle dispensed with, and the gatekeepers didn't bother to pump out the lock completely. Air, after all, was cheap in the Emir's prosperous domain. On the Jovian moons, Hamid-Jones had heard, one actually paid an air tax.

The buggy climbed the long ramp on its six elephantine tires and emerged into the thin pink sunlight. Hamid-Jones craned forward to peer through the plastic windscreen at the rubbled landscape as the driver left the narrow track that headed east toward Xanthe and took off across the desert.

Even after a thousand years of greening, the Martian surface would have been recognizable to the early pioneers. The same tumbled rocks littered the terrain, and the sky was still brownish with suspended dust. The air was still thin despite all the carbon dioxide brought in from Venus and the oxygen liberated from

Mars itself—men and animals still had to wear breathing masks, though pressure suits were no longer necessary for the hardier breeds, like Marscamels. The bioengineered plant life hardly showed through the ruddy soil, except to give an occasional greenish tinge to a ridge or depression, or to form a faint reticulated pattern along fractures where water had collected.

The horizon was sharp and near, hiding the peaks of the Tharsis Range, but Hamid-Jones knew that Ascraeus was just past the planetary bulge, only a few miles away, and beyond it, Olympus Mons, poking its crater rim into the stratosphere. He raised his eyes to the sun, small and bright in a butterscotch sky. The glinting mote that attended it was one of the mirrors that hung in synchronous orbit some ten thousand miles up, making the Emir's days brighter and his domain somewhat warmer.

A lone nomad appeared from nowhere, sitting cross-legged atop an impossibly tall Marscamel. Carpeting draped the flanks of the beast, hiding bulging saddlebags that would have been stuffed with homemade survival equipment. The Bedouin was swathed in flowing robes, an antique submachine gun slung over his shoulder. Both man and camel wore leather breathing masks. The apparition veered to avoid intersecting the path of the sand car, loping in dreamlike fashion in the Martian gravity.

"Bedu!" the driver spat.

The guard muttered under his breath. He didn't care much for the lone rider either, though he was a desert tribesman himself.

"He's a bit off his territory, isn't he?" the Clonemaster remarked. "He'll be sorry if one of the Emir's patrols catches him. No wonder he's not too anxious to rub elbows with us."

Hamid-Jones murmured assent. The camel, bobbing in slow motion, seemed to float over a ridge, the rider bouncing upward like a tethered balloon.

"They caught two of those fellows near a severed pipeline last month," the Clonemaster went on. "Skinned them alive and mounted the skins on poles to serve as an example. They swore they hadn't done it. Said that the *Bedu* had been taught long ago not to interfere with the Emir's air supply—and that they had their own tribal penalties against it. They said the camels had led them to the break—that they couldn't hold the beasts back—and that they were only taking advantage of the spill."

The guard twisted around in his seat with a scowl. "That one belongs to the Banu-Shu'bah tribe. Very bad people. They would slit a man's throat for his gear, even in defilement of the rules of hospitality.''

He turned round again with a righteous grunt and kept his eye on the dwindling camel.

''Personally,'' the Clonemaster mused, ''I think they were telling the truth—*Bedu* don't interfere with oxygen lines. Why would they? Oh, they'll tap a pipeline whenever they can get away with it, but they restore the seals when they're done. No, it's the terrorist *mujahidin* who sabotage pipelines and blow up pumping stations—the Christian fedayeen or the followers of al-Sharq, the Pretender. What do you think, *ya* Abdul?''

He thought carefully before he replied. ''It is true that people are prejudiced against the children of the desert, *sidi*, and that they are blamed for every missing traveler and every other misfortune in the wastelands. It is hard for a city dweller to understand their ways. But it is also said that al-Sharq could not exist without the support of the desert people . . . that he swims among them as a fish swims in water.''

The Clonemaster's face was unreadable. Hamid-Jones couldn't tell if he had said the right thing.

''They're picturesque, that's for certain,'' the Clonemaster said after a pause, ''and a great deal of nonsense is written about their romantic ways. But they're out of place in a modern world.''

''Yes, *sidi*,'' Hamid-Jones agreed quickly.

The Clonemaster sighed. ''They were becoming city dwellers a thousand years ago, when the Great Resurgence was getting under way. And they came to Mars with the early settlers, looking like everyone else and telling tall tales about their desert ancestors. But all those centuries of city life failed to tame them, it seemed. Earth was overdeveloped—there was no place for them there—but when they were confronted with the wastes of Mars, they reverted to their earlier life-styles. They began slipping away into the desert a few at a time with whatever primitive life support equipment they could buy, borrow, or steal. By then, of course, the basic enhanced camel had come out of the genetic laboratories, part of the effort to establish an ecology. It was already capable of sustaining the nomadic life, though that wasn't the planners' intention. The *Bedu* have done wonders with their herds in the centuries since then—and by old-fashioned selective breeding, without benefit of further genetic engineering.''

Hamid-Jones held his tongue. What was the Clonemaster leading up to?

"Perhaps we could learn something from them, *ya* Abdul." The Clonemaster pulled reflectively at his iron-gray beard. "Oh, everyone pays lip service to the old desert virtues, the simple, free way of life. We all like to boast about that trace of the pure tribal blood flowing through our veins, no matter how attenuated it may be."

Hamid-Jones stiffened, as he always did when ancestry was mentioned. Was this the reason for the Clonemaster's disquisition—to put him subtly in his place? Did he somehow suspect about Lalla? The little framed holo portrait lay like a stone against his heart; Hamid-Jones with an effort kept his hand from straying toward it. The Clonemaster could trace his ancestry back to the house of Saud; the blood of the Anizah tribe flowed through *his* veins—and through Lalla's veins, too, though her mother had been only an Omani handmaiden whom he had taken as his fourth wife in the passion of his youth.

But no, the Clonemaster was still going on about nomads.

". . . there's no place for them, really, in this brave new world of ours, despite our nostalgia. They're a nuisance and embarrassment to the Emir—for all the ceremonial kissing and protestations of loyalty. Obsolete. Eventually the population will expand and the *Bedu* will become extinct again. Assimilated, forced to live like the rest of us."

Hamid-Jones was bewildered. He didn't know what reply was expected. Was the Clonemaster testing him—trying to draw out an indiscreet or disloyal remark about the Emir's rule?

He settled on something bland and conventional: "Sacrifices must always be made for the sake of progress, *sidi*, isn't that so?" The words of Mr. Fahti the night before came back to him. "We're entering the second millennium of the Awakening, and some say a new golden age is on its way."

The Clonemaster's eyes flashed irony in the instant before he hooded them. Then he became brisk. "Yes, *ya* Abdul, you've hit the nail on the head. A new age is certainly waiting to be born. And Mars, with the Emir to guide us, will be the beneficiary. He sits on the second most valuable piece of real estate in the solar system, after all. With the two natural space stations we have in Deimos and Phobos, more interstellar traffic passes through our terminals than even Luna. And the Emir collects *zakat* on every bale of merchandise, on every pilgrim transshipping for Mecca." His tone was thoroughly genial, and Hamid-Jones decided he'd been mistaken about the irony. "Yes, *ya* Abdul, a ruler of Mars will certainly be in a favorable position to take advantage of the second millennium of the *Nadha*. You are lucky to be young at such a time.''

He measured out a wide, white smile to Hamid-Jones, then seemed to become preoccupied again.

Hamid-Jones let himself relax. He had passed the test, whatever it was. Surreptitiously he wiped away a drop of sweat that had collected above his eyebrow.

The Mars buggy topped a dune, its gigantic tires spinning in gravel before it caught itself, and then as it rolled forward, an enchanted vision of vanilla domes and peppermint minarets rose from the desert.

"The palace, *sidi*,'' the driver announced unnecessarily.

The crazy splendor of the Emir's brainchild could be perceived even at a distance. The glazed wall, glittering in the sunlight, enclosed a hundred square miles of desert. Within was spread an intricate architectural fantasy of towers and pavilions, harems and guest palaces, private mosques, pearly bubbles containing pools and gardens—the whole sprawling complex exposed to the Martian sky. The Emir, when he had replaced his brigand father, had scorned to burrow underground. The Martian atmosphere, he had decreed, had become thick enough to screen out the worst of the heavy primaries and the killing ultraviolet. All that was required, the architects had been told, was to enclose the pleasure gardens, polo fields, boating ponds, and other outdoor playgrounds in their own pressurized domes, and to glass in the lacy arcades that connected one building with another. The buildings themselves were to be individually sealed—at ruinous expense to the treasury.

Most lavish of all were the outdoor pools and fountains, boiling off enough water vapor in the thin atmosphere to have supplied all of Tharsis City twice over. Hamid-Jones could see the fleecy white clouds hovering over the royal grounds like a benediction from Allah.

And now, as the Clonemaster's vehicle drew closer, Hamid-Jones could see further evidence of the Emir's extravagant ways. Acres of rich carpet were spread out across the desert to provide a welcome mat for today's visitors.

The *khad-al-lakh*'s swollen tires bit into the thick woolen nap and found a grip. It would be a smooth ride for the remaining three miles to the palace gate. The driver turned round to grin in delight, then swiveled back to watch where he was going.

A lumbering eight-wheeler cut in front of them. The driver cursed and hit his horn, which made a thin, futile wail in the three-hundred–millibar atmosphere. He caught up with the eight-wheeler and passed it, and then Hamid-Jones became aware that he was slowing down.

There seemed to be a vehicle jam up ahead. Hamid-Jones's eyes traveled down the line of rollers and crawlers to the base of the wall, where there was much milling around of people-size specks.

"Hello, what's going on up there?" the Clonemaster said with a frown. "Some kind of trouble?"

By the time the driver, with skillful maneuvering and a combative zeal for jousting with other chauffeurs, got them within striking distance of the gate, increasing congestion had brought the churning mass of vehicles to a virtual halt.

The driver switched off the motor. "I go see what's wrong, *sidi*."

He took a respirator from under the dashboard and cranked up the glass partition to the passenger compartment. The Bedouin guard sat impassively, disdaining the use of a respirator for himself as the driver skinned through the door without bothering to use the sleeve, though it would be long minutes before the pumps brought the pressure up to par again; desert people prided themselves on their ability to hold their breath.

The driver hung by one hand and dropped lightly to the ground, not taking the trouble to lower the chassis. Hamid-Jones watched as he disappeared into the maze of stalled vehicles.

The driver was gone about fifteen minutes. Back inside the cabin, he rubbed his hands together for warmth while the pressure built, then removed his mask and turned to the Clonemaster.

"They've had some sort of security warning, *sidi*. They're very nervous. I almost got myself shot by approaching one of the guards from behind. No vehicles allowed through the gate—they're parking them about twenty miles away in the desert, inside a crater, in case of nuclear devices. They had a car-bomb scare about a week ago, but it was discovered and disarmed." He gave the guard a sidelong glance. "No bodyguards with weapons allowed inside the palace wall—he'll have to check the gun or wait with the car."

The guard's knuckles whitened on his microdart spitter. It was an insult both to the Clonemaster and himself to take his gun away from him. The fiction was that sheiks and their retainers were trusted without question, though in practice, bodyguards usually found themselves cooling their heels in an anteroom, generously provided with refreshments to remove any sting.

"Never mind, my son," the Clonemaster said softly. "What harm could befall me under the protection of the Emir's hospitality?"

The guard made no reply. There was no question that he would willingly go hungry, thirsty, and comfortless for as long as it took, rather than be separated from the weapon on which his honor depended.

"Always the terrorists," the Clonemaster said wryly. "Was there ever a time when they were not a part of our way of life? But they seem to be more of a nuisance than usual lately. Their causes multiply. That Deimos ferry that was hijacked to Pallas last month—they claimed to be Byelorussians, seeking to liberate their homeland."

The driver had been waiting diffidently for the Clonemaster to finish speaking. "At least two, three hundred cars waiting to be parked, *ya rayis*, and more arriving every minute. Not enough parking attendants—security was just starting to press the stableboys into service when I left."

His eyes expressed a mournful apology that he had not been able to get the Mars buggy closer to the gate.

"We'd better walk, *ya Abdul*," the Clonemaster sighed. He handed Hamid-Jones a respirator. "Would you like a heatcloak?"

"Thank you, no, *ya sidi*, it's not that far," Hamid-Jones said. It was high noon outside, and the temperature must be above freezing by now, to judge by the disappearance of frost that had left wet spots on the nearby rocks. He didn't want the Clonemaster to think he was any less rugged than the driver or the guard.

"Fine," the Clonemaster said absently, popping the door. Hamid-Jones hastily jammed the respirator over his face and followed the Clonemaster down the step stool that the driver had extruded as the car knelt.

He regretted his bravado as soon as he was outside. The wind cut through the thin indoor clothing he had donned that morning, and the light dress cloak the Clonemaster had loaned him wasn't much help. The Clonemaster, he saw too late as the other pulled a stretchcuff over his fingers, was wearing thermal underwear.

He tried not to let his shivering show as they picked their way through the confusion. A babble of complaints and arguments carried through the thin air as security men in thermal suits with red-checked keffias over the hoods hammered on drivers' compartments with the butts of their automatic weapons and explained the situation to the chauffeurs.

Every sort of vehicle was represented: big, sleek limousines sitting atop their eight-foot tires, beat-up desert pickups with caterpillar tracks and scarred plastic bubbles, expensive little sports Hovercraft, bright as toys, a spider-legged walking bus full of schoolchildren—even a sprinkling of camels; both the classic Marscamel in its primitive leather mask, steed for the fierce desert chieftains who had come to pay homage to the Emir, and the later six-legged model, like as not wearing a full set of electronics and carrying a fancy pressurized howdah containing some effete urbanite whose closest approach to the desert was ordinarily the sand in his asparagus vinaigrette.

Hamid-Jones skipped out of the way as a camel hissed at him from fifteen feet overhead, bumped into the keglike drum of a high-roller, and hurried to catch up with the Clonemaster as he rounded the slab-sided bulk of a luxury hovercamper. The Clonemaster was heading, with a dignified no-nonsense tread, straight for a group of security guards who were manning one of the long folding tables, checking people's identities and handing out receipts for weapons before sending them through the row of portable detector booths that had been set up in front of the gate.

The Clonemaster gave up a jeweled dagger and was showing his retinal patterns to an eyeprint machine as Hamid-Jones came up behind him. Up ahead, a man was making a fuss about going through a detector with a caged falcon.

"I tell you, this is a gift for the Emir," the man was protesting. "A royal bird, the rarest of its kind—it may be owned by no one but the Emir himself. The Falconmaster is expecting it! It is too sensitive to go through a muon scanner."

Hamid-Jones looked at the bird with interest. It was an enormous snow-white mutation derived from an arctic gyrfalcon—the bird that indeed was reserved for kings. It would have weighed at least twenty pounds on Earth, and from the exaggerated jut of its keel he estimated a wingspread of possibly thirty feet when its triple-jointed sails were unfolded. Such birds were splendidly equipped for soaring high in the Martian atmosphere when provided with breathing masks, as this one had been; the gaily tufted hood it wore incorporated a respirator connected by tubes to the cage's life-support system.

The cage itself was an open one, not the closed travel cage that one might have expected. It was a typical field cage of the type that cadgers wore on their backs during a hunt—a cumbersome framework that loomed high above the shoulders and that would have been staggeringly heavy on Earth. The pumps and pressure cylinders of the life-support system were installed below the bird's block perch, to keep the center of gravity as low as possible.

The heater with its heavy-duty batteries seemed superfluous, Hamid-Jones thought. Gyrfalcon variations were comfortable at any Martian daytime temperature down to 140 below.

"My poor darling," the man cooed to the bird. "First they subject you to all this noise and confusion, and now they want to bombard you with muons!" He appealed to the crowd of admiring onlookers. "Do you know what a strong magnetic field can do to a bird like this? The structures in their brain are very delicate—it can destroy their orientation, make them worthless!" He turned to the guards again. "Do you want to take the responsibility for damaging this magnificent creature, a gift of state for the Emir?"

The onlookers murmured in sympathy. The falcon trainer acknowledged their support with a shrug of elaborate martyrdom. Interesting, thought Hamid-Jones: around the edges of the man's transparent mask were beads of sweat, despite the biting cold. Perhaps the heater of his thermal suit was defective.

"For shame, to molest a bird like that," a brave soul in the crowd said, loud enough to be heard, and there were mutters of agreement.

The security guards were inclined to be lenient. After all, they admired the bird, too, and—the Emir's proprietorship aside—were not especially anxious to inconvenience it.

Now they were trying to persuade the man to remove the bulky harness. They would make a concession; the man could go through the security booths without the falcon—they would inspect the cage by visual and nonintrusive means only and meet him around at the other side with it.

But the man still balked. "She is my beloved, my child, my eye!" he whined. "She is too used to my presence to be separated from me! Can't you understand how sensitive such a noble creature is?"

"It's only for a moment." The guards did their best to pacify him, while one took the cage and another unobtrusively patted the man down, removing a dagger and a short decorative scimitar that, if sharpened, might have cut butter.

"What are you doing? Don't poke around in the cage like that! You'll upset her!"

One of the guards was waving a short wand around between the bars—a Geiger counter or explosives sniffer.

"Don't worry," one of the man's escorts soothed him, pushing him with firm insistence toward a curtained booth. The guards inspecting the cage lost interest in it after a cursory look-through and were just in the process of passing the falcon along to be rejoined with the owner on the other side of the booth, when the man lost his nerve and, wresting himself from the grip of his escorts, broke and ran.

A dozen weapons swung toward him and brought him down with a firehose stream of explosive microflechettes that turned him into a pink cloud of mincemeat that jerked in different directions before raining in fragments to the ground.

Screams came from bystanders hit by stray darts, sounding nightmarishly distant and tinny in the thin air. A couple of security guards went down, too, victims of the crossfire. There was another spattering of blood and tissue on the carpet at Hamid-Jones's feet. A guard had fired deliberately into the crowd at the man who had expressed sympathy for the falconer, possibly mistaking him for an accomplice.

Another guard had flung himself instantly over the falcon cage with the first shots, to shield the bird with his body, and now he was buried under a pile-up of red-shawled security agents who had belatedly followed his example.

The crowd screamed and scattered. Some dropped to the ground to flatten themselves, or burrow under the edges of the carpeting. Security men fell on those trying to flee, cutting them down with long curved swords. In a flash of horror, Hamid-Jones saw a grimly intent palace guard sawing away with a knife at the throat of a man he had pinned to the carpet with his knees, and recognized the hapless victim as one who had been standing too close to the falconer's sympathizer.

He turned around in time to see a sizable guard bounding enthusiastically toward him, teeth bared behind his transparent mask, brandishing a sword. He dived to the ground and hugged the rug, trying to protect his head with his forearms. Through eyes squeezed half shut with terror, he was able to note that the part of the pattern he was lying on was the *mihrab*, or prayer niche, of a rug large enough to accommodate the devotions of an army, and thought irrelevantly, in the clarity of pumping adrenaline, that at least he was going to die in the best possible place.

He waited an eternity for the blow to fall, and then he felt the shadow over him move away. After a few moments he mustered enough confidence to roll over and chance a look. The Clonemaster was there, talking with calm authority to the scowling guard and, from his gestures and the holographic credentials he was waving around in front of the guard's nose, vouching for Hamid-Jones.

Sheepishly, Hamid-Jones rose to his feet. The Clonemaster said, "Come, *ya* Abdul, they're going to let us through now. It's all over. I have your documentation, and you'll just have to give your eyeprints and go through the detectors."

The crowd was assembling itself in some kind of order. The security men stood around looking fierce. Medical teams were beginning to move among the dead and wounded, administering to those who could still be helped, and tagging bodies for removal. The carnage had been terrific. Scores of people lay about. The rich oriental carpeting was soaked, but drying fast as the coagulating blood gave up its moisture to the thirsty Martian atmosphere. A haze of steam was rising into the air.

As Hamid-Jones followed the Clonemaster through the immense carved portals leading through the series of airlocks, he gathered enough courage to ask, "What happened?"

"It was a nuclear device," the Clonemaster said through tight lips.

Hamid-Jones hurried to keep up with the Clonemaster's long strides. "The falcon cage?" he said, horrified by the enormity of it. "A backpack nuke?"

"These terrorists will stoop to any depths, it seems," the Clonemaster said, his face grim. The air curtain behind them slid massively shut, and he slowed down a little to let the mob surge past them down the wide corridor and pile up in front of the next air curtain down the line.

"But who . . ."

The Clonemaster seemed reluctant to speak. "There's no telling yet what group's responsible. Apparently the Palace got an advance tip that someone was going to try something today, but they didn't know who or what."

He paused for a moment to let a couple of stragglers pass by out of earshot, then went on with more animation. "These people were very clever, whoever they were. Who would suspect a bird in an open cage? The falcon was a rare specimen, and the Palace's Falconmaster was expecting it. The man was legitimate, too—at least his retinal patterns must have passed the test." He pursed his lips. "It's ironic that he lost his nerve at the last minute, like that. The device contained no fissionables—it wouldn't have been detected by any kind of a scintillation counter, only the kind of X ray or muon scanner that no one would put a valuable bird through. But the pressure tanks of the life-support system were actually cryocontainers with deuterium and tritium, and the heater batteries were heavy duty capacitors for the laser assembly. There was probably no more than a pint of air for the bird—just the minimum necessary to keep it alive long enough to go through security." His lip curled to show what he thought of people who would do *that*. "Except that they failed to anticipate the size of the mob and the added delays. I suppose that's why the fellow panicked. He was afraid the bird would keel over at any minute. You'll be glad to know, *ya* Abdul, that the falcon's safe. One of the guards gave it his air until the medics arrived—they attended to the bird first. They think the guard's going to be all right, too." He sighed. "I wonder where the bird came from. It's a brilliant job of bioengineering—good enough to rival anything we do at the Royal Stables. There'll be a massive investigation—we'll have to be prepared to answer a lot of questions, *ya* Abdul."

The Clonemaster seemed unusually subdued. His professional pride must have been hurt, Hamid-Jones decided.

"Perhaps it was one of those bootleg cloning outfits, *ya sidi*," he ventured. "The kind that grow back illegal hands for convicted thieves."

"Yes, *ya* Abdul, that must be it." The Clonemaster halted as they caught up with the mob waiting in front of the barrier. He seemed disinclined to offer more conversation, and when the huge arched *bab* opened to let them through, Hamid-Jones trailed along in silence.

There were wonders enough to hold Hamid-Jones's attention as the security people herded them through the corridors and great public rooms of the palace. The public coffee hall was fully an eighth of a mile high, encircled by level after level of colonnaded porticoes, its honeycombed roof lost in the distance. Stately arcades bordered the walls, their columns dripping with carved abstractions. A lily pool an acre across and graced by tall fountains sat in the middle of the tiled floor; around it, reclining under manicured plum trees and potted date palms, even the poorest of the Emir's subjects could enjoy a taste of magnificence while waiting to be called to the hall of the *majlis* to present a petition.

Hamid-Jones gawked unabashedly at all the sights, dragging his feet as he passed the open doorways and glassed arches. One enormous room contained a whole mechanical zoo, including a life-size clockwork giraffe that grazed on the silver foil leaves of a platinum acacia tree. Another domed chamber was a gallery presenting holographic scenes of the life of Mohammed; Hamid-Jones particularly enjoyed the holo of the veiled Prophet, surrounded by angels, ascending to heaven on the back of Buraq, the magical mule with a woman's head and a peacock's tail. Another room was a museum of ancient vehicles, including a gold-plated antique *khad al-lakh* with fat desert tires, also gold plated, that looked as though it had once been owned by some old-time sheik on earth.

The views visible through the glass arcades they hurried through were no less astonishing. There was a tremendous falcon dome, big enough to hold an indoor gazelle hunt in, with a poetic glimpse of a single swooping hawk high overhead that suddenly folded its great wings to dive for the reward offered by some trainer. There were enclosed gardens of terran flowers and trees, and outdoor parks, through which one would stroll with a respirator, planted with exotic Mars-adapted vegetation. There was even a whole lake, boiling away water at a fearsome rate despite what must have been a floating molecular skin to retard evaporation, on which sailed a fleet of naval vessels. The Emir, Hamid-Jones had heard, liked to relax now and then by donning an admiral's uniform and staging mock naval battles.

But all those wonders paled in comparison to what he saw next. At the broad intersection of one of the main routes leading to the *majlis*, the guards suddenly herded everyone against the wall, not hesitating to use their clubs on those who were too slow to move. A gorgeous procession of eunuchs, resplendent in gold lamé vests and crimson pantaloons, marched down the corridor with drawn scimitars.

The personage they were escorting was grander still. He was an immense blubbery creature all aglitter in jeweled brocades topped by a great puff of a turban, carrying a horsehair switch of office. His vast charcoal cheeks were smooth as a baby's, but the eyes buried within the globular features were sly and quick. Despite his bulk and the considerable weight of all the gold chains and oversize keys he wore, he waddled along at a surprising pace, so that the small boy who was trying to hold a yellow silk parasol over his head had to scurry to keep up.

"*Al-Ustador*, the Intendant of the Eunuchs," whispered the man squeezed next to Hamid-Jones against the corridor wall.

Hamid-Jones drank in the brilliant sight avidly. So this was Ismail, the Chief Eunuch and Chamberlain of the palace, the second or third most powerful man on Mars. He had seen him on the holovid, of course, during broadcasts of state occasions or the occasional homey feature on palace life. But it was not the same as seeing him in person. A dozen quick steps, Hamid-Jones couldn't help thinking, and he could reach out and touch Ismail's jewel-encrusted sleeve—not that he had a chance of covering half that distance without being beaten to the floor by a dozen swinging clubs.

The procession swept by and disappeared round a corner, leaving a scent of perfume and spices hanging in the air. The security guards allowed Hamid-Jones and the others to continue.

But Hamid-Jones's day of marvels was not yet complete. Before his group reached their destination, the security guards pulled them over to the wall again. This time it was the Grand Vizier and his party, on their way to the behind-the-scenes preparations for the great event.

Hamid-Jones recognized Rubinstein, the Vizier, at once, even before the whispers around him confirmed it. After Ismail, Rubinstein was a disappointment. He was a small, stooped, tired man with a lined face. Take away his magnificent costume, the leopard-collared cape and the silver staff, and he might have passed for a nobody. His assistants were more impressive: stalwart fellows with a crisp authoritative air about them, comfortable in their well-fitting regalia. One of them carried a padlocked case that was chained to his wrist, and Hamid-Jones wondered if that contained the box of coded algorithms that would launch the Emir's nuclear arsenal on that never-to-be-thought-of day when Islam would fall apart, and the rulers of the Faithful themselves would bring about the day of splitting skies and scorched worlds foretold by the Prophet.

"A steady man," the Clonemaster said unexpectedly. "He serves the Emir well."

Hamid-Jones was surprised. The Clonemaster was not in the habit of discussing matters of state with his underlings, but here, for the second time today, he seemed to be inviting comment from Hamid-Jones. Perhaps, Hamid-Jones told himself, he was misconstruing the Clonemaster's tone, but the remark had come out sounding more like criticism of the Emir than praise for the Vizier.

It was not his place to pass judgment on his betters—whether approbation or disapprobation. That was a privilege reserved for gentlemen of the Clonemaster's class. "May God bless his hands," Hamid-Jones said piously.

The Clonemaster gave him that peculiar look again. "Ah, here we are, *ya* Abdul. I'll be leaving you now. They'll take good care of you. It won't be too long."

They had arrived at some kind of anteroom. Receptionists were there to sort people out, consulting lists and counting heads all over again. A number of palace officials in the colorful costumes of their offices waited at the doorway to pick out the VIPs. One of them, in surgical grays, scanned the arriving crowd and made straight for the Clonemaster. The Clonemaster got into an electric cart with him and went off with the other notables to scrub for the ceremony.

Hamid-Jones looked around the waiting room. It was relatively austere despite the two-ton chandelier that hung from its marble dome and the hundreds of low tables with identical flower arrangements that stood in front of the grouped divans. A gray-bearded *farash* moved about with a tray, offering coffee. There was a small adjoining paradise with roses and nightingales, and a few of the earlier detainees were taking advantage of this chance to stretch their legs.

He estimated that about two thousand people were gathered in the room. They were of every sort—minor sheiks, muftis in their judicial robes, a few well-dressed mullahs, businessmen with pull, a delegation of handpicked *fellahin*, and some carefully selected foreign observers recognizable by their dress, including a crinolined and sunbonneted Arcturan whose family and friends would have died of old age by the time he returned home. What they all had in common was the coveted ticket that made them witnesses.

With a sigh, Hamid-Jones sat down on the nearest divan and picked up a magazine, prepared to cool his heels with the rest of the nobodies.

CHAPTER 4

From his seat high in the bleachers, Hamid-Jones had a fine, clear view of the *majlis* chamber. The great audience hall had been converted into an operating theater. At the far end, a hundred yards from where he sat, the raised dais that held the throne was now a stage that displayed two gleaming stainless steel tables, side by side, each with its own full panoply of life-support equipment, blinking monitors, and microsurgery apparatus, and each with its own fully staffed surgical team in bubble helmets and sterile grays.

He squinted at the stage through binoculars he had rented from a vendor at the entrance. He was able to spot the Clonemaster, masked and gowned, sitting with the other dignitaries in the rows of slender gilt chairs that had been set up on either side of the stage.

Even over the muted babble of voices that filled the amphitheater, Hamid-Jones could hear the steady hiss of the positive-pressure air curtain that preserved a sterile operating field without "separating" the Emir from his loyal subjects. In theory, at least, the Emir was as accessible as if this had been an ordinary *majlis*.

The great canopied throne on its marble base had been moved out of the way, but the black leather carpet and the chopping block in front of it were grisly reminders of the more usual uses of the chamber. They were there for the convenience of the executioner, whose ropes, stanchions, winches, and double-headed axe could be seen leaning against the far wall. Here, in the public hall where every citizen of Mars, no matter how humble, had by immemorial custom the right to personally petition the Emir, justice was meted out on the spot. Hamid-Jones shuddered as he thought of all the beheadings, amputations of right hands, and other statutory mutilations that had been carried out on the sinister Carpet of Blood. But the Emir's justice was tempered by mercy. Under his enlightened rule, the loss of a hand, foot, or other body part need not be a life sentence. A lesser miscreant might be sentenced to only ten or twenty years of handlessness or footlessness, then have the missing part legally recloned.

"Pardon me, brother. Could I borrow your binoculars?"

Hamid-Jones turned to face the speaker, a small fussy man with a smear of black beard, wearing a business suit and a black-and-white reticulated headcloth that proclaimed him to be a Shi'ite.

"Here you are, brother," Hamid-Jones said, handing the binoculars over.

The man at once began to scan the platform for celebrities. He showed no inclination to hand the binoculars back.

"To think, brother," he gushed, "that we are among those honored to be asked to sign the *qadi*'s certificate on this auspicious occasion!"

Hamid-Jones was not sure of how much an honor it was, not when he looked around the auditorium and saw at least six thousand people there to do the same thing—not counting the women who were hidden behind the grille set in the rear wall. Women, of course, were forbidden in a court of law, but at the weekly *majlis* were allowed to testify from "another room"—a woman's word being legally valued at half that of a man's. Hamid-Jones supposed the same rule applied today.

Even the luminaries sitting onstage in their surgical masks and gowns were there as part of the mob. Like the lesser witnesses, they were there only to certify in person that the composite individual resulting from the operation would indeed be entirely the true Emir—the shopworn original head that had uninterruptedly contained the Emir's brain and will for the past two hundred years, and the spanking new body had been grown from the Emir's own cells and that had been warranted by the highest *mujtahid*s in the land to be legally a part of the Emir himself.

Still, Hamid-Jones had to admit, it was a thrill being here as a part, however small, of this historic event—not consigned to watching it on the holovid, like everyone else he knew. His eyes went to the banks of holoscan cameras in the press gallery— already feeding live images to assure the multitudes that the Emir was indeed legally succeeding himself today in an unbroken line of succession.

"Yes, brother," Hamid-Jones agreed, "we're fortunate to be chosen."

The little man wasn't sure he liked that. He gave a self-important frown. "Of course it's understandable why someone like myself would be chosen. I'm a physician—a podiatrist—with some claim to expert judgment in medical matters." He peered doubtfully at Hamid-Jones. "And what kind of work do you do, brother?"

"Uh . . . I'm a lab technician."

"Oh . . . well, at least you're familiar with scientific procedures. Not like some of those who've gotten past the gatekeepers today."

He sniffed loudly and tilted his head toward the stolid, slack-jawed delegation of token *fellahin*, who doubtless had been trucked in from some nearby bubble village.

The man sitting in front of the podiatrist turned around at that and fixed him with a cold, dangerous stare. He was a rough type, a laborer or factory worker to judge by the cheap shirt and trousers and the rag of a headcloth, knotted in place without benefit of headrope. Hamid-Jones noticed something peculiar about his hands: the left hand had black fingernails, while the right hand looked pink and manicured.

"I was speaking only in general terms, brother," the podiatrist said nervously. "About the technical qualifications of a witness. Nothing personal."

The man looked him over without answering, a long, chillingly impersonal examination that ended with an apparent dismissal, then turned his attention back to the stage, where two teams of scrub nurses had begun to lay out sterile drapes around the operating tables.

The little podiatrist mopped his brow, then after reassuring himself with a glance that the man in front of him was no longer interested in him, raised the borrowed binoculars for a look at the proceedings.

"They must be about to start," he reported to Hamid-Jones. "The technicians are wheeling in a stand with a sort of bird cage attached to it. They're plugging it into the computer. But there's only one of them. There's no cage for the other operating table."

Hamid-Jones refrained from pointing out that he might have seen it for himself if he had his binoculars. He leaned forward to squint at the tiny figures below. He had a fair idea of what was going on. He'd seen stereotaxic cages before. The Clone-master used an oversize one to hold a horse's head in place while implanting embryonic brain tissue for minor neurological repair of valuable animals with learned behavior—specialized training or a repertoire of tricks—that could not be duplicated by a simple cloned replacement.

The operating table that was being fitted with the stereotaxic hat would be for the Emir. The clone wouldn't need one.

"That must be the Emir's table, then," he said to be helpful. "The body donor will be on the left."

Confirming his words, one of the circulating nurses lugged in a laundry hamper lined with a rubber sheet and unceremoniously dumped it next to the left-hand operating table.

"How could you possibly know that?" the podiatrist said in dismissal. "Let's wait and see." He lifted the binoculars again to study the activity more closely.

Down below, the electronics technicians were swiveling the cage this way and that on its jointed stem to check it out. Hamid-Jones could make out flickering movement on the banks of displays as the computer responded with random coordinates from its mapping program. The computer contained a precise atlas of all the major and minor blood vessels, peripheral nerves, spinal cord and the vertebral architecture, as well as a microscopic cross-section of complex structures like the trachea, esophagus, and neck muscle fibers, within the crucial slice of the Emir's neck. Depending upon where the cut was made, Hamid-Jones supposed, resection of the thyroid and parathyroids might be necessary, too.

Specialists from the various subteams—neurosurgeons, osteoplastic surgeons, angiologists, and all the others—clustered thickly around the screens, fiddling with knobs and making last-minute adjustments with the help of the technicians. Even with most of the microsurgery done from a distance, and the thousands of microsutures done by a high-speed computer program, it would be tremendously complicated to reconnect all the major systems at once. Like too many men trying to dig a well, Hamid-Jones thought.

At last they seemed satisfied. The surgeons stepped back from the displays and took their stations. The chief of surgery, a portly man with an embroidered skullcap over a shaved head showing through his bubble helmet, nodded, and a circulating nurse disappeared through an archway to the left.

"Excuse me," Hamid-Jones said. "Do you mind if I have a look?"

His neighbor reluctantly yielded the binoculars. Hamid-Jones kept them focused on the archway, and a few minutes later was rewarded by the sight of a rolling stretcher guided by two orderlies.

The clone was wheeled in, smiling and woozy from the preliminary anesthetic. He raised himself on one elbow to get a better look at the packed tiers of people surrounding him. He waved at the crowd while the surgical team hooked him up to the life-support equipment. He seemed to be enjoying the attention.

Hamid-Jones did not think the clone could have grasped what was about to happen. He was acting as if he thought this was some kind of coronation ceremony, with himself as sovereign-to-be. The poor creature could only have absorbed the vague impression that after the operation, he—or most of him—would somehow "be" the Emir. Hamid-Jones was not surprised. From hints he had picked up over the years from the Palace technicians who were his own low-level counterparts at the Garden of Clones, he knew that the stable of spare bodies grown from the Emir's cells—though they were pampered and maintained in superb physical condition—were kept in a state of blissful, vegetablelike ignorance. They remained mental infants, offering no threat of usurpation. Those who showed signs of independent thought were quietly erased.

The Emir had cause to fear himself. He knew his own character too well.

Hamid-Jones trained the binoculars on the clone's face. It was uncanny to see the Emir's distinctive lineaments in the unformed, characterless features. There was the same parrot's beak of a nose, not as fleshy as it became in later life; the same full lips without the downward twist that had later become permanent. The sloppy chin was firm and youthful. The clone looked to be about twenty years old. Did the Emir really look like this, Hamid-Jones wondered, before the lines of cruelty and self-indulgence were etched so deeply into his face?

"How long are you going to hog the binoculars, brother?" the podiatrist complained with a sharp tug at his sleeve.

Silently, Hamid-Jones gave up the binoculars again. The little man snatched at them eagerly and lost himself in the scene below.

Even without close-up detail, Hamid-Jones could tell that they were putting the clone under. He seemed to slump in the middle of one of his cheerful waves at the crowd, and the anesthesiologists gently eased him to a prone position. When the anesthesiologists moved away from him, Hamid-Jones could see that two white dots had replaced the clone's eyes. Foam pads. Other electrical contacts had been pasted over the mastoids, or perhaps plugged into previously implanted sockets, and a violet light was blinking on a small machine. They had knocked him the rest of the way out with electric anesthesia instead of using the IVs that were already in place. Hamid-Jones wondered why.

A hush fell over the auditorium. Hamid-Jones raised his eyes and saw the Emir being wheeled in through the great arch behind the throne. He lay easily on the stretcher, his hands folded on his chest. He was clad simply in two seamless lengths of white cloth—the pilgrim's *rida* and *izar*—with the upper length thrown toga-fashion over his shoulder. It was a nice touch, and a convenient garb for surgery. He was bareheaded, also in the fashion of a pilgrim—the first time any living subject had seen him that way. Hamid-Jones thought he looked no less imposing, even with his bald pate and the few strands of greasy hair around the fringes. His stretcher was surrounded by household guards, big men whose gold-frogged robes had been replaced by sterile gowns and bubble helmets, their automatic weapons sealed within transparent plastic bags that would allow them to be fired in a hurry if necessary.

As orderlies transferred the supine Emir to the operating table, the guards took up positions within the already overcrowded operating arena. They were facing inward, not outward, their guns trained loosely on the surgeons and nurses.

Hamid-Jones hoped they'd been briefed thoroughly on every possible medical contingency.

From the forest of IV poles surrounding the twin operating tables, there was plenty of fresh blood available, anyway. Dozens of clones must have been bled in preparation, and more would be standing by in case of emergency.

He got the binoculars back from the podiatrist long enough to see the Emir's lip curl as he snarled at the technician who was clamping the stereotaxic cage in place. One of the padded pins must have pinched his temple. A guard's finger felt for the trigger of his weapon within its plastic wrapper, and he took a step forward. The technician's bearded face turned ashen, but to his credit he continued screwing in the wing nut until the clamp was firm.

There was another touchy moment when the IV nurse slid his transparent catheters into the carotids and jugulars in preparation for the dangerous interlude between bodies when the heart-lung machine would have to take over. The Emir didn't care for the sensation at all, even though he'd been desensitized with an anesthetic spray followed by an axillary block. His lips writhed with what must have been inventive abuse, and the nurse's hand began to tremble so that there was a bright spurt of arterial blood that soiled the linens. The nurse, a large burly man, slipped to the floor in a dead faint.

The chief surgeon signaled, and another IV nurse stepped in to finish the job. Two orderlies dragged the unconscious man away. Hamid-Jones didn't envy him. He was in for it, whether the Emir lived or died. Hamid-Jones felt sorry for the chap. But you had to have steady nerves to be around royalty.

A few moments later, Hamid-Jones understood the reason for the axillary block. A pair of neurosurgeons were slitting open the Emir's neck and teasing out—if Hamid-Jones remembered his human anatomy correctly—the first four cervical nerves. A web of fine platinum wires was attached to them with tiny clamps, and a computer screen went wild, then settled down. The Emir grimaced but said nothing.

Next, the neurosurgeons rotated the cage slightly to get at the back of the Emir's neck and inserted electrical leads between the second and third cervical vertebrae directly into the Emir's spinal column. The Emir turned pale and opened his mouth, but fortunately for the surgeons, he was now unable to talk. A larger computer screen flashed a complicated display, and after a few dicey moments, two sets of multicolored geometric pulses got into rhythm and canceled each other out.

The Emir would remain conscious throughout. He was far too wary and distrustful to allow general anesthesia.

Hamid-Jones was astounded. The computer-mediated nerve block would make the amputation of the Emir's body painless, of course. And after a thousand years of Arab medical renaissance, techniques for eliminating shock were well advanced. But still, the psychic shock of seeing oneself beheaded, of knowing oneself—however temporarily—as a disembodied head, must be enormous. Hamid-Jones couldn't begin to imagine what thoughts must go through a brain at such a time.

But now he could figure out why there had been no general anesthesia for the clone either—why he had been put under with electric anesthesia instead. When the Emir was finally connected to his new body, he might become a little woozy from the traces of preliminary anesthetics still in the clone's bloodstream, but he would not lose consciousness.

"They've begun to behead the donor," his irritating seatmate said peevishly. "I don't want to miss it, brother, if you don't mind."

With a sigh, Hamid-Jones relinquished the binoculars once again.

It took more than twenty minutes to amputate the clone's head, even with a high-speed computer program doing most of the mechanical work while relays of surgeons made their thousands of microscopic slashes by light pen on the highly magnified images of the holo simulacrum. They couldn't simply lop the head off. It had to be done millimeter by millimeter, millimicron by millimicron, so that all the necessary structures were properly exposed and accessible for precise alignment.

Finally the last tendon, the last shreds of tissue, were parted. The head rolled an inch or two from the intubated stump of the neck and came to a stop. Two surgeons, working at either side, quickly clamped the remaining small blood vessels, attached tubes to join the spaghetti tangle already connected to the heart-lung machine. A nurse picked up the severed head by its hair and disposed of it in the laundry basket.

Now it was the Emir's turn.

There was a short wait while the computer checked its catalog and certified that all systems were go, and then the Emir gave the nod, figuratively, to the surgeons by forming a silent *yallah* with his lips.

The guards moved in a little closer. A whole battery of anesthesiologists bent over their consoles, ready to damp out the least twinge, while two more, just to play it safe, sprayed the Emir's neck with a surface anesthetic and administered a shot of succinylcholine to paralyze the Emir's respiratory muscles for the few moments it would take to begin oxygenating the bloodstream directly through the machines.

A trio of government mullahs onstage began praying in a reedy chorus. Over their voices, Hamid-Jones could hear the thin buzzing of a small circular saw, as the microinstruments on their jointed arms descended on the Emir's neck like the fingers of a gigantic skeleton hand.

The procedure took only thirteen minutes this time. A nurse pushed the operating table to one side and threw a sheet over it. The cage containing the Emir's head rose on its stem with a whirring of small motors and tilted to present the stump of the neck with its trailing skeins of tubes and wires. It swiveled toward the table containing the clone's headless body, then began to lower itself into position.

"Excuse me," Hamid-Jones said, "but could I just borrow those back for a minute?"

The podiatrist surrendered the binoculars with ill grace. He'd gotten the eyepieces steamed up, and while Hamid-Jones was busy polishing them on a corner of his cloak he missed what happened next.

The first thing he was aware of was that the tough-looking man who had given the podiatrist a dirty look was standing up, and that there was something wrong about his right arm. With an effort, Hamid-Jones made sense out of what his eyes were reporting: the man was pulling off his right arm and fitting the bent crook of its elbow into his left armpit.

There were hoarse cries as men in the surrounding seats scrambled to get out of the way. The detached arm was pointing at the stage and spitting fire from its extended index finger with a sputtering sound. Display screens shattered below, and Hamid-Jones saw red stains suddenly blossom on several of the gray surgical gowns.

It was all happening very fast. Now Hamid-Jones noticed that five or six other men had also risen to their feet in various parts of the audience, and were raking the stage with automatic fire. Some of the people there still hadn't realized what was taking place, but in the VIP section gilt chairs were overturning as the more alert observers scurried to get out of the field of fire.

One of the terrorists heaved what looked like his own sandal-shod foot at the stage, and it exploded with a gout of orange fire. The explosion brought Hamid-Jones out of his fog of bewildered disbelief, and he moved instinctively to act without thinking of the consequences.

The left-handed *mujahid* had climbed up on his seat and was standing straddle-legged for a more commanding field of fire. With only one arm, he wasn't able to balance very well. Hamid-Jones shoved as hard as he could with both hands. The man toppled over and landed headfirst, two rows ahead, his weapon still spitting fire.

A rain of small missiles spattered around him, and Hamid-Jones realized that security men in the balconies were indiscriminately hosing down the foci of terrorist activity in the audience. Other security guards were climbing over the rows of seats, trampling people, as they tried to reach the terrorists. Hamid-Jones came to his senses then and dived under the seats. He collided with something soft, and there was a grunt from the podiatrist, who babbled: "Please, brother, get away from me! Find your own hiding place!" Hamid-Jones wedged himself in without apology as a murderous crossfire filled the chamber.

The firing fizzled out after a minute. Hamid-Jones cautiously raised his head and saw a frenzied tangle of guards with scimitars hacking away with great industry at the dead body of the one-armed man.

Below, blue smoke was trickling from the smashed life-support machines and computer screens. People in red-splashed gowns writhed on the floor. A rain of blood had exploded from the burst IV reservoir, drenching the stage in crimson.

Some fluke of damaged machinery had made the stereotaxic cage, with the Emir's head still firmly clamped in place, rotate to an upright position. The head seemed to be undamaged. Several connections dangled loose, but the four main tubes to the carotids and jugulars still seemed to be connected to the smoking, badly leaking heart-lung machine. A technician was trying to stanch the flow, and a gaggle of surviving surgeons, some of them wounded, scuttled about on frantic errands of salvage.

The elaborately prepared headless body of the clone was badly damaged. Hamid-Jones could see where it was stitched from groin to sternum by explosive microflechettes—a perfect butcher's mess. The machines were still pumping blood through it, but red fountains were spurting out all over the torso while the physicians stood by, helpless.

Beside Hamid-Jones, the little podiatrist risked a peek. He gasped at the carnage. "I don't see how they can get another clone here and prepare it in time, not with the surgical machines out of commission," he said in a shaking voice. "They'll have to reattach the Emir's head to the old body!"

Hamid-Jones said nothing. Even if the head could be saved, the Emir's own body was so much dead meat.

The security force had begun to hustle the audience out of the *majlis* chamber, steering them away from the stage. The great hall emptied faster than Hamid-Jones would have believed possible, as the guards, with shouts and blows, pushed the stragglers along. Up in the press gallery, guards were beating up a holovid cameraman who hadn't stopped taking pictures fast enough.

Hamid-Jones and his seatmate joined the flow. As he stumbled along in the thick crowd toward the exit, Hamid-Jones found that he was still holding the binoculars. He raised them for a last look at the wrecked operating theater.

A security guard knocked the binoculars from his hand. But not before he had a chance to see the Emir's severed head, mottled with fury, mouthing silent commands as it gasped away its last moments of awareness.

CHAPTER 5

"**M**ake believe you don't see him, and maybe he'll sit somewhere else," Ja'far said.

Rashid was standing like an ox at the far end of the cloning section's canteen, balancing a tray loaded with the day's specials and looking around at the crowded tables. His meaty forearms, covered with golden fuzz, bulged out of his short-sleeved lab coat, and he looked very *ferengi* despite the red-checkered keffia clapped over his head.

"Why?" Hamid-Jones said, chewing on a mouthful of the canteen's greasy mutton and eggplant. "I thought he was a chum of yours. You were going to go paradise-hopping with him last night."

"I think he's under suspicion," Ja'far said, lowering his voice. "He was called in for questioning this morning."

"Everybody's being called in for questioning," Feisel said. "It'll probably be our turn this afternoon."

"Shh, I think that fellow sitting by himself is a Greenie," Ja'far warned.

Hamid-Jones sneaked a look at the man in question. He saw a square-jawed, humorless type in dark blue who fit the popular stereotype of a dedicated agent of the Department of Rectitude, or the Green Bureau, as it was more generally known.

"The place is crawling with plainclothes *shurtayeen*," Feisel complained. "Snooping around the labs, poking into everything. You know little Ali, the bottle washer in protein assembly? They took him away for a scourging this morning. And all because someone overheard him making a remark about the fedayeen being clever to get past the eyeprint machine at

54

the Palace security check yesterday. Poor Ali wouldn't know a terrorist from a six-legged racing camel."

"Not so loud." Ja'far glanced nervously around the canteen. "Oh oh, he's seen us."

Hamid-Jones followed his glance. Rashid, holding his tray high, was coming toward them across the crowded canteen floor with a smile on his face.

"You two should be ashamed of yourselves," Hamid-Jones said. "Rashid may be a bit meddlesome, but he means well. He's always been a good friend to the both of you." He swallowed, not comfortable in the role of a defender of Rashid, but knowing why he was doing it. "To the three of us," he amended firmly.

Ja'far's dark, liquid eyes shifted away from his. "Oh, I like Rashid, but he talks too much. He's the sort who gets himself into trouble. And other people as well."

"You talk too much yourself, brother," Feisel said. He gave a serpentine smile to Hamid-Jones. "What he means, ya Abdul, is that Rashid likes to know too much about other people's affairs. And he likes to show that he knows. And so he digs himself in too deep . . . just the type the *shurtayeen* love to recruit."

"He's no informer!" Hamid-Jones burst out indignantly.

Feisel and Ja'far exchanged a glance. "Oh, no, of course not," Feisel agreed.

"Anyone might have thoughtlessly repeated what Ali said . . ." Ja'far trailed off.

"Certainly," Feisel supplied. "Protein assembly's a large department."

Hamid-Jones's face burned. He didn't think for a moment that either of them believed that Rashid had informed on the little bottle washer. The trouble was that Rashid, big, bluff, and florid-faced, was too obviously *mawali*—just the type that attracted scrutiny during security flaps—and they didn't want to be seen with him. Hamid-Jones had just as much *mawali* in his blood, but with his lean, aquiline features and flashing black eyes, he looked all right.

Feisel and Ja'far smiled at him in brotherly fashion, showing how unprejudiced they were.

"Whew, what a morning! Thanks for saving a place for me, brothers."

Rashid was at the table, hooking a chair into place with his foot. Hamid-Jones moved his tray aside to make room for him.

"*Sabah il-khayr, ya* Rashid!" he said loudly, determinedly effusive. "Have a seat."

"Yes, do, *ya* Rashid," Feisel and Ja'far murmured.

Rashid set all his dishes in a row preparatory to attacking them. "They grilled me for an hour," he said between mouthfuls. "Awfully interested in what we do here in the stables cloning department. Particularly in our recent bird projects. Seems they've decided that the incident yesterday, with the falcon that was supposed to be a gift for the Emir, was intended as a diversion to get Palace security to relax. What do you fellows think?"

"The Clonemaster thinks it was a coincidence—two different terrorist groups happening to pick the same day for an attack," Hamid-Jones said recklessly, not caring that he was repeating the Clonemaster's indiscretions. The Clonemaster had been unhurt in the operating theater assault, but had been badly shaken, and during the ride back home perhaps had talked more freely than he ought to have to a subordinate.

"Oh?" Rashid raised his eyebrows. "You were there, weren't you, *ya* Abdul? What really happened? They're not letting much out in the newscasts."

Ja'far and Feisel looked everywhere except at Hamid-Jones. Feisel's lips pursed a silent warning.

"They had weapons disguised as body parts," Hamid-Jones said defiantly. "Plastic the same density as flesh to get through X rays and muon scanners, barrels and firing assemblies in the shapes of bones. At least that's what the Clonemaster theorized."

"Right arms mostly?"

Hamid-Jones nodded.

"I thought so. I caught a split second of something that looked like that before they cut off the live holovid. It must have been the Christian Jihad, then. Only Christians would be fanatic enough to be willing to sacrifice their right arms."

He looked around the table, pleased with his analysis.

"Yes, you may be right, *ya* Rashid," Feisel said smoothly.

"Of course I'm right. I'll tell you something else I managed to pick up. You want to know how those dogs got past the eyeprint machine? Each of them sacrificed one eye as well. They were given false eyes imprinted with retinal patterns to match their other identification."

"Is that what you told Ali?" Ja'far said.

Rashid's pink face turned a shade pinker. "He may have overheard me. He should not have repeated it in front of the wrong people.''

'''Don't distress yourself, *ya* Rashid,'' Feisel said. ''It was not your fault. Poor simple-minded Ali. He should have known better.''

Rashid looked at him suspiciously, then went on. ''At any rate, that's what the fuss is about here today. The suicide bomber with the falcon also was equipped with a false eye. And the gyrfalcon derivative he was carrying was a very sophisticated job of bioengineering. It could only have been done with the most advanced cloning techniques. The little bootleg shops that grow back hands and feet for convicted thieves don't have the technical capacity to handle something like that.''

''They can't believe that anyone here was responsible!'' Hamid-Jones cried. ''A project like that couldn't be covered up except at the highest level.''

''Don't worry about it, *ya* Abdul,'' Ja'far said soothingly. ''It'll soon be cleared up. There was that investigation a couple of years ago about some fugitive with a half-regrown hand they apprehended, and the chief soon set them straight.''

Rashid stuffed a handful of rice and gravy into his face. He chewed and swallowed hastily, obviously bursting to tell them his next tidbit. ''I don't know about that,'' he said, licking his fingers. ''The Clonemaster himself may be under suspicion. At least they asked me an awful lot of questions about his comings and goings—if I'd noticed any suspicious characters visiting his house late at night, and so forth.''

''What did you tell them?'' Hamid-Jones said, horrified.

Rashid's bluff face contorted with naked jealousy, and he looked straight at Hamid-Jones. ''What could I tell them?'' he said bitterly. ''I told them I don't hobnob socially with the Clonemaster. *I'm* not his fair-haired boy around here. Not like some who're always hanging around his house at all hours.''

A crawling sensation went down Hamid-Jones's spine. Could Rashid possibly know anything about his unrequited attentions to Lalla, the Little Sugarplum? No, it wasn't possible—not unless Rashid himself had been hanging around the house in the Street of the Peacock. Hamid-Jones shook off the notion. Rashid couldn't possibly be as idiotic as he himself was. There had been many junior assistants over the years, he was sure, who thought that wooing the Clonemaster's daughter would be a shortcut to advancement. But they would have been young men of good family, not *mawali*. Rashid might be pushy, irritating, socially inept. But he was not stupid or unrealistic.

The crawling sensation persisted. He suddenly remembered something that had happened during one of his all-night vigils below the harem window. It had been about three in the morning. Two men in dark cloaks had appeared, keeping to the shadows. There had been something foreign about one of them, though Hamid-Jones couldn't put his finger on it—perhaps the drape of his keffia, that reminded him vaguely of the star travelers one saw around the big hotels, trying to dress like the locals and getting the Martian style wrong. Hamid-Jones had slipped out of sight behind a tunnel support. The men, after looking quickly about, had gone straight to the Clonemaster's gate and let themselves in without knocking for the sleeping porter; the door had been left open for them. Hamid-Jones had shrugged the incident off; it was none of his business who the Clonemaster entertained, or at what hour.

He realized with a start that he was frowning with concentration, and that he had missed Rashid's next remark. Feisel came to his rescue.

"The Clonemaster plays no favorites. He's a hard taskmaster, but fair. We've all been to his home at one time or another, either for the department banquets or because he had some business to discuss. If Abdul's been getting his attention recently, it's because of the project he's working on that the Palace is interested in—and as for yesterday, the Palace probably wanted to look him over."

From the knowing look that Feisel and Ja'far exchanged, Hamid-Jones realized that the cloning job on the Emir's precious stallion must be common knowledge. Rashid had been unable to keep from blabbing.

The resentful look on Rashid's face gave way to curiosity. "At least you can give us the real scuttlebutt, *ya* Abdul. The official news reports say that the Emir's head and the new body survived the attack without a scratch. But they aren't showing any pictures, and the Emir hasn't made the postoperative pronouncement that was scheduled. Is it true? Is his Majesty really all right?"

Hamid-Jones didn't need the nervous glances of Ja'far and Feisel in the direction of the Rectitude agent to remind him to exercise extreme caution in his reply.

"The Emir's head was alive and undamaged when I left the *majlis* hall. That's all I can tell you."

"But—"

"All I know is that the Palace bulletins say that the transposition was successfully completed by the surviving surgeons after the hall was cleared for security purposes."

Hamid-Jones was sweating. He and the other members of the audience had been warned in no uncertain terms, before they were allowed to leave the palace, to keep their mouths shut. Apparently the warning had not been heeded by some of those present. Hamid-Jones shuddered as he recalled the grisly segment on the morning news program. Some thirty of his fellow witnesses had been executed at dawn for "spreading false and malicious rumors." The method of execution had been braising. Another twenty or so, whose degree of culpability had been less serious, had had their tongues publicly cut out. Security agents had appeared the night before at Hamid-Jones's lodgings to interview his neighbors; doubtless they were still working overtime to interview the friends, neighbors, and relatives of the other 6,000 people who had witnessed the operating theater attack.

He stole a glance at the Bureau cop and froze as the man paused in the act of shoveling a ball of falafel into his mouth and met his eyes.

"I don't think you should ask anymore questions, *ya* Rashid," Feisel cut in.

"I only wanted to know if—"

"According to the official bulletins, the Emir will remain in seclusion until the nerve connections are fully knitted and his Majesty is up and about. That seems quite reasonable. It must have been a harrowing experience for his Majesty."

"We should all go to the mosque this evening and pray for his speedy recovery," Ja'far put in.

The Rectitude agent was grazing peacefully on his falafel, his eyes no longer on Hamid-Jones. Hamid-Jones gave Feisel an oblique, grateful grimace.

Ja'far and Feisel rose to their feet. Hamid-Jones rose with them. "Well, back to work," Feisel said.

Rashid was in a sulk. He flung a parting shot at Hamid-Jones. "When they call you in for questioning, remember what I said. They'll want to know how much you know about the Clonemaster. Maybe it's not so good to be his favorite. That's all I'm saying, so be prepared."

It was midafternoon before they sent for him. Yezid the Prod appeared unannounced in the doorway of his cubicle and stood there looking him over, an expression of sour satisfaction on his stubbled face.

"They want you in room aleph-five," he grunted.

Hamid-Jones was in the middle of synthesizing an oligonucleotide probe. "All right," he said. "I'll just finish condensing this blocking group."

"Now," Yezid growled.

He glared redly at Hamid-Jones, tapping his wooden rod impatiently against his leg, and waited while Hamid-Jones shut down his console. The nucleotides on the screen blinked out one by one. Hamid-Jones hoped they would remain stable till he returned. He had spent most of the day catching up on his sequencing work. The work on the Winged One's genome was stalled until he could get another DNA sample, and the Clonemaster had not been seen all day. Hamid-Jones wondered if the project would go on now that the Emir's sponsorship was moot; though it might, he supposed, remain on the Palace books.

His mind skittered away from the dangerous thoughts. He had seen with his own eyes the life draining away from the Emir's caged head, and even if the demoralized surgeons had somehow managed to hook the major vessels up to an auxiliary blood supply within minutes, the head could be nothing more than a vegetable. But with nobody admitting that anything was wrong, it was best not to think about such things.

"Never mind locking up," Yezid said. "I'll take care of it."

Room aleph-five had been cleared out for the convenience of the interviewers. Ordinarily it was a small conference room. The long table had been pushed haphazardly against a wall, but the Green Bureau personnel had brought along their own portable equipment and folding furniture. Hamid-Jones's eyes rested briefly on a collapsible aluminum flogging bench that was spotted with old bloodstains, and he quickly glanced away.

The interrogator was a narrow-skulled man in a military blouse and a headcloth bound into place by an *agal* made of twisted silver cord. The *agal* bore no insignia, but the silver probably implied the rank of colonel. He had two assistants: a thin young man with a voice-activated tachyscriber for taking dictation, and a muscular fellow of undetermined function.

There was also a stainless steel utility cart dangling an assortment of wires and tubes equipped with every sort of monitoring lead, from alligator clips to blood-sampling needles. Among the interrogation instruments on display, Hamid-Jones recognized an EEG recorder and a rather wicked-looking dolorimeter. A green smock draped over the handle of the cart may or may not have indicated an absent third assistant.

The colonel motioned Hamid-Jones to a low stool. He sat down gingerly. Nobody moved to hook him up to any of the equipment, which led him to hope that the interview might not go too badly.

"Abdul ben Arthur Hamid-Jones?" the colonel asked, consulting a file folder.

Hamid-Jones developed a frog in his throat but managed to say, "Yes."

The stenographer's pad beeped. Out of the corner of his eye, Hamid-Jones saw it begin to scroll.

"You're an assistant to the Clonemaster of the Royal Stables?" the colonel asked.

"Uh . . . one of several assistants," Hamid-Jones said nervously. "Actually there are eight cloning technicians as such, that is, not counting those whose job is bringing the clone to term and so forth—"

He cut himself off, conscious that he was showing a tendency to babble. Guilty people did that. He told himself that he was not guilty of anything.

"What are your duties here?" the colonel asked, looking sleepy and bored.

"Uh, I work with original genetic material, sometimes to manufacture a simple duplicate genome, sometimes to modify the pronuclei by adding or subtracting various genetic elements. Uh, am I being too technical?"

The colonel gave him no help, his expression masked by the curved green lenses that blanked out his eyes.

Hamid-Jones swallowed hard. "I, uh, sometimes have to design a gene or part of a gene, or put together a hybrid," he went on. "Or redesign recognition sites to accept cross-species splices—" He stopped again, wondering if he was going into too much detail. "I, uh, that is, my responsibility basically stops after I give the epigenesis department the fertile egg or early stage blastocyst . . . in the same way as I get some of my nucleotide sequences ready-made from protein assembly or other departments . . ." He trailed off.

"Have you ever made a falcon?" the colonel asked lazily.

Hamid-Jones became aware that a small light was flickering somewhere on the utility cart, so perhaps in some fashion he was hooked up after all—possibly to a voice stress analyzer or a sniffer that examined the airborne molecules of the perspiration being given off by his skin.

"Well . . . yes, of course, but—"

"Specifically, have you recently worked in any way on a Mars-adapted arctic gyrfalcon derivative?"

"No." Hamid-Jones was glad to be able to say it truthfully.

"Could you have contributed unwittingly to any part of such a job—say, on some special order authorized by the Clonemaster?"

"No." He spoke too quickly. Sweat broke out on his forehead as he suddenly realized that the thing hinted at was not entirely impossible. There had been the glowing nightingales for the Vizier's garden, a spinoff of the singing peacock project. Some firefly genes had been added to the nightingale genome. But he had prepared great batches of a falcon-compatible DNA polymerase that bonded well to both species. Some of it, just conceivably, could have been used after hours without his knowledge.

"Go on," the colonel purred. "I believe you had something more to say."

The light on the utility cart began to flicker more rapidly. The muscle man made a small adjustment to the equipment, then stepped back again.

Hamid-Jones floundered. "Well, uh, of course in the sense that the genetic code for all forms of life uses basically the same raw materials, I suppose you could say theoretically that there are a lot of shortcuts to gene synthesis. But the coding for DNA templates involved in protein manufacture is very specific to species, and I'm sure I would have recognized—"

"Have you ever been involved in the cloning of human hands or feet?"

Hamid-Jones was shocked. "Certainly not!"

"Are you sure?" The colonel drummed his fingertips on his collapsible desk.

"You need a medical license for prosthetic cloning—it's illegal for a veterinary practitioner!" Hamid-Jones protested, his face hot for no reason. "Anyway, the preparation of the bud is a delicate procedure. It has to be grown in vitro and then grafted. That qualifies as minor surgery. But first the desired portion of the genome must be isolated—you can only work with the patient's own DNA. Otherwise there's the problem of rejection you see in some bootleg jobs—hands falling off and that sort of thing."

He was saying too much. He ought not to know about such things. He faltered, stopped. Relays clicked on the utility cart, and Hamid-Jones heard mechanical pens scratching on paper.

Unaccountably, the colonel dropped the subject. "Tell me, *ya* Abdul," he said silkily, "is the Clonemaster a good chief to work for?"

"Oh, yes," he said in a rush, pleased at the opportunity to switch to a harmless topic. "I like it here very much."

"He treats you kindly, then?"

"He is fair, yes, and gives his assistants credit for the work they do."

The colonel consulted his file. "And you are welcome in his home, are you not?"

Hamid-Jones saw the trap then. "He is a generous employer," he stammered. "He has made all of us welcome in his house on occasion."

"And what sort of people frequent his home?"

Hamid-Jones spread his hands over his chest in token of earnestness. "How would I know, *sidi*? I am only a subordinate."

"You haven't seen any Centaurans there, then?"

"N-no, *sidi*."

"Who might know, then? The Clonemaster has a marriageable daughter. Are any of your coworkers courting her?"

The question, coming suddenly, was a shock. "N-not that I know of, *sidi*."

The colonel sighed. "It's a serious matter to withhold information, *ya* Abdul. You know that, don't you?"

"Yes, *sidi*." Hamid-Jones sweated. What had he gotten himself into?

"You don't want to get yourself into trouble by trying to protect a friend?"

"No, *sidi*."

The colonel leaned across his portable desk and spoke almost kindly. "The girl is a flirt, *ya* Abdul. We know all about her. Quite a few young men have stood in the Street of the Peacock mooning up at the window of the women's quarters, and we have located most of them. No blame attaches to them, do you understand that? We only want to question them about what they may have seen. If you know of such a person, you'll be doing him a favor by telling us his name. Now, do you have anything to say?"

Hamid-Jones dry-welled the question. "No, *sidi*."

The little light on the utility cart was blinking madly. The muscular assistant peered intently at a readout, and a look passed between him and the colonel. Hamid-Jones expected the worst, but the colonel seemed satisfied. The rest of the interview was perfunctory. After another quarter hour, he was dismissed.

"Keep your eyes open, *ya* Abdul," the colonel told him on the way out. "We may have more questions for you later."

It was only when Hamid-Jones was outside the door that he realized what a fool he'd been. It was one thing to admit to aspiring to a girl above one's station. It was quite another to deliberately attempt to deceive the Department of Rectitude. He had put himself squarely in the frying pan. Rashid probably suspected his vigils at Lalla's window, and sooner or later he would spill the beans to Ja'far and Feisel. Mr. Najib and the other lodgers at his digs knew he was moonstruck over some girl, and they had already been interviewed once, so far. The eunuch who had seen Lalla drop her note into the street might have recognized him. Or Lalla herself might be questioned.

Thinking about the note reminded him that he had better do something about answering it. Had it only been yesterday that he had retrieved Lalla's token from under the Clonemaster's eyes? So much had happened since then!

Come to the little gate tomorrow, the note had said, *and look for a silken thread.*

It was clear. Lalla was not very imaginative, but she did not need to be. It was a classic ploy. The thread would dangle, invisible to casual passersby, invisible to the household eunuchs. He would pour out his impassioned heart in a reply and attach the message to the thread. Lalla would haul it up. And then what?

Hamid-Jones's knees went weak. His mouth was dry. He was filled with sudden longing. What did it matter that the Emir was dead, that a kingdom hung in the balance, that the security men were running around like ants in a kicked-in anthill? What did he care for danger? All the poets had written of the fickleness of woman. He dared not wait.

His room had been ransacked while he was at work. Hamid-Jones closed the door softly behind him and inventoried the ruins with dull dismay. They hadn't even bothered to be careful. His mattress had been slit, and the rude hand that had rummaged around inside had left stuffing hanging out. His wardrobe drawers hung open, spilling clothing. His prized Turkish rug from Earth had been taken up for a look underneath and left in a crumpled heap in the center of the floor. They had even un-screwed the top plate of his alcohol stove and not taken the trouble to put it back together again.

He stared resentfully at the mess they'd made of his writing desk. Holocards were strewn helter-skelter across the surface, leaving him the tedious job of putting his library back in order. The screen of his reader, still blinking a page of text, showed that they'd spot-checked his books for righteousness. He hoped they hadn't sampled the unexpurgated *Maqamat* or his English-language *Chatterley*.

They'd been more thorough with the hard copy. Open books lay about where they'd been riffled through and discarded, print-outs were dumped on the floor, and every piece of unfiled paper-mail had been removed from its envelope, unfolded, and left in an untidy pile.

The little locked drawer had been broken open and its con-tents scattered. Praise Allah that there'd been nothing in it but paper clips, stamps, spare stylus batteries, and some old good-luck beads he'd had since boyhood.

He sat down and thanked his stars for the good fortune that had made him keep Lalla's note and her holo portrait on his person all day. He'd intended to lock them up in the drawer while he was at work, but had absentmindedly left them in his pocket.

After taking a few moments to get over the jitters *that* thought caused, he shut off the blinking screen and settled down to an-swer Lalla's note. He rummaged around and found a real pen and paper. He took a long time over it, laboring over the flowery *thuluth* script used in the language of love, and taking care to get the rhymes and rhythm just right.

The Street of the Peacock was queerly quiet for the early evening hour. The unrest caused by the previous day's assassi-nation attempt was keeping prudent people indoors. The Palace had not gotten around to officially canceling the three-day hol-iday it had announced to celebrate the Emir's beheading, but with nervous security forces patrolling the city corridors, and the Green cops and the religious police stopping suspicious pe-destrians at random and questioning them, a damper had been put on the celebration.

Hamid-Jones cursed himself for a fool again as he crossed the plaza of the Golden Gate, trying to look like any innocent eve-ning stroller. He'd already been stopped twice by the *mutawain* and asked what his business was, but he'd been able to satisfy them by saying he was on his way to the mosque to pray for the Emir's swift recovery. Fortunately he'd been able to produce a dog-eared prayer holo that Mr. Faqoosh had pressed on him some time ago and that had lain forgotten in his pocket. They had let him go with a warning and a few routine baton raps across the knuckles. But the next time he was stopped, he might not get off so easily.

A small party of halfhearted celebrants came toward him across the plaza—men and boys in holiday finery, carrying electric sparklers and paper flowers. They must have been on their way to a banquet that someone hadn't made up his mind to cancel. They gave Hamid-Jones a wide berth—people were skirting one another in the streets tonight—but one of the boys called out *"Masalaama!"* as they passed.

"Masalaama!" Hamid-Jones returned.

He slowed down as he approached the Clonemaster's house. A party of women swathed in black hurried by, crossing to the other side of the street to avoid him. The street in the vicinity of the Clonemaster's gate seemed to be quiet; a man in a striped djellaba was ambling past, and there was a parked delivery truck a few doors away, with no driver in sight.

By the time he saw the shadowed figure loitering in the niche in the wall, it was too late to stop without being conspicuous. Hamid-Jones thrust his hands deep in his pockets and walked on, trying to appear nonchalant.

The lurking figure across the street had emerged from the niche and was doing something at the wall near the Clonemaster's gate. His hands fumbled in the air for something invisible; he located whatever it was, and then his fingers were busy with a small white packet.

Hamid-Jones's heart almost stopped. The man was tying something to Lalla's silken thread!

As Hamid-Jones passed, the man looked up and their eyes met. Hamid-Jones received a second shock.

It was Rashid.

Rashid recognized him with a start and turned away guiltily. Hamid-Jones saw the florid face flush suddenly in the harsh streetlights. Neither of them spoke. Hamid-Jones walked on.

A few steps later hot fury welled up in him. Why the hell was he worried about being seen by Rashid? It was the other way around. Rashid had better worry about being seen by him! The effrontery of that ruddy *mawali*, with no prospects and the dust of the Australian Protectorate still between his toes, hanging around under Lalla's window and imagining the silken thread was for *him*!

An instant after that, the realization that he and Rashid were two of a kind let the air out of him. But he was double-damned if he was going to stop to think about that now! Holding onto what was left of his rage, he turned to give Rashid a piece of his mind.

And froze in place.

Four men in dark robes were erupting from the parked delivery truck with truncheons raised high and piling on the unfortunate Rashid. The man in the striped djellaba, a dozen yards down the street by now, turned and pounded across the pavement to join the quartet. Two more men who'd been hiding behind potted palms in the center strip burst out of concealment and added themselves to the scramble.

Hamid-Jones's first thought was that these were the religious police, reacting to Rashid's *mawali* face in a good neighborhood. Then he realized that the arrest was too organized; it had been a planned stakeout of the Clonemaster's house.

He caught a glimpse of Rashid's face as they dragged him to the delivery truck. His headcloth had been knocked off and blood was running down his forehead, but he didn't seem to be seriously damaged. He'd only received the normal clout on the head that you'd expect on being picked up by the authorities. Rashid's mouth was hanging loosely open, and his dazed eyes flickered in Hamid-Jones's direction, but he didn't say anything. He wasn't able to.

Yet.

Hamid-Jones turned and walked away, being careful not to hurry. No one noticed him.

The Clonemaster was arrested the next day.

Not much work got done at the stables lab that morning. Everybody seemed subdued. Whispers of Rashid's arrest had started making the rounds early; Hamid-Jones wasn't able to figure out how they got started. People clotted together at the water fountain or the *farash*'s coffee cart and spoke together in low tones, until Yezid the Prod broke them up. Yezid seemed to be everywhere that day, squelching rumors before they got started, issuing warnings—in a couple of cases using the rattan on members of the office help.

Hamid-Jones managed to see the Clonemaster about midmorning, but the Clonemaster wasn't much help. He seemed preoccupied, distant.

"Just go on as you've been doing, *ya* Abdul," he said vaguely. "I'll let you know later about the pronuclei transfer."

"But is the Winged One project still on the schedule?"

"That remains to be seen."

"But—"

"Just carry on as best you can."

"But I'll need some additional nucleotide samples, and I've got to know if—"

"That will do, *ya* Abdul. I'll speak to you later."

But he never did. Shortly before the noon prayer, a security squad swooped down on the lab—four burly gorillas in camouflage keffias and a plainclothes officer in charge. Yezid the Prod swept in ahead of them and brayed at everyone to close the doors of their cubicles and not look out. Hamid-Jones heard a thud and a yelp as Yezid applied his rod to somebody who had remained in the way.

After a few hushed minutes, Hamid-Jones opened his door a crack and risked a peek. He could hear voices down the hallway—polite, dignified tones of protest from the Clonemaster and the coldly formal, harsh inflections of the officer. The Clonemaster gave it up—his pride would not have let him continue—and Hamid-Jones watched as the knot of men marched in silence past his door, the Clonemaster boxed in by the four gorillas and the officer walking a little ahead. The Clonemaster hadn't been touched, and Hamid-Jones wondered if someone of his rank would be exempt from the usual preliminary beating during the ride to the station.

Yezid appeared a moment later, looking as if he had swallowed a pickle and enjoyed it, and stood watching the security men depart, the rod in his hand twitching absentmindedly, like a cat's tail. Hamid-Jones quietly shut his door before Yezid could turn in his direction.

The rumors flew all afternoon, despite Yezid's efforts. He couldn't be everywhere at once. At the ablutions font before the noon devotion, Ja'far sidled up to Hamid-Jones and said, "Odd, isn't it, that they pick up Rashid, and the very next morning they come to take the Clonemaster away. Remember what I said about how the Greenies recruit informers? They get the goods on someone, and then they blackmail him."

"What could Rashid possibly know about the Clonemaster?"

Hamid-Jones protested. "Besides, why would the *shurtayeen* beat up one of their own informers?"

"To make it look good, of course," Ja'far retorted. He paused in his ablutions, water dripping from his forearms. "How did you know they beat him up?"

"I . . . uh . . ." Hamid-Jones cursed himself for the slip. "I guess I just assumed . . ."

"My cousin saw it from a window," Ja'far confided. "He works in one of the big houses on Peacock Street. He says the Green police set Rashid up. They sent him a note that was supposed to be from the Clonemaster's daughter, and the poor fool fell for the bait. Now they own him."

Hamid-Jones began to sweat. How much else had Ja'far's cousin seen? And would the man know him by sight? He couldn't recall ever having met a cousin of Ja'far.

"I wouldn't pay any attention to such rumors," he said desperately. "The *shurtayeen* are probably just interested in what Rashid may have seen at the Clonemaster's house. He told us that himself. And they asked me if *I* knew anything when they questioned me. Didn't they ask you?"

"And what did you tell them, *ya* Abdul?" Ja'far said, giving him an odd look.

Hamid-Jones wasn't able to reply, because Yezid came along just then, swinging his rod. "Hurry it up," he rumbled. "The *zuhr* prayer starts in a minute. Why don't you do your ablutions in the morning?"

Hamid-Jones spent a sleepless night. If Ja'far's cousin had been right and Rectitude agents provocateurs had set Rashid up, then last night had been the first time that Rashid had camped under Lalla's window. He couldn't have seen men who looked like Centaurans slipping through the gate in the middle of the night—or anything else of interest to the Bureau.

Except Hamid-Jones's presence in the Street of the Peacock! He could toss *that* nugget at the *shurtayeen* to get himself off the hook.

And even if he didn't, there were Ja'far's newly awakened suspicions, and Ja'far's cousin, and the eunuch in the Clonemaster's household, and—

Hamid-Jones groaned as the muezzin's wake-up call cut through his disordered thoughts. He rolled out of bed, washed, dressed, and made a breakfast of sorts out of a stale disk of bread and some cold *fool* that he found in the cupboard.

He was thoroughly resigned by the time he got to work. He only wanted to get it over with. All he hoped was that the *shurtayeen* wouldn't beat him up too badly.

When he walked into the cloning section, he got a surprise. All the employees were standing around in the central atrium, looking nervous and worried. Yezid poked his rod in his direction and bawled, "You're late! Get in there with the others, and don't hold things up any longer!"

A Rectitude officer stood over to one side, conferring in low tones with one of his subordinates. It was the colonel, this time in uniform, with tabs on his shoulders.

Hamid-Jones did as he was told, though he smarted at Yezid's uncalled-for tone. He was not late—he just wasn't ten minutes early, as usual. As it was, Yezid had to wait another few minutes for the rest of the latecomers to straggle in before herding the cloning section to the main hall, where the other sections were also assembling.

He took his place in the crowd and stood patiently with them, waiting for the purpose of the assembly to be revealed. At least he could be sure of one thing—it didn't have anything to do with him. If they were going to grab him first thing this morning, they wouldn't do it this way.

The colonel took his time about relieving the suspense. He dawdled with his subordinates, going over some documents in a plastic binder with them. Finally he mounted the steps to the narrow platform and stood in front of the gigantic rotating model of the DNA helix that formed the hall's central decoration.

He unrolled an official-looking scroll. "This is to dispel any harmful speculation," he said by way of preamble. "Be informed that Hassan bin Fahd al-Hejjaj, Clonemaster of the Royal Stables, was executed this morning for conspiring against the person of the Emir and other high crimes. In view of his lineage and high position, Hassan bin Fahd al-Hejjaj was granted the merciful death of strangulation by the silken cord, by the express command of his Majesty himself."

Nobody dared to make a sound, of course, but somehow the crowded chamber was filled with a generalized suspiration of cautiously released breath and the rustle of shuffled feet.

"The Emir's justice is swift," the colonel went on. "Let this be a lesson to you all. Long live the Emir!"

"Long live the Emir!" the crowd recited obediently.

"The proclamation of execution will be posted for all to see. Now go about your work. Be vigilant."

And that was all there was to it. No details of the charges against the Clonemaster, nor did Hamid-Jones think there would be in the parchment notice that a Rectitude agent was now nailing to the wall, even if he'd had the nerve to go over and look at it.

He was dizzy with disbelief. Somehow, at the bottom of his mind, he'd believed that the whole thing would be straightened out—that the Clonemaster would return with the apologies of the *shurtayeen*, remain discreetly tight-lipped about the whole misunderstanding, and that things would return to normal. The Clonemaster had always been the most solid of solid citizens and had kept himself aloof from the petty Palace intrigues that swirled about him.

Ja'far was at his side as he shuffled out of the hall with the others. "I guess it was only to be expected," he said in a shaken voice. "But I didn't think it would be this soon."

"Expected?" Hamid-Jones choked. "For God's sake, who could expect such a thing?"

"Shh, control yourself, *ya* Abdul. I know you were a favorite of his. That's why you should watch out for yourself now."

"What do you mean?"

Ja'far looked about nervously. "I'm a friend of yours, *ya* Abdul. Otherwise I wouldn't be seen even talking to you. Just don't do anything foolish. Like going back to the Street of the Peacock."

With that, he pushed ahead, leaving Hamid-Jones by himself.

It was only when he was back in his cubicle, trying to look busy whenever Yezid's patrol took him past the door, that Hamid-Jones stopped to think about the wording of the execution notice. The Clonemaster had been granted a merciful death by the express command of the Emir himself. But it was not possible that the Emir was still alive.

Who was issuing edicts in his name? And what did it all mean?

By the time of the *'asr* prayer in the late afternoon, the rumors had grown all out of proportion, fed by the lack of specifics in the execution notice. There was nothing Yezid could do to stop them. People whispered together at the tea break, found plausible reasons for desk-hopping. Yezid had only to pass down a corridor for a new outburst of buzzing to follow in his wake.

"I have it from a friend who has a second cousin who works as a file clerk at Rectitude headquarters," one of the protein technicians told Hamid-Jones when they bumped into each other in the cryocontainer stockroom. "The Clonemaster's had connections with one of the terrorist underground organizations for years. He was a secret royalist sympathizer—wanted to bring back the former dynasty—you know, the Pretender. Well, what could you expect, with his family background?" He lowered his voice prudently. "He had princely blood himself, you know, way back."

"I don't believe it," Hamid-Jones said.

"I'm telling you, I just had lunch with my friend who has the second cousin in the Bureau. It'll be all over town by tomorrow. They've been watching the Clonemaster for a long time. At first they only suspected him of donating money to the al-Sharq organization. Then they got evidence that he was hiding fugitives in his house." He lowered his voice again. "He recloned severed hands and feet with the help of a veterinarian."

That was more serious. Terrorist organizations often supplied the convicted amputees among their members with realistic computerized prostheses—but such mechanical devices could not pass spaceport inspections or other security checks.

"Nonsense," Hamid-Jones said stoutly.

The protein technician suddenly remembered that Hamid-Jones was supposed to be one of the Clonemaster's protégés, signed out for the amino acid kit he had come to the stockroom for and, with a vague mumble, hurried off.

Hamid-Jones heard the same story a dozen times that day. Only the name of the supposed terrorist organization varied. Some versions connected the Clonemaster to the Christian Jihad. Others favored the Israeli Liberation Organization, the Syrtis Major separatists—even the Popular Front for an Assassins' Homeland.

But all the rumors agreed on the main point: the Clonemaster had been running a safe house and recloning service for terrorists.

As a child of his culture, Hamid-Jones began tentatively to draw conclusions from the rumors—or rather from the vector sum of the rumors and all their tantalizing gaps and divergences. It was a necessary survival skill in a society where the hard-copy media were long on polemics and short on facts, and where the state-controlled holovid served up officially approved news along with a dismal diet of sermons, sports, the safer classics, and a sprinkling of heavily censored holodramas from Earth.

The Clonemaster, it appeared, had simply been the victim of bad luck.

It had been the bioengineered gyrfalcon, the one that had provided a diversion for the Emir's assassins, that had originally thrown suspicion on the Clonemaster. But the Green Bureau's investigators, try as they might, had been unable to find any link between the attempted nuking of the palace and the attack in the *majlis* chamber. It had been an unfortunate coincidence for the Clonemaster, that was all. The Bureau cops had quietly dropped that line of inquiry.

The Bureau also had reluctantly abandoned the theory that the Clonemaster had been involved in the assassination attempt itself—though the charge would remain on the books to avoid embarrassment.

Autopsies on the terrorists had squelched the notion that a sophisticated shop like the Clonemaster's had taken part; the surgery had been crude, and any hole-in-the-corner clonelegger could have regrown the sacrificed body parts for the fedayeen. The focus of the investigation now was not cloning, but the electronics and prosthetics expertise that had provided the disguised weapons.

What remained was the Clonemaster's more generalized guilt. There seemed no doubt that, for all his aristocratic background, the esteemed scientist had been playing at revolution.

Even Hamid-Jones, despite his protestations to the contrary, now believed that.

All that remained to be established was the identity of the shadowy group or groups that had used the Clonemaster for its purposes. They would have had good slogans, at least—of that, Hamid-Jones was sure. The Clonemaster had been a man of the highest moral character.

"Now the purge starts," Feisel said bitterly at the sunset prayer. "That's what he's let us in for. The *shurtayeen* won't rest until they've found the Clonemaster's accomplices here at the stables. And taken in a few lukewarm religionists and closet hedonists for good measure."

"I don't believe there *were* any accomplices," Hamid-Jones insisted loyally. "The Clonemaster was an idealist. If he was involved in anything, he would have used outside help. He wouldn't have wanted to incriminate any of us here in the shop." The words stuck in his throat. "We were his children."

"It doesn't matter, does it?" Feisel said. "Scapegoats must be found."

It didn't take long. By quitting time that day, the purge had claimed its first victim, a palsied old veterinary's assistant whom the Clonemaster had kept on out of charity. Hamid-Jones stood well back with the others and watched as they dragged the old fellow away, cringing under the blows and sobbing his innocence.

Feisel spoke softly from behind him. "Don't count on your friends, *ya* Abdul. It's every man for himself."

Just a look, Hamid-Jones promised himself. Just a look down the street, and if he saw the least indication that the Clonemaster's house was still under surveillance, he would walk past the corner, take a roundabout way to the tube station, and go home.

But as he hurried across the intersection with the sick excitement still coiling within him, he knew very well that he was deceiving himself. Some devil deep within his mind had worked it all out for him: *ya* Abdul, you can afford to gamble that the stakeout's been removed now that the file's been closed on the Clonemaster.

And if he were caught he could still brazen it out, the seductive whisper in his brain insisted. He was only making a sympathy call on the bereaved. What was wrong with that? The Clonemaster had been his chief. It was all open and aboveboard. Politics had nothing to do with it. After all, this was Mars, not Callisto or the South African People's Sultancy, where whole families down to babes in arms went to the chopping block with the guilty party.

Still, his heart thumped. His reason must be entirely gone, he told himself despairingly, to even think of trying to approach the Little Sugarplum after all that had happened. But his feet continued to carry him across the intersection.

He skipped back a step to avoid being grazed by a delivery trike. Traffic was back to normal in the plaza of the Golden Gate; that was a good sign. It had been four days since the assassination—"attempted assassination," as the official account had it—and life had to go on, after all. The three-day Feast of the Head was over without ever having been declared canceled, and the Palace was issuing bulletins hourly on the Emir's condition. He was displaying a remarkable amount of activity for a man whose recently severed spinal cord was still knitting. He was receiving visitors, issuing edicts, conferring with his ministers, signing documents with the help of an eyeblink scriber. The Vizier was with him constantly and emerged from time to time to make his

Majesty's wishes known. The holovid reporters were permitted to film the tongueless slaves who brought refreshments to his Majesty and filed out with the empty trays.

The weekly *majlis*, however, would be suspended until the Emir was on his feet again and felt up to facing crowds. Petitions could be presented in writing until then, and the Chamberlain would transmit his Majesty's decisions.

Clearly, despite the unavoidable dislocations caused by the planetwide security sweeps and the gathering purge, the Palace wanted to encourage people to go about their business, shops to reopen, and a normal surface to be presented to the rest of the Solar system.

Halfway across the intersection, Hamid-Joncs slowed to a saunter and stole a long glance at the yawning tunnel entrance. He stiffened when he saw a delivery van across from the Clone-master's gate, but it really *was* a delivery van, with a driver unloading a caged sheep onto a dolly; Hamid-Jones had a look through the van's open tailgate and there were no men inside, only caterer's supplies.

No one seemed to be loitering anywhere along the street, though he could see passersby slowing down as they passed the Clonemaster's house, then resuming a normal walking pace. Rubberneckers. That was a good sign, too. They'd heard about the Clonemaster's arrest on the holovid and felt safe in indulging a little morbid curiosity. People didn't do that when the grape-vine told them that the security goons were grabbing bystanders for lack of anything better to do.

He joined the sidewalk parade, staying alert for any signs of skulking Greenies. If he saw anything he didn't like, he'd just keep walking. When he drew abreast of the small wicket gate past the main gate, he stopped and began rattling it authorita-tively. Someone was bound to be within earshot; the household would still need water deliveries, after all.

"Open up!" he demanded in a voice that he hoped sounded sufficiently commanding to be taken for official.

The stream of foot traffic bent into an arc around him and went by without slowing down. People smiled vacantly to show their harmlessness.

"*Eftah, eftah*, open up!" he shouted, pounding on the door.

He kept pounding and making a fuss until the gate opened a crack and a frightened face peered out. He pushed hard and bullied himself inside past a scrawny kitchen boy who was too scared to try to stop him.

He pulled the door shut behind him, his heart thudding. It had taken less than a minute, but it seemed to him that he had been standing exposed in the street forever.

It was no time to be fainthearted. "Go find the majordomo," he told the gawking boy. "Tell him that Abdul ben Arthur Hamid-Jones is here to pay a call."

The boy scuttled off. He returned with a eunuch whom Hamid-Jones recognized from previous visits, a pale, hollow-chested man named Yusif from the Soviet Islamic Republic, who had had the operation performed on Earth in the hope of bettering himself and had come to Mars looking for employment in one of the great houses. He was not the chief eunuch, and he wasn't very impressive; the Clonemaster had given him the job out of pity.

"Salaam, master," the man said nervously. "There is no one to receive you; haven't you heard that the lord Hassan bin Fahd al-Hejjaj is dead?"

"I'm here to call on the respected Lalla bint Hassan al-Hejjaj, to offer my condolences as an associate of her father. Set up a *q'ata* in the visitor's hall so that I may talk to her through it, and inform her of my presence."

The eunuch wrung his hands. He was so obviously demoralized by events that Hamid-Jones had hopes his bluff might work.

"Murad went away this morning and left me in charge," Yusif wailed. "He didn't say when he'd be back. I don't know what to do."

At least it didn't sound as if the head eunuch had been arrested; more likely he had deserted a sinking ship. Hamid-Jones had no way of telling. Murad was a wily man, prized for his talents; a top-notch eunuch like him would have no trouble finding another job. He had run the Clonemaster's household with an iron-fisted efficiency. Without him, things would fall apart. The pitiful creature in front of Hamid-Jones proved that.

"Do as I tell you," Hamid-Jones said sharply.

If Murad had been there, he never would have gotten away with it. He would have found himself in the street, lucky to retain his manhood. But Yusif blinked and after a moment said, "Wait here."

He came back looking chastened, and it occurred to Hamid-Jones that Lalla must have worked on him, too—wheedled or even produced a display of temper that caved him in. The thought heartened him. Lalla wanted to see him, despite everything. It must be frightening for her at a time like this. Isolated from the world and helpless, she would need an ally. A wave of tenderness swept over him.

"Follow me, please, *sidi*," the eunuch said.

He led Hamid-Jones up the stairs. Hamid Jones's heart fluttered; the meeting was not going to take place in the impersonal spaces of the visitor's hall, but in the heady territory of the harem.

As he climbed the carpeted steps, Hamid-Jones became aware that the familiar twitterings from the women's section were absent. There was only silence. The women ought to have been crowding the grille wall that ringed the balcony, straining for a look at a male visitor. Even the threat of Murad's willow switches had never intimidated them before. The Clonemaster's concubines and female dependents must be wondering what would happen to them now. There were no wives, Hamid-Jones dimly recalled. The Clonemaster's cherished first wife had died many years ago, without issue. He had taken three new wives in succession and found that none of them could replace her; he had divorced them all with handsome settlements and sent them back to their families. Lalla was the daughter of the second or third wife, a girl from neighboring Araxes, who had been one of his first wife's servants.

As he continued climbing, Hamid-Jones saw servants peeping up at him from the hall below—further evidence of a demoralized household. One was giving him a slack-faced stare from around the edge of a doorway; another had ventured into the hall itself, pretending to dust. Murad, if he had been here, would never have allowed such impertinence.

Yusif took him to a small salon adjoining the harem. It was still technically the *raba'a*—the men's section, but such rooms could be used to entertain close family friends or authorized suitors. Hamid-Jones controlled his excitement. A latticework screen had been set up in front of a tall archway. A couple of junior eunuchs in chartreuse livery were at the far end of the salon, pretending to arrange flowers and plump up pillows.

Hamid-Jones was invited to sit down and offered tea and cakes. The refreshments were slow in arriving—the kitchen, too, must be in a state of confusion. Yusif, looking uneasy, stationed himself in a doorway some distance off.

The servant who brought the refreshments, an unveiled slave girl in pantaloons and halter, set down the tray with a frightened glance at the arrangements and scurried off. Hamid-Jones bit into a cake. It was stale—at least a day old. Nothing had been freshly baked since the Clonemaster's arrest.

But music was being played somewhere within the women's quarters: an improvisatory tune on a one-stringed *rabába*. Someone was making an effort. It could only be Lalla's doing.

He waited.

After an eternity, a whisper of sound came from the other side of the screen, like silk on silk. A heady scent drifted toward him: jasmine perfume. He lifted his head and saw a flash of movement behind the latticework.

The young eunuchs at the other end of the salon stopped what they were doing and glanced at Yusif, then went back to their flower arranging and dusting with elaborate unconcern. In the doorway, Yusif's hand strayed to the handle of the little curved knife thrust into his sash and stayed there. He looked unhappy, his sickly complexion more pallid. Hamid-Jones had no attention to spare for him.

"Fair is she, though veiled and guarded," he whispered, quoting the classic ode by Imru'lqais, "and yet she welcomed me."

He was rewarded by a giggle from the other side of the screen. Encouraged, he went on.

"I passed between her tent ropes, though her guardians slept near in the dark, thirsty for my blood . . ."

The sensual imagery soon brought gasps and little squeals of delighted outrage from the other side of the screen. Hamid-Jones stole a glance at his watchdogs, but they were all looking the other way. The requirements of *muharram* had been satisfied, technically at least, and who was to say that the visitor was talking to Lalla? She was not in the room. If Hamid-Jones wanted to sit there quoting poetry to himself, it was his own business.

When Hamid-Jones finished, there was a pregnant silence. Then a whisper came from behind the screen.

"Have you brought me something?"

All of a sudden, the poem he had written in reply to her note no longer seemed enough. He worked off the heavy gold ring he had bought at the *suq* after he had received his scanty patrimony. A good part of his savings were in it. The sapphire, the merchant had assured him, was genuine. He wrapped the stiff paper of his reply around it and folded it small, then made a low underhand toss toward the edge of the screen. A white arm snaked out and retrieved it.

Greedily, he fixed the brief glimpse in his memory; the arm

had been plump, smooth, deliciously bare but for the gold bracelets and pearl wristlet it wore. He shivered with anticipation.

He heard the crinkle of unwrapping and a tinkle as the ring fell out. There was more rattling—paper being smoothed out—and the gratifying sound of deep breathing. His senses swam. He heard the sound of giggling—more than one voice. Was there someone with Lalla, or was some harem busybody peeping from somewhere behind the screen? It didn't matter.

All discretion forgotten, he poured out his heart in a hoarse whisper. He declared his love, offered any assistance he was capable of giving. *"Ya Halawiy-at,"* he said soulfully, giving her a pet name. He had not the right to call her "Little Sugarplum," but he could call her "Candy." "Ask me for the moons and I shall fly to heaven and bring them back to you."

The eunuchs did nothing to interfere. Hamid-Jones was an unknown quantity. Despite his cheap garb, he might be anything—scion of an important family, rising star in the bureaucracy, police spy. Lalla, as the despised orphan of a convicted traitor, was not the only one who needed protection. The entire household had better find powerful friends—fast! The absent head eunuch, Murad, would know Hamid-Jones for what he was—a down-at-the-heels lab worker without family or influence—but Yusif and the two junior eunuchs he had brought with him to spread out the responsibility were not about to take chances at this point.

Lalla heard him out in silence. Hamid-Jones waited in suspense for anything that might be interpreted as a response.

There was a languid sigh. Then Lalla said in a distinct whisper, "My poor head is swimming. You are very inconsiderate to say all those things. I must go now."

With a swirl of fabric, the figure behind the screen rose. By chance or design, she passed too close to the edge of the screen as she withdrew, and Hamid-Jones was vouchsafed a fleeting view of her form shrouded in a light print fabric, one bare arm emerging from the folds, an embroidered headcloth drooping to reveal a creamy profile and the flash of dark lashes. A scrap of fabric floated to the floor, and then she was gone.

Hamid-Jones got up to leave. The eunuchs paused in their mock chores to watch him. On the way out, he passed close to the screen and stooped to pick up the piece of fabric. The eunuchs stiffened but made no attempt to stop him. The token was some kind of drawstring from her garments—the symbolism of it made him dizzy with surmise. He held it to his nose. It was impregnated with jasmine perfume, and he felt like swooning.

He was walking on air as Yusif led him through the house. At the outer door he had a moment of indecision: ought he to tip? In the end he pressed a gold dinar into the eunuch's hand. Yusif accepted the coin with indifference, dropping it into a pocket of his vest, and Hamid-Jones wondered if he'd made a fool of himself.

When he rounded the corner to the Golden Bab tube station, he got the shock of his life. Feisel and Ja'far were emerging from the platform, holding hands. He ducked back before they could see him. What were they doing in this neighborhood? They couldn't be heading for Peacock Street. Not after what had happened to Rashid. And especially not after Ja'far had warned him about indulging in the same kind of foolishness.

He gave them time to get out of range, then went back to the station and took the levitrain home. He half dozed in his seat, tired but happy. Associating with Lalla could only make matters worse for him, but he didn't care. As for Ja'far and Feisel, he couldn't be bothered worrying about them. If they wanted to get into trouble, it was their own business. Perhaps their reasoning had been the same as his—with the Clonemaster disposed of, his house was probably no longer under surveillance, and if it was, they could beat a hasty retreat. In the meantime they could satisfy their curiosity with a look. One thing was for certain—they weren't going to call on Lalla; Feisel was too cold-blooded and practical to allow that.

He forgot about the matter.

When he arrived home, ibn Zayd, his landlord, was waiting up for him. "You'll have to leave, *ya* Abdul," he said, intercepting Hamid-Jones at the foot of the steps. "The *shurtayeen* were here again tonight, asking questions. I can't have this. My other tenants are very upset. I may lose Mr. Najib."

He peered sidewise at a lighted window in Mr. Najib's ground-floor apartment, where a curtain had parted a crack, then had been drawn shut again. The light abruptly went out.

"But hajji," Hamid-Jones protested, "I've always paid my rent on time—"

"I can't help that," the landlord said. "You'll have to find another place to live, that's all there is to it. You have until the end of the week to pack up."

* * *

The next day, Feisel and Ja'far failed to show up for work. Word went quickly round that they'd been arrested during the night. Hamid-Jones had a sinking feeling in the pit of his stomach. The Clonemaster's house must have been watched after all.

He spent the morning doing his pointless work on the Winged One's genome automatically. He found, when he left his cubicle, that he was in a sort of quarantine. Nobody spoke willingly to him. When he needed anything from another department, he was given it quickly and gotten rid of.

The other cloning techs avoided him like the plague. He didn't blame them. He had been the Clonemaster's most recent protégé, and no one wanted to be around a possible source of contagion.

But they avoided one another, too. There were only five cloning techs left. It was impossible to know where the axe would fall next.

As the day wore on, Hamid-Jones's apprehension grew. He kept picturing Feisel and Ja'far in the cellars of the Department of Rectitude. The things that were done there could only be whispered about. He had no illusions that either of them would stand up under torture. They both must suspect by now that Hamid-Jones had lied to the Rectitude interrogators about loitering outside the Clonemaster's house and failing to report on any suspicious callers.

And if they didn't, they could make things up. People did that under severe questioning, just to make their inquisitors happy and get themselves off the hook. When it came to that, God only knew what Rashid had spilled. They had had him for four days now.

By quitting time, Hamid-Jones was thoroughly resigned. He would be next; he was sure of it. There was nothing to do but wait for the axe to fall.

CHAPTER 6

Hamid-Jones struggled out of sleep. For a moment he didn't know where he was. He was mired in a dream of a vast silken plain where sticky cords kept wrapping themselves around his legs. A great mouth was in the sky, opening to swallow. A heavy pounding came from above, and a veil dropped to cover the mouth.

He moaned and sat up. The sound that had awakened him grew insistent: a booted foot was kicking methodically at his door.

"Come on, open up!" a voice shouted. "Open up in the name of the Vizier!"

He turned on the light and reached blearily for a pair of trousers. But before he could put them on, the door burst open at a particularly violent kick and two enormous men, tall even for Mars, rushed into the room and hauled him upright.

"On your feet, *ya* buddy, you're coming with us," one of them rasped, clamping Hamid-Jones's arm in a painful grip.

They wore black, silver-tabbed capes over green and gold uniforms. They were some kind of police, but they were not Greenies.

"B-but what's this about?" he stammered.

His arm got a painful twist for that. "You don't deny that you're Abdul ben Arthur Hamid-Jones?"

"N-no, but—"

"We just pick them up, friend. What they do to you at the Palace isn't our department."

They allowed him to get dressed. He fumbled with shirt, trousers, and sandals while they towered over him, hemming him in. "Hurry it up," the arm-twister said, smacking a metal rod into a meaty palm for emphasis. Both of them were equipped with the rods, which dangled from their wrists by leather thongs. They also wore sidearms, bulky riot guns in stiff holsters. The holsters stayed buttoned; evidently Hamid-Jones wasn't considered dangerous.

He reached for a cloak. "You won't need that," his oversize captor said, pushing him toward the door.

They herded him down the stairs, one giant keeping his arm imprisoned, the other going ahead with a flashlight. A window opened somewhere and a voice quavered, "Who's there? What's going on?" Hamid-Jones recognized the voice as Mr. Fahti's.

"Shut up, you! Go back to bed. Mind your own business." The man with the flashlight played the yellow beam over the window. There was a gasp, and the window slid quickly shut.

They propelled him across the shadow-pooled courtyard, one on either side of him now. The forced pace made him stumble, but the implacable grip kept him upright. Somewhere behind a darkened window a woman's voice sobbed with fear, and a man hissed her to silence.

The outer gate was ajar. Old Ibrahim, the porter, stood paralyzed beside it in his nightclothes. He hadn't had the nerve to close it behind the two cops. He opened it all the way with a trembling hand to let them through, keeping his good eye averted from Hamid-Jones.

A low, black vehicle with curtained windows waited outside the gate. Its oily sheen and the way it rode low on its springs showed that it was laser-baffled and armored. Armored vehicles were standard for transporting prisoners—quite as much to protect crowds in the street from undetected explosives carried by suspects as to protect the passengers.

The two men shoved Hamid-Jones into the rear seat and climbed in with him, walling him in. Two more men, just as big as the first pair, sat in front. The rear was caged off from the front by a mesh whose spaces were too fine to allow a gun barrel to be poked through it. Hamid-Jones wondered idly what good an extra guard beside the driver was if he couldn't bring his weapon to bear on a prisoner who acted up.

The heavy door thunked shut, and there was the sound of electronic tumblers clicking into place, isolating the cage and rendering its occupants inaccessible to the threats of hijackers. The driver spoke briefly into a microphone, and the vehicle moved smoothly into the sparse predawn traffic.

As the car hissed through the dark streets, Hamid-Jones had

time to reflect on his situation. It dawned on him that no one had hit him yet.

He ventured a sidelong glance at his captors. They sat like blocks of granite, not inclined to knock him about at the moment. Covertly, he examined the markings on their uniform tabs. The inscriptions were in an ornamental Kufic script, something from the Koran about striking down wrongdoers. What was it these gorillas had shouted before they kicked in his door? He frowned in concentration. They had invoked the authority of the Vizier, and they wore the Palace colors.

Hamid-Jones felt worse. He shrunk down in his seat. It was bad enough to be in the hands of the Greenies or the religious police, but being in the hands of the Palace was more fearsome. The executive tended to make a painful example of those accused of offenses against the throne—like feeding the miscreant piecemeal to a Cerberus, or simmering him slowly in cooking oil, with full medical support to keep him alive and conscious until the last possible moment.

He racked his brain trying to figure out why he personally should be singled out for the special attention of the Palace itself. Surely he was too unimportant. Even the Clonemaster had been swept up in the general security net, though the Palace had intervened to mitigate his sentence.

He worked up enough courage to try to engage his captors in conversation. "Are we going to the district guard station in the Old Palace quarter?" he said, clearing his throat.

"Shut up, kid," the stony presence next to him said without heat.

The other guard loosened up a little. "We're going to take a little ride in the desert."

"Then what?"

Up ahead there was a bark of malicious laughter from the driver. "You've got him worried, Qasim." He glanced over his shoulder at Hamid-Jones with a nasty grin on his face. "What do you think, donkey? We dump you. The idea is to see if you can walk back without a respirator. But first we—"

"Shut up, Musa." Qasim turned to Hamid-Jones and said, not unkindly, "Don't listen to him, kid. We turn you over, that's all."

The driver chuckled.

The ride continued in silence. At the Bab al-Dahub, the gate-keeper let them through with a salute, not attempting to collect a toll. The car sealed itself with a hum of small servos and rolled out into the desert.

The mesh of the cage prevented a clear look through the windshield, but one of the guards had left his side curtain open. It was still dark outside. The bright fleck of Phobos was coming over the horizon, visibly rising, and the brilliant stars that were the Earth-moon pair hung low in the east, heralding sunrise.

The car sped across the desert, keeping to the palace road. It used the reserved lane, though there was no other traffic. Gradually, a rosy light spilled across the landscape, revealing a pebbled bleakness. A milky fog filled the low spots as pockets of frost began to sublimate. By the time they reached the first checkpoint, dawn was breaking.

Hamid-Jones's guards paused to say the dawn prayer with the sentrics. A rough hand pushed him to a kneeling position. It was awkward in the cramped interior; he was unable to touch his forehead to the floor and had to settle for burying his face in the seat cushions. Outside, the checkpoint sentries in their heated coveralls and face masks took turns prostrating themselves, keeping their weapons within reach.

At the second checkpoint, the guards were more difficult. They insisted that everyone get out of the car so it could be searched. Two of Hamid-Jones's captors donned respirators and got out to argue with them. Tempers flared, and Hamid-Jones saw both sides bring the muzzles of their guns up, fingers on triggers. After a brief stand-off, everyone became amicable again. They were permitted to proceed after a peek into the interior and a look in the luggage compartment.

At the third checkpoint, an iron-barred gate on wheels had been rolled across the road between two domed shelters equipped with firing slits. Here, the credentials of the driver and three guards were checked carefully, a call made to the Palace, and detectors run over the vehicle. Hamid-Jones was made to get out. Holding his breath and numbed by the bitter cold, he hurried across to one of the shelters, where he was strip-searched. The contents of his pockets and his wrist communicator were taken from him and sealed in a plastic bag, which was labeled and put in a cupboard.

There were two more checkpoints, and then a long delay at a guardhouse in the palace wall, where nobody seemed to know what to do with Hamid-Jones. The matter was finally settled after a series of phone calls, and Hamid-Jones's guards were permitted to take him to a receiving point inside. Once again, Hamid-Jones drank in the splendors along the palace corridors, as they hustled him along. At the receiving point, the two black-cloaked giants

surrendered Hamid-Jones to another set of guards. Again, he was
strip-searched, and he had to explain why his pockets were empty.
They pried open his mouth to look at his teeth, investigated his
body orifices with fiber optics, and tried diligently to unscrew his
fingertips. When they were finished, they tossed him his clothes
and told him he could get dressed.

In due course, a Palace official came for him, accompanied
by two hulking bruisers in the Vizier's livery: corkscrew turbans,
broad pantaloons, and green brocade tunics. The official was a
fleshy man with a large jaw and a bulging dome of forehead,
his robe trimmed at collar, cuffs, and hem with silver fur.

"Hurry, you mustn't keep him waiting," the official said.

"Who?"

The official pursed his lips. "The Vizier."

"What, the Vizier himself?" Hamid-Jones exclaimed, unable to hide his astonishment.

The official looked at Hamid-Jones as if he were a ticking
bomb that somehow could not be gotten rid of. "Come, *ya*
Abdul," he said with a grimace of forced courtesy.

There was one more body search at the entrance to the Vizier's apartments—this time an almost deferential pat-down and
discreet magnetometering by two slim, efficient young men who
apologized as they worked.

A page ushered him into an enormous garden room hung with
caged songbirds and dripping with exotic vegetation. A solitary
figure sat at the far end, its outline blurred by a dazzling radiance
of artificial sunlight pouring through the glass doors behind it.

The page urged Hamid-Jones forward. Hamid-Jones was
amazed to find that he was being permitted to approach the Grand
Vizier without a guard at either elbow. He glanced around the
room, but could see no sharpshooters ranged along the walls either.

The only concession to security was a Cerberus stretched out
on the floor beside the Vizier, its three heads chained by their
jeweled collars to a sturdy stanchion. But the Cerberus seemed
more a pet than a watchdog; as Hamid-Jones watched, the Vizier
stretched out a many-ringed hand and absently patted the one
head that was awake.

The Vizier was eating breakfast—Spartan fare of green figs,
yogurt and Turkish coffee from a large brass tray that was set on
a low stand before him. Seen up close, Rubinstein was even
more shrunken than Hamid-Jones remembered him. His wiz-

ened face and pipestem neck with its prominent Adam's apple seemed lost in the opulence of his sumptuous silk robes and conical turban ringed with gold.

He looked up with a gnomish twinkle. "*Salaam, ya* Abdul," he said. "Sit down. Have you eaten breakfast yet?"

"Uh, no, your .. uh, Mightiness. That is . . ."

He looked around for a seat and started to pull a leather camel saddle toward him, keeping a wary eye on the Cerberus. The fractionally sleeping beast showed no inclination to snap at him, but you never could tell with Cerberi. They were high-strung creatures, derived from Russian wolfhounds, and their three narrow heads, taken together, scarcely contained the brains to be found in one enhanced Doberman or neo-Alsatian.

"No, no, sit here with me," Rubinstein said, patting the cushions beside him. "What would you like?" He clapped his hands and a servant appeared. "Bring our guest something tasty—some of the anaerobic bluemelon in nectar, I think, and a caviar omelet with nightingale's tongue, and maybe a little camel sausage on the side." He turned to Hamid-Jones with a benevolent smile. "And you've got to try some of the new honeyberries in cream. I believe you had a hand in their creation—didn't the Royal Stables supply the altered honeybee gene that went into the berry genome?"

Overwhelmed, Hamid-Jones could only nod. He sat down gingerly, still smarting from the fiber optics and lubricated finger cots of all the body searches.

"Well, Abdul," said the Vizier, "these have been difficult days, have they not? But perhaps things will settle down before too long. And perhaps you can help to settle them. You would perform a service for the Palace if you were asked, would you not?"

"Of course, your Uppermost," Hamid-Jones stammered. "Anything . . ."

"Good, good," Rubinstein said. He passed Hamid-Jones a dish of candied dates. "Here, try these. They're from my own oasis in Tithonius Lacus. I have them flown in by tethercraft."

Numbly, Hamid-Jones took one of the sticky confections and sampled it, while the analytical portion of his mind reckoned up the ruinous cost of having one of the east-west freight satellites drop its tether just for the purpose of hauling up a basket of fruit.

"We've heard fine things about you, *ya* Abdul," the Vizier went on, peeling a fig with a little gold knife. "Your talent for bioengineering, your industry, your discretion . . . you're not one to go bragging about what he knows, are you?''

"N-no, your Supremacy."

"I thought not. The Palace has had its eye on you for some time now—even before the recent unfortunate events. Did you know that?"

"No, your Transcendence."

Rubinstein dipped the fig in yogurt and popped it into his mouth. "Yes, that's why we asked your late employer, the Clonemaster, to bring you along to the palace for the decapitation ceremony. We'd had nothing but the most glowing reports about you. We wanted to have a closer look at you, see how you handled yourself in an important situation. And I must say that you acquitted yourself well—in the face of the unexpected. We have holostats of your quick thinking in knocking one of the assassins off his feet."

"Thank you, your Uppermost."

Rubinstein dabbed at his mouth with a silk napkin. "Yes, we always have use for a young man of talent and discretion. And your family background need not be a hindrance to your advancement." He struck his thin chest and laughed. "After all, look at *me*!"

Hamid-Jones laughed self-consciously along with the Vizier, hoping he was not showing too much familiarity. Rubinstein was living proof that a loyal and energetic non-Moslem could get ahead in an Islamic empire. Jewish executive officers were not that uncommon; in fact, many monarchs, like the Emir, preferred them as viziers for the same reason they preferred eunuchs as palace chamberlains—there was no threat of overthrow or succession from them; eunuchs because their imperfection in the sight of Allah barred them from the throne itself, and Jews because they remained outside the Faith. They could govern, but not rule. Though they might attain great power, they possessed none of the inconvenience of legitimate male heirs to the throne—the sons and brothers who had to be strangled in their cribs as infants or kept imprisoned for life in gilded palaces where deaf-mute guards were forbidden to communicate with them. Rubinstein was uncommonly able as Grand Viziers went. Even in that exalted company, his reputation reverberated throughout the Solar system. It was he who kept the Martian Emirate fiscally stable and moderated the worst excesses of the Emir.

Still, Hamid-Jones couldn't help reflecting, Rubinstein must have been very nimble all these years to have stayed on the good side of the Emir and to have kept his head intact.

"Yes indeed," Rubinstein continued, "there's no limit to how far an ambitious young man can go if he perseveres and keeps his wits about him. I myself was nothing more than a penniless *dhimmi* when I emigrated from Israel and went to settle in Saudi Arabia." He gave a wry grimace. "The Israeli constitution guarantees equal opportunity, but let's face it, the opportunities for the Jewish minority are limited. But the Saudis prize us as civil servants—must be our reputation for incorruptibility. In less than six years, I saved up enough to emigrate to Mars, joined the civil service here, and finally came to the attention of the Emir."

He paused and, waving away a hovering servant, poured Hamid-Jones a cup of coffee with his own hand.

"But we're not here to talk about me, *ya* Abdul," the Vizier said. "Forgive the meanderings of a garrulous old man. We're here to talk about you and your future."

Hamid-Jones kept his face blank. A whisper of alarm went off in his head. The Vizier was definitely buttering him up, but he couldn't imagine for what purpose.

"It's unfortunate about Hassan bin Fahd al-Hejjaj," the Vizier said with a sad shake of his head. "He was a fine gentleman of the old type and the best Clonemaster to ever hold that office. I had the highest regard for him. But he *would* involve himself in intrigues and politics! I myself did not take his activities that seriously. He was the sort of hazy, well-meaning reformer that is sometimes thrown up by his class, but he listened to the wrong people. Yes, this unfocused yearning for a better world gets a lot of people in trouble! I did my best to save him, but unfortunately things had gone too far." He sighed. "But life must go on, *ya* Abdul, and now you have yourself to consider. Tell me, would you consider yourself disloyal to your old master if you were to take some of his tasks upon your own shoulders?"

Hamid-Jones's mouth went dry. His mind reeled at the vistas he saw opened to him by the Vizier's casual words. "No, your Mightiness," he whispered.

"Ah, here's your breakfast!"

A small procession of servants, bowing low, unloaded trays of food in front of Hamid-Jones. There were golden serving dishes of eggs, melon, berries, cheeses, preserves; piles of breads and confections; tall brass pots of coffee and hot water; an enormous salver heaped high with steaming camel sausages. It was enough to feed an army.

"Eat, eat," Rubinstein urged. "Don't be bashful!"

Hamid-Jones helped himself to a small portion of the omelet, wondering how he was going to get it down with his mouth as dry as it was. He took a sip from a goblet of some kind of peach slush. The Cerberus, its sleeping heads awakened by the smell of food, stirred on the floor, and Hamid-Jones instinctively shrank back.

"Oh, Pluto won't hurt you," Rubinstein assured him. "He just wants a little snack. Here, boy!"

He began feeding the creature pieces of camel sausages from the salver. The three heads snapped at one another, competing for the scraps, and Rubinstein had to admonish them: "Stop that, Aidoneus, that's not nice, Hades!" It appeared that he had named each of the three heads separately. Hamid-Jones could not help being nervous, despite the Vizier's assurances. The bioengineering tour de force that had created Cerberi had also screwed up their hereditary instincts. They made marvelous watchdogs, with at least one head being awake all the time, but the third head interfered with the natural borzoi instinct to hunt in pairs; millennia before, the big white wolfhounds had bracketed a running wolf, easily keeping pace with it, and when the wolf turned to snap at one, the other had seized its throat. Hamid-Jones wondered that Rubinstein had kept all his fingers.

The Cerberus settled down to a low intermittent growl as it fed on the diminishing heaps of sausage, and Rubinstein made a small signal to some computer sensor somewhere. A soft background wash of music began to fill the room, *ferengi* music with its strange, oddly soothing scales and thick harmonies.

"Beethoven," the Vizier explained. "How do you like it?"

"It's . . . different," Hamid-Jones said tentatively. He searched the other's face for a clue as to what was expected of him. "But . . . but somehow *large*."

The Vizier's expression radiated approval at the choice of words. Encouraged, Hamid-Jones went on. "As if . . . if it were trying to *say* something, even though there aren't any words. I suppose you could grow to like it once you got used to the foreign sound of it."

"By which you mean you haven't had the opportunity to hear much music in the Western tradition."

"No, your Peerlessness."

"And yet it's a part of your heritage," Rubinstein said with a sigh. "Once every cultivated man among your forebears was familiar with music like this—was *expected* in polite society to be familiar with it."

Somehow it did not make Hamid-Jones uncomfortable to have the Vizier refer to his *mawali* origins. Perhaps it was because Rubinstein was an outsider himself.

"I'm sorry, your Uppermost. We were very strict at home. Music wasn't allowed."

"Ah yes, it's a sin. The Prophet denounced music as a temptation of the devil, and the little ayatollahs have continued to mistrust it down through the ages—*ferengi* music most particularly. We're enlightened now, of course. The Emir's father was the last ruler to actually forbid it."

He turned his head to listen to the Beethoven. The spacious chords had been augmented by a soloist who was playing slow cascades of notes on an instrument something like an oud, but more resonant.

"I . . . I guess I haven't thought much about it."

Seeing his stricken look, Rubinstein said, "Never mind, *ya* Abdul. It's not your fault. Large, you said. Yes, that's a good way to describe it. It's the slow movement of the *Emperor* Concerto, by the way. I don't suppose that means anything to you."

"No, your Mightiness."

"But you know something of your vanished culture. You read books in English, don't you?"

Hamid-Jones wished the Vizier would drop the subject. He didn't particularly want the weight of a "vanished culture" on his shoulders—not when Rubinstein had begun by telling him he was as good as anybody else.

"We spoke it at home, your Mightiness. And when I went to school, I took English as my second language."

"Ah, yes, one of the three languages of an educated man, along with French and Russian. And all three relics of a colonial past, when the ancestors of our present ruling class were economically subservient to those vanished powers. Yes, even today you can generally tell an ethnic Arab's origins by his second language—French for the North Africans, English for the gulf protectorates, Russian for all the Tajiks and Kazakhs and Azerbaijanians and so forth. Do you know what I'm talking about, *ya* Abdul?"

"I studied history in school," Hamid-Jones said stiffly.

"You studied *a* history," Rubinstein gently corrected. "History is written by the winners, someone once said. What books do you read in English, *ya* Abdul?"

"Uh, there's not much after the twenty-second Christian century, at least not much that's interesting—it's mostly translations from the Arabic after that. And it gets hard to understand before the seventeenth century. I guess I like the nineteenth and twentieth centuries best—Kipling, Huxley, Maugham." He forbore to mention the English-language *Chatterley* by Lawrence and hoped the Vizier had not had a police report on it after the ransacking of his room. "And I like the Americans a lot. They're exotic—Fitzgerald, Hemingway, Sinclair Lewis."

To his surprise, Rubinstein seemed to be familiar with this odd corner of literature. His respect for the Vizier as a man of broad culture grew.

"Yes, exotic is the only way to describe it—as exotic as your ancestors once found the *Arabian Nights*. The societies described by these forgotten scribblers are almost incomprehensible to us in our present reality, and yet these fanciful tales are the echoes and shadows of great empire, of world dominion. Perhaps something in you hungers for those days, eh?"

"Oh, no, your Maximum, this is the—the—" He stopped in confusion.

"The best of all possible worlds?" the Vizier supplied. "Don't worry, *ya* Abdul, I'm not questioning your devotion to actuality. We're all entitled to daydream, aren't we? Yes, history is merely clouds that blow away to be replaced by new clouds. It's our present existence that's important. And for an able and ambitious young man like yourself, there are limitless opportunities in this twenty-fifth century of Allah."

"Yes, your Uppermost."

The Vizier seemed to withdraw within himself. Abstractedly, he patted each of the three heads of the Cerberus in turn. The beast responded by wagging its collective tail, thumping the floor hard enough to rattle the utensils on the brass tray.

"But indulge an old man," the Vizier finally said, turning a mischievous smile on Hamid-Jones. "It's not often that a sequestered old party like myself has the chance to prattle on with someone who actually has a modicum of feeling for that decadent past. Tell me, *ya* Abdul, have you thought very much about the origins of this best of all possible of Allah's worlds?"

"It was the *Nadha*," Hamid-Jones said promptly.

"And what was that?" the Vizier pressed him.

"Why—uh, the Great Awakening. The Resurgence."

"And what brought this rebirth about?"

Hamid-Jones strived to remember the teachings of the mosque school he had attended as a boy. "Uh, it was a historically favorable moment when a surge of renewed Islamic faith happened to coincide with the availability of great wealth, at a time when the Western faiths of Christianity and Communism were in decline.''

Rubinstein's head bobbed with a vigor that threatened to dislodge his blimplike turban. ''Yes, that's part of it, though the mullahs in charge of your education tended to mix cause and effect. Hear me out, *ya* Abdul. The *Nadha* had been predicted for centuries. When it finally came, it was because of a convergence of historical forces—four of them, principally.'' He ticked them off on his bony fingers. ''Demographics. Oil. Fervor. And the historical coincidence of a newly available frontier in space that was able to give shape to them.''

''Yes, I know about the first man on the Moon. An American. But then the Americans lost their purpose and gave the Moon to the Russians. But the Russians lost their vigor, too, and so the first man on Mars was a Moslem.''

''That's not quite how it happened,'' Rubinstein said. ''But you're close enough. The first manned expedition to Mars lifted off from Baikonur, of course, which we now know as part of the Kazakh Islamic Republic, but at that time Kazakhstan, with its Moslem population, was part of the Soviet Union. And one of the Soviet cosmonauts—both for propaganda purposes and as a sop to a growing Soviet Moslem population—happened to be a Kazakh: Colonel Abai Akkul, whose name went down in history along with Neil Armstrong's when, after the crew drew lots, he became the first man to set foot on Mars.''

Hamid-Jones gave a starry-eyed nod. ''I don't think any schoolboy ever forgets those famous words of his from the history tape—'This, too, is Allah's world.' ''

Rubinstein smiled thinly. ''Thrilling indeed. But not what he was supposed to say.''

''Huh?''

''What he was *supposed* to say was, 'This is the first footprint, but not the last.' I'm sure he received a rebuke when he returned home, though they wouldn't have dared to administer it publicly. At first they tried to claim that he *had* said the words that had been written for him, but there were too many amateur cryptographers in the West who had been able to unscramble the transmission and play it back for the press of the day.''

Once again, Hamid-Jones marveled at the depth and breadth of the Vizier's knowledge. Rubinstein could have inferred this refinement of historical fact only from an exhaustive familiarity with twentieth-century press accounts buried in some moldering data dump.

"Truth is like an onion, *ya* Abdul," the Vizier said, seeing the expression on his face. "It has many layers that must be peeled away, and in the process it may bring tears."

"Yes, your Undiminished."

Rubinstein went on: "Eventually there *were* more footsteps on Mars, as we all know, but they belonged mostly to ethnic Russians through the first two decades of the twenty-first century, as your forebears styled time." He smiled gently. "*My* forebears, of course, styled it the fifty-seventh century. But both calendars became increasingly irrelevant as the century wore on and a growing Moslem population gradually absorbed the Soviet space program—while at the same time their oil-rich brethren on the southern tier invested in American and European space programs and eventually preempted them." He sighed. "And so, with Allah controlling the purse strings and setting the agenda, we arrived at the Solar system we know today."

He settled back, poured coffee for them both, and as the majestic, irrelevant music of Beethoven rolled out of the concealed loudspeakers, said: "Attend me, *ya* Abdul, and I shall tell you something of those blurred days when the Arab world, which once had stretched from Spain to the Pacific islands and then had gone into decline while Europe and its American scion had *their* day in the sun, rose to dominion again . . ."

Demographics.

In the Soviet Union, Tajiks, Uzbeks, Kazakhs and other Moslem peoples simply outbred their Russian masters. The trend was clear by the final decades of the twentieth century. The southern Soviet republics were sixty to ninety percent Moslem, and the birth rates were five times as high as those in European Russia. Now, by weight of sheer numbers, the original inhabitants began to crowd out the Russian immigrants who had been sent to them by Stalin in the 1930s to change the racial balance and to sovietize them.

As early as the 1980s, the Russian minority in the southern republics actually found itself suffering job discrimination. Modernization had worked too well. They were no longer needed as technicians—nor wanted as party bosses. They began moving back to European Russia in droves.

In 1980, and again in 1987, there were riots in Alma Ata, capital of Kazakhstan, heart of the Soviet space program. The first time, the issue was Islamic burial for the bodies of the Kazakh soldiers who had been sent to Afghanistan to fight their

Moslem brethren. The second time, the issue was a Kazakh party leader who had been replaced by an ethnic Russian.

Both times, Moscow had to back down.

Next door to Kazakhstan, in the Kirgiz Soviet Socialist Republic, the prime minister was murdered—victim of rising nationalist feeling. In Moscow, the Supreme Soviet hastily called a session, admitted publicly to "political problems" in the area.

The Islamic population had begun to feel its oats.

Official Soviet policy grew increasingly irksome—particularly the prohibition of pilgrimage to Mecca. Thousands of closed mosques—still highly visible as cinemas or antireligious museums—fueled more resentment. So did the continued suppression of Islamic rites; for two generations the faithful had tried to pass off circumcision as "hygiene" and pretended that those who persisted in fasting during Ramadan were "dieting."

Then came the winds of *glasnost*. The ban on travel to Mecca was relaxed, along with other restrictions. Soviet Moslems had the chance to mingle with their co-religionists from every corner of the world, and to reaffirm their sense of identity in Islam.

That was a mistake.

But the Soviet policymakers had no choice. The Islamic nations on their southern border, newly vigorous and assertive, had to be placated. And the USSR's own Moslem population, growing by leaps and bounds, had to be kept within the fold.

Moscow, drowning in a Moslem sea, had to grin and bear it.

By then, charismatic Moslem religious leaders were working within the Soviet power structure; there was no way to keep them out. They walked a thin line, these officially sanctioned *ulama*. Communism, they preached to their growing flocks, was compatible with the social ideals of the Koran. As for official atheism, it was not to be considered as *kufr*, or unbelief, but as *jahiliya*, the innocence of the yet-to-be-converted.

As the twenty-first century reached its midpoint, the ties of the Islamic republics to European Russia loosened and their ties to their Islamic neighbors to the south grew closer. They became autonomous in fact as well as in name. Eventually the USSR lost its southern tier—which happened to contain the Baikonur launch complex and about ninety percent of the Soviet civilian space program.

The Islamic presence in space—already considerable through private investment in the West and the Saudi-Iranian launching facilities built with Japanese technology—received a quantum boost. Within a generation, the Soviet colonies on the Moon,

Mars, Ceres, and the outer Jovian space habitats were largely Moslem . . . and rapidly expanding.

There had been no sudden break—no secession, no bloody revolution. There didn't need to be. By the twenty-second century, European Russia itself was more than fifty percent Moslem.

"Yes, demographics," Rubinstein said, pouring them another cup of coffee. "The gradual replacement of one population by another. The same thing had happened in Israel a century earlier, on a smaller scale. The Arabs simply had a higher birth rate. The Arabs never had to defeat Israel in the all-out holy war their firebrands had threatened. They simply became the majority."

As Hamid-Jones reached for his cup, the middle head of the Cerberus, suspecting food, opened its eyes and stretched its long neck to sniff at his hand. He jerked back his hand, rattling the cup in its tiny saucer, but spilled only a few drops.

Rubinstein laughed. "I think he likes you, *ya* Abdul. Why don't you feed him a sausage?"

But Hamid-Jones's courage did not extend quite that far. The other two heads had turned to give him a doggy stare, tongues lolling. Their teeth looked very sharp.

The Vizier clucked and broke a camel sausage into three parts. He tossed a piece to each head in quick succession, then wiped his hand on a napkin.

"The demographic tide crept steadily northward and eastward," he said, returning comfortably to his subject. "The West was slow to realize the extent to which a Moslem foothold had always existed. Albania had already been seventy percent Moslem in the twentieth century—a heritage of the last Islamic invasion—and the rest of the Balkans had significant Moslem populations, Yugoslavia in particular. Mohammed's empire had been stopped at the gates of Vienna in 1683; this time it swept on. The Germans, the French, the Dutch, and others had a habit of importing their former colonials as 'guest workers' who then found ways of staying on and sending for their families. As early as 1990, ten percent of the Dutch population had been Moslem—Indonesians, Surinamers, Turks, Moroccans, Pakistanis. Once they got control of the trade unions—incidentally, that was a quaint institution I must tell you about some time—they brought in still more 'guest workers' and their families. As for the French, they had never been able to digest the Algerians; now the Algerians digested them. Islam returned to Sicily via Tunisia and Libya, and from there got a toehold in the Italian boot. Spain once again became a Moorish country, as it had been under the Caliphate of Cordova.''

He paused for a birdlike sip of coffee. ''In England, demographics received a small boost from snobbery. Always a potent force in human affairs, eh, *ya* Abdul? The children of the rising class of Arab proprietors and managers went to the best schools and became the new gentry. Their former classmates paid them the sincere compliment of imitation. Once upon a time, your British ancestors had been Romanized, then Normanized; now they were Arabized.''

He broke off as he saw the embarrassed expression on Hamid-Jones's face. The Vizier's eyes, buried in a parchment network of crinkles, looked very ancient and very sad as he resumed:

''America was a slightly harder nut to crack, but Allah has time—all the time in the world—and a myriad of paths to His will. Listen to me now while I speak of wealth and the power of wealth. . . .''

Oil.

The second of the great historical forces that converged to create the *Nadha* (said the Vizier).

The West failed to learn its lesson during the first ''energy crisis'' of the 1970s when the Arab world, in the first flush of *Nadha*, had experimentally flexed its economic muscles.

Fusion power came too late to let the West off the hook. By the time the second—and much more devastating—oil crunch came along in the early twenty-first century, the Arab oil producers had learned *their* lesson well.

This time they did not fritter away their wealth—and their economic and political clout. During the precious moment of history when they had the West over a barrel, they did two things.

First, they invested massively in the promising frontier of space and all but preempted it. In the 1970s, the Saudis alone had accumulated surplus revenue at the rate of a billion dollars a week—enough to pay for three new space shuttles a *month* at the prices then current. The rest of OPEC could have bought the U.S. Moon program twice over annually with their spare cash. The surpluses had been an embarrassment then, rattling around in British and American banks and not accomplishing much of anything except drawing interest. But this time—as the West indulged in a final oil splurge with the last of the mideast reserves—all the loose money was put to work. Japan, the hungry and underutilized U.S. aerospace industry, and the Anglo-

French consortium—whose Hermes spaceplane had gone into service in the 1990s—were kept busy supplying space vehicles. Competition kept the hardware cheap. Huge launch complexes sprang up in Saudi Arabia, Moslem Africa, and Indonesia with its favored position on the equator.

The second thing the oil-rich nations did was to buy into the West in a big way, to make their temporary affluence permanent. They worked to gain control of banking, real estate, basic industries, agriculture. Farmland was a popular investment. So were the luxury hotels and the posh playgrounds that Arab visitors had become familiar with.

England was the first to be swallowed. The stately country homes were taken over, one by one, by Saudi and Kuwaiti royalty, or by the sterner commissars of Democratic Yemen and the nouveau riche mullahs of post-Khomeini Iran. Claridge's and the Ritz became Arab preserves, and at the Connaught Grill, the sign "No English or Dogs Allowed" appeared one day after complaints from the new clientele about the British habit of carving meat with the right hand and eating with the left. At the Savoy, the omelet Arnold Bennett gave way to boiled sheeps' eyeballs, and alcohol of any sort was prohibited. The overworked tailors of Savile Row learned to make burnooses, and at Epsom Downs, camel races came into vogue after the Queen set the tone with an entry of her own. The Scots held out a bit longer than most, but it is generally conceded that Arab money had won the day when shooting parties wearing tartan djellabas and toting sports Kalashnikovs took over the grouse hunting at Balmoral.

The United States was glad of the business, too. After inexplicably abdicating its leading role in space following the Moon landings, and allowing what was left of its civilian space program to wither during the budget disasters of the 1980s, it had never caught up again. It was forced to watch helplessly as the lucrative aerospace contracts went to Japan's Mitsubishi, France's Aerospatiale, China's cut-rate Long March rocket, and the Soviet Union's powerful Energia booster—which for a time during the 1990s was actually hired out sub rosa for the launching of American spy satellites. When a trickle of business finally came America's way, U.S. industry's capacity was largely given over to the burgeoning Arab space programs.

Status follows money. Things Arab became fashionable. It was chic for a woman to wear the veil in public, for the modish male to add a curved dagger to his wardrobe. It became smart and up-to-date to segregate the sexes socially, and as always, manners and customs filtered down. The whole roasted sheep became haute cuisine; the fast food joints switched from beef to mutton. Sports buffs replaced baseball with falconry and polo in their Sunday afternoon television repertoire, and the big Thanksgiving game changed from football to soccer. It was faddish at first to sprinkle your conversation with a few Arabic words—then a social and business necessity. As in England, the pampered children of the Arab influx attended the best schools, and as old grads, made their influence felt on the boards of trustees. Mosques sprang up everywhere. Even in the 1980s there had been more Moslems then Episcopalians in America. Now upwardly mobile Americans converted to Islam in increasing numbers. The sound of the muezzin was heard in the land.

The new sensibility began to be reflected in public morals, in laws and in social institutions—most states went dry, blue laws sprouted like mushrooms, and women's social gains were chipped away at by state legislatures. The Supreme Court, in a landmark decision, finally allowed school prayer—plus the use of public funds to provide a *mihrab*, or directional niche, for those children who, in the free exercise of their constitutional rights, chose to face Mecca. Oddly enough, anti-Semitism was no longer fashionable in the troglodyte clubs where up to now it had survived; the Arab nations no longer had a quarrel with Israel since—with demographic inevitability—it had evolved into an Arab state.

The Vizier passed a weary hand over his face, then continued with a sigh. "The same story of Arab money and Arab influence on manners and mores could be seen in the other industrialized nations; a healed Lebanon had become the banking capital of the world, and the big financial institutions in the U.S., Switzerland, London, and the Far East danced to its tune. But I don't imagine that the mullahs at your mosque school taught you much about ancient banking history, eh, *ya* Abdul?"

"No, your Eminence," Hamid-Jones said humbly. "Only that the *ferengi* banks were wicked institutions that bloated on loaning money at interest, which is forbidden by the Koran."

"Ah, yes," said the Vizier gently. "Nowadays we call it something else—a commission for services paid by the lendee, or some such. But you studied history at university, I believe you said."

"Yes, your Supremacy—the required survey courses. But it was mostly courses in my specialty."

"Perhaps you've heard of something called an AIDS virus?"

Hamid-Jones furrowed his forehead. "I don't believe so, your Mightiness."

"I thought you might have run across it in your technical studies, at least. An interesting footnote in the history of molecular biology. It's an English acronym for a disease that attacked the immune system. Transmitted sexually. Of course it's of little interest in these advanced days when all viral diseases have succumbed to tailored synthetic molecules that sop up the viruses as soon as they emerge from their hiding places and gradually leach them entirely from the body."

"One of our science survey courses touched on the history of the fight against oncogenes, but I don't remember anything about . . . *ayuds*?"

"No matter. It was only a final lagniappe in the saga of the *Nadha*—a postscript in God's hand—though it frightened society badly at the time. It took less of a toll in the Arab world because sexual opportunity was more strictly regulated behind the household walls. But it was the final push into the grave for a bankrupt Western society—one that helped the blue laws along and contributed to making conversion to Islam an attractive proposition. Yes, *ya* Abdul, if status follows money, so do styles in morality. One is tempted to say that when the Prophet needed a clincher, Allah obliged by sending along a biblical plague at the psychological moment."

Hamid-Jones smiled uncertainly. It was hard to figure the Vizier out; though he represented the inner circle of power in Hamid-Jones's circumscribed world, it sometimes seemed as if his attitudes were those of an outsider, skirting the edge of mockery. There was no doubt about it; Rubinstein was a very complicated man.

Rubinstein poured the third and final cup of coffee. Hamid-Jones raised his cup for a ceremonial sip and waited for the Vizier to complete his tale.

"Finally," the Vizier said, "let us not forget faith, the power that moves mountains. Without that simple zeal, the other historical forces of which we have spoken are engines without fuel. Strange, is it not, that the will of one inspired man should make itself felt across so many centuries?"

He waved aside Hamid-Jones's attempt at a reply and continued:

"Yes, *ya* Abdul, even at the dawn of the space age it was single-minded fervor that prevailed, as it had in the great days of the Omayyad and Abbasid conquests, when Allah's empire overran three continents and stretched from Spain to India, and the second great wave under the Ottomans, which lapped at the very gates of Vienna before spending itself. Now came the third and greatest swing of the pendulum. The sheer energy of the newest Islamic revival overwhelmed a tired, demoralized Western culture and cast its influence eastward as well. China was trod by Islamic missionaries, where Christian missionaries had trod before them. The Japanese, who had taken eagerly to Christmas carols and Christmas shopping, now gave themselves with equal enthusiasm to Ramadan and Ali's birthday. Once again, Arab traders spread the word of the Prophet across the islands of the Pacific, as they had in the days of the Malay sultanates. Spain's posthumous influence waned in the Philippines and the Moros regained the independence lost to the conquistadors. Even in South America, Islamic missionaries began to make headway in a population whose Catholic faith had been exhausted by poverty and social injustice. In the end, Islam's glowing promises had more credibility than those of the homegrown guerrillas, whose decades of inconclusive struggle had brought nothing but more suffering. Ironically, in a replay of that sorry region's colonial past, the Islamic evangelists followed in the wake of the bankers, investors, and Arab industrialists looking for cheap labor.''

He drained his tiny cup and set it down carefully in its saucer. ''This time the Prophet did not have to conquer by the sword. Money and demographics were his weapons, a spaceship his marvelous steed, and a vacant universe his prize.''

The Beethoven came to a noisy end with a crash of open chords, and the Vizier turned it off with a snap of his fingers. Gathering his skirts about him, he rose to his feet.

''But the dead past is the dead past, eh, *ya* Abdul?'' he said. ''A young man like yourself must look to the future. And here, on Mars, the future lies in the Garden of the Clones. Come with me; you'd better have a look at it before you assume your new duties.''

CHAPTER 7

Everywhere he looked he saw the Emir—the Emir as a young man, a pimply-faced adolescent, a middle-aged man growing portly, a toddler playing in the garden path, a pasty-faced infant being wheeled by a nurse. Some were bearded, some clean-shaven; some were smooth-cheeked or sprouted the downy fuzz of pubescence. But at any age, the great fleshy beak and droopy eyelids were recognizable as the Emir's. All had the same vacuous expression punctuated by slyness.

"Ordinarily they're not preserved much past the age of forty, and that's the problem," the Vizier said, not bothering to lower his voice so as to spare the sensibilities—if any—of a juvenile Emir who stepped out of the bushes, eating a pomegranate with one hand and scratching his crotch with the other.

"Uh, yes, I can see what you mean," Hamid-Jones said.

"They're not in great demand for organ transplants after that, not when there's a plethora of young donors available. But the occasional oldster does slip through the winnowing process for one reason or another, and of course the doctors like to keep a few control naturals of advanced age around so that they can continue to do geriatric studies on the Emir, or in case any unexpected medical problems crop up that call for destructive tests with autopsies before trying a treatment on the Emir himself."

"Er, that's good, then . . . in the present situation, I mean," Hamid-Jones said uncomfortably.

"But they do tend to get unruly as they grow older. Their way of life, you see."

"I suppose . . . um . . . that's understandable."

The fledgling Emir, pink juice dribbling down his chin, peered at them and said something unintelligible, spraying them with pomegranate seeds.

The Vizier said benevolently, "Run along, my darling—I think they're arranging an orgy for the fifth form in the recreation hall."

The clone gave a witless giggle and ran gawkily down the path toward one of the pleasure domes.

Rubinstein continued walking. "So in spite of everything, we do have a few marginally plausible candidates available. I'll show you the best of them. I'd value your opinion."

"Er . . . what about their mental capabilities?" Hamid-Jones ventured.

Rubinstein grimaced. "They're in possession of their faculties, if that's what you mean. In the beginning they were lobotomized, but it tended to affect their body tone. They have to be kept in tip-top physical shape, as you can appreciate."

As if to underscore his words, they passed an open court where a quartet of twentyish Emirs in satin shorts and athletic shirts were being put through their paces by a muscle-bound exercise instructor who coaxed them on with a fixed, gritted smile. The Emir had never been particularly athletic at any age, to judge by these sorry specimens, who were puffing and sweating their way through the simple calisthenics and who were identically flabby around the middle despite their youth. All were openly sulking. A fifth proto-Emir had already dropped out, to be comforted by an attending houri in a small pavilion at the rear.

"It's a job keeping them fit," Rubinstein remarked. "They're spoiled rotten."

"Uh, I suppose they would be." Hamid-Jones was uneasy at seeming to criticize the Emir—even these blank simulacra of him.

The Vizier flashed a sardonic smile. "They're only living beef, of course, but they *are* the flesh of the Emir's flesh. It's unnerving for the attendants. They're terrified of tantrums. They're afraid of committing an act that might be construed as lèse-majesté, so they let these tadpoles have their way. The Emir complicated the situation by occasionally conceiving a tender affection for himself at an early age. He liked them best at about the age of fourteen."

Hamid-Jones winced at the Vizier's show of disrespect but was somewhat mollified by the use of the past tense. Even after what he had seen in the audience chamber, it was hard to think of the Emir as dead when embryonic replicas of him kept popping up on every side. Somehow he couldn't shake off the sneaking suspicion that the Emir's gory demise had been a trick—the Emir's unlamented father had delighted in having his own death announced from time to time, then swooping down on those who showed insufficient sorrow and having them hideously executed.

"Perhaps living beef isn't the best way to describe them," Rubinstein mused. "Milk-fed veal would be more like it. We've turned them all into pampered, mindless infants—but infants with all the Emir's underlying traits in undeveloped form. And that's what worries me. We could deal with a stand-in who was merely simpleminded—limit his appearances, coach him to perform in controlled situations, say with an implanted electronic prompter at the *majlis*. Condition him with mild stimuli to the pleasure and pain centers. But willfulness—that's the real problem! And the Emir was a very willful man."

He paused, then apparently decided to confide further. "The Chamberlain exerted influence on the Emir by pandering to his worst vices. He thinks he can control the substitute the same way." He spat in the garden path. "Eunuchs are a corrupt lot at best, but the corps of eunuchs that this Ismail creature has gathered around himself is the worst in the Solar system."

Hamid-Jones gulped at the Vizier's indiscretion. The Garden of the Clones must surely be full of listening devices. Any pebble in the path might be one. Or that ladybug crawling on a leaf. The Vizier must be very sure indeed of his grip on power!

Rubinstein went blithely on. "But it's an age-old problem. All that's new about it is clones. There were gilded cloisters hidden away in the seraglios of the past, too. Potential heirs to the throne spent their lives in solitary confinement, with only their sterilized harems to amuse them. The poor creatures became deranged. When a sultan died, the court officials would lead one of these pathetic rattlebrains out of his cage. But they quickly got the hang of absolute power. And they used it for stupidities and slaughter. One of the Ottomans, for example, executed a thousand of his most competent officials for permitting a drought. Another used members of his court for target practice—and appointed a chicken as Grand Mufti. They invariably led the sultanate to disaster. In the end, the janissaries would have to strangle them and trot out another royal prisoner. Some of the smart ones—those who were smart as well as mad—murdered the janissaries as soon as they were self-confident enough. And that, *ya* Abdul, is why our glorious past is written in blood."

The ladybug flew off with what to Hamid-Jones's imagination

sounded like a distinctly metallic rattle of wings. Hamid-Jones turned white.

The Vizier noticed his distress and let him off the hook. "Ah, here we are, *ya* Abdul. There are the apartments of the Keeper of the Paradise around the bend. Let's drop in and have a look at our ringer."

"And here," the Keeper of the Paradise fussed, "is Number Forty, a very early edition. He's almost sixty years old. In fact, he was around at the time of the *last* transposition of heads, and he was judged by the decapitation committee to be too old, even *then*, to be a body donor. But somehow they never got around to disposing of him during the next few weedings, and he just hung on. He'd learned enough to make himself useful to the staff in little ways—informing on his broodmates and so forth—and I suppose that accounted for it. We call him Bobo."

Hamid-Jones looked through the spyhole. The clone was sitting naked in a shallow tiled pool, splashing away happily. Rubber toys bobbed in the water around him—a duck, a fish, a pneumatic mermaid. Two plump, rosy houris were in the pool with him: one scrubbing his back, the other scrambling around on her hands and knees, blowing at the sails of a little full-rigged schooner to make it go for the clone's amusement.

"Yes, we've all grown quite fond of him. He seems to have developed a little more personality than most of them—I suppose because he's older. Somebody actually taught him to read a little."

Rubinstein's brow darkened. "Who?"

The Keeper's hands fluttered nervously. "Oh, it was all some time ago. One of the gardeners, I think. He'd been transferred from the Phobos floating palace without being muted—sloppy paperwork—and managed to conceal his condition. He was executed as soon as it came to light. But there's nothing to worry about. Bobo can only spell out a few simple words—and of course he's never had access to any printed material from outside."

"I don't like his having a nickname," Rubinstein said. He turned to Hamid-Jones. "Well, *ya* Abdul, what do you think?"

"He's the best I've seen so far," Hamid-Jones said cautiously. The Keeper of the Paradise, atwitter at the Vizier's visit and fawning over the two of them, had shown them more than a dozen clones, most of them still too young to be suitable. "But the left eye doesn't droop enough, and there aren't enough lines in his face. And his color's too good."

"A little plastic surgery can take care of that," the Vizier said impatiently. "And we can give him a touch of jaundice for the color. What I mean is do you think he can pull it off?"

"Well . . . he isn't morose enough."

Rubinstein nodded vigorously. "That's it exactly. None of the clones have felt the weight of empire on their shoulders, or had to hold onto a throne by their wits. Fortunately the Emir wasn't very talkative. We thought of tranquilizing the ringer, but that's only going to make him happier. We need somehow to induce the Emir's characteristic sour expression."

"Have you thought of giving him a mild stomachache before his public appearances?" Hamid-Jones suggested.

"That's it!" the Vizier cried in delight. He squeezed Hamid-Jones's arm in fellowship. "I knew I was right to bring you aboard." He turned to the Keeper of the Paradise. "Our esteemed Abdul will act as liaison between the Palace cloning staff and the laboratory of the Royal Stables. We lost half of the managerial staff during the terrorist attack, and the rest of them are so used to covering their rears after a lifetime of working at the palace that they've forgotten how to act boldly. We'll need some young blood taking charge of things if we're to pull this thing off."

The Keeper of the Paradise inclined his head gravely. "We shall show him every courtesy."

Rubinstein turned back to Hamid-Jones. "We're going to give you the Clonemaster's old office at the palace—you'll be spending more time here than in Tharsis City. And we'll see that you have all the perks needed to boost your status." He waved off Hamid-Jones's protests. "No, no, your new rank has to be made visible in all the small ways, if you're to impress some of the popinjays you'll have to work with. They'll step all over you otherwise."

"Thank you, your Preeminence," Hamid-Jones stammered.

A scream came from within. Rubinstein frowned. The Keeper of the Paradise hastened to peer through the spyhole. "Oh, dear!" he exclaimed. "Sami, Musa! Come quickly!"

He fumbled with the lock with clumsy fingers and managed to get it unfastened after a moment. He pushed the heavy door and hurried inside, scolding.

"Bobo, what are you doing? Stop that immediately! That's not nice!"

Hamid-Jones looked through the open door and got a confused glimpse of a naked rump rising high out of the water, amidst a flurry of splashing and churning. It belonged to the girl who had been playing zephyr to Number Forty's sailboat. The clone had her head underwater and was earnestly trying to drown her. Her arms were still beating at the water, but the splashing seemed to be getting feebler. The fine little schooner lay capsized, victim of too strong a gust or a careless wave. Tears streamed down the clone's aged cheeks.

"Bad nonny!" he was blubbering. "Bad, bad!"

He seemed to be remarkably strong in the arms, despite his age and generally flabby state.

The Keeper of the Paradise was wringing his hands ineffectually at the edge of the pool, afraid of getting his gold slippers wet. "You mustn't *do* that, Bobo!" he pleaded. "Do you know how long it takes to train a new girl?"

A pair of hefty bath attendants burst in just then and jumped into the pool, clad in trousers and T-shirts. Gently they tried to pry the clone's hands from around the houri's neck. It wasn't easy, constrained as they were from hurting him. He kept slipping out of their grasp and getting a fresh grip. But one of them managed to get her head out of the water so that she could breathe, while the other got a lock on the furious clone. Even then, Number Forty got an arm free to pick up the schooner and start flailing away at the girl's bare skin. He was nasty about it. He aimed deliberately at all her tender parts, holding the toy so that the sharp edges and masts drew blood.

The attendant heaved the houri over the rim of the pool and leapt out after her, hauling her out of reach. He dragged her over to the Keeper of the Paradise, who recoiled from the droplets of water and blood shaking from her.

"What did you do to provoke him?" the Keeper said sternly.

"Nothing, master, I swear," the houri sobbed. "He overturned the boat himself by splashing at it."

Bobo was having a fit. "Cut off her head!" he screamed.

"No, Bobo," the Keeper of the Paradise said soothingly. "You don't want to do that. She's the one you like, remember? We'll have her whipped. Would you like that?"

The clone nodded vigorously, a crafty smile lighting up the tearstained face. "Bobo watch," he said slyly.

"Of course, darling," the Keeper of the Paradise said. He turned to Hamid-Jones and the Vizier. "By tomorrow he'll have forgotten all about it," he said. "It was lucky that we were able to stop him in time. He's been dyspeptic lately. In the last couple of months he's killed two girls and maimed another badly enough to make her useless."

The attendants hustled the weeping girl out of the room quickly, and the clone settled down. The other houri, after a moment's hesitation, offered him one of the rubber bath toys, and soon he was blissfully making waves to see it rock back and forth.

Rubinstein's forehead was like a thundercloud. "I think you had better show us Number One Hundred and One," he said. "He's a few years younger, but he's a little more tractable."

The Keeper grew flustered. "I'm afraid I can't do that, your Greatness."

"What? Why not?"

"The Chamberlain removed him several days ago. He's being kept in the eunuch's wing."

"He is, is he? We'll see about that!" Rubinstein scowled at Hamid-Jones. "I'm afraid Ismail's up to his old tricks. He thinks he can groom his own alternate, then spring him at the last moment."

"Please don't tell him I told you, your Greatness," the Keeper quavered.

The Vizier looked disgusted. He said to Hamid-Jones, "You'll have to find your own way back, ya Abdul. We'll talk again later. In the meantime, my staff has set things in motion. Be at the palace tomorrow morning after prayers." He reached for a purse at his waist and handed it, clinking, to Hamid-Jones. "And do something about your wardrobe. This ought to hold you until your new credit transfer is cleared."

"Yes, your Excellence."

"Will you see about arranging a ride back to town for him?" the Vizier said to the Keeper of the Paradise. "And you'd better scare up a guide to get him back to Reception."

The Keeper bowed. "It shall be done, your Greatness."

"And don't let anyone near . . . Bobo. I'll send someone to remove him later. I don't want him within the Chamberlain's reach."

"Yes, your Greatness," the Keeper whispered, trembling.

Rubinstein left, fuming. "Underhanded son of a camel," he muttered, shaking his head.

A tall eunuch was waiting in the corridor just outside the Garden of the Clones. He stepped away from the wall to bar their way.

"I'll take care of him," he said.

The bath attendant, Sami, started to speak, then thought better of it. He gave Hamid-Jones a sidelong glance, then slipped away without a word.

"Come with me," the eunuch said in a normal baritone voice that indicated that the operation must have been performed later in life. The billowing pantaloons of the Chamberlain's entourage hung loose on a frame that lacked belly and rump; from his bearing he might once have been a military man, perhaps a paroled prisoner.

"But where are you taking me? A car's being brought round for me at Reception."

"You'll be taken there later. Come."

Bewildered, Hamid-Jones followed the eunuch through the gilded corridors to an electric bath chair equipped with a sealed canopy for outside detours. He squeezed in beside his taciturn escort, and the vehicle began moving at once, without benefit of a driver. The eunuch sat with folded arms as the little three-wheeler whizzed through branching tunnels, jerking round sharply at each bend, then scooted through an airlock to travel the palace roadways. There was no doubt that the remote operator could see where he was going: control had to be via muon beam, able to penetrate the tunnels and thick palace walls. It worked two ways—muons made excellent spy beams. Hamid-Jones wondered if he was being scrutinized en route.

They dipped underground for a couple of shortcuts, but surfaced long enough before the final approach for Hamid-Jones to get a good look at their destination. It was a particularly gaudy palace of pink and green marble, puffy with domes, set in its own hundred acre park. It looked like an enormous gelatin mold inlaid with glazed fruit.

The little runabout turned down an avenue lined with feathery anaerobic palm trees and pink statuary and bounced up a flight of broad marble steps into a turntable-style airlock. The lock pressurized with an extravagant puff, and a simpering page sprang forward with a footstool.

Five minutes later, Hamid-Jones was in the blubbery presence of Ismail, the Chamberlain and Intendant of the Eunuchs. Four of the five minutes had been consumed by a brutally thorough security frisk that left him black and blue in several unlikely places. Despite the speed of the examination, the clever probing and pinching by knowing eunuch fingers made the previous security checks seem naive.

He limped forward, hemmed in by a cluster of oiled and perfumed eunuch guards whose nasty little crescent knives stayed unsheathed. The caged parrots surrounding Ismail's dais screamed in warning as he got too close, and the eunuchs tugged at Hamid-Jones's clothing to bring him to a stop.

Ismail, his immense bulk spilling over the splendid gilt chair he lolled in, beckoned to him. "You may approach us," he said in a piping voice like a child's.

Released from the press of scented flesh, Hamid-Jones advanced to within ten feet of the Chief Eunuch before a puffy, ring-encrusted hand again waved him to a stop. Two of the eunuch guards had followed close behind, and one of them was holding on with all his might to the tail of Hamid-Jones's shirt.

The vast globular head rolled in his direction. Little hippopotamus eyes, embedded deeply within the swollen slate-gray flesh, stared redly at him.

"So, you've been given a promotion, *ya* Abdul?" Ismail said.

"Y-yes, *al-Ustador*," Hamid-Jones replied, impressed that Ismail had found out so quickly.

Ismail continued his liverish scrutiny of Hamid-Jones for several moments. Then he burst into a high-pitched giggle.

"That's all right. I have no objection. But you'll want to earn your new privileges, won't you?"

"Uh, certainly, *al-Ustador*."

"Fine. Do what the Rubinstein person tells you. He seems to think you can do a good job. But you are to report everything to me. Is that understood?"

"Y-yes, *al-Ustador*."

"You needn't look so stricken. You aren't likely to betray any confidences. The Vizier is a sly old dog. He isn't apt to let anything slip that he wouldn't *want* to reach me."

The eunuchs holding onto Hamid-Jones's shirttail snickered. Ismail rolled his eyes for their benefit.

"Just keep me informed of your progress. And let me know what the Palace cloning staff are up to. Any changes in their instructions, for example. You needn't bother informing me of the Vizier's insults to my person."

The eunuchs guffawed openly at that. Hamid-Jones felt an unpleasant chill crawl down his spine.

Ismail toyed with the little ceremonial sickle-bladed knife that hung from a silver chain around his neck, testing its edge with his thumb. It was a family heirloom, according to the Palace public relations releases—the very knife that had gelded Ismail's father before him, and that Ismail's father, in turn, had personally used to geld Ismail in order to guarantee that he would inherit the Chamberlain's job. He had a sentimental attachment to it, so it was said. But the Chamberlain's job had stopped being hereditary with Ismail. His father, a former slave assigned to the harem, had been neutered as a grown man, but Ismail himself could never have had any issue to succeed him in the post.

"You wouldn't even dream of trying to hold anything back, would you, *ya* Abdul?" he cooed at last.

"N-no, *al-Ustador*."

The Chamberlain's gelatinous bulk quivered with silent laughter. "Good, good," he said unctuously. "You are my brother, my eye. We will be the best of friends, yes?"

"Y-yes." Hamid-Jones gulped.

A chubby page hurried up and whispered in Ismail's ear. Ismail nodded, and struggled to his feet.

"Speak of the satan. The old fox didn't waste any time. We got you here only a few minutes ahead of him." Ismail clapped his hands to get the attention of the splendid functionary at the door. "Tell his Mightiness that I am honored by his visit, and that I am hastening from my private quarters to receive him." He waggled a finger at Hamid-Jones. "Come, little brother, we mustn't let the old devil see you here. I'll let you out the back way."

Propelled from behind by the two eunuchs, Hamid-Jones followed the Chamberlain's mountainous figure through a beaded curtain and into a dim enormous grotto whose air was thick with the sickly sweet smell of incense. Hamid-Jones had only a moment to gawk at a huge, billowing jellybed surrounded by caged parrots and the narrow cot at its foot where some attendant evidently slept. Then, on a stand beside the bed, a grotesque sight caught his eye.

At first he had taken the ovoid object for some kind of padded rack to hold a turban. Now he saw a twitch of movement and caught a whiff of a medicinal smell that had been masked by the incense.

Ismail giggled. "I jumped to his tune for many a year. Too bad he has no legs to do a little jumping himself."

It was the Emir's head, like a wilted cabbage in a sconce. Plastic tubing sprouted from the base of the sconce and disappeared beneath the ruffled skirt of the dressing table. A soft wheeze of hidden pumps could just barely be heard.

There could have been no brain function left in the putrid thing—at least Hamid-Jones hoped not. The head had been deprived of oxygen too long, and surely the hemorrhage that blotted out one eye was evidence of a series of massive terminal strokes. It was simply that no one had had the nerve to pull the plug, and some frightened attendant, not knowing what to do with the grisly souvenir, had brought it to Ismail.

But as Ismail's bulk got in the way of the light, the pupil of the Emir's good eye dilated. It might have been only an autonomic reflex, but its effect was to give an expression of alarm to the Emir's face.

Ismail, grinning broadly, waddled over to the Emir's vegetable head and picked up a brass incense burner lying next to it. He blew with pursed lips for a moment to get the embers glowing, then puffed a cloud of smoke into the Emir's face.

The good eye blinked. A tear trickled from the corner and ran down the ravaged cheek.

Ismail found it tremendously amusing. "Ha ha, if he could only speak," he chortled. "It was Ismail this and Ismail that and Ismail move your fat behind when he held the whip hand! But he'd be singing a different tune now!"

The blink and the teardrop had only been another reflex, like the dilated pupil, Hamid-Jones devoutly told himself. It was not possible that any vegetable thoughts could still be flitting about behind that dusty one-eyed stare.

And there was no possible way that Ismail could be planning to use his awful trophy as an ace in the hole. Otherwise he would not be secretly grooming clone number one hundred and one. Still, the Vizier ought to be informed that the Emir's head was being kept alive.

As if reading his thoughts, the Chief Eunuch said indifferently, "Tell Rubinstein if you like. When the head cannot be found, you'll be whipped for lying to an officer of state."

Then, with Ismail's mirth echoing in his ears, Hamid-Jones was whisked through a series of small, curtained doors to a deserted corridor where the tall eunuch who had delivered him to the Chamberlain's palace waited for him with the motorized bath chair.

"Get in, my lord," said that lugubrious individual. "I'll take you back to the transportation pool. There's a limousine waiting for you now to take you back to Tharsis City."

CHAPTER 8

Someone had left the door to his room ajar.

Hamid-Jones distinctly remembered the Palace cop kicking it shut when they had dragged him out early that morning. He listened for a moment on the dark landing, then cautiously pushed the door open a few more inches.

The intruder was still inside, moving furtively about. The pale beam of a handlight was playing stealthily on the interior of a cupboard. The shelves were almost bare, and the thief, with cool aplomb, had already stacked a neat pile of Hamid-Jones's possessions next to the door, ready to be taken out.

Hamid-Jones's heart hammered in his throat as he alternated between rage and resignation. People who were taken away by the police were an inevitable target of a district's burglars, always on the lookout for easy pickings. He should have gone home while it was still daylight instead of procrastinating by walking about the *suq* and tarrying for a meal at the ibn-Donald booth.

He started to back out slowly. No point in taking chances. He could get help from the night porter or one of the tenants, and they could wait at the bottom of the stairs for the thief to come down.

But then there was suddenly a dazzle of light in his face, and a sharp intake of breath over by the cupboards.

There was nothing for it but to launch himself at the intruder and hope the fellow didn't have a weapon handy.

His shoulder thudded into beef, and he heard a gasp of pain. The handlight clattered to the floor, and Hamid-Jones had a wiry, malodorous body pinned against the wall. The fellow had a sour reek of cheap wine on his breath, and that would be another mark against him when the constables arrived.

It was like trying to hold on to a wriggling snake. Hamid-Jones was unable to get in a solid punch. But finally he had a firm grip on flesh, and his Earth-born muscles prevailed. The man stopped struggling at once.

"Please, master, don't hurt me!" the intruder whined. "I wasn't doing anything!"

"Let's have a look at you," Hamid-Jones grunted. He tightened his grip with one hand and groped for the wall switch.

His captive was a scrawny, ferret-faced individual wearing a carelessly knotted turban and a long gabardine whose ample pockets were weighed down by their ill-gotten contents. Hamid-Jones forced a grimy sleeve back for a closer look at the wrist under the light, and was not surprised to see the signs of past knavery—a right hand that was about ten years younger than the left one. It must have been regrown after the rogue had served a limited sentence for some previous offense. It was too bad, but he would have to lose it again.

"Speak quickly, you misbegotten miscreant," Hamid-Jones said pityingly. "What are you doing in my room?"

"Let me go, master," the man whimpered. "I'm no thief!"

"No?" Hamid-Jones said ironically with a glance at the stripped cupboard. "What then?"

"I'm Aziz, your servant."

Hamid-Jones was startled enough at that to let go of the man's wrist. Aziz straightened himself up and dusted off his clothes with dignity.

"I've just begun to pack up your things. A man in your position can't live in a place like this. It's not dignified. And don't worry about paying me. My first month's wages are taken care of. You can start picking up the tab when your new stipend comes through." He cocked his head hopefully. "Though if you happen to have a few extra dinars on you, you might let me have a little extra on account. It's going to be expensive getting you set up—the bribes I've already had to pay tonight, and out of my own pocket!"

"Wh-who hired you?" Hamid-Jones managed, the wind taken out of his sails. "Was it the Vizier?" A sudden suspicion struck him. "Or was it the Chamberlain?"

"How would I know?" the spindly man said evasively. "Such as myself don't question the authorities. Somebody from the Palace paid me, gave me my instructions, that's all I can tell you."

"But what office did he say he was from? What did he look like?"

"He looked like any of those Palace flunkies with fancy titles who run errands for the bigshots—too many jewels, too many furs, and a couple of flunkies of his own to follow him around and yes him." Aziz licked his thin lips. "They came and sort of got me out of a jam I was in, so I wasn't about to ask for any details."

Hamid-Jones didn't think he'd get anywhere trying to question Aziz about what kind of "jam" he'd been gotten out of. "And what instructions did they give you?" he said.

"Just what I told you, master. They said that now that you're moving up in the world, you needed a servant—one who knows the ropes." He went on quickly, "Don't worry, *sidi*, I'll take good care of you, see that you live the way you're supposed to, and make sure that no one cheats you."

"And did your instructions also include reporting back on me?"

Aziz gave him a stare of wide-eyed innocence. "Master, how can you suggest such a thing?" he protested. "I'm your man!"

"Never mind." Hamid-Jones fumbled in the purse the Vizier had given him and tossed Aziz a five-dinar gold piece; Aziz caught the spinning coin deftly and tucked it away out of sight. "You can start by putting back my things. The landlord's given me notice, but I suppose he'll give me a few days to look for new digs. In the meantime, you can help me shop for a new wardrobe first thing in the morning."

Aziz's mismatched hands fluttered. "Don't bother your head about it, *sidi*. I've already arranged—"

He was interrupted by a commotion on the landing. The landlord, ibn Zayd, stood swaying in the open doorway, panting from the long climb.

"Ah, *ya* Abdul," he said with a wraparound smile. "I'm so glad you've arrived. I've been trying to explain to your servant here that there's no need to move you out so precipitously."

"You mean I can keep my room, hajji?" Hamid-Jones said uncertainly.

Ibn-Zayd looked shocked. "Keep your room? No, no, we're preparing larger quarters for you. You won't have to spend even one more night in this little cell—we can have you moved within the hour!"

Aziz took charge of the situation before Hamid-Jones could replay. "What? My master stay in a fleabag like this? In a neighborhood full of pensioners and clerks? It's unthinkable. Are you aware that my master has been named Custodian of the Royal Nucleotides, with access to the Grand Vizier himself? He needs an address worthy of his station.''

The landlord's sallow face twitched. ''But my dear friend! Aziz, *ya aini*! Have you forgotten our little discussion? I thought we were about to come to an understanding—''

Aziz cut him off before he could say more. ''I'm a reasonable man and always willing to listen. But this place won't do at all. The master will need a place suitable for receiving important visitors, enough space for servants, surroundings that won't shame him. I think we can do better elsewhere.''

Ibn Zayd appealed to Hamid-Jones. ''I've already evicted Mr. Najib. He's packing up now. It's the best flat in the house, with its own courtyard, ample room for a harem, servants' quarters. You couldn't be more comfortable anywhere! It's true that some may consider my establishment a trifle unfashionable, but we've had many eminent tenants in the past—jurists, *mujtahideen*, a *chereef*, even princes of the blood. I would be honored to have you stay.''

''I couldn't think of having Mr. Najib evicted on my account—'' Hamid-Jones began.

But a look had passed between the landlord and Aziz, and Aziz cut in: ''Well, I suppose it won't hurt to have a look at it— though mind you, my master promises nothing.''

''Bless you, bless you!'' the landlord said, rubbing his hands together. ''You won't lose by it, I promise you.''

With Hamid-Jones feebly protesting, they trooped together down the stone steps to the courtyard. The porters were carrying out Mr. Najib's furniture and stacking it in neat groups. The members of the Najib household stood around, looking glum. The rug manufacturer's small harem—a wife, a couple of daughters, a mother or mother-in-law, and a scrawny servant girl— were sequestered in a tight group to one side, swathed in black from head to foot and guarded by a male relative.

Hamid-Jones was desperately embarrassed, but Mr. Najib came hurrying over to him with an effusive smile.

''Mr. Najib, it's all a mistake!'' Hamid-Jones blurted. ''I've told the hajji that I don't want your flat. I'm sure this can be straightened out.''

''Think nothing of it, my dear young friend,'' Mr. Najib said lightly. ''I'm glad to make the sacrifice for an important Palace official such as yourself—and congratulations on your appointment, by the way. I know you won't forget your old friends in the luster of your new post, the way some people are inclined to do. Feel free to call on me if your department ever needs rugs, tapestries, or anything in that line. Anything from a prayer rug to a pavilion, that's our motto.'' He winked broadly. "It could be that it might be worth a little something to you—but we need not speak of that now.''

His eyes gave the merest flicker toward Aziz, who looked away at once, his hands in his pockets.

"But you can't uproot your whole family like this!" Hamid-Jones cried. The porters were still lugging out household possessions; as he watched, they wrestled an overstuffed divan over to the pile in the center of the courtyard.

"I'll hardly be inconvenienced at all," Mr. Najib said with an airy wave of his hand. "Arif ibn Zayd is moving out his relative, Khaled, and getting rid of Mr. Daud—who was behind in his rent anyway—and promises to knock out a few walls to provide me with a new flat almost as large as the one I'm vacating. I'll be honored to still be your neighbor.''

Several of the other tenants had come crowding round Hamid-Jones by that time, keeping a respectful distance of three or four feet. "You only deserve it, *ya* Abdul," the little *farash*, Mr. Fahti, said vehemently. "I always knew they'd recognize your worth one day.''

Even Kareem, the supercilious hotel clerk, came over to congratulate him. "You're in the big time now, *ya* Abdul," he said with no cynicism that Hamid-Jones could detect. "Make the most of it.''

Aziz sidled up to him and said in a lowered voice, "That thief of a landlord thought he could get away with overcharging a trusting person like yourself, but never fear, I set him straight.''

Hamid-Jones bowed to the inevitable. "All right, Aziz, move me in as soon as it's convenient for Mr. Najib.''

Yezid the Prod stood before Hamid-Jones's desk, surly but respectful. Hamid-Jones looked him over, seeing him in a new light, as he could now afford to. The overseer didn't seem quite so intimidating a figure any more. He was bare-chested under the metal-studded leather vest, and the tufts of hair standing up on his beefy shoulders and pectorals were noticeably gray. The biceps still looked like carved rocks, but the belly could be seen to sag under the weight of Yezid's sixty years. And the indented scar on Yezid's shaved skull, running all the way from under the leather skullcap down behind one cauliflower ear to the thick neck, no longer seemed an emblem of toughness and brutality, but poignant evidence of a hard life.

"I've been keeping them in the detention room till you got here," Yezid growled. "I didn't know what you wanted to do with them."

"Quite right," Hamid-Jones said. "I mean, not to take any harsh steps till consulting me. After all, they've been released." He glanced at the Department of Rectitude report on his desk. "There doesn't seem to be anything against them."

"Shall I bring them in now?" Yezid asked with a scowl, the knotted flail in his hand twitching like a cat's tail.

"Er, yes. That is, you can tell them I'd like to see them."

Yezid stomped out on his bandy legs, looking like an overgrown chimpanzee in leather pantaloons. Hamid-Jones sat back and waited. He felt like a imposter behind the imposing desk, an antique carved from comet-grown cedar. He hadn't wanted to appropriate the Clonemaster's old office, but Aziz had insisted on the point before allowing him to leave for work in his new finery. "You've got to take charge from the first moment," he had chided. "Otherwise they won't respect you."

Yezid reappeared, pushing Ja'far and Feisel in front of him. The two cloning technicians were pale and drawn, blinking as if unaccustomed to light. Yezid folded his hairy arms and posted himself next to the door.

"Er, you can go, ya Yezid," Hamid-Jones said. "I won't need you."

For a moment, Hamid-Jones thought Yezid was going to stay, but then the overseer, with a snort of disgust, unfolded his arms and clumped off.

"Well . . . uh . . . have a seat," Hamid-Jones said.

The two settled themselves with alacrity. After an awkward moment, it came to Hamid-Jones that they were waiting for him to speak first.

"I, uh, hope everything's all right," he said fatuously.

"Oh, yes," Feisel said quickly. Ja'far hastened to nod agreement. "They let us go this morning. Everybody was very nice. We were treated quite well."

Hamid-Jones could see the livid bruise on Feisel's cheek, and the missing fingernail on Ja'far's right hand, but he did not press the point. "That's fine, then," he said with imitation heartiness. "It's good to have you back at work. Things were in a state of confusion for a while after all the, er, events, but it seems to have calmed down now. I don't expect there'll be any more, uh, problems."

The pair exchanged a worried glance. "*Ya* Abdul," Feisel began, "you understand that under certain circumstances a person may say things he doesn't exactly wish to . . ."

His sharp eyes had caught the Department of Rectitude dossier on the desk, and he was afraid that Hamid-Jones had been reading some of the accusations against him they had doubtless been forced to make. He needn't have worried; the Greenies had expunged any such references in Hamid-Jones's copy.

"None of that matters anymore," Hamid-Jones assured him. "As you can see, the authorities have closed the books. My own situation is secure, and I can assure you that yours will be, too."

They broke into relieved grins. "We heard that things had changed around here. Is it true that you're in charge of the Palace cloning operation, too?"

"Don't get too far ahead of yourselves," Hamid-Jones cautioned. "I'm only acting as liaison between us and the Palace. But yes, I'll report directly to the Vizier, and we're to be given an expanded role in the medical cloning program."

"See, Feisel, I told you!" Ja'far said.

Feisel nudged him to silence. "You'll have an office at the Palace, too?" he said.

"Well, yes, but I'll spend as much time here as possible."

"You'll need a deputy, then," Feisel declared. "Someone to keep an eye on things for you."

"Um, let's all get settled in and see what happens. Now, if—"

"*Ya* Abdul," Ja'far said. "There's just one thing."

Hamid-Jones frowned. "Yes?"

"They're still holding Rashid. The charges against him are more serious. He was caught red-handed sneaking into the Clonemaster's house for a clandestine meeting. He's in terrible shape. We saw him once in the exercise yard. He could hardly walk."

"Don't bother the chief," Feisel admonished. "I'm sure he'll do everything for Rashid that he can."

"I'll look into it," Hamid-Jones said.

He got some indication of the extent of his new clout by the end of the day when, after an hour's worth of phone calls that ended with him being bucked to the Department of Rectitude's Second Assistant Deputy Director himself, a battered and bedraggled Rashid limped into his office.

"They just kicked me out," he said wonderingly. "Handed me my clothes and told me to beat it."

He swayed and would have fallen, had not Hamid-Jones hurried from behind the oversize desk and helped him to a chair. "Just take it easy," he said. "Do you want a glass of water?"

He was shocked by Rashid's appearance. He was missing an eye, and the inflamed lid drooped over an empty socket. The eye could be regrown, but worse still was the fact that Rashid seemed to have lost his spirit. The irritating brashness had given way to a tentative smile that kept switching anxiously on and off. There was a sag to Rashid's shoulders, and the big, florid face was unhealthily mottled.

"Thanks, old man, but I'll be all right in a minute. Just got caught dizzy there for a moment."

"I'm sorry."

Neither of them referred to the unfortunate moment under Lalla's window when they had pretended not to recognize each other, or to the undoubted fact that Rashid had been an informant, willing or unwilling, against Hamid-Jones while in the hands of the Green police.

"We'll see about getting that eye taken care of first thing," Hamid-Jones rattled on. "It'll be about two years before you have any useful vision in it, but at least with the new Palace medical priority I can get you put on, you won't have to waste time on a waiting list."

"I say, that's jolly decent of you," Rashid said awkwardly.

"And of course your old job is waiting for you."

"That's fine, really fine. I'll do my best for you, ya Abdul. You can count on me."

"The Royal Stables have been given a rather important new assignment. We'll be coordinating with the Palace cloning program."

"So I gathered."

Hamid-Jones did not dare to tell too much about the Royal Stables' new role. Rashid, as meek and chastened as he was at the moment, was fully capable of piecing things together from a few clues, and it was too much to hope for that he had permanently given up his gossiping ways. "Er, the Emir is still mending after his ordeal, and while no particular problems are anticipated, we're to be on standby, just to be safe. If any touch-up surgery is needed, it'll be the surgeons' show, not ours. Uh, with the strain that this recent business put on the Palace's resources, though, we might be asked to help bring a few more clones on line, in order to keep the regular program going—that sort of thing."

"How *is* his Majesty? Did you see him?" Rashid's good eye shone with dangerous interest.

Hamid-Jones thought of Number Forty in his bath, flailing away at the unfortunate houri with his toy boat, and of the moribund head ensconced by the Chief Eunuch's bedside.

"Yes," he said shortly. "In a manner of speaking."

When he got home that evening, he found that Aziz had been shopping again. An entire sports wardrobe was laid out in his bedchamber—electric jodhpurs, vacuum-rated riding boots, a houndstooth jacket cut generously enough to be worn over a pressure suit, heatcloak, deluxe respirator and thermal hood combination, handgear ranging from skintight thermaplast gloves to heavy-duty mittens with retractable trigger fingers. A fortune in expensive accessories completed the outfit. Hamid-Jones saw matching sets of lightweight air tanks with gold-plated valves, miniaturized survival gear including an inflatable walktent that fit in a pocket-size pouch, radar binoculars, a sports Kalashnikov designed to look like a twentieth-century antique but carrying a two thousand round microflechette magazine, a laser smartpistol, a rocket-assisted fragmentation grenade launcher for bringing down small game anywhere within a twenty yard radius.

"What's all this?" he asked a beaming Aziz.

"Hunting clothes, *ya* Abdul. Don't worry about the cost. I charged everything."

"What are you talking about? I'm not going hunting."

"Ah, but you are, master. And in company with the finest gentlemen. A sand car and driver will be sent round to pick you up first thing in the morning."

"Look, she's flushed something!"

The hunting party reined in and watched the circling hawk, a distant black dot against the orange sky. Hamid-Jones followed the example of his companions and pulled his horse to a halt. The Mars-bred stallion quivered on its nine-foot legs, breathing hard through its respirator; a small snowfall of carbon dioxide floated from the nosebag to the desert gravel.

"What did I tell you?" the hawk's owner exulted. "She can spot gazelle in a dustfog from twenty miles up!"

"Gazelle?" drawled another member of the hunting party. "More likely it's another bustard—or some small burrower that caught her fancy." He was a young blue blood named Thamir, a lean, dandified man who hadn't spoken a word to Hamid-Jones all day beyond a bare, obligatory acknowledgment when they had been introduced.

Hamid-Jones looked around at the others, sitting easily on their stilt-legged thoroughbreds as if they had been born to the saddle. Except for Thamir, they had been decent enough to him—though none of them could have been overjoyed at having been asked to accept into their tight midst a plebeian upstart whose clothes were too new and whose horsemanship was decidedly awkward. Hamid-Jones couldn't blame them; he was none too comfortable about being here himself—but the Vizier's wishes were not to be taken lightly.

He let his gaze wander back to the little group of mounted cadgers, carrying the rest of the birds on the open frameworks strapped to their shoulders, and the dog handlers, struggling with a yapping pack of salukis who looked goggle-eyed and elephant-faced in their long-snouted breathing masks. The dogs were straining at their leads; they were watching the circling falcon, too, and they knew something was up.

Waiting discreetly further back was a small fleet of sand cars and halftracks. Aziz was somewhere among them with the other personal servants, basking in the warmth of an enclosed van and no doubt showing off the expensive outdoor wardrobe he had bought on Hamid-Jones's credit.

"She's going for more altitude! She's going to stoop!"

Hamid-Jones snapped his eyes back to the dot in the sky. He raised his binoculars in time to see the great kitelike wings fold on their double-jointed metacarpals, and then the Marsfalcon dropped like a stone.

The radar autofocus and the image compensator kept the shape in view as it plummeted, then it disappeared behind the horizon. He kept the binoculars trained just above the skyline so the radar could pick it up again, and a few minutes later saw the bird rise, circle, and drop once more.

"Whatever it is, it's too much for her to handle alone—and too big for a quick kill!" someone said.

"It's gazelle, I tell you!" the bird's owner insisted. "Maybe a whole herd of them!"

"Perhaps it's a Bedouin, Aswad," Thamir said lazily. "Remember the time when that tiercel of yours put out the eyes of some dirty fellow's camel, and there was all that fuss about blood money?"

The cadgers were busy readying a new cast of falcons, unscrewing the air tubes from the cadge tanks and attaching them to the little streamlined nacelles the birds carried in flight. Within seconds, the jesses were loosed from the leg restraints, the hoods removed, and the magnificent birds thrown into the air to spread their huge sails. The dog handlers gave them a minute's head-start, then released the straining salukis. The gangling hounds took off joyfully, their silky ears flopping, keeping the falcons in view.

Omar, cloaked and masked in the quietly expensive togs of the true upper crust, pulled his horse alongside Hamid-Jones. "Try to stick close to me," he said. "That's rough country up ahead, and we're bound to get split up."

"Thanks, I will," Hamid-Jones replied.

Omar was his ascribed sponsor, though Hamid-Jones had never met him until this morning. He was the son of a rich family with property in Xanthe, a field of oxygen wells in Cimmerium, and extensive shipping interests, who had nothing much to do but amuse himself. But he had been kindness itself to Hamid-Jones, loaning him one of his best horses—a gentle, easy-to-manage animal that wouldn't embarrass him—and generally taking him in hand.

"I hope Aswad's right and that it's not bustard," Omar said. "It could be an all-day chase in terrain like this, and it's dangerous to the birds to try to make a kill that close to the ground. Bad for the horses, too—too easy to break a leg."

The other riders were spurring their horses on, following the dust of the salukis. Omar took off at a gallop, and Hamid-Jones did his best to keep up. He suspected that Omar was holding his horse back to make it easy for him.

The chase was a long one. The gazelle hadn't waited for the salukis to arrive but had taken off in all directions, separating the wheeling falcons and fragmenting the hunting party. Hamid-Jones lost Omar in a labyrinth of boulders and rifts, but by keeping his eye on the same group of dive-bombing falcons, managed to head in what he hoped was the right direction. He heard automatic fire and the high-pitched keening of the hounds up ahead and, holding onto the reins for dear life with one hand, snapped out the folding stock of his reproduction Kalashnikov.

The horse picked its way through the desert rubble on its spidery legs, and as he rounded a house-size boulder, Hamid-Jones found himself in on the scene of a kill.

Two gazelles had already been slaughtered, cut to pieces by automatic fire. It had been body shots, leaving the heads more or less intact as trophies, though the gaping eye sockets showed the birds had blinded them first. It was hard, in all that mess of raw meat, to tell what the dogs had done.

A third gazelle was somehow managing to keep a pair of salukis at bay, driving them off with its curved horns. It was handicapped by the falcon still impaled on one of the horns, its twenty-foot wings trailing broken struts, but as Hamid-Jones watched, the gazelle managed to get rid of the bird with a toss of its head.

That explained why the other birds were so wary, hovering in slow circles overhead.

Fifteen yards away, a lone rider sat motionless atop his tall steed, calmly watching the bloody little drama and making no attempt to finish the wounded gazelle off. From the jeweled heatcloak and the rich caparison of the horse he rode, Hamid-Jones recognized Thamir.

Hamid-Jones hesitated, torn by admiration for the gazelle. The graceful creature was putting up a brave battle, but it was running out of air. The Marsgazelle had been a marvelous feat of bioengineering for its day, when an earlier generation of sportsmen had turned it loose to stock the Martian deserts. It had a lot of rabbit genes to enable it to survive in its sparse environment—its "hooves" still retained vestigial claws from the toes they were derived from, and its "horns" were sidetracked bicuspids, channeled up through the skull—and its breathing apparatus owed a lot to porpoises. But the real marvel was the biochemical sleight-of-hand that enabled it to extract oxygen from the carbon dioxide of its waste products and reuse it, in a reverse oxidation process similar to photosynthesis, and store a reserve in its tissues. It had been a much more complicated job than the redesign of the Marsbustard, whose creators had simply modified the enormous existing throat pouch to store oxygen under pressure and provided an electrical organ derived from electric eels to manufacture oxygen from the electrolysis of water.

Still, the poor creature had passed its design limits during the cruel chase. Hamid-Jones could see the huge accessory bellows heaving in a vain attempt to extract more oxygen from the thin Martian atmosphere. And internally, the gazelle's system must be clogging up with the sugar that was a byproduct of the photosynthetic-like metabolic process that released oxygen—it was what made gazelle flesh taste so sweet.

Now one of the salukis, emboldened by the gazelle's flagging strength, darted in and tore an ugly strip of flesh from the animal's flank. They weren't supposed to do that—they were trained to harry prey and hold it at bay to be dispatched by the hunter—but the game had gone on too long and it was getting excited.

Thamir made no attempt to stop the dog or call it off. The other saluki, give this tacit permission, dashed under the threatening horns and buried its teeth in the gazelle's belly.

Sickened, Hamid-Jones unslung his Kalashnikov and thumbed it for single fire.

A hand on his shoulder stopped him. He hadn't even noticed the other rider come up beside him, so intent had he been.

"It's Thamir's kill—best not to interfere," Omar said gently.

Hamid-Jones lowered his weapon. Thamir's cowled form sent a veiled glance in his direction, then he shouted at the salukis.

"La, la, la! Kiff! Kiff!"

The salukis refused to let go of their victim till Thamir fired a warning shot. Another burst of fire over their heads sent them skittering away, yelping. Then, coolly, Thamir emptied his entire magazine on full automatic into the gazelle's panting form.

At two thousand rounds per minute, it was over quickly, but it seemed to Hamid-Jones to go on forever. When Thamir was finished with his bloody work, there was nothing left of the gazelle but a fan-shaped spray of stew meat across the desert floor. He had made no effort to preserve the head as a trophy.

Omar raised his hand in greeting and started forward. But Thamir, with another look at Hamid-Jones that seemed baleful even through the mask and hood, spurred his horse and rode off without a word.

Hamid-Jones, still shaky with disgust, said, "I spoiled his fun. He wanted it to go on longer."

Omar gave him a hard look. "He was upset, that's all. The animal speared one of his best falcons."

Up above, the remaining birds had stopped their circling. The enormous sails fluttered, beating the thin air for altitude, and then the kitelike creatures wheeled about and soared back in the direction of the waiting cadgers.

"They must be on their reserve tanks—hunt's over for now," Omar said. "Let's get back and have some lunch."

A refreshment pavilion had appeared as if by magic while they were away. A halftrack with a small 'dozer blade had scraped a thousand square yards of the desert floor flat, and a clutch of air tents had been inflated, like gaily striped eggs in a rocky nest. The fleet of service vehicles was drawn up in a circle around the rubbled rim, and masked servants were flitting between the still-billowing shelters with trays and insulated carryalls.

Omar and his friends didn't believe in roughing it.

Hamid-Jones surrendered the reins of his gangling steed to a groom, who led the creature off to a barn-size tent that had been set up as a stable. He followed Omar into the most festive-looking of the fabric structures, a double ovoid with a scalloped marquee extended on poles.

Within was a miraculous feast laid out on draped trestles—cheeses and dips, cold chicken, little meat pastries, bowls of Scotch eggs, heaping platters of moussaka and falafel, trays piled high with tarts and confections, silver pitchers of tea, sherbets.

"Let's get something hot," Omar said, and led him over to one of the tables. Hunters stood around, their masks doffed and their cowls thrown back. Servants hurried back and forth with steaming dishes.

Hamid-Jones accepted a flaky cornucopia of stuffed pigeon and eggplant and listened to the boasts of the hunters. ". . . by the time I arrived the birds had felled one beast on their own and were feeding on the liver, but the dogs were running circles around the other three and keeping them pinned down. I could have used the Kalashnikov, of course, and not risked losing any, but I had the antique Weatherby Magnum, and I thought, Why not?" He held up three ungloved fingers. "Three bullets, three gazelle . . ."

One of the hunters turned to Omar and asked politely, "Get anything?"

"Not yet. Maybe this afternoon."

The man nodded sympathetically, then sent a discreet glance somewhere past Hamid-Jones. His meaning was clear: having to play nursemaid to the yokel must have held Omar back.

Hamid-Jones flushed. Omar noticed, and with impeccable courtesy made a point of edging closer to include him in the group. "Abdul beat me to the birds' pitch—he must have ridden like the wind—but we both got there too late. Isn't that so, Abdul?"

Hamid-Jones mumbled an acknowledgment, but eyes slid away from him. A newcomer strode into the group, and the others turned to greet him. It was Thamir; he flung back his hood and snapped his fingers, and a servant put a glass into his extended hand. Thamir raised it to his lips without looking.

"Bad luck, Thamir," one of the hunters commiserated. "My cadger told me that your prize peregrine, Thunderbolt, got speared."

Thamir took a gulp of mint tea. Hamid-Jones could smell scotch in it. "I raised her from an eyas," he said. "Trained her myself."

"A noble creature. She must have had gyrfalcon genes from the look of her."

Thamir's lips twisted as he made an effort not to appear boastful. "That would have been illegal."

"But she came from the Royal Stables, didn't she?" the hunter persisted. "Wasn't she a gift from the Emir to your father?"

Omar inclined his head toward Hamid-Jones. "Abdul here could probably settle the question about gyrfalcon genes. What about it, *ya* Abdul?"

"Well, er . . ." Hamid-Jones looked at all the expressionless faces that were suddenly turned in his direction. ". . . we weren't allowed to use actual gyrfalcon genes themselves for gift birds, of course, but we constructed close analogs." He added quickly, "You couldn't have told them apart, really."

"Well, there we are," Omar said brightly.

Thamir shot Hamid-Jones a murderous glance. "I knew the family of Hassan bin Fahd al-Hejjaj very well," he said. "I wasn't familiar with his servants."

He spilled the rest of his tea into the ground at Hamid-Jones's feet, dropped the glass and stalked off.

"You can have the night off," Hamid-Jones said.

He took a last critical look at himself in the mirror. The image he saw was a haberdasher's triumph—crisp white djellaba gleaming with optical brighteners, dark cloak discreetly bordered with kaleidotape, silver dagger with a jeweled pommel stuck in his sash, silk foulard headcloth from Harrod's of Tharsis, English leather wingtips.

Aziz wrung his hands. "Please, master, don't go!"

"Hold your tongue!" Hamid-Jones said angrily. Then, curiosity getting the better of him, he asked, "Why not?"

Aziz was evasive. "The woman is not good for you, that's all. You have a fine new position. The world is opening up before you. You can easily afford a nice little concubine who won't be any bother to us. Why go out of the way to cause trouble for yourself?"

"Nonsense! My position is secure. I'm no longer under suspicion. I have the sponsorship of the Grand Vizier himself. I owe it to the memory of Hassan bin Fahd al-Hejjaj to look after his daughter, who is all alone in the world, and vulnerable to anyone who wishes to take advantage of her.''

Aziz flicked invisible dust off Hamid-Jones's cloak with a whiskbroom. "She may not need your protection anymore," he said at last.

"What do you know, you rascal?" Hamid-Jones demanded.

"Nothing, master, nothing at all. I just have your best interests at heart. Stay home tonight. I'll send for a dancing girl."

"You're an impertinent rogue. Where's the gift I bought for her?"

"Here, master."

Hamid-Jones peeped into the excelsior nest at the orbital pearl in its sterling silver setting. They were grown in a globe of artifically heated water that had once been a comet before a Japanese syndicate had nudged it into orbit somewhere past Deimos, and this one was the size of a billiard ball. It had cost Hamid-Jones a month's salary, but by God, it was heavy enough to give the woman who wore it a crick in the neck!

He snapped the lid back on the box. "You had better learn to show some respect," he admonished Aziz. "Lalla bint Hassan al-Hejjaj may be your new mistress after this night, so you'd better get used to the idea."

He glared at Aziz to forestall a reply, and left with the pearl under his arm.

This time he went openly to the front door. "God be with you," he said to the liveried eunuch who answered. "I am here to see Miss Lalla bint Hassan al-Hejjaj."

"The *sayyidati* is seeing no one." The man made as if to close the door.

"You're not the judge of that. Please have me announced immediately."

The eunuch gave him a surly look. "Whom shall I say is calling?"

"You know very well who I am!" Hamid-Jones exploded. "Don't be insolent!" The eunuch was Yusif, the same pathetic specimen he had browbeaten on his last visit. Yusif seemed to have acquired some backbone since then; someone had spruced him up and given him the courage to be cheeky.

Yusif blinked. Hamid-Jones pushed past him before he could decide to close the door.

"I'll go see," Yusif muttered, and went upstairs without offering Hamid-Jones any refreshments. Hamid-Jones was too full of anticipation to notice the slight. He began rehearsing what he was going to say to Lalla.

But he was left cooling his heels so long that he began to smolder all over again. He looked around and began to take some notice of his surroundings. It dawned on him that there were no loafing, dispirited servants hanging around as before; those who passed through the great hall on errands seemed busy and purposeful. The indefinable background sounds he could hear were those of a household that once again was humming normally.

He was about to collar one of the passing servants when he saw movement on the staircase. It was not Yusif returning but the head eunuch himself, Murad, a pear-shaped, mud-colored man in resplendent mauve silks and corkscrew turban.

That explained it. It was Murad who had whipped a demoralized staff back into shape. If Murad had returned, it could only be because he thought the fortunes of the house had improved—that it was no longer under a shadow.

"Salaam, *ya* Abdul. You can go up. The *sayyidati* will see you."

If Murad saw him as a potential protector, he was not being overly cordial. Well, that was the man's way—he was a sour one. It was what made him a good majordomo and guardian of the harem. There was no nonsense about him.

Still, Hamid-Jones was piqued that Murad seemed unimpressed by the expensive new togs that Aziz had shopped for, and that he showed no recognition of Hamid-Jones's new station in life—news of which certainly must have reached him. Hamid-Jones might still have been the junior assistant whom the Clonemaster rewarded with an occasional dinner invitation.

"Peace to you, *ya* Murad," he said stiffly, and headed for the stairs.

He forgot his pique when he saw Lalla. She was no longer behind a screen—the room was technically separated into harem and *raba'a* by a symbolic *q'ata* composed of a row of tasseled cords hanging from a ceiling frame. The old latticed screen was leaning casually against a door frame and a eunuch chaperon was sitting in a far corner—both concessions to a surprise inspection by the morals police. They kept a special eye on households like this, with new widows or orphans. That was why it paid to have a first-class chief eunuch like Murad in charge; he had an impeccable reputation.

"Now I can die," he said recklessly. "*Ya helwa*, Little Candy!"

She reached across the dividing line and patted the cushions there, motioning him to sit down. "*Marhaba, ya* Abdul," she said in a voice that thrilled him to the core. Her face was concealed by a designer veil and she was wearing a billowing long-sleeved gown that left a lot to the imagination, but her plump little hands were bare.

Hamid-Jones started to open his mouth again, but a high-pitched yapping interrupted him. Two tiny pug faces peeped from the folds of her gown, showing little needle teeth.

"Quiet, Bijou," she said. To Hamid-Jones, she said, "He's so jealous!"

The creature was a miniature Cerberus, made from Pekingese stock. Such toys were not produced on Mars—it had to be a Terran import, and frightfully expensive.

"Uh . . . so I see."

He settled into the cushions. The diminutive creature growled at him, a sound like two gargling piccolos. Hamid-Jones produced his gift package. "Uh . . . I've brought you a little . . ."

The two-headed mini-Peke didn't like him reaching across toward Lalla. It leapt from her lap like an animated dishrag and sank its thumbtack teeth into his hand.

"Bijou, that's not nice!" Lalla scolded. "Isn't he adorable? He's trying to protect me. Don't worry, he's too small to hurt you."

Hamid-Jones was not so sure. It felt as if the skin were broken. He tried to shake the tiny creature loose, but it held on with both sets of jaws.

"That's *enough*, Bijou! Don't be a silly!" Lalla said.

Reluctantly it let go and, with a final squeaky growl at Hamid-Jones, retreated to Lalla's lap. It had left twin rows of puncture marks across the back of Hamid-Jones's hand, oozing pinhead drops of blood. "It's nothing," he said, wrapping his handkerchief around it.

"A woman alone needs protection," Lalla apologized.

"Yes . . . yes indeed," he agreed hastily. "Uh, is he new?"

"An old friend of the family gave him to me," she said, her eyes shining above the designer veil. "Thamir bin Thamir, of the Memnonia Thamirs."

"What?" he cried. "Thamir bin Thamir al-Sarook?"

"Do you *know* him?"

Hamid-Jones was affronted. She needn't have acted so surprised! "I've gone hunting with him," he said in a surly tone.

"Oh," she gushed, "then you know what a dear, kind, thoughtful man he is. So *democratic*, don't you think?" She saw

Hamid-Jones starting to sulk and gave an immediate tinkling laugh. "But *you've* been such a good friend, too, *ya* Abdul. I don't know how I could have gotten through those first, awful days without knowing that I had your support. Even Murad deserted me."

That was better, although Hamid-Jones didn't like being compared to a eunuch. "Aren't you going to open your present?" he said gruffly.

"Oh. Yes. Of course." She lifted the lid of the box, gave a perfunctory squeal over the orbital pearl, and held it up on its silver chain. Hamid-Jones hoped that she was going to try it around her neck, but she lowered it back into its excelsior packing and replaced the lid. "It's very nice, *ya* Abdul," she said indifferently.

Hamid-Jones shrank a little. He really couldn't blame her. As expensive as it was, the space-grown bauble couldn't compare in cost to a toy Cerberus. And he himself, despite his Palace patronage and brand-new title, must seem rough around the edges next to someone like Thamir, who had been born to wealth and position.

"Listen, *ya* Lalla," he said desperately, "I know I'm not worthy of you, but I worship the ground you walk on. Give me a chance to make you happy. All that I have is yours!"

"*Oo, la*, you mustn't talk like that, *ya* Abdul! If Murad heard you, he'd have you thrown out!"

She giggled.

"Say that you care—just a little!" he begged.

"Don't spoil it," she said with the hint of a pout. "Be nice, *ya* Abdul."

"*Ana bahebik!*" he declared. "I'm burning for you!"

He had leaned too far forward, and the miniature Cerberus showed its two sets of teeth and growled.

"See, you've upset Bijou. Now don't be silly and tiresome, *ya* Abdul. We'll have some tea and talk of pleasant things."

She clapped her hands. A computer chime confirmed that the order had been relayed to the kitchen.

"What is Thamir to you?" he demanded.

"He's just a friend . . . like you," she soothed him. "Please, *ya* Abdul, you mustn't carry on this way. Think of my reputation."

She indicated the eunuch in the corner with a roll of her eyes.

The tea arrived a few minutes later with a tray of exquisite little cakes that proved that the kitchen, at least, was back in commission. It was agony for Hamid-Jones to sit there making small talk, with the Little Sugarplum separated from him by no more than a few strands of braided cords, but it would have been worse agony to leave. When his time was up, Yusif arrived with another junior eunuch, and the two of them began aggressively polishing lamps and doorknobs.

"*Mumtaz*, it was enchanting," Hamid-Jones said, rising stiffly to his feet. The twin heads of the little lap pet started yelping hysterically at him. He raised his voice to make himself heard. "May I call again?"

She lowered her gaze demurely. "I'm all alone in the world. How can I stop you?"

"Why didn't you tell me about Thamir?" he stormed at Aziz.

"Please, master. I wasn't sure he meant business till you came back and told me about the toy Cerberus. I got to talking to his servant at the hunting camp when we were setting up the tents and getting lunch ready. I was hanging around the cook tent with the rest of the personal servants, and you know how they like to gossip about their employers."

"No, I don't know," Hamid-Jones shot out.

"Not me, I swear," Aziz protested, spreading his hands. "My lips are sealed where your business is concerned."

"Well, what about Thamir's servant?"

"A bibulous man named Shaban, sotted with the scotch that had been entrusted to his care. A babbler and a boaster. I thought he was only wagging his tongue—"

"Well, out with it!"

"Don't be angry with me, master," Aziz whined. "I'm only repeating what he said."

"What *did* he say, damn you?"

"He asked me who my employer was, as was natural, and I told him it was the illustrious Abdul ben Arthur Hamid-Jones, the Clonemaster of the Royal Stables, and not omitting your new title, Custodian of the Royal Nucleotides. And he laughed, and made several unkind remarks about your background, which I won't repeat, and said that he had been to the house of the old Clonemaster many times with his master, who was on an equal social footing with the al-Hejjaj family, and a good deal richer to boot. And that since the house now had no protector, there was a plum in it that was ripe for the plucking."

"The rotter!"

"Yes, master. He winked at me and said that in referring to

Miss al-Hejjaj, his master Thamir had made a pun on the word 'sugarplum'—I don't have to tell you what rhymes with *baroo*.''

"The utter swine!" Hamid-Jones raged. "I must go back to Lalla and warn her of his intentions!"

"No, master!" Aziz looked genuinely alarmed. "You'd better forget about the woman. Thamir is a serious man. It doesn't pay to cross him.''

"I don't care how rich he is. The bounder needs to be taught a lesson."

"How do you think his family made all that money? They're not fussy about dealing with people who get in their way." He lowered his voice. "When I said that Thamir is a serious man, I meant that he has connections."

"What are you babbling about?"

"I told you that this Shaban didn't know how to keep his mouth shut. He let slip that the Thamirs, father and son, are tied in with the Assassins. Do you remember that big contract to crash a Saturnian iceberg into Utopia and make a new oasis out of Tithonius Lacus? It went to the Thamir firm. The only serious rival bidder wound up orbiting Phobos without a spacesuit."

"Oh, a lot of nonsense is written about the Assassins. They're just another Ismaili sect with an image problem."

"No, master, the old customs still flourish. Murder is a religious duty for them, and after two thousand years they're very good at it. Their children are raised with a dagger and instructed in the ritual techniques of killing by stealth from an early age. When their imam accepts a contract, the thing is as good as done."

"Balderdash! People have been sued for defamation for saying such things."

"It happens all the time. The Derby Day killing last week had all the earmarks of an Assassin contract hit. The one where the severed head of the owner of the odds-on favorite was found in the horse's stall the morning of the race. It unnerved the horse so that it came in third. The man had been warned to throw the race, but he didn't take it seriously. Nothing annoys an Assassin as much as a lack of respect."

"You can't blame every professional killing on the Assassins."

"When they found the headless body, it had a poem about death in its pocket. And there were crumbs on the bed."

"So?"

"Those are the three warnings: a poem, a flat hot cake—hot to show how recent the Assassin's visit was—and a dagger. In this case, the dagger was found between the ribs."

"How do you know so much about such things?"

Aziz saw Hamid-Jones's involuntary glance at his mismatched right hand and immediately adopted his usual subservient cringe. "Don't be angry, master. I've had a hard life."

"I want you to go shopping tomorrow. I'll need a suitable gift for Lalla. You can try the Pet Boutique on the upper level for a minigiraffe or a pair of bioluminescent lovebirds—no, I can't give her any kind of tailored animal; she'll think I made it myself. You'd better try the jeweler's again—maybe a diadem or something."

"Master, please," Aziz pleaded, close to tears. "You're making a big mistake."

"Do as I tell you. I'm going hunting again on Thursday. I want to see the look on Thamir's face."

"Don't you already have enough trouble in your life—getting yourself caught in the middle between the Vizier and the Chamberlain?"

"What are you talking about?"

Aziz arranged his features in an expression of stiff disapproval. "Rubinstein isn't a vindictive man, but all the same, it would be better if he didn't find out you were spying on him for the eunuch."

Hamid-Jones grabbed Aziz and, forgetting his Terran strength, shook him like a rag doll. "Where did you hear that, you scoundrel?"

"Please, master. Let go." Hamid-Jones released his grip, and Aziz gave him a hurt look. "I happened to be talking to one of the vendors who supplies the Chamberlain's palace, that's all. He says it's common knowledge."

"Well I'm not spying for anyone, damn you. And you can tell that to anyone who asks."

"Yes, master. About the diadem. I'll have to get it on credit. You've been spending money like water."

"That's enough! I don't want any more of your impudence. Money is no object, do you understand?"

"Yes, master," Aziz grumbled. "All the same, I'll do what I can to knock down the price. We'd better save a little something for your winding sheet and coffin."

CHAPTER 9

"**Y**ou need a medal," Aziz fretted, chewing on his lower lip.

"Don't be ridiculous," Hamid-Jones said. "I've never done anything to deserve one."

"That doesn't matter," Aziz said firmly. "If only those who deserved them wore them, the electroplating booths at the *suq* would go out of business. You're representing the cloning department at a state function. You have your position to consider. Everybody else at the reception will be covered with decorations that no one will know the meaning of. You can't go without one."

"Never mind all that," Hamid-Jones said, pushing away the hands that were fussing at his evening clothes. "Did you get the tiara?"

"Yes, master," Aziz said grumpily. "It's fit for a sultana, though I don't see why you want to be so foolish as to spend all that money just to make trouble for yourself. I saw Thamir's servant at the *suq*, and he saw me coming out of the jeweler's. He hung around till I turned the corner, pretending to be interested in a brassware display, but I outfoxed him and ducked back in time to see him go into the jewelry booth to find out what I bought. You can be sure he's already carried the tale back to Thamir."

"Let's see it."

His face set in stiff lines of disapproval, Aziz produced a glittering diadem that dripped with jangling baubles of chased gold tipped with jewels. "She'll love it," he said. "It's just this side of the sumptuary laws."

"You've done well, *ya* Aziz."

"It's my job to serve you, even when you're bent on committing suicide," Aziz said sarcastically.

Hamid-Jones handed the tiara back. "Lock it up in a safe place. I'll have to postpone giving it to her till tomorrow night. I don't see why I'm expected to attend that foolish reception."

"It's your duty to attend. It's the annual reception for the entire diplomatic corps. All the department heads are expected to be there. Since the Emir is still indisposed, and the Vizier is standing in for him, a show of governmental solidarity is essential."

Hamid-Jones glanced sharply at him. The subject of the Emir's health was dangerous ground, and if Aziz were to let anything slip while gossiping with his cronies at the *suq*, suspicion would fall on Hamid-Jones himself for betraying state secrets.

"May the Emir's recovery be swift, *inch'allah*," Aziz said innocently.

"Bless you for your concern." Hamid-Jones frowned and turned to leave.

"Just a moment, master." Aziz rummaged in a small chest and extracted a brassy gewgaw hung from a broad green ribbon.

"What's this?"

"Your medal, master," Aziz said, deftly slipping it around his neck.

"Where did you get this?"

"At the *suq*, master. At a secondhand booth. Doesn't it look impressive?"

"I can't wear this! What the devil is it supposed to be *for*?"

"I don't know, master." Aziz stepped back to admire the effect. "But no one else will know either."

Hamid-Jones stood with his back against the wall, well to one side of the mammoth buffet, where he would be out of the path of the harried waiters, balancing a demitasse in one hand and trying to remain inconspicuous.

It wasn't hard to do. The Foreign Ministry's great ballroom was filled to capacity. He was just one more white robe among thousands. From the honeycomb ceiling a hundred feet overhead, the vast tiled floor must have looked like a milling swirl of fat snowflakes, sprinkled with the more colorful specks of those diplomatic guests who wore exotic costumes.

He sipped his coffee and listened to the wailing orchestra whose music could be heard through the hubbub. The musicians were sitting cross-legged on a raised platform behind the buffet, a live ensemble of oboists, percussionists, bagpipers, and one-string violin players in the plaid tribal robes of the Islamic Kingdom of Scotland and Wales.

But he hadn't removed himself far enough out of the way after all; a waiter jostled his arm, spilling coffee. *"Eh-sif,"* the man apologized automatically, and then there was a sudden embarrassed pause of mutual recognition.

"Kareem!" Hamid-Jones exclaimed involuntarily, and was immediately sorry that he hadn't pretended to look the other way.

His dapper neighbor, the hotel clerk, was in an ill-fitting waiter's uniform, looking not at all like the supercilious fashion plate who condescended to the shabby old fogies in the Street of the Well.

"That's all right, *ya* Abdul, it's honest work, and at good pay, too," Kareem said with a derisive smile that increased Hamid-Jones's discomfiture. The clerk glanced distastefully at his borrowed uniform. "All the major hotels were pressed into service to help cater this shindig—the Palace still doesn't seem to have got its act together. Our assistant manager is in the kitchens, skewering kebabs."

"Everything looks very nice . . . that is . . ."

"We all serve the Emir in our own way, eh? How *is* his Majesty, by the way?"

"He's doing fine . . . er . . . . so I'm told."

"Here, have a canapé," Kareem said, and deftly whisked a deviled egg on toast from his tray into Hamid-Jones's free hand. Hamid-Jones had to grab awkwardly to keep from dropping it on the floor, and then he realized that a small, stiff envelope was folded in the paper napkin.

"What's this?" he said.

"Somebody asked me to give a note to the gentleman wearing the Order of the Green Star," Kareem said. "No, I wouldn't open it now, if I were you. It may be something private."

And then Kareem was gone with his tray of canapés, leaving Hamid-Jones to puzzle over why what was evidently a planned encounter had been made to look like an accidental bumping. Hamid-Jones fingered the envelope, and after a moment put it into his pocket. He promptly forgot all about it when he saw one of Rubinstein's splendidly dressed assistants striding purposefully toward him.

"The Vizier's been watching you," the functionary said. "He

says you're not doing your part. You've been standing like a stick. He told me to tell you to mingle.''

Hamid-Jones looked over to where Rubinstein was holding court in the middle of a dazzling, ribbon-bedecked company, all of whom were competing for his attention. The Vizier smiled at him and flapped both hands at him in an encouraging gesture.

With a sigh, Hamid-Jones deposited his cup and the uneaten canapé on a passing tray and looked around for someone to talk to. He spotted an unhappy little man in blue sunglasses and a feathered shawl standing by himself and staring wistfully at the glittering group surrounding Rubinstein.

He walked over and introduced himself. "How do you do? I'm Abdul Hamid-Jones, the director of cloning for the Royal Stables. How are you enjoying yourself?"

"*Tashar rufnah*, I'm glad to meet you," the little man said gratefully. "I've just arrived here from Gamma Virginis B. Everything's still a little strange to me."

He had a peculiar accent, with a slurring of consonants and a lot of elided vowels that made it sound like some of the backward dialects to be heard in the asteroids.

Hamid-Jones was impressed. Gamma Virginis, more than thirty-six light years away, was about as far as starfarers had ventured—even farther than the thriving civilization that had taken root on Delta Pavonis. Starships probing much beyond that radius invariably disappeared, never to be heard from again. The fundamentalists liked to say it was because man was not meant to push beyond his allotted sphere—that there were djinn waiting in the void to swallow up overreaching spacecraft—to which the moderates replied that it was blasphemous to suggest that Allah's fiat was limited.

"I don't wonder," Hamid-Jones said sympathetically. "You're a long way from home."

The little man became weepy. "Forty years out, forty years back—or close to it, counting the boost—plus a ten year tour of duty. The better part of a century will have gone by when I return. No one will remember me. My dear wife will be long dead, and even my youngest baby, if he's still alive, will be a doddering old man with one foot in the grave—and me still in the vigor of my years!"

Hamid-Jones was a bit taken aback despite himself. Gamma Virginis must have developed into a queer society indeed, for its inhabitants to show so little compunction about discussing their wives and their family business with casual strangers.

But it wasn't up to him to find fault with a visitor's ways. "Uh, you didn't bring your, er, spouse with you then?" he said in a carefully neutral tone.

"Certainly not," the Gamma Virginian replied. "I had to leave her behind to raise the children. I took a couple of concubines along with me for solace." He drew himself up virtuously. "I believe in family life."

"Well . . . uh . . . it's a great honor to be chosen to represent your planet. I'm sure that's some consolation, at least. I imagine you'll be finding yourself quite a celebrity here in the Solar system. The news from your part of the sky is so scanty, and so outdated by the time it gets here, that I'm sure that most people couldn't even name your ruler."

"Even there I get the short end. The celebrity is the ambassador from Gamma Virginis *A*." Bitterly, the little man drew Hamid-Jones's attention to a large, florid personage with the group around Rubinstein. "They got the best real estate just because their colony ships arrived a few years ahead of us. Two yellow suns only a little hotter than Sol, and *they're* the ones blessed with a terrestrial world far enough out to stay cool at closest approach. Their star scorches us every time it comes round every hundred and eighty years. The climate's terrible. All our resources go into underground shelters and orbiting sunscreens. We never had a chance to develop the way they did."

"I'm sure you'll catch up. Who knows what's happened in the last forty years? You may have passed them already."

"That's hardly likely. When I left, less than two subjective years ago, their population was ten times ours, and growing faster. They treat us like a satrapy." A tear trickled from beneath the blue sunglasses. "In fact, our ambassador to Gamma Virginis A has a higher diplomatic rank than *I* do as ambassador to Mars. No offense, but they're much more important to us than all you nations of Sol put together, being next door to us as they are."

"They're quite a power, then?"

"More than you Solarians realize, here at the center of Allah's sphere. You'll be hearing a lot more about them one of these days. They're an overweening people. You can be thankful that they're far away."

He broke off to stare glumly at his rival, who sported a chestful of medals that blinked in different colors, and who was holding forth self-importantly to a captive audience of Rubinstein and some of the bigger diplomatic guns, comporting himself as if he were the equal or superior of the ambassadors from the older civilizations of Alpha Centauri and Tau Ceti.

"They've already taken over all the best worlds of both stars in our double system," the little man went on, "including the moons of *our* gas giant that we hadn't gotten around to yet, and they've sent an expedition to Mizar—two double stars in close orbit around each other, plus the Alcor binary only a quarter light year away. Six stars in one convenient cluster—now *there's* fertile ground for expansionist ambitions!"

"Mizar? But that's . . ."

"More than twenty light years beyond us."

"But Earth sent an expedition to Mizar almost two hundred years ago, during the last great wave of exploration. It disappeared—like all the other ships that went too far."

"*Theirs* didn't."

Hamid-Jones was amazed. "I'd always been taught that there was supposed to be some natural law that limited relativistic space travel to about the radius of Arcturus and Capella—and of course Gamma Virginis—though there are slower automated probes that are still broadcasting from as far away as Aldebaran. That it probably has something to do with the relativistic reference frame and the curvature of our local space, but that until some Einstein or Harun al-Mudarris comes along to explain it, man's access to the rest of the universe is limited." He turned his head to stare at the medal-bedecked ambassador from Gamma Virginis A. "Have your neighbors found some way of cracking the barrier?"

"How would I know? The news reached Gamma Virginis just before I left. I brought it with me to Mars. Your foreign office people turned me over to a scientific committee for debriefing—they pumped me dry, then dropped me. Now I'm a nobody again." His chin trembled with self-pity.

"Hmm . . . you know, once upon a time sailors used to think that if they sailed too far, they'd drop off the edge of the world. We got in the habit of thinking that way about space when the disappearances started, centuries ago. I know that some religious people say that Allah did not intend for man to travel beyond the possibility of pilgrimage to Mecca. But what if there's no *absolute* prohibition on the distance relativistic ships can travel from Earth? What if you only have to start out afresh from a second locus, provided you travel no further than the old disappearance radius? It would open the possibility of doubling the size of Allah's sphere."

Hamid-Jones had only a layman's knowledge of astrophysics, but as he mulled over the implications of what he had just said, he turned back to the ambassador with a growing sense of excitement.

"Tell me, has Gamma Virginis A sent any expeditions *farther* than Mizar? If so, and they stopped transmitting at the critical distance of thirty-five or forty light years . . ."

"That's the same question your debriefers kept asking," the emissary said peevishly. "Maybe they have by now. I'm sure I wouldn't know. No one would. It's been sixty years since Gamma Virginis A reached Mizar, and you're just finding out about *that*. God alone knows what's been going on *there* all this time. The Sultanissimo sent his most contentious son there to get rid of him. Blood's supposed to be thicker than water, but you can't keep a pasha under control when it takes forty years to check up on him, and anyway he must long since have been succeeded by a son or even a grandson."

The thought reminded him anew of his long exile, and he suppressed a sob.

Embarrassed, Hamid-Jones tried to console him. "Now, now, you'll still be a young man when you return to your home world, and you'll be full of honors for your sacrifice. The trip will take only two years of subjective time, counting boosting and deboosting. You can start over again—have a new life, a new family. And your own grandchildren and great-grandchildren will be there to help you."

The Gamma Virginian produced a large handkerchief and honked loudly into it. "You're very kind . . . *salaam ideek* . . . blessed be your hands . . ." He wandered off into the crowd, still blowing his nose.

In the next hour or so, Hamid-Jones tried dutifully to circulate as much as possible. He had a long conversation about atmospheric mining with a commercial attaché from the Venusian Habitat, discussed horse breeding with a minor consular official from the Texan Dependency, was gracious to the chargé d'affaires for the Titanian government-in-exile, and chatted about nothing in particular with an English-speaking sheik from the little desert kingdom of Iowa, whose ancestors had been wheat farmers before the greenhouse effect had shifted the American breadbasket northeast to the Islamic Commonwealth of Quebec.

Most of his conversational partners seemed pleased by the attention, except for the squat, high-G deputy ambassador from Sirius, who began by complaining that everyone confused his mission with the Syrian delegation from Earth, and who became obviously miffed when he realized that a medium level civil servant like Hamid-Jones had been delegated to entertain him. But just when the Sirian was being his rudest, Rubinstein caught Hamid-Jones's eye and winked as a sign that he was pleased to have his difficult guest taken off his hands.

When the Sirian finally stalked off, jangling the platinum chains and weights that held him down in Martian gravity, Hamid-Jones looked around for some other minor official to pay attention to. He saw the Centauran ambassador working his way in his general direction but thought nothing of it until the ambassador stopped in front of him with a smile and said, "Quite an affair, isn't it? I haven't seen so much pomp and glitter since the al-Saud XLII inauguration."

Hamid-Jones glanced around to confirm that the ambassador was indeed talking to him and not to someone else, then summoned the presence of mind to reply: "Uh, yes, I guess they've gone all out."

The Centauran looked him over benignly. He was an imposing man with the chest of a bull and a squared-off beard of beribboned curls. He was quietly but richly dressed in the Centauran manner, with a togalike cloak pinned with a brooch at one shoulder, a braided tarboosh in place of a headcloth, and red slippers with turned-up toes.

"They certainly have," he agreed. "It's much grander than last year's diplomatic bash—I suppose to compensate for the Emir's absence. Give a sense of continuity of government."

Hamid-Jones realized belatedly that the ambassador was talking to him in English, not Arabic. Very good English, at that.

"Uh, his Majesty's still indisposed," he said carefully. "I'm sure he'd be here if he could." Then, more briskly: "Allow me to introduce myself, your Excellency. I'm Abdul Hamid-Jones, acting Clonemaster for the Royal Stables."

"Yes, I know." The Centauran waved a careless hand.

"You know? But how . . . that is, I'm flattered that you recognized me."

"I had you pointed out to me. You're being far too modest, ya Abdul. It's come to my attention that you've been given additional responsibilities with the Palace cloning program."

The turn of the conversation made Hamid-Jones nervous. He glanced involuntarily over his shoulder, to the Centauran's politely concealed amusement.

"Uh, very minor responsibilities, your Excellency. My job's still mostly veterinary cloning."

The ambassador laid a hand on his arm and began unobtrusively to steer him to one side. "It's reassuring to know that the Emir's health is in capable hands such as yours. One hears such disquieting rumors." He coughed delicately. "Such as that the Emir—may Allah always smile on him—didn't survive the recent attempt on his life."

Somehow the ambassador had maneuvered them both next to the musicians' stand. Hamid-Jones had to raise his voice to make himself heard over the squealing of the bagpipes.

"I don't know where you could have heard anything like that."

"Such rumors, of course, will be scotched as soon as the Emir shows himself in public," the ambassador said, watching Hamid-Jones's face.

"That might be some time," Hamid-Jones said quickly. "If you saw the assassination attempt on the holovid, you can appreciate that his Majesty might need some additional recovery time."

"Such as a remedial body transplant?"

A chill went down Hamid-Jones's spine. How much had the Alpha Centaurans guessed? And how much did they actually know? "I don't have any inside knowledge," he said stiffly, "but I'm sure his Majesty is recovering nicely with normal medical attention."

The ambassador went on imperturbably. "If there *were* to be a remedial body transplant, the Emir would have to appear in public as soon as possible, to put to rest any loose talk of a substitution."

"I don't know what you're talking about," Hamid-Jones said, reddening.

The ambassador's eyes were glued to his face. "Of course not," he beamed. "You have no inside knowledge, as you just said. We are just supposing."

Hamid-Jones cursed himself for his lack of a poker face. The Centauran was pumping him—that was the reason for his flattering attention to someone several rungs down the ladder of protocol—and he was very good at extracting information from the unwary. An amateur was no match for him.

"Don't be angry, *ya* Abdul," the ambassador said, putting a restraining hand on his arm to prevent him from walking away. "Your devotion to the Emir is admirable. I wouldn't have it any other way. I can see why the Vizier thinks so highly of you."

"Your Excellency gives me too much credit," Hamid-Jones growled.

The ambassador pulled him a little closer to the bandstand. The pipes and drums were deafening. He leaned toward Hamid-Jones's ear. "You mustn't take my curiosity amiss, *ya* Abdul. The Emir's welfare is very important to us on Alpha Centauri. Sol is our nearest stellar neighbor, and Mars is the jewel of the Solar system, more important than any single nation on Earth. The Sultan has the highest regard for the Emir—they are brothers in Islam, equals in power and circumstance. Certainly they are the two most plausible contenders for the Caliphate. Wicked people have tried to stir up dissension between them, it is true. But the Sultan's affection for his fellow monarch is boundless. It would set his mind at ease to know that his brother, his eye, is well. And who can tell us better than someone involved with the Palace cloning program?"

"You're an officially accredited ambassador," Hamid-Jones said rudely. "You can make your inquiries through the Foreign Ministry."

"Ah, yes, the authorized version," the Centauran said. "The considered statements of public information officers. I had in mind a more intimate evaluation of the Emir's condition, from someone with scientific judgment. And most particularly information about those factors which might have a bearing on the Emir's future behavior, such as the dispositions of some of the older clones . . ."

He knows about Number Forty, curse the man for a devil! was the first thought that flashed through Hamid-Jones's mind. Then, getting a grip on himself, he thought, No, he's only fishing. He turned away so that his face wouldn't betray him.

"You'd find us most grateful," the Centauran said softly—so softly that his words almost could not be heard against the blare of the orchestra. His eyes swept the room, as though he were looking for a friend.

"I've got to go," Hamid-Jones choked. The bribery attempt had been too blatant. He did not have the same faith as the ambassador in the efficacy of loud music against listening devices. If any guests at the reception were monitored, it would be the Centaurans.

"By all means," the ambassador said. "I've enjoyed our little chat. 'Profit from your encounters,' the *Hadith* says. I hope I've given you food for thought. Perhaps we'll have the opportunity to talk again, eh?"

"Ma-a issalaama," Hamid-Jones mumbled, and beat a hasty retreat.

He served out the rest of his time at the reception by diligently keeping several minor embassy staff people socially occupied—attachés, cipher clerks, translators. He expected someone from the Vizier's staff to come over and question him about his conversation with the Alpha Centauran ambassador, but no one did. Nor was he aware of any special scrutiny from the security people, though he knew they must have taken an interest in the encounter.

When next he caught sight of the Centauran's red tarboosh and beribboned beard, the big man was accepting a drink from Kareem's tray, bending his head graciously to exchange a few affable words as guest to waiter. The Centauran had returned to the vicinity of the bandstand by then, and it couldn't have been easy to make himself heard over the din of the instruments. The ambassador's good breeding was evident—the Sultan must have sent only the cream of his aristocracy to represent him—in the fact that, though he didn't have to, he left a tip on Kareem's tray. Hamid-Jones could see the folded banknote, quickly pocketed.

He decided he couldn't fault the Centauran for trying to bribe him. The man was only doing his best to serve his Sultan loyally. The ambassador was right about one thing. With its early start at colonization and the two stars of its system close enough to be under the thumb of their powerful ruler—three stars, if you counted dim Proxima and its marginal world only a sixth of a light year from the main pair—Alpha Centauri was Mars's only serious rival for the prestige of the Caliphate. One had to expect a certain amount of upper level skulduggery.

Hamid-Jones was glad not to be involved. He congratulated himself on the way he had handled it—just walking away without answering. No one could make anything of that. Still, he was relieved when the end of the evening came and no one from security had invited him into a little anteroom for a talk.

He stifled a yawn as he filed out of the ballroom past the phalanx of undersecretaries and foreign service officers who were lined up to accept farewells. The upper-level guests got a hug and a peck from the Vizier or one of his deputies; Hamid-Jones got a fixed smile and a wiggle of white-gloved fingers from a department junior.

His rooms were dark when he got home. Aziz had not waited up for him. He was glad of that. He was too tired to have borne a servant's chatter when all he wanted to do was sleep. He flung his clothes at a chair and crawled gratefully into bed.

Something woke him in the middle of the night: a whisper of sound that might have been part of a dream, or a feathery touch at his throat that might have been the fringe of the blanket moving across his skin as he twisted in his sleep. He had been dreaming of tiny two-headed butterflies—a rush order for the Vizier—only they had all turned out with miniature raisin-size faces like the Chief Eunuch's and little sharp teeth like the points of sewing needles, and one of them had fluttered to a landing on his throat.

He lay motionless in the darkness. An almost imperceptible square of ghostly light where the window ought to be told him that it was within an hour of dawn. The light was still too dim for him to see more than the humped silvery outlines of furniture. He listened and decided he had been mistaken about the sound. Sleep dragged at him once more, and he knew nothing until the salmon light of a Martian sunrise poured in from the outside mirrors.

Aziz was standing at the foot of the bed, making a queer choking sound. His eyes were fixed in horror on Hamid-Jones's torso.

"What's wrong?" Hamid-Jones said, and sat up. A piece of paper that had been lying on his chest fluttered to the floor. He twisted his head and saw a knife resting next to his pillow.

"Now you've done it!" Aziz wailed.

"Done what?" he said irritably. He sat up and put his hand down on something warm. He snatched his hand away, then saw that the thing was only a small, flat cake.

"The knife, the poem, the cake—it's your death warrant, just as I tried to warn you." Aziz wrung his hands.

"What are you talking about?" But he was afraid he already knew.

"The Assassins! This is their notification that a contract has been taken out on you."

Hamid-Jones retrieved the piece of paper from the floor. It was a poem, written in an old-fashioned gliding Kufic script.

> Death is the posy, waiting to be plucked,
> Death is the fruit, waiting to be tasted,
> Death is the jewel, waiting to be pawned,
> Death is the maiden, waiting for consummation,
> Life is old, but death is new,
> Death is life's last deed.

There were more verses in the same vein. The author would never win a prize for elegance of style, but the Arabic rhymes were good enough to get by, and the meaning was plain enough. He crumpled it up and tossed it aside.

"I told you to stop seeing that two-faced bint, but no, you wouldn't listen," Aziz nagged at him. "You had to go on buying her expensive presents to boot. You might have given some thought to me. What am I going to do for employment when they come and cut your throat?"

He stopped his scolding long enough to break off a corner of the cake and taste it.

"What are you doing?" Hamid-Jones cried. "What if it's poisoned?"

"No, no, that's not their way," Aziz said. "Poison is against their religion." He rolled the crumbs around in his mouth. "Hmm, still warm. It must have been left here less than an hour ago. But there are no nuts, thank God! Just a touch of cardamom for flavor."

"What are you babbling about?"

"It's only your first notice, master. The second notice has nuts and anise. Don't worry, there's still time to call the whole thing off. But we mustn't waste any time. I'll get word to the imam of the local Assassin's chapter through a fellow I know first thing this morning. We'll assure them that you won't see the Lalla bint anymore, and they'll notify Thamir that the contract's off. We'll have to pay compensation, of course, but don't worry—it's on a fixed scale."

Hamid-Jones was not yet totally awake, and it took a moment for Aziz's meaning to penetrate. When it did, he roared, "You'll do no such thing, you scoundrel! Do you think this idiotic flummery with cakes and bad poetry would make me renounce my love? And I've warned you to be more respectful when you speak of Miss Hassan al-Hejjaj!"

"Be reasonable, master. The Assassins are being more than fair with you. It's custom for them to issue a warning, but it's not binding on them." He pointed a quivering finger at the knife beside the pillow. "They've demonstrated that they can get to you anytime and anyplace they choose. This was just a practice run. They usually send a novice the first time. He's supposed to draw a feather across your throat and leave before you wake up."

Hamid-Jones remembered the tickling sensation that had been a part of his dream and felt a finger of ice run down his spine. Then he became stubborn and said, bristling, "They're not supernatural beings! A door must have been left unlocked, or they forced a window. We'll just be careful—take precautions—till this blows over."

"It won't blow over," Aziz said, just as stubbornly.

At Hamid-Jones's insistence, they inspected every window, every door—even the utility company's air ducts, though these would scarcely have accommodated an anaconda—for signs of forced entry. But all locks were secure, and there was not so much as a scratch or a displaced mote of dust.

"You see?" Aziz said triumphantly.

"I see that no one could have gotten inside during the night. How do I know that you didn't plant all this mumbo jumbo here yourself? You've been trying hard enough to make me give up Lalla! Telling me she'll hurt my career! Filling me with childish stories about the Assassins! You've got yourself a soft job here, and you're afraid a wife will spoil it for you. You probably bought that cake at the *suq*."

"How can you say such a thing, master?" Aziz said in an injured tone. "You don't even believe it yourself."

Hamid-Jones felt ashamed of his outburst. He disguised it with brusqueness. "Never mind," he said. "You said yourself that there's usually a second warning. We'll let things ride for a while, and worry about it when the time comes."

"Does that mean you'll hold off on seeing the woman?" Aziz asked hopefully.

"I didn't say that, you rogue!" Hamid-Jones snapped.

Aziz wrung his hands. "You can't count on a second notice, master," he whined. "They might skip it if they see you're being intransigent."

"Enough!" Hamid-Jones bellowed. "Get me some breakfast. I've got to get ready to go to work. I'll give Lalla the tiara tonight. See that you have it gift wrapped by the time I get home."

"Oh, master," Aziz said mournfully.

His ablutions and prayers done, Hamid-Jones dressed quickly and sat down to a breakfast of yogurt, toast, and jam on a tray brought to him by Aziz. While he ate, Aziz straightened out the room, clucking like a mother hen as he picked up the clothes that Hamid-Jones had carelessly tossed over a chair the night before.

"What's this?" Aziz said as a slim envelope fell out of one of the pockets. He bent to retrieve it from the floor.

"Let me see. Oh—someone gave it to me at the reception last night. I forgot all about it."

He took the envelope from Aziz and opened it. Inside was a sheet of stiff, cream-colored notepaper folded in half over a small square of flimsy semitranslucent tissue with a hyphenated number imprinted on it.

The notepaper contained only a line from the *Hadith*, written in a flowery hand. It was the same verse that had been quoted to him the previous evening by the Alpha Centauran ambassador. There was no signature.

"Where did you get this?" Aziz said with uncharacteristic sharpness.

"I told you. Someone left it for me with a waiter at the ball last night."

"How long have you been carrying it around?"

"Well . . . all night. What does it matter?"

Aziz snatched the sheet of notepaper from his hand and tore it in half. He held the torn edges up to one eye and squinted at them.

"What are you doing?" Hamid-Jones cried.

Aziz put a finger to his lips for silence and tore the paper across several times more until it was reduced to a handful of confetti.

"What did you do that for?" Hamid-Jones demanded. "I wanted to have a closer look at it."

"Have a closer look, then," Aziz said, thrusting the scraps at him.

Puzzled and a little annoyed, Hamid-Jones took a couple of the scraps and peered at them edgewise as Aziz had done. He saw thin gold wires, fragile as a spider's web, sandwiched within the paper, and little dark flecks, insubstantial as soot. Tiny specks like grains of pepper spilled out.

"It was a listening device," Aziz said. "Battery patches, ion-implanted field effect devices, thin-film mike, FM transmitter. No telling what the range is. The pickup could be anywhere in the street, in a crack in the rock—anything."

"B-but why?"

Aziz sighed. "Exactly who did you talk to last night? Tell me everything you said."

Hamid-Jones wrinkled his brow, trying to remember. He began with the little emissary from Gamma Virginis B, summarized his encounters down through the ill-tempered Sirian. Aziz cut him short impatiently till he got to the Alpha Centauran.

"That's it," he said. "They want to pick up anything you might drop about the Emir and his clones, and in case they don't get anything, they've also recorded you so they can blackmail you later if necessary."

Hamid-Jones was getting miffed at Aziz's know-it-all tone. "I'm not stupid," he said testily. "I didn't say anything they could blackmail me with."

Aziz spoke to him as if to a child. "Try to remember your exact words."

Hamid-Jones repeated the conversation as best as he was able. "So you see," he finished, "I didn't volunteer any state information. And when he started to make those hints, I just said good-bye."

"Pardon me, master, but you're too honest a man to understand the villainy of the world. Your words can be edited to make you say anything they want. It can be done phoneme by phoneme. If all else fails, they can dub in your yesses and noes to new leading questions. And if that isn't enough, there's the bribe evidence."

"What bribe evidence? I told you I didn't accept a bribe."

Aziz picked up the little square of tissue that had been enclosed with the note. "See this? It's a secret numbered account on the Bank of Ceres. It's on rice paper. They provide these edible slips as a service to their foreign clients. You memorize the number, then eat the slip. The deposit was probably made sometime yesterday."

"But I didn't ask for it!" Hamid-Jones said in horror.

"It doesn't matter. The deposit's in your name. But the Centaurans know the number. If you get difficult, they can produce the records."

Hamid-Jones started to protest, then realized that Aziz was right. It would look bad no matter what. His face turning purple with fury, he reached for the slip. "Edible, you said? Well, we'll soon find out."

Aziz grabbed his wrist and held the slip away from him. His grip was surprisingly strong, despite his scrawny build.

"The harm's already done," Aziz said. "You might as well keep it."

"But I don't want it."

Aziz placated him with a weasel's grin. "You're in a pickle, master, and so am I. They don't listen to excuses from my sort. If we have to leave Mars in a hurry, you may be glad to have an off-planet bank account."

The slip of paper disappeared into a fold in Aziz's greasy djellaba.

"Leave Mars? Why would I want to leave Mars?"

"Face it, master. The fat's in the fire, one way or the other. It's all bound to come tumbling down on your head—and soon! The Assassins have your life dangling by a thread. You're a pawn in the struggle between the Vizier and that fat eunuch—bound to be sacrificed eventually. And now the Centaurans have you in their pocket. What more could happen to you?"

Hamid-Jones took his cloak off the peg and headed for the door. "Don't forget to wrap the tiara for tonight."

Aziz made a grimace of despair. "After all I've said, you're still bent on self-destruction?"

"You said it yourself. What more could possibly happen to me?"

CHAPTER 10

Lalla was in a coquettish mood. "You're a naughty man to lead a poor helpless woman on so, *ya* Abdul," she said in mock reproof. "My poor head is spinning."

"I meant every word, Little Candy," he said fatuously. "I have only the deepest respect for you. Admit me to your heart and I will die with joy."

"*Oo, la,* I don't want you to die. Compose yourself."

He settled back on the cushions facing her across the symbolic screen of dangling cords. Her dress this evening was more revealing, gathered at the bodice to suggest the outlines of an opulent bosom, and the designer veil had dropped an inch and a half. She had allowed him to take her hand, and he had crushed it to his face and smothered it with kisses. She had sat passively, not snatching it away. The young eunuch at the opposite end of the room had carefully looked in the other direction, though Hamid-Jones had not bribed him. So it must have been Lalla herself who had bribed or cajoled him into leniency before Hamid-Jones had been ushered up the broad stairs. The thought made Hamid-Jones's heart beat faster.

"I can't live without you," he said recklessly. "My intentions are honorable—not like some others I could mention. Little Sugarplum, make me happy and say you won't see anyone else!"

Her brow above the designer veil's monogrammed headband clouded with momentary annoyance. Recovering, she fluttered her lashes and said coyly, "What's that I see in your lap, *ya* Abdul? Have you brought me something?"

"Oh." He fumbled with the package. Aziz, despite his unwillingness, had outdone himself in the gift wrappings. The

152

wrapping paper was a thin film of trapped holo scenes from the *Arabian Nights*, shifting and changing with the angle of vision. Lalla giggled as one of the more indecent scenes flashed into view—a tableau from *The Five Ladies of Baghdad*—then lowered her eyes demurely.

He tried to pass the package through the dividing line of cords, but an ill-tempered snarl in the piccolo range came from the mini-Cerberus nestled in her lap. The two tiny heads lifted one at a time to bare their teeth, then burrowed again into the folds of Lalla's skirts.

"Haven't you gotten rid of that thing yet?" Hamid-Jones bristled.

"What, give up my little Bijou? How could you make such a cruel suggestion, *ya* Abdul?"

"I only mean . . . couldn't you leave him in your quarters or something?"

"Poor little boojums," she cooed at the squirming little beast, hugging it protectively. "The bad man doesn't like you."

Miserably, Hamid-Jones apologized. She relented and reached through the hanging cords to take the package from him. She ripped off the holopaper and a scene from *Sindbad* expired, blinking.

She inspected the tiara in an offhand manner. "Very nice," she said. She called over the eunuch, who took it from her. "Take it away," she told him. "I'll wear it Thursday for my outing. It will go with my new bracelets."

"What outing?" he said. "What bracelets?"

"*Eh, fi!* Don't look so fierce! A very dear friend has invited me for a weekend in Memnonia."

"Thamir!" He spat the name.

"*Ya* Abdul, I won't tolerate such a tone. You're acting as if you own me." She softened. "Anyway, it's all perfectly proper. I'll stay in the women's quarters. I'll have his sisters as chaperons."

"And the bracelets?" he said bitterly. "I suppose they cost a fortune."

"Don't worry, *ya* Abdul," she humored him. "They can't compare with your tiara. Won't his sisters' eyes pop out when they see it!"

Hamid-Jones was in despair. It was all perfectly clear. Lalla had progressed from using Thamir to make him jealous to using him to make Thamir jealous.

"Thamir's intentions are not honorable," he said desperately. "He's the sort of man who boasts of his conquests."

"I won't hear such talk, *ya* Abdul! It's insulting to *me*! My reputation is beyond question!"

She tried out a sob. It seemed to go well, so she extended it into a small but fetching fit of weeping.

Some devil made Hamid-Jones persist. "All the same, you'd better take a couple of your own eunuchs with you."

He immediately made an abject apology, and after keeping him dangling for a suitable interval, she forgave him.

"May I see you again?" he said as he rose.

"All right," she said. "If you're very nice."

As he went down the stairs with his eunuch escort, he tried to think of what to give her for the next gift. Thamir would be sure to top the tiara. If Aziz had been telling the truth about seeing Thamir's servant at the jeweler's, Thamir already knew about the tiara—in fact, had a full description, including cost.

He stomped past the porter in a foul mood. There was no way he could compete with country weekends in Memnonia. Thamir must think him no more than an irritating flea. He tried not to imagine the lavish reception that would await Lalla—the servants, the feasts, the private hunting parties at which women could observe male prowess from screened palanquins.

He was fuming too much to notice the man in cheap robes loitering across the street, who spoke into a thumbphone as he came out the door.

He got as far as the corner. There were not many people about at this hour, and the few Hamid-Jones passed in the street were, like himself, walking swiftly, hurrying to get home. He was too preoccupied to notice at first that the intersection was darker than usual; then he looked up and saw that somebody had smashed the streetlight. Shards of glass lay at the base of the pole, and he wondered briefly why anyone would have thought this act of vandalism was worth the risk of punishment.

Then some whisper of sound made him turn his head and look behind him. He had just time enough to register the long black car that had been shadowing him at a walking pace and that now picked up speed. A rear door opened outward, and his disbelieving eyes saw a net stretched along its frame to make a sort of scoop.

He tried to get out of the way, but the car was already crowding him against the curb. The net scooped him up, the door swung shut, and he found himself deposited on the car's floor, amidst several pairs of knees.

The timing had been very professional. It had happened so

quickly and quietly that no one in the darkened street could have had time to think that anything unusual was happening. The car screened him from the opposite side, and anyone walking behind would have seen only a car door opening and closing; if they noticed the absence of the pedestrian who had been ahead of them, they could only have assumed that he had turned the corner.

Hamid-Jones tried to lift his head, but rough hands shoved him down to the floor. "Get out of here, Hafez," a tense voice said, and the car leapt ahead.

A knee in the small of the back and a hand on the top of his head forced him to remain kneeling, facedown, out of sight. He could see only three sets of cracked shoes, the hems of dark robes, the blackened barrels of guns held below seat level.

"Who . . ." Hamid-Jones began, then kept his mouth shut. He could think of only one answer to his question.

"It's not good to talk right now," the man holding him said, giving his neck a little push for emphasis. He'd been eating onions; that was all Hamid-Jones could tell about him.

"Take the next left, Hafez," another one said. "We're liable to meet a police patrol if we keep going this way."

One of the gunmen didn't believe in bathing; he had a rank, goatish body odor and greasy robes that smelled of natural fiber—probably camel wool. He had to be some kind of tribesman, only recently arrived from the desert. The others might have been city men. Hamid-Jones wondered why Assassins would recruit a Bedouin. They had no need to hire strong-arm men. Then it came to him that their organization, in order to function, would have to have all kinds of contacts. Maybe the Bedouin was there to take his body out into the desert and dispose of it.

"How did you know where to find me?" he said.

He got another shove for his trouble, but his captor answered him. "We've kept you under observation. We don't like to attract attention."

Hamid-Jones could appreciate that. He kept his silence while the car zigged and zagged through side tunnels. Even if he had been able to see out the windows, he would have lost all sense of direction. When the pressure on the back of his neck finally eased up a bit, he was able to see that the car was bumping through sparsely settled slum areas, where only a few rock rats eked out a living in stale air, without piped water or electricity. Even the scattered cave mouths petered out after a while, and the car's headlamps bored through gloom to the old, abandoned excavations beyond.

He was just about to complain that he had not received his second warning when the car bounced to a halt behind a pile of rubble from an old fallen ceiling.

"Get out," the gunman said.

"Can't we talk this over?" Hamid-Jones said.

"But of course, *ya* Abdul," was the reply. "That's exactly what we're going to do."

The hands shifted their grip, and two of his kidnappers helped Hamid-Jones out of the car. Holding him by the arms, they led him farther into the rubble, while the Bedouin followed behind, cradling the antique submachine gun that he had probably been born with and that never in this life would he relinquish. The driver stayed with the car.

They stopped at a scarred face of rock and released his arms. They backed off a pace or two, and Hamid-Jones was able to see them more clearly in the light of the headlamps. They were stocky men in cheap black robes shiny with wear and dark headcloths wrapped to conceal their faces. The Bedouin was taller and more wiry. His face was hidden, too, but Hamid-Jones could see that his eyebrows were set in a scowl.

"All right," he said bravely, "let's get this over with."

He got a nod in return, and the two city men tucked their guns away somewhere inside their robes. One of them loosened his keffia enough to reveal a coarse, rather shopworn face with predatory eyes.

"Aren't you going to shoot me?" Hamid-Jones said in surprise.

"Shoot you? Why would we do that?"

"Well, for—" He stopped. It wasn't up to him to supply reasons.

"The Clonemaster trusted you," the other man said. "He loved you like a son. He said that you were politically innocent, but that you had a good heart, and that when he had time to develop you, you would come around to the right way of thinking."

"That's why he was building you up, getting you noticed by the Palace," the first man chimed in.

They both looked at him expectantly.

Hamid-Jones's mind raced furiously. They weren't Assassins after all. They were members of the underground, and the suspicions of the authorities had been correct—the Clonemaster had been guilty as sin.

But it was a shock to discover that the Clonemaster had considered him to be a likely recruit as a terrorist fellow-traveler.

Had been sure of him, in fact. Probably because of his *mawali* birth. It went to confirm that the Clonemaster, for all his aristocratic background, had been an idealistic dreamer, naive about human nature. No wonder these men had used him.

"Uh . . . what do you want with me?" he temporized.

"Information," the unmasked man said promptly. "The Clonemaster was going to report to us on the outcome of our Decapitation Day strike. But the Rectitude pigs arrested him before he could contact us."

"We can't get any definitive information out of our sources at the Palace," the muffled one elaborated. "They can't get into the clone garden. We know they have enough spare parts to assemble fifty Emirs, but the head's the thing. So . . . did our martyred comrades succeed in doing away with the tyrant?"

Remembering the cabbagelike thing in the Chief Eunuch's bedroom, Hamid-Jones was able to tell them truthfully that the Emir was not entirely dead.

The terrorist sighed. "We were afraid of that. Some dog of a spectator tackled our lead sharpshooter before he could make sure of the job. If we could get our hands on the fool, we'd kill him."

Hamid-Jones gulped. "Bad luck."

"We'll have to try again, that's all. Hold yourself in readiness, brother."

"I'll certainly do that," Hamid-Jones hedged.

"In the meantime, you can assist the brotherhood by recloning severed hands and other body parts. That's our greatest ongoing need."

Hamid-Jones shivered at this reminder of the group's fanaticism. The only question remaining was which group was it? They could be anything from militant Twelvers to Syrtan separatists.

"To the Cause!" the other *mujahid* said in a ringing voice.

"To the Cause!" cried the first man.

"To the Cause!" Hamid-Jones echoed. "Er, I know it's silly, but at first I thought you were Assassins."

They laughed heartily at the idea. "With the Assassins, you don't get a ride in a car. Just a cake, then a knife between the ribs."

"Or a wire around the neck," the other amplified.

"No, no, that's the Syrtis Major chapter," the first one corrected. "With the Tharsis chapter, it's always a knife."

"The Assassins aren't interested in any cause but their own," explained the unmasked one. "The restoration of the Assassin's homeland. It's supposed to be somewhere in Syria. The Earth

Syria, that is, not the one on Mars. They're extremely narrow-minded. They don't think about the good of all, the way we Legitimists do."

Legitimists. It was a clue. Hamid-Jones racked his brains.

"Of course the Assassins cooperate with us, when it's to their advantage, just as we cooperate with them. All *mujahidin* should mutually cooperate, isn't that so? Even the Christian Jihad."

"Even the Christian Jihad," the second terrorist agreed. "But none of them are really interested in the Restoration, except as it suits their own purposes."

That was it. The fedayeen with whom the Clonemaster had been flirting were the Committee of Restoration, the followers of the mysterious al-Sharq, pretender to the throne. Of course it made sense. Al-Sharq, "the Shining," as his followers styled him, claimed to be the legitimate heir of the royal dynasty that had been unseated by the Emir's father a couple of centuries before. The blue blood would have appealed to an old monarchist like the Clonemaster.

"You're with us, of course," the unmasked *mujahid* said, his eyes boring into Hamid-Jones's face.

"Of course," Hamid-Jones replied.

"To the Shining!" the two *mujahidin* declaimed, and waited for his response.

"To the Shining," Hamid-Jones said weakly.

He was in for it now, if he were bugged. Convicted out of his own mouth. He thought of all the ways a listening device could have been slipped into his clothing—as a button, an adhesive patch, a lump in a seam, as the very cloth of the gold-threaded *keffia* that Aziz had bought for him and insisted he wear tonight. And if no one else in the growing number of interested parties was eavesdropping, the terrorists themselves might be recording this for leverage over him.

He visualized the various ingenious methods of public execution reserved for traitors, and his knees went weak.

"We'll take you back now, brother," the first terrorist said, wrapping his face up again in the black scarf. "We'll be in touch with you very soon."

They dumped him a block from his quarters, and he walked the rest of the way. That was all right with Hamid-Jones; if his front door was being watched, he didn't want to be seen getting out of a car that was probably stolen. Ibrahim, the porter, complained bitterly about having to get out of bed to let him in, and he placated the old man with a dinar.

Aziz had been waiting up for him with the lights on. The seedy little man was frantic. "Thank God you're back alive! The Palace has called twice in the last hour. I've been putting them off."

"What did they want?"

"They wouldn't say. Security. You'd better call them back right away."

"All right." Hamid-Jones headed for the phone. On the way, he suddenly stopped. "What do you mean, thank God I'm back alive?" he said suspiciously. "What do you think you know?"

"Nothing," Aziz said hastily. "It's just that the hour is late. You should have been back from your rendezvous with the lady a long time ago. Who knows what misfortunes might befall a person late at night in this wicked city?" He spread his hands. "And after all, you're a marked man."

"You weren't that worried about the Assassins when I left tonight. You pointed out yourself that I haven't received my second notice."

"It isn't the Assassins you're in immediate danger from. They're steady sorts. They've been around a long time. It's the other sort of fedayeen who are unpredictable—" He stopped abruptly.

"Go on, say it," Hamid-Jones snapped. "You had me bugged, didn't you?"

"It was only for your own good, master," Aziz whined. "How am I to serve you faithfully when I don't know what trouble you're getting yourself into? Especially when you have the poor judgment to get yourself mixed up with these fanatics who follow al-Sharq, the Pretender."

"Bad judgment?" Hamid-Jones roared. "If you were listening, you know that I had no choice in the matter!"

"I'm sorry, master," Aziz said with downcast eyes.

Hamid-Jones forced himself to be calmer. "All right, where is it, you scoundrel?" he demanded.

Aziz dropped to his knees and took Hamid-Jones's shoe in his hands. "If you'll just lift your foot . . ." He pried a flattened wad of something unidentifiable from the sole of the shoe. It was about the size of a small copper coin and looked unpleasant—distinctly not the sort of thing a good Moslem would touch with his bare hands.

"That's it?" Hamid-Jones marveled.

"That's it, master."

"But how . . . I mean the range?"

For answer, Aziz pinched the edge of the thing between thumbnail and fingernail and peeled off a layer that resembled a piece of brown leaf. "Each relay transmitter has a range of about a thousand feet. There are fifty layers of them, each no more than a few microns thick. All together, they add up to a thickness of less than a millimeter. Each contains a simple counter on a nanochip, so one layer comes unstuck about every two hundred paces the wearer takes. So all told, that adds up to a ten-mile range. The last one contains the microphone pickup. It stays stuck."

He peeled away something that looked like a small leather patch that matched the sole of Hamid-Jones's shoe.

"It's only a cheap disposable, master," he said anxiously. "The battery would have run down in a couple of days anyway."

"You miscreant! Where did you get such a device?"

"They're easy to buy if you know who to approach in the *suq*," Aziz grinned. "It's an ordinary off-the-shelf item used by businessmen."

"I can imagine what kind of businessmen. Aziz, you're a blackhearted knave."

"Yes, master."

"Did you make a recording?"

"Of course not, master," Aziz said resentfully. "What do you take me for?"

There was no way to check on Aziz's statement, Hamid-Jones realized. His life now hinged on the uncertain discretion of a slippery rascal whose very origins were uncertain; at best, Hamid-Jones could hope that his servant had been foisted on him by the Vizier—whose trust he had audibly betrayed when he pretended to go along with a terrorist faction whose stated goal was to overturn the throne.

He stared sourly at the shabby little man who held his fate in his grimy hands. It rankled that he had overheard his exchange with Lalla.

His distaste must have showed. "It's not me you have to worry about, master," Aziz said in a tone of injured innocence. "It's others. Like that so-called hotel clerk, Kareem, who's probably a police spy, or the porter, Ibrahim, who blabs everything he knows to the four winds."

"I gave Ibrahim a dinar."

"Oh, fine. Now he'll be sure to remember tonight."

"Listen to me, I—"

"Master, you're a babe in the woods," Aziz said, shaking his head. "You're lucky to have me to look after you."

"You knew in advance that the underground was going to contact me tonight, didn't you?"

"It was a fair guess," Aziz protested. "After the Centauran bribe. The Centaurans bankroll the Legitimist faction."

"They bankroll everybody who can make trouble for the Emir."

"Yes, but al-Sharq is a special case. The other fedayeen groups have no program but destruction. Or some crazy cause that nobody could rally behind. Al-Sharq is the only one who could plausibly take over the throne."

"Careful," Hamid-Jones gibed. "Now you're the one who's uttering treason."

Aziz showed yellowed teeth in a ferret's grin. "I was only referring to his royalist claims. All of these fedayeen are a pox on the landscape."

Hamid-Jones was opening his mouth to reply, when the phone beeped.

"That's the Palace, master," Aziz said. "I told you that you should have called them back right away."

Hamid-Jones took the call with his back to Aziz. It was an official from the office of the Vizier. Hamid-Jones answered him in uninformative monosyllables.

"Surgery will be at six o'clock tomorrow evening," the voice at the other end said. "Do you understand?"

"Yes," Hamid-Jones said.

"You're to be there at five to scrub."

"But . . ." Hamid-Jones bit his lip. "All right."

"Needless to say, this is under a triple seal of secrecy. Do I make myself clear?"

"Yes. Er . . ." Hamid-Jones cupped the mouthpiece and lowered his voice. ". . . what exactly is my role in this?"

"Your presence has been required by one whom you know," the voice said sternly.

There was the click of a broken connection. Hamid-Jones hung up and turned to see Aziz busily brushing his cloak and putting it on a hanger. "You can leave that," Hamid-Jones said. "I'm going to go to bed. I've got to get up early."

"Are you going to the palace?" Aziz inquired innocently.

"None of your business!" Hamid-Jones said sharply. "Go to bed. I won't need you in the morning."

Aziz gave him a bland stare. "Pray Allah that all will go well for the Emir," he said.

CHAPTER 11

This time there were no spectators. The operation was scheduled for a small surgical amphitheater in the Palace hospital. For secrecy's sake, the entire floor had been hastily cleared out for the procedure, and Hamid-Jones had been escorted to the scrub room through white corridors that were deserted except for the green-robed guards with riot guns who were stationed every thirty feet.

The only witnesses were Rubinstein and Ismail, and they seemed more interested in keeping an eye on each other than watching the operation. They were safely behind glass—there was no rigamarole of a positive-pressure air curtain this time. Hamid-Jones raised his eyes to sneak a look at the observation gallery where they sat. Rubinstein smiled and gave a little wave with his fingertips. Ismail sat, grim and preoccupied, his usual toothy smile gone. His bloodshot eyes rolled in Hamid-Jones's direction with no sign of recognition.

Hamid-Jones turned his attention to the operating theater. It was the same setup as before in a smaller space—two stainless steel tables side by side, but only one stereotaxic hat. The donor clone's table was equipped only with a laundry hamper for the discarded head. Platoons of medical personnel in bubble helmets fussed with banks of equipment, rehearsing their various subprograms on the tiered screens, while coveralled technicians checked out a small thicket of jointed mechanical arms bearing the computerized microsurgical instruments.

Hamid-Jones himself was at least twenty feet from the action—his own contribution, if there was one, would be decidedly minor. He glanced down at the surgical grays he was

162

wearing and unconsciously flexed his gloved hands in readiness
for anything that might come up.

"You're blocking the centrifuge," the Palace Cloning Director said, breaking into his thoughts.

"I beg your pardon?" Hamid-Jones said.

"You're blocking the centrifuge," the cloning exec repeated
testily. He was a crabbed, fussy man named Rafiq ig-Gabal,
whose hands were knobby with jeweled rings under the transparent gloves. He had made it clear when they had been introduced before scrubbing that he wasn't overly pleased at
Hamid-Jones's presence.

The fact was that the Palace cloning staff were decidedly minor players at this stage. It was the surgeons' show from this
point on. The cloning department had worked overtime growing
new batches of Emir embryos for the fetal neurons and glia they
could supply and prepared appropriate annealing solutions of
disaggregated cells with which the surgeons would bathe the
central nervous system splices. Now they were expected to stay
out of everyone's way.

Ig-Gabal didn't see it that way, however. He was far too puffed
up with his own importance—he had too many assistants dancing attendance on him. Hamid-Jones had done his best to stay
unobtrusive and to avoid stepping on the man's prerogatives.

"Oh, sorry," Hamid-Jones apologized. He moved a couple
of steps to one side of the equipment.

"We might have to get to it in a hurry, you know," the cloning
exec huffed.

One of ig-Gabal's simpering assistants came scurrying over, a
young fashion plate named Mustafa, who had a beautifully
groomed mustache that filled up the lower half of his bubble helmet.

"Here's a fresh preparation of myelinating cells, *effendi*," the
assistant said, with a sidelong glance at Hamid-Jones. "Schwann
cells in the green tray, oligodendrocytes in the red tray. The
Dewar flasks have the laminin and the nerve growth factor, both
labeled. Do you want me to blend it yet?"

"No, it will settle too soon," ig-Gabal said. "I'll do a mix
when the time comes. You can get started on a second batch
now."

Mustafa's dark-lidded eyes flicked insolently over Hamid-
Jones before he returned to his place with the other assistants.
In the scrub room he had amused his coworkers at Hamid-
Jones's expense by running on about fashion and Tharsis City's

lack of it, in a tone that fell just short of an open sneer that one could take offense at. Nevertheless, when the cloning party had filed into the OR, it was Mustafa and his chittering fellows who had been relegated to the sidelines along with the circulating nurses and standby technicians, while Hamid-Jones had been assigned to stand with ig-Gabal in the place of honor at the surgical interface, though there was nothing, really, for him to do. They had been placed like chessmen. It was Rubinstein's way of driving home the point to all those present that Hamid-Jones had received his favor, and that the Royal Stables were to be considered to be on a par with the well-entrenched bureaucrats of the Palace cloning establishment.

"I'll be glad to do the laminin blend for you," Hamid-Jones offered. "You're likely to have your hands full with the peripheral glials when they start the grafting."

"That won't be necessary," ig-Gabal said stiffly. "I'll manage just fine." He added unneccessarily, "This is the Emir's line of cells, you know. It isn't a horse."

Hamid-Jones choked off a reply. He transferred his gaze to the rubber-gasketed doors at the end of the aisle that had been cleared through the jumble of equipment. The first of the clones was being rolled in. The murmur of helmet-muffled talk ceased as the various medical teams turned to look.

It was the donor clone, evidently. He was a well-muscled youth of about twenty—as well-muscled, at least, as the intimidated fitness instructors in the Garden of the Clones had been able to manage with the material at hand. He was strapped down, woozy from the preliminary drugs that had been administered by the anesthesiologists. He was bald, and his face, neck and upper torso to midchest had also been shaved.

It wasn't necessary to bother preserving the facial hair on the body donor.

Hamid-Jones got a close look as the clone was wheeled by and felt an unexpected gush of pity. The callow face, unmarked by experience, was as yet innocent of the cruelty and despotism that lay buried like a seed within the Emir's genetic heritage. This was a blank of nature, as helpless as any puppy or kitten. His greatest sins heretofore would have been nothing worse than pushing aside a junior at feeding time or pinching a houri. It was a strange thought, distinctly unprofessional, and Hamid-Jones shook it off with an effort.

A pair of muscular nurses unstrapped the body clone and lifted him to the operating table. He made a few uncoordinated body movements, like a fish removed from a creel, and one of the surgeons nodded. An anesthesiologist turned a valve and knocked him the rest of the way out. There was no electric anesthesia machine. Apparently it would not matter this time if drugs remained in the bloodstream.

Quickly, impersonally, the nurses covered the body with sterile drapes from the chest down, propped the head into position on a stainless steel chock, positioned the sonic and muon beam generators that would keep track of the internal structures catalogued in the computer.

When all was ready, the chief of surgery—a younger one, Hamid-Jones noted, than the one who had been killed by the terrorists—stepped forward and, with the casual ease of a virtuoso, drew a line around the clone's neck with an indelible pencil. A dozen display screens riffled through their sheaves of bright images as their operators fine-tuned for an exact match.

The double doors flew open again, and the second clone was trundled in. He, too, was heavily sedated. A portly man in protective clothing trotted beside the rolling stretcher, clasping the clone's hand and burbling endearments.

"There, there, my darling, don't worry about a thing," he cooed, though his charge could hardly have been conscious enough to understand him. "Uncle's here with you, and he won't let anything bad happen. Before you know it you'll be waking up in your own little room."

Hamid-Jones peered through the attendant's tinted bubble helmet to identify him. He was a rouged old man with a marcelled beard and a silver lamé headcloth bound in place by a string of baroque pearls. It was the Keeper of the Paradise himself.

He craned to get a good look at the clone as the stretcher passed. It would have to be one of the older clones, of course, for verisimilitude, but the plastic surgeons had done a remarkable preliminary job. The left eye drooped realistically—they would have cut a nerve—though that particular mishap hadn't happened to the Emir till he was past a hundred and sixty. And they'd matched all the age spots and added wrinkles. The details of the chin line were hard to discern because of the snood that confined the scraggly beard, but Hamid-Jones was sure that was authentic too.

They all looked alike, but this had to be Number Forty; Hamid-Jones was sure of it.

A moment later, the Keeper of the Paradise confirmed his suspicion. "Bobo's a good boy," he prattled on. "That's my precious. Now Bobo go sleepy-sleep for a little while."

Evidently Rubinstein had been unable to pry the substitute clone loose from Ismail. That did not bode well. He should have been able to make his will felt. Hamid-Jones was not familiar with the power plays of high-level politics, but it seemed a bad sign.

He looked up at the observation gallery. The eunuch's gross bulk was leaning toward Rubinstein, whispering something in his ear. Rubinstein looked annoyed. His lips were set in a tight frown. Ismail leaned back and laughed, showing rows of oversize teeth. He signaled lazily and an attendant hurried forth to fan him.

Bobo's stretcher had reached the stainless steel table. Four orderlies hoisted the comatose form to its surface. The Keeper of the Paradise clung to the clone's hand throughout. The neurosurgeons had to speak to him twice. Finally he raised the liver-spotted hand to the faceplate of his helmet and gave it a kiss through the plastic, then allowed himself to be chivied to the sidelines.

The surgeons fitted the big stereotaxic birdcage over Number Forty's head and fixed the clamps in place. An anesthetist unceremoniously pried open the snooded jaw and sprayed cocaine down the windpipe, while an IV team deftly slipped catheters into the carotid arteries to oxygenate the brain directly after severance.

The sight of the trapped head gave Hamid-Jones an uncanny sensation. He forgot that the mottled, parrot-nosed visage was Number Forty's. It was the Emir in every particular—an impression so strong that it exorcised the hideous memory of the cabbage-thing on a stand in Ismail's bedroom.

The two teams of surgeons got into position around their patients, the technicians hunched over their consoles, and all the little whirring knives descended to do their work.

It all went off without a hitch this time—the surgeons had been practicing on some of the surplus clones and gotten the procedure down pat. There was only one awkward moment. When it came time to paint the spinal cord graft with a solution of myelinating cells, ig-Gabal, the Palace cloning chief, became rattled, and tried to hand the circulating nurse a syringe of unenriched oligodendrocytes. Hamid-Jones had no choice but to intervene; the oligodendrocytes were needed for central nervous system repair, but they secreted a substance that inhibited axon growth. Without an admixture of laminin and nerve growth factor derived from Schwann cells, the graft might not have taken, and the composite Emir would have remained paralyzed from the neck down.

Ig-Gabal began to sputter as Hamid-Jones tried discreetly to explain the mistake, and with the circulating nurse holding out his hand impatiently, it was Hamid-Jones himself who quickly had to fill a syringe from the right tray and slap it into the waiting glove. Ig-Gabal shot him a stare of pure hatred but did not dare to berate him within earshot of the surgeons.

As the surgical teams worked outward, layer by microlayer, ig-Gabal recovered his composure and played his small part to the hilt, bestowing his batches of cloned cells with a lordly air. There was nothing much that could go wrong now that they'd reached the peripheral nerves. Hamid-Jones stood tactfully to one side, maintaining a self-effacing silence. But the incident had not gone unnoticed. When the ligature of the carotid branches began and the neurosurgeons could take a small break, Hamid-Jones saw the circulating nurses touch helmets with the neurosurgery chief, who sent a thoughtful glance in his direction. Ig-Gabal saw it, too, and turned an angry shade of red.

The last stitches went in, joining the cutaneous muscle, and a transparent dressing was slapped in place. The stereotaxic cage was removed. The chief anesthesiologist slapped Bobo's face and said sharply, "Bobo, can you hear me?"

He got a mumbled response. He slapped the sagging face again, and this time the eyes flew open. Then, as the face grew gray with pain, the anesthesiologist pushed a plunger attached to an IV line, mercifully putting the clone under again.

Bobo's old, headless body lay obscenely uncovered until a nurse remembered to throw a rubber sheet over it. They'd capped the stump of the neck to cut down on spillage of blood. Hamid-Jones got a clear look at the new composite Emir as the attendants tenderly lifted him from the operating table to the rolling stretcher. It was odd to see that bloated purplish face topping the slim, white boyish body—as if someone had clapped a grotesque mask over a sleeping youth.

The Keeper of the Paradise rushed forward, getting in everyone's way, but no one stopped him. He picked up one smooth pale hand and held on to it tightly as he followed the stretcher and the linked service carts, piled with blinking equipment, out to the recovery room.

The army of people in the chamber stood aside while the little train was rolled out. Then a cheer went up. Helmets and gloves were peeled off, and people began to babble to one another in a rush of released tension. A ragged flow to the exits started, but many of the team members seemed strangely reluctant to admit that it was over and leave.

Hamid-Jones stood forgotten behind the cloning department's utility table. Ig-Gabal had swept past him without a word of thanks for saving his skin. Hamid-Jones waited until the exit flow thinned out, then unlatched his helmet and filed out with the stragglers.

"It went well, wouldn't you say, *ya* Abdul?"

Rubinstein had been waiting in the corridor to congratulate the key team personnel and pump everyone's hand personally. Hamid-Jones didn't expect to get noticed until the Vizier got down to the nurses and support staff, but to his surprise, Rubinstein had cut short his conversation with the orthopedics chief and come over to talk to him.

Hamid-Jones began to stammer a conventional reply about the brilliance of the surgery, then gathered his courage to speak out boldly. He owed it to Rubinstein. If the Vizier had singled him out for advancement, it was because he valued frankness.

"Your Uppermost, you told me before that willfulness in the clones was the problem that worried you most—that they all inherited it from the Emir. Some of them are spoiled rotten, you said. Er . . . I know that Number Forty was the best match for the head age-wise, but I'm . . . ah . . . surprised that you decided to use him."

He left delicately unspoken the question of Ismail's barefaced kidnapping of the Vizier's alternate candidate, Number One Hundred and One, but it was clearly implied in his remark. For a moment, Hamid-Jones wondered if he'd gone too far.

Rubinstein's face darkened. "I know," he admitted grudgingly. "I wanted to use a more manageable candidate, but time was running out on us. We can't wait much longer to show a live Emir to the masses. But not to worry, *ya* Abdul. We have an ally in the Keeper of the Paradise. He's a foolish old man, I know, but—" he made a grimace of distaste "—he knows Bobo better than anybody. He's on our side, and if anyone can keep our miraculously resurrected Emir under control, he's the one."

Both of them sent glances toward the door of the recovery room, now being protected by at least two squads of the Household Guard, who were piling up sandbag barriers and who were armed to the teeth with everything from flamethrowers to grenade launchers. The Keeper of the Paradise had not made an appearance. Evidently he was prepared to sit with Bobo all night if necessary.

Ismail was nowhere in sight either. Anticipating Hamid-Jones's question, Rubinstein said, "Our caponized friend disappeared before they'd even stitched together the windpipe.

Sometimes I wonder if he's as cunning as I give him credit for. It would have been good politics for him to glad-hand the medical team. As one of the Emir's predecessors used to say, a smile is cheaper than a knife.''

He lost his worried look and gave Hamid-Jones a crinkly smile. ''But there's no point in worrying unnecessarily, eh, *ya* Abdul. Things are going swimmingly. We've retrieved the future with this morning's work. So let's turn our thoughts to pleasant things, my boy. You're a young man who's about to go places—don't think that ass ig-Gabal's mistake went unnoticed. The chief of neurosurgery told me how you saved the day. We won't rock the boat too much right away—not till the public settles down and stops noticing things—but ig-Gabal and fossils like him will shortly be eased out of the way. He'll be retired with honors, by the way, so don't worry about midnight stranglings or bloody purges. That was the old way. With Bobo under our thumb, we'll evolve a more humane administration. And we'll need bright young go-getters like you, my boy, to make things hum.''

He waved off Hamid-Jones's stumbling attempt to thank him, and went on: ''You'll stay close by here for a while, won't you? There's a staff coffee shop down the hall that they'll open up now. Let me know as soon as Bobo is out of the recovery room—I can't depend on the doctors to inform me promptly. Call no matter what the hour. I want to be sure to be at Bobo's bedside the moment he opens his eyes.''

Hamid-Jones promised. He had probably condemned himself to stay awake all night after all, decapitation was a major trauma, no matter how skilled the surgeons—but he faced the chore willingly. The Vizier needed someone he could trust.

Rubinstein pressed a high-security scrambler into Hamid-Jones's hand. It was a tiny cylinder, hardly large enough to accommodate the phone jack that was meant to fit into it, but it carried the Imperial seal. Unauthorized possession of one of these was worth the loss of a hand, a foot, and an eye.

''A private line's been left open for you. This will let you through at any time, night or day.''

Rubinstein shook more hands all around and left. Most of the remaining medical personnel departed soon thereafter, except for a few diehards who were still too keyed up to let go of their brush with glory.

It was a good time to get a cup of coffee and something to eat; even if Bobo and his new body showed remarkable recuperative powers, there could be nothing doing for several hours at the earliest. Hamid-Jones was at the brink of exhaustion; he'd had only two hours sleep and nothing to eat since the night before.

But before he could sneak round the corner, he was detained by a talkative technician who insisted on replaying the operation. Hamid-Jones nodded, eyes glazed, until the man ran down. At last they were all gone, except for the belligerent-looking guards in their sandbagged command post, who kept eyeing Hamid-Jones suspiciously as they fingered their appalling weapons.

Hamid-Jones turned to make his escape, but just then there was a stir of activity around the door to the recovery room. The guards stood aside to make way for the lone figure who emerged.

It was Ismail, his gaudy costume half concealed by a smock. He looked pleased with himself. The guards fell all over themselves to bow and salaam as he pushed through them, but the eunuch Chamberlain paid no attention to them. He sashayed grandly down the corridor without a glance in Hamid-Jones's direction, grinning hugely.

Hamid-Jones hurried through a cup of coffee and a microwaved tahina sandwich, wondering if he ought to disturb the Vizier. Rubinstein had wanted his to be the first face Bobo saw, except for the nurses. But on reflection, he decided that the clone could not possibly have imprinted on the Chamberlain; the last jolt of happy juice after the anesthetist had checked his responses would have knocked him out beyond the possibility of recall, no matter how imperious the importunities of the eunuch. No, Ismail had simply wanted to have a look.

As short as he had made his break, it wasn't short enough. He knew something was wrong as soon as he turned the corner. The guards were standing around, fidgeting, trying to act tough but not knowing where to point their weapons. A scared-looking nurse was holding the door to the recovery room open. Two orderlies came through, pushing a draped stretcher.

Hamid-Jones intercepted them halfway down the corridor, far enough from the itchy guards not to make them nervous. They didn't want to stop for him, but he produced the security scrambler the Vizier had given him—the only authority symbol he could think of—and tried to keep his voice firm.

"What happened?"

"We don't know how he died, *sidi*," one of the orderlies said unwillingly. "We weren't even in the room."

"Please, *sidi*," the other one begged. "We're only from the morgue. They sent for us. We had nothing to do with it."

Hamid-Jones was numb. It was all over now. Heads were

certainly going to roll over this, no matter how humane the Vizier's intentions. There had been no indication that anything had been awry with the composite Emir. Certainly the surgical team never would have evaporated if there had been. The recovery room team should have been able to keep Bobo alive.

"Nothing's going to happen to you," Hamid-Jones assured them with more confidence than he felt. "Let's have a look."

But they were too frightened to touch the sheet. Hamid-Jones had to peel it back himself. And then he had the shock of his life. The corpse was not Bobo.

It was the Keeper of the Paradise.

The old man's face was bright purple, the eyes popping, the tongue horribly lolling. The thing that had strangled him had cut so deeply into his neck that it was out of sight.

Hamid-Jones did not want to touch it, but he could identify it by the loose ends, now flecked with the Keeper's blood. It was a silken bowstring—the traditional instrument of execution used by the Palace eunuchs for those highborn victims who, for one reason or another, could not be brought openly to the Carpet of Blood.

Bobo began to cry when he saw the anesthetist.

"Hurt Bobo!" he sniveled. "Bad man hurt Bobo!"

Rubinstein whispered swiftly to the chief of staff, "You'd better get him out of here," and the anesthetist was hustled quickly out of the hospital room, looking as if he were on the point of protesting.

Rubinstein turned back to the bed, but he was not fast enough to forestall Ismail from leaning into Bobo's field of vision and saying in his clear soprano: "Don't worry, your Majesty, we'll see that he's punished."

Rubinstein glared. Ismail leaned back with a broad triumphant smile.

"Now Bobo," the Vizier said ingratiatingly. "How do you feel?"

"Bobo hurt," the clone sobbed. "Make hurt go away."

"You'll feel better soon, Bobo," the Vizier soothed him. "There's going to be some pain for a while, but we'll try to keep it under control." To the surgical chief of staff, he said in an undertone, "Can't you increase the dosage?"

The chief of staff pursed his lips. "We don't want to oversedate him," he said without bothering to lower his voice. "We can't take a chance on depressing his breathing at this point.

The pain really shouldn't be all that severe with what we've given him. He ought to be able to bear it.''

Rubinstein looked dissatisfied. Hamid-Jones interjected: "How about electric anesthesia? It's used for postoperative pain in infants. I've used it myself for high-risk foals.''

The chief of staff gave him a scathing look. "My dear chap—'' he began.

"Do it,'' the Vizier cut in.

The chief of staff said stiffly, without looking at Hamid-Jones, "I'll send for a machine. It will take a few minutes.''

While they waited, Hamid-Jones took the opportunity to study Bobo. The clone lay supine on a crisp white bed, the upper sheet folded down to his groin to accommodate all the monitor wires and tubing attached to his body. He was shaved down to the nipples—a poignant reminder of the body's last owner—but they'd removed the snood from his jaw and someone had combed out the thin, scraggly beard, turning him into a perfect copy of the Emir. Hamid-Jones, though an insider, couldn't help being struck by the uncanny match. The lips of the wound that encircled the neck were slightly everted, showing raw and red beneath the transparent dressing, but in time the incision would heal outward, leaving a ropy scar like the gorget of flesh that the old Emir had worn. That, too, would add to the verisimilitude.

The body was of no use to Bobo for the time being—he was still unable to move from the neck down. But the autonomic functions worked fine, and a host of clever machines were plugged in to help with the body's housekeeping chores. And since the cut had been made below the larynx, he was able to talk.

There was a brisk traffic in and out of the room—nurses and various specialists keeping tabs on the bewildering array of monitors. The number of people in on the secret was well over a hundred, but that couldn't be helped. It was only to be hoped that Rubinstein, despite his humane instincts, would be ruthless about leaks if he had to. He had been the Emir's right-hand man for decades, after all.

The only nonmedical visitors present were Rubinstein, Hamid-Jones, and Ismail—and Hamid-Jones had been allowed in only because the doctors had stretched a point at the insistence of the Vizier, who pointed out that Hamid-Jones had assisted in a minor way at the operation and so could be considered part of the medical team. The Vizier's other aides had firmly been made to wait in the hall.

Ismail, surprisingly, had come alone. It was unprecedented

for him to be seen publicly without a buffer zone of eunuch assistants. As the Chamberlain, of course, Ismail himself could hardly have been refused by the doctors.

Nor could Rubinstein plausibly have refused him. When Ismail had shown up, clad in a visitor's gown, the Vizier had sourly accepted the situation.

"An excellent suggestion, *ya* Abdul," Ismail said smoothly. "It's wicked to let his Majesty suffer unnecessary discomfort."

The clone's eyes rolled in gratitude in Ismail's direction, and the eunuch gave him a toothy smile.

Rubinstein looked furious, but there was nothing he could do. "The doctors are doing their best, Bobo," he said. "They only want to make you get better."

It had been a hectic twenty-four hours. Hamid-Jones was dead on his feet, kept going only by the stimulants he had cajoled out of one of the younger doctors. He had used his scrambler right away to notify Rubinstein of the garroting of the Keeper of the Paradise, and an executive team had immediately descended on the recovery room. Two members of the household guard and four investigators had died in the misunderstanding that followed, and in the end only one agent, suitably sterile in a body condom that someone had had the improvisatory wit to provide for him, had been allowed in the recovery room itself. The recovery room personnel to a man had denied seeing anything; they had thought the old man was "asleep," they insisted. The Keeper had been slumped, apparently dozing, in a chair by the wall where they had put him to get him out of the way while they worked. No one could remember seeing the Chamberlain approach him, and it would not have mattered anyway if anyone had admitted it. One did not tangle with the Chamberlain.

Ismail had been blithe, mocking, when they had met him at the hospital room. Rubinstein was not willing to confront him directly. The deed was already done. It could not be altered. Hamid-Jones got a small lesson in the exercise of statecraft from the Vizier: one does not squander power unnecessarily. An unresolved clash with Ismail would only have weakened Rubinstein's position.

"I'm sorry," a shaken Hamid-Jones had said miserably to the Vizier before Ismail's arrival. The brazen insolence of the execution had staggered him. It was a deliberate affront to the Vizier. The silken bowstring was an instrument of state, and it was supposed to be used discreetly.

"It's not your fault, *ya* Abdul. There was nothing you could have done."

"But I know you were counting on the Keeper to manage Bobo for you. He's the only family Bobo's ever known—Bobo called him 'Uncle.' What are we going to do now?"

"It's unfortunate about the old fellow, but we'll have to do without him," Rubinstein had replied grimly. "Bobo's an unformed lump of clay. He's never seen anything except the Clones' Paradise. He's very impressionable. We'll have to work a little harder to gain his confidence, that's all."

Then he had tried to pin down the chief of staff. "How long before the nerve connections knit? I don't mean until he's walking around normally. Just till he can be propped up in a chair and show some arm movement and so forth?"

The doctor hedged. "It's hard to say. Nerve regrowth is always slow. Perhaps a month."

"Not soon enough. We'll have to display him at a *majlis* within two weeks at the outside."

"Impossible."

Hamid-Jones cleared his throat. "May I make a suggestion?"

The doctor stared down his nose at him. Rubinstein said encouragingly, "Go on, *ya* Abdul."

"Why don't we put a light mechanical framework on him under his clothes? Control his movements by radio, like a puppet?"

"That's it," the Vizier said. "We can prompt him through an earpiece. Keep it all very simple—a few words at a time. I'll be next to him, and he can bend to my ear—I'll 'interpret' for him. The public will expect him to be weak." He rubbed his chin. "He'll have to be intensively coached, of course."

"And if he absolutely *has* to say something lengthy or complicated, we can lift an arm to veil the mouth and do it through a little loudspeaker. Program a voice synthesizer with some of the Emir's old pronouncements. A computer can take the words apart and put them together again."

Rubinstein was caught up in the idea. "In the meantime, we can speed up the coaching with a little reward and punishment. A small jolt to the pleasure center when he obeys the FM prompter—not enough to glaze him over, just enough to make him feel good . . ."

Hamid-Jones was brought back to the present by a small moan from Bobo.

"What's the matter, darling?" Rubinstein said.

"Bobo hurt."

"I know, darling. The machine will be here in a few minutes."

"Bobo can't move!"

He had just realized that he was paralyzed as he grew more alert, and it frightened him. Hamid-Jones could see panic starting in the sagging old duplicate of the Emir's face. It hadn't dawned on Bobo yet that he was young again from the neck down, and when it did, that was going to cause more fear and confusion.

"There, there," Rubinstein said, but Bobo was working himself into a fit.

"Bobo want Uncle!" he wept.

"Uncle's . . . not here," Rubinstein said. "Just try to relax, Bobo. I'll be here with you."

"Want *Uncle!*" the clone screamed. He would have been thrashing around if he had been able to move, but as it was he could only toss his head back and forth.

"He shouldn't be doing that," the chief of staff said worriedly. The display screens of the monitors began to show peaks and swoops, and the various beeps speeded up, like a forestful of small twittering creatures.

The feeble neck movements had begun to cause pain, and that alarmed Bobo even more. He began shrieking at the top of his lungs. Rubinstein exchanged a helpless glance with Hamid-Jones.

"Where's that machine?" Rubinstein demanded.

Just then it arrived. The chief of staff took it from the hands of the nurse and personally plugged it into the bedside cart. In moments he had the little foam pads pasted on over the forehead and mastoids.

"This will call him down," the chief of staff said, as if Bobo were not there. "It sends a mild impulse through the thalamus and hypothalamus—but I'm sure your assistant knows that." He favored Hamid-Jones with a baleful glance. "It stimulates the release of endorphins, works on the pleasure center. That'll take away the pain, make him happy."

He fiddled with dials, and the ugly lines of tension in the clone's face smoothed out. Bobo stopped the twitching movements and smiled.

At that moment, Ismail leaned into the clone's field of view again. "Do you feel better now, your Majesty?" he said.

"Yes," Bobo said dreamily. "Thank you, Auntie."

* * *

The *majlis* chamber was jammed to capacity with a handpicked crowd to make it look good for the news cameras. Hamid-Jones marveled that Palace security had been able to screen so many thousands in such a short period of time. They sat in a teeming, buzzing mass that filled the balconies and bleachers and over-flowed the main floor, while carefully selected cameramen, each with an armed guard at either elbow, prowled the aisles to get human-interest closeups of the Emir's loyal subjects.

Hamid-Jones was one of the favored fifty or so sitting on the dais behind the throne. His immediate seatmates were one of Rubinstein's aides, a sober young man named Mashur, and a beady-eyed sheik who had something to do with the Ministry of Planning.

He had to admit that Bobo looked good, propped upright on the massive gilt seat—satisfactorily dissolute and pouchy and, against all reason, possessing that indefinable *presence* that defined a monarch. It was a quality that evidently came with the Emir's genes. As far as Hamid-Jones could tell, even the household guards who had served the Emir for years had been taken in.

The light tubular framework under the clone's robes didn't show. It worked by microhydraulics—a bit slow, but consistent with the progress of the peripheral nerve knitting to be expected from the earlier head transposition. A man with waldoes operated the living puppet from the next room. Bobo himself had not yet succeeded in wiggling a toe or moving a finger independently.

A petitioner approached the throne and knelt. He was a substantial-looking businessman in a gray herringbone robe and headcloth to match. He tried to thrust a piece of paper into Bobo's inert hand, but Rubinstein, stationed beside the throne, took it from him and added it to the pile stacked on a small table tended by a clerk. The puppeteer in the next room, watching through a screen, made Bobo bend at the waist and tilt his head. The businessman whispered in Bobo's ear. Bobo wore an expression of ineffable boredom.

Hamid-Jones glanced discreetly at the thin-film display pasted to his thumbnail. It already had scrolled past the petitioner's name, and when Hamid-Jones tried to flick his nail, he kept rewinding it too far.

Mashur whispered to him, "Name's Kazimi. North Tunnel importer. Has something to do with an easement dispute."

Bobo spoke, coached by the mole in his ear. "Granted," he said laconically. The dyspeptic expression on his face softened for a second as a little jolt to the pleasure center rewarded him for his performance.

The tutors had done a marvelous job in the short time available; there wasn't a trace of the old baby talk in his inflection. Of course the brief responses did not tax Bobo beyond his capacity.

Rubinstein stepped in unobtrusively to fill the gap. He handed the importer back his petition, stamped and initialed by the clerk, and told him to present it at the Palace business office. Kazimi backed away, gushing his thanks past Rubinstein to the throne.

Bobo was getting tired and irritable, despite the little rewards he was getting from Rubinstein's palmed transducer. Hamid-Jones couldn't blame the clone. The court had been at it for over an hour already—a tedious parade of one dull petition after another. Rubinstein had planned it that way purposely. He wanted no surprises. Everybody would be lulled by monotony and glad when it was over. Eventually the crowd would be thrown a little of the red meat that was expected at the Emir's *majlis*, but it would be strictly rationed.

"We'll have to have at least one execution, of course," Rubinstein had confided to Hamid-Jones the day before. "It would be remarked on if we didn't. But we've chosen a condemned murderer—so the executioner will only be carrying out a legal sentence. And it will be someone who indubitably deserves to die—the ghoul who ran the travelers' rest house at the Bathys oasis and minced his victims for kibba. His lawyer will ask the Emir for clemency, and Bobo will deny it. The existing sentence will be carried out on the spot. But with no inventive cruelty. We're going to wean the public away from that sort of thing."

Hamid-Jones sneaked a look at the executioner, a meaty, hairy man who was stripped to the waist and masked with a blue veil. He wore a broad leather belt hung with the tools of his trade—hooks, awls, hammers, tongs, a graduated set of knives. He stood at ease at the center of the Carpet of Blood, next to a well-worn butcher's block. His assistant squatted nearby, heating a metal plate in an archaic charcoal brazier.

Hamid-Jones shuddered. The metal plate was supposed to be used to cauterize stumps—a barbarity that the old Emir had revived at the instigation of Ismail. Ismail had taught him a further refinement. If the executioner yelled "Run!" in the instant before beheading a man and then applied the plate to seal the stump of the neck, the headless man, by reflex, might take a few jerky steps—sometimes more than a few. The Emir, on several memorable occasions, had amused himself by sending the headless body charging into the crowd, laughing himself to tears as they scrambled to get out of the way.

The Emir, since his first renewal, was understandably obsessed by anything to do with decapitation; Ismail had gauged his master's psyche well.

But the metal plate was only there for effect this time, Rubinstein had assured Hamid-Jones. No amputations were scheduled for this first *majlis*, and when they were resumed—sparingly—under Islamic law, the Vizier intended to have a physician standing by with a tourniquet and painkillers.

"Next," Rubinstein called.

Hamid-Jones had finally got his thumbnail working properly. He scanned the docket and saw that the next item was another dull piece of business—this time a family quarrel involving breach of marriage contract.

"I think the . . . the Emir's getting cranky," Hamid-Jones whispered to Mashur.

Mashur raised his eyebrows at the clone. Bobo's expression was growing more peevish. He was definitely pouting. His mouth twitched and he started to say something on his own. Rubinstein was quick. He leapt to whisper in Bobo's ear, forestalling the clone's outburst. A moment later, the pout was washed away to be replaced by a brief moment of sunshine.

"Nipped it in the bud," Mashur said.

"I think he's beginning to adjust to the pleasure," Hamid-Jones said.

"Not a chance. It's not like drug addiction. You can't acquire tolerance."

"How much longer is the Vizier going to work him?"

"Don't worry about it. There's only another hour to go. Then the execution. Then it's over. The old man can keep him going until then easily. He's playing him like a fish on a line."

"I hope you're right."

Hamid-Jones cast a worried glance in Bobo's direction. For a moment he thought he saw the clone's finger move, then he told himself that he must have been mistaken. Bobo had undergone a series of tests that morning. There was still no sensation in his extremities.

His attention was diverted by a disturbance at the far end of the carpeted runway leading to the throne. Two soldiers were dragging a terrified man forward. He was sobbing and pleading.

He must have received a pretty good preliminary beating, because he had a nasty nosebleed that was running down the front of his shirt.

"What's this?" Mashur said sharply. "There's nothing like this on the agenda."

The battered face was familiar, and as the soldiers hauled the man to the base of the throne, Hamid-Jones recognized him. It was the anesthetist who had slapped Bobo to consciousness after the operation.

Bobo's little pig eyes flew open with sudden interest, and then he seemed to shrink back as much as the limited mobility of his head and neck would let him. Rubinstein must have stabbed several times at the button in his palm, because Hamid-Jones could see the conflicting emotions of happiness and fear flicker back and forth across Bobo's face like a badly-cut film. But the synthetic pleasure couldn't compete with Bobo's real feelings, whatever they were, and almost visibly it could be discerned that Bobo had set the induced sensations aside to serve as a disregarded background to his own emotional state.

Ismail, unnoticed in the surprise of the moment, had heaved his ponderous bulk out of the peacock chair behind the throne and reached Bobo's side.

"He can't hurt you, your Majesty," the eunuch said with oily glee. "He's under arrest."

Bobo's face lit up and stayed that way. It wasn't Rubinstein's transducer this time. "Good," Bobo said. "Good."

There was nothing much that Rubinstein could do except make the best of the situation. He wouldn't have wanted to reinforce Bobo's behavior with another jolt to the pleasure center, Hamid-Jones knew, and the cameras and microphones had irrefutably picked up the Emir's approval of the arrest.

"What's the charge?" Rubinstein asked sourly.

Ismail made a motion with his hand, and a bailiff stepped forward with a docket book.

"The charge is lèse-majesté," the bailiff said. "On the Chamberlain's warrant."

"He committed an affront to the person of the Emir," Ismail amplified.

"I only slapped his Majesty's face to get a reaction!" the anesthetist blabbered, his teeth chattering with fright. "It has to be done, to bring someone out of deep anesthesia. It could be dangerous otherwise."

"You see, your Majesty," Ismail said. "He has convicted himself out of his own mouth."

Rubinstein gave the small signal that would alert the waldo operator in the next room to have Bobo raise an arm as if he were adjusting his headcloth, effectively screening his lips. A crack speechwriter was standing by to punch in the instructions to the computer that would search a century's worth of *majlis* footage to find the Emir in a lenient mood, then feed the appropriate words to a voice synthesizer and get the anesthetist off the hook.

Bobo's arm rose a few inches, then stopped. It rose jerkily a few inches more, then stopped again. The microhydraulics were very weak, and Bobo, somehow, was finding the strength to resist them.

To his astonishment, Hamid-Jones saw the fingers of the clone's right hand curl themselves, straighten out, then clench again.

"I don't like this," Bobo said clearly.

Rubinstein signaled the hidden puppeteer to stop. Hamid-Jones saw disaster yawning before them all. Beside him, Mashur was staring in disbelief.

"What shall we do, your Majesty?" Ismail said unctuously.

"What shall we do?" Bobo repeated. There was the faintest hint of infantilism in his inflection, but it was doubtful that anyone who was not looking for it would notice.

"Shall we cut off his head?" Ismail suggested.

Bobo smiled with glee. "Yes, cut off his head," he chortled.

The eunuch bent to whisper in Bobo's ear. Bobo laughed aloud. One had the impression that if he had been able to, he would have clapped his hands with delight.

Rubinstein had gone ashen, but he made no further attempts to interfere.

The soldiers dragged the anesthetist to the black leather carpet with the chopping block on it. He screamed and kicked, but two assistant executioners with their faces wrapped in gauze grasped him by the ankles and the four men bore him at the horizontal to the block. Holding him stretched out, they lowered him so that his neck rested on the block. He tried to thrash about but could only succeed in twisting his neck back and forth.

The blue-veiled executioner came over, the bright axe balanced in an expert grip, and spoke to the anesthetist. "Don't move your head like that," he said kindly. "It will go easier for you."

The anesthetist stopped wriggling at once. He held himself rigid, poised above the block. The executioner stepped back and raised the heavy axe in a two-handed grip.

Bobo giggled. "Run!" he cried.

The axe whistled down. The head fell with a thump into a padded basket, and the assistant with the cauterizing plate applied it with a sizzle of steam. The legs of the headless body twitched a couple of times and fell limp.

Bobo turned to Ismail, disappointed.

"Never mind, your Majesty," the eunuch said. "Sometimes it doesn't work. We'll just have to try again."

The next hour was a horror. Ismail must have had it all planned, and he had done his research well. There was a steady parade of prisoners against whom Bobo had grievances, both real and imagined. They all had been taken into custody by eunuch sergeants at arms during the night.

The first was the bath attendant, Sami, from the Garden of the Clones, who had prevented Bobo from drowning the houri. The charge against him was interference with the prerogatives of a monarch. "Let the punishment fit the crime," Ismail suggested, and Sami's head was held in a bucket of water provided by the executioner until the bubbles stopped.

The next was a fitness instructor who had prescribed jogging for an overweight and middle-aged Bobo; his legs were hacked off, and he was allowed to bleed to death on the leather carpet. He was followed by a dietician who was force-fed boiling pabulum until he choked to death, a cook who was microwaved, a carpenter-handyman who was sawed in half, a manicurist who was fatally trimmed, a houri who was impaled. The beheadings, though, were mostly disappointments, except for one responsive victim whose decapitated corpse managed four or five floundering steps before toppling. But Ismail was able to gloss over the failures by immediately occupying Bobo with another victim.

Bobo passed out capricious sentences with sadistic glee, avenging all the nursery slights he had stored up during his sixty years, until the leather carpet was slippery with blood.

The last to go was the executioner. He was seized without warning by soldiers and beheaded by one of his gauze-masked assistants for disappointing the Emir in the performance of his duties.

Rubinstein was forced to stand by helplessly. The cameras were rolling, the crowd had settled back to watch the turn of events in a curdling silence. It would have been out of character for him to have made a fuss about the carnage; he had presided at many another bloody *majlis* on the Emir's dyspeptic days.

The charade had worked all too well. There was no doubt in the minds of the witnesses in the *majlis* chamber and all those huddled in front of their holo sets throughout the warrens of Mars: the Emir was back, and fully in charge.

The summons from Ismail came a week later. Hamid-Jones had been dreading it. When the eunuch had failed to follow up on his demand that Hamid-Jones spy on the Vizier for him, Hamid-Jones had begun to hope that he had forgotten the matter. But evidently some sort of report was still expected of him.

"Er, right now?" he asked the aide who had delivered the message. It was the tall eunuch with the baritone voice who had come to fetch him before.

"Immediately after the afternoon prayer," the dour aide said. "Don't be late."

A small reprieve was better than none. Hamid-Jones had been thinking his situation over, and he had come to the conclusion that the risk of being straight with the Vizier was preferable to sinking into a bottomless morass of double-agentry.

"Will I have any trouble being admitted to the Chamberlain's palace?"

"You're not going to the Chamberlain's palace. You're to present yourself at the Royal Apartments. Here's your security pass. It tells you where to go."

The eunuch handed him a ticket that was stiff with electronics.

As soon as the Chamberlain's creature left, Hamid-Jones went to Rubinstein and was admitted with a minimum of fuss by his secretary.

"Yes, yes," Rubinstein said, waving away Hamid-Jones's explanations. "I know that the gelded wonder enlisted you to spy on me for him. It doesn't matter. Go on. You may learn something useful."

"But what shall I tell him?"

"Tell him anything. It's of no moment."

The Vizier seemed smaller, more shrunken. The *majlis* had been a terrible blow to him. "There's no denying it—that treacherous capon outmaneuvered me," he had told Hamid-Jones afterward. "I'm cancelling next week's *majlis* till I can figure out what to do. Ismail is pandering to our pastiche of an Emir, currying favor by bringing him slave girls from the royal harem."

"But I thought that Bobo . . ." Hamid-Jones began. He finished delicately, ". . . couldn't."

"Oh, the sacral nerves are intact," Rubinstein said. "It's just that there's no connection to the brain yet. I believe that Ismail is supplying Bobo with an electric suppository. It stimulates the sacral nerves directly and makes consummation possible—harem eunuchs have a whole bag of tricks for dealing with the little problems of their masters. I don't know that there's any feeling, but that's not the point of the exercise anyway. It's a question of dominance. Bobo is simply asserting himself, with Ismail's encouragement. What he's doing is symbolically taking possession of the old Emir's property."

"But . . ." Hamid-Jones sputtered. "What are you going to do about it? If the Chamberlain keeps insinuating himself into the Em . . . Bobo's confidence this way . . ."

"He'll overreach himself soon. It's a failing of eunuchs. They don't know when they've gone too far. Ismail may think he's pulling strings, but he'll shortly find the strings are pulling him. Let him supply a few slave girls for now! Bobo is still raw, new to the game. He'll soon discover that he has a wider stage to play upon than the Palace harem. He'll discover the greater pleasures of wielding power. And then he'll find that he needs me."

Rubinstein had spoken with self-assurance, but Hamid-Jones could detect a note of worry in his voice. The Vizier was a badly shaken man.

Now, a week later, he seemed to have regained his confidence. Hamid-Jones wondered what he had up his sleeve.

"I want you to know that you can count on me, your Uppermost," Hamid-Jones said. "For anything."

The Vizier patted him on the shoulder. "You're a good boy. I never doubted it. Now you'd better run along and see what the Chamberlain wants."

"I won't tell him anything that he can use against you . . ."

"There's nothing you could say that would hurt me. Go on, *boychick*, Ismail's scheduled a tentative news conference for after the evening prayers. Maybe you can find out what he's up to."

He stepped out of the elevator into a lobby filled with aimlessly loitering reporters and mosque correspondents. They set up a clamor as soon as they saw him.

"Is he anybody?"

"That's Hamid-Jones—he's a high muck-a-muck in the cloning department!"

"*Ya sidi, ya sidi,* look this way! Give us a smile!"

"What's going on, *ya sidi*? Can you tell us anything?"

"*Ya beyshah* Jones, would you comment on the report that you're going to take over the Palace cloning department?"

"Is it true that the Emir's going to announce some kind of shuffle?"

"What's the Chamberlain doing in there with him?"

"This is the third time the Chamberlain's called us in here like this! What's it all about? Is he going to make an announcement his time?"

Hamid-Jones put his head down and walked through. The guards clubbed reporters out of the way, clearing a path for him. He showed his pass to the security desk set up in the exit at the far end, stuck his finger in a slot where a needle jabbed it and a high-speed identoscanner compared his DNA with his file records, and breathed a sigh of relief as an electrified door clanged shut behind him.

One of Ismail's eunuch secretaries immediately took him in hand. "Go straight on through and join the others. We're still waiting for the Ayatollah Hashemi."

Bewildered, Hamid-Jones allowed himself to be led through a swinging door. Hashemi was one of Mars's most distinguished jurists, respected by the most learned Sunni *ulama* and acceptable to the Shi'ite minority as well. His presence was a must when unanimity was required.

He found himself in a high-ceilinged apartment that had been set up as a private hospital suite, with luxury touches. The screen beside the bed, now folded, was of white brocade silk on a gold-plated tubular frame, and plumbing had been brought to the bedside in the form of a pink marble sink and commode with solid gold fixtures.

Bobo lay on the bed with a towel draped across his loins, a silly expression on his face. Four nude slave girls were posted at the corners of the bed, their faces decently veiled.

Ismail was standing in the middle of a cluster of robed dignitaries, a huge smile creasing his balloonlike face. When he saw Hamid-Jones, he motioned him over.

"This is my dear friend Abdul; he is like a son to me," the eunuch said. "Never mind his youth—he is an educated man, with good sense. He has risen far and fast in the cloning department, haven't you, *ya* Abdul?"

Hamid-Jones gave an embarrassed mumble. The graybeards, after a perfunctory murmur, resumed their conversations. Hamid-Jones felt out of place in his hastily thrown-on djellaba with the cuffs of his work trousers peeking out from under the hem. He was somewhat mollified to see a few men dressed as casually as himself—mostly young professionals by the look of them. One he recognized as the neurosurgeon who had presided at the glial graft.

"Ah, here's the Ayatollah now," Ismail announced. "We can begin."

The door had opened once again to admit an august personage dressed all in black. Two roly-poly eunuchs backed in before him, bowing and scraping. The newcomer was a tall, stern man with a chest-length beard set in corn rows.

Ismail giggled. "Most of you will have to wait outside. For decency's sake, only the four allowable witnesses may remain. I do not matter, of course, being an imperfect person, nor do the slave girls who will physically assist the Emir, since they are not persons at all."

Hamid-Jones snagged one of the professional men. "What's he talking about?"

The man shook him off. "Shhh."

"The chosen four are beyond reproach—a doctor, the Ayatollah, and two *ulama*," Ismail went on.

The two *ulama* stepped forward, looking very serious. They were sober, well-fed men in legal robes, wearing black skullcaps.

"For those of you who do not know them, the *ulama* are two of our most distinguished jurists," Ismail said. "The estimable Murrwan Murrwan bin Yusuf bin Wadiah bin Ibrahim al-Malfoof, and Neweaf bin Arif bin Hamza al-Wazza. Their word cannot be doubted."

Hamid-Jones tried one of the circulating eunuchs. "What are we all here for?" he said.

The eunuch edged away from him. "The Chamberlain is speaking," he murmured irritably.

Ismail paused to locate the source of the distraction. "Ah, *ya* Abdul, you are in the dark," he said with exaggerated solicitousness. "You were somehow notified late, and missed the briefing. Forgive me, it is entirely my fault. How could I have been so careless? You are to be one of the news-spreaders." His smile was full of malice. "His Majesty is feeling well enough to resume his conjugal responsibilities. He has called for his favorite wife, Umm Nour."

Hamid-Jones could only stand there with his jaw sprung at Ismail's presumption and impudence. Rubinstein had seriously misgauged the audacity of his rival.

"I know you'll want to help pass on the joyous tidings," the Grand Eunuch leered at him. "Most especially to the Vizier."

A door leading to the inner suite opened, and a walking pyramid came out, escorted by two magnificently dressed eunuchs wearing jeweled swords. The woman under the heavy shroud was enormously fat, to judge by her waddle and the few defining contours of her shape that could be guessed at through the stiff cloth, but the eyes just barely visible through the veiled slit at the top seemed young and lively.

"Your Majesty, your beloved is here," Ismail piped in his child's voice. "The beautiful and bounteous Umm Nour, delight of your life."

The invisible woman giggled beneath the shroud. The veiled eyes fluttered modestly. Hamid-Jones caught a reek of perfume and henna.

Incredibly, Umm Nour seemed totally unaware that the towel-draped figure on the bed, with its slim white body and bilious head, was not the husband she was accustomed to, but a collection of stitched-together spare parts. Hamid-Jones had supposed that if anyone could tell, it would be the Emir's favorite wife. But then, when he had taken her to wife, he had been another pastiche, with a borrowed body that was probably still on the right side of middle age, and a head that might not have been much more than a century older than Bobo's. Perhaps, if there was any thought at all behind that vacuous giggle, she assumed that somehow the body transplant had a rejuvenating effect on the head as well.

"See—your husband brings a strong young body to you now, ya Umm Nour," Ismail said with a broad wink. "Are you prepared to be a good wife to him?"

Umm Nour giggled again. The eunuchs urged her forward.

"His Majesty still hasn't much movement in his arms and legs," Ismail said, addressing the learned men, "but the slave girls have been well instructed, and they will do all that is necessary." He gave an insinuating grin. "And after all, it's not strength in the arms and legs that make a man a man, is it?"

"Auntie, Auntie, look!" Bobo called from the bed.

Hamid-Jones turned his head and saw the clone wiggling his toes, a proud smile on his puffy face.

"Ah, that's wonderful, your Majesty," Ismail approved. "You see, gentlemen, he already has some control over his extremities. It won't be long now. I'm counting on all of you to help put an end to those wicked rumors that the Emir or his body prosthesis were damaged in the terrorist incident. As you see, there's not a mark on him. We had to finish the surgery under trying conditions, but praise Allah, all turned out for the best. He'll soon be walking about, and with more spring in his step than formerly."

He turned to stare at Hamid-Jones with eyes like a pair of cracked marble eggs. "And I'm sure the Vizier will be glad to know that his Majesty's will is intact, as is proved by his calling for his favorite wife."

The slave girls had begun to prop the clone up, one to a limb. They were chunky, well-muscled girls, strong enough to move the helpless man in any position—even hold him in midair if that was required.

"Shoo, gentlemen, shoo, shoo, shoo!" Ismail said in high good humor, flapping his hands. "Everybody out except the four attestors. The rest of you wait outside in the anteroom. This shouldn't take long. Then we can all go out and talk to the reporters."

Ismail pressed a button in a small transmitter in his palm. The towel rose. Umm Nour giggled coyly, and the four slave girls made encouraging sounds. Hamid-Jones filed out with the rest.

They were seated in an armored bath chair, hurtling through a dark, dank tunnel at terrifying speed. It was Ismail's private way between palaces—an old, disused sewer system that must have been part of the original plumbing complex.

Hamid-Jones was alone with the Chamberlain on the broad wicker bench, though there was room for a bodyguard. It was almost insulting—a contemptuous demonstration that the eunuch had nothing to fear from him. But even if Hamid-Jones had been so inclined, he would have had to have been very brave—or desperate—indeed to want to tangle with Ismail's quarter-ton of deceptively soft blubber in the hampering confines of the bath chair. Mass would be more than a match for strength and swiftness in the circumstances; and Ismail was practiced in the use of the little sickle-bladed knife that hung from a chain around his neck, to say nothing of the great thick hands that must have personally strangled hundreds during his long career.

"You don't mind coming with me, my dear Abdul?" the Chamberlain purred. "You have nothing pressing?"

"No, your Immensity," he replied.

Ismail was doing this to prevent him from reporting to the Vizier, Hamid-Jones was sure. The eunuch wanted to rub Rubinstein's nose in this latest chess move by having him find out from the evening holocast.

"The Vizier has canceled Friday's *majlis*, I understand," Ismail probed.

"I believe so, your Irreplaceability."

"He'll have to resume them sometime, you know. The public won't be denied."

"That's true, your Splendor." The immediate pressure was off now that Bobo had shown himself, but Rubinstein was all too aware that the period of grace would be short. Hamid-Jones had no idea of how Rubinstein intended to gain control of the situation, but he had all of the machinery of the state at his disposal, while Ismail had only the resources of the harem.

"His Majesty should be able to move about a bit on his own in another week or two. You saw how well he wiggled his toes?"

"Yes."

The eunuch gave a great chuckle, setting all his jelly aquiver. "He's feeling quite frisky now. Full of beans. He won't tolerate that mechanical harness anymore, you know. He hates it."

"Well, it was only . . ."

"He wants to be his own man." The eunuch simpered. "In every way."

"But he's only a clone!" Hamid-Jones burst out. "A spare! Two spares! He's not qualified to run the kingdom of Mars!"

"Who's to know, *ya* Abdul?" the eunuch said silkily. "Nobody can tell the difference, and the number of people who are in on the secret is limited." He shook with silent laughter. "And will soon be more limited."

A crawling sensation began at the base of Hamid-Jones's spine. "Limited, your Immensity?"

"We've had to dispose of more than twenty operating room personnel who were inclined to talkativeness. And I'm afraid there will be more to come. I'm drawing up a little list."

The bath chair jerked to a stop in a tiled chamber whose vaulted roof was supported by bulbous masonry pillars. Ismail raised the clamshell hood and they stepped down to a fine carpet that was getting a little soggy from residual moisture. A cherubic little page offered to take the Chamberlain's towering turban and replace it with one that, to Hamid-Jones's eye, seemed no less elaborate, but Ismail brushed him aside.

"Let's call on his Former Majesty and see how he's doing," the eunuch said.

There was a fetid smell in Ismail's bedchamber that could not be entirely masked by the thick clouds of incense. Hamid-Jones searched the dimness and located the stand on the low chest beside the jellybed. The Emir's head looked much as it had before—a greenish lump resting in a sconce—but it had been turned to face a small portable holo screen.

"His Excrescence has been entertaining himself while I was absent," Ismail said, curling his lips. "I had a camera set up so that he could watch his Umm Nour being serviced."

He laughed heartily and turned the stand around so that Hamid-Jones could see the face.

"Did you enjoy the show, your High-and-Mightiness?" the eunuch chortled. "Your Umm Nour doesn't need you anymore. No one does."

At first Hamid-Jones thought that the despoiled face was too far gone in decay to show any spark of a living process. Then he saw the putrid lips twist in a simulation of rage.

"Cat's got your tongue?" Ismail taunted.

The marred face writhed in helpless fury. Tears trickled down the dilapidated cheeks. Hamid-Jones tried to persuade himself that awareness in the usual sense could not be possible—this was a behavioral residue, the reflex of a choleric personality left in the synapses.

"The thing stinks," Ismail said.

He reached under the stand and pulled out a plug. A soft background chugging of pumps stopped abruptly. The Emir opened his mouth in a silent scream. A small green light winked out.

Color drained out of the face, leaving it pale and patchy. The ravaged lips mouthed silent obscenities for fully half a minute, then became flaccid. The marbled eye turned dull.

A white-jacketed orderly hurried into the room with panic in his face. "The monitors all went dead . . ." he began, then saw the plug in the eunuch's hand.

"Take this thing out and throw it in the garbage," Ismail said. "Still better, you can feed it to the fish in my lily pond."

When the orderly left, holding the disagreeable object at arm's length, Ismail turned to Hamid-Jones and said, "There's no need to keep useless things around, don't you agree?"

Hamid-Jones managed a strangled, "N-no, your Splendor." He could not help reflecting that, like the rest of the operating team, his own usefulness was at an end.

In fact, his knowledge was as great a threat to the Vizier as to the Chamberlain, should Rubinstein choose to regard it that way.

"You can go now," Ismail said indifferently. "The old fox must be wondering what's keeping you."

CHAPTER 12

"**B**ack, back," the soldier ordered, prodding with the butt of his riot gun, and Hamid-Jones obediently gave way with the rest of the crowd to let the palanquins through.

The first arrival was only the Minister of Housing and *Zakat*, a colorless little man whose chair was borne along on the shoulders of two sweating civil servants in department livery. He waved daintily at the onlookers through parted curtains, a shy smile on his face.

"May his tribe decrease," growled the man who was pressed up against Hamid-Jones's right side. "I don't mind state alms going to widows and orphans as the Koran commands, but by the Prophet, I don't like to see my tax dinars disappearing into the pockets of bureaucrats!"

Hamid-Jones edged away as much as the crush would allow. Another palanquin was coming through, this one a larger conveyance carried by four trotting bearers in the gay floral trappings of the Department of Parks and Recreation. A cheer went up from the crowd; the Minister was a popular figure since the opening up of the Hellas dome to bathers, and the public entertainments he had thrown to celebrate the executions of the surviving terrorists taken after the *majlis* hall attack had only cemented that popularity.

Hamid-Jones looked around the enormous public square that fronted the Hall of Ministers and the other government buildings. It was crammed with people hoping to catch a glimpse of the Emir on his way to his cabinet meeting. High overhead, the immense translucent dome hung like a proper sky, letting in a bloody Martian light that turned white robes pink and made faces ruddy.

News teams on mobile platforms were present in force, to record this latest evidence of a recovering Emir taking command of his government. "One symbol is worth a thousand protestations," Rubinstein had told Hamid-Jones when he had set it up. As the litters passed, the multiple snouts of the holo cameras swiveled with one accord to follow the arriving ministers up the wide stairs to the marbled entrance.

An impromptu zoo was parked in the square outside the Hall of Ministers, protected for the moment from the crowd by portable barriers. It was more of the Parks and Recreation Minister's handiwork; the Emir had generously consented to share with his subjects a traveling circus that had been imported for his private amusement. There would be animal acts, acrobats, fire-eaters, and jugglers after the ministers' meeting.

Hamid-Jones cast a jaundiced eye over the cages with their moth-eaten bears and monkeys and shabby lions, and the towering giraffe that never would be able to return to Earth again after its sojourn in Martian gravity.

Hamid-Jones knew the real story. Ismail had freighted the circus all the way from Earth at ruinous expense to the treasury, as part of his campaign to divert Bobo. But Rubinstein had outmaneuvered the eunuch. "I offered Bobo the chance to play the statesman," he had told Hamid-Jones. "He was quite taken by the chance to play the benefactor to 'his' people. He loves grandstanding. And why not? It's in his genes."

Rubinstein had waited three weeks before calling a second *majlis*. He didn't dare postpone it any longer. But he spent every possible minute with Bobo, cementing his influence, and in the end he was satisfied that his strategy was working.

"The key is to work him hard," he told Hamid-Jones. "Give him no time to be seduced by all these gaudy temptations that Ismail is throwing at him. Eventually there is always a surfeit of physical sensation and tawdry diversions. Boredom sets in. But the exercise of power is a pleasure that never palls."

He had started Bobo out in easy steps—minor decisions on matters of Palace architecture or public works. Bobo could see results almost immediately—Rubinstein made sure of that. He was entranced by the fact that he had *accomplished* something, not merely titillated his nerve endings or amused himself.

"The original Emir took a keen interest in the smallest details—sometimes too keen an interest," Rubinstein said. "It wasn't hard to awaken the predilection in our current pastiche. Nucleotides will tell.''

All had been carefully orchestrated by Rubinstein's staff. None of the decisions were hard or irksome. Simple, carefully prepared options were presented for his signature. The options, of course, were stacked in favor of Rubinstein's intentions. The bad ones were made to look outrageously bad—and sometimes, not often, Bobo would perversely gravitate toward them, but that was a risk that had to be taken. As Rubinstein summarized the position papers aloud, Bobo had merely to say yes or no, or make a multiple choice—and the rewards of decision were always manifest and prompt. Bobo became highly enthusiastic—sometimes so much so that Rubinstein had to gently stop him from stamping the documents over and over again with the seal that he had given him.

Rubinstein's strategy seemed to be succeeding. At least Ismail was going around looking disgruntled. Rubinstein's intelligence apparatus was, of course, aware of a steady parade of distractions and entertainments stage-managed by the corps of eunuchs. There were the cloned blond octuplets from the circus high-wire act who were smuggled into the harem and out again the next morning with a gift of a fortune in jewels for their services; the expensive mechanical gewgaws and electronic toys that were obtained by commission agents who scoured the Solar system for them, and that were turning Bobo's quarters into a junkyard; the orbital fireworks displays that lit up the night side of Mars and kept a marveling populace awake.

But next morning Bobo, though bleary, was always ready to work again. Rubinstein tried to show him how much the orbital extravaganzas cost the Palace exchequer in terms of its annual budget, but when he saw that Bobo was becoming bored, he wisely stopped.

Bobo's physical condition was improving rapidly. Once the first nerve connections had established their bridgeheads, message traffic flooded the available channels; dendrites could grow at their leisure. Bobo could walk with two canes, lift anything that wasn't too heavy, feed himself, and have sex without the assistance of the quartet of brawny slave girls—though he was getting into the habit of keeping them around anyway. Seated on his throne at the *majlis*, he was an imposing and plausible figure. He was acquiring the speech patterns of his father-body, the original Emir, and it was one of Rubinstein's recurring chores to keep him from talking too much in public.

There had been no repetition of the disaster of the first bloody *majlis*. The supplicants and the accused were carefully screened to make sure that Ismail hadn't slipped in any ringers. Rubinstein's own security forces controlled the order of precedence of those who approached the throne, and bribees were severely punished. Ismail was able to cause some minor mischief, but Rubinstein's damage control procedures held it in check. Executions were limited to one or two per session, all of them certified by a *qadi*, and though Bobo's eyes glittered, he did not get carried away again.

The crowd's roar brought Hamid-Jones to attention. He'd only half noticed the arrivals of the last several officials in their ceremonial travel chairs, and the crowd hadn't been that impressed either. But Ismail was something else again.

He had outdone himself in plumage today. His turban stood two feet high, precious jewels winked all over his costume, and his gold lamé vest and flowered silk pantaloons had been enhanced by optical brighteners. Eight grunting eunuchs in costumes almost as splendid as his own staggered under the weight of a mammoth sedan chair of polished teak inlaid with gold leaf and ivory.

Rubinstein, as usual, was almost dowdy by contrast, despite the magnificence of his official robes. Four plainly dressed bearers carried him along, though he was entitled to eight. It seemed to Hamid-Jones that the Vizier carried his dislike of pomp to an extreme—it was a disappointment to the expectations of his public. But some in the crowd cheered and called blessings on him; Rubinstein had his supporters, and their numbers had been growing these days because of the moderation that had come to the *majlis*.

The crowd's real excitement was reserved for the Emir.

Bobo arrived in a sixteen-man palanquin with bulletproof glass. Armored bodyguards trotted alongside, pausing only to swing a cudgel at the occasional incautious onlooker who pressed too close. The crowd bobbed and salaamed. Bobo smiled and waved, then spoiled the effect by scratching his crotch—a habit that Rubinstein hadn't been able to break him of.

The doors clanged shut behind the pseudo-Emir. Soldiers pushed the crowd further back to provide an open space in front of the steps. Vendors were starting to circulate through the square; Hamid-Jones bought an ice cream cone and wandered over to look at the zoo while he was waiting.

* * *

"But where is the money? Show it to me!" Bobo demanded.

The Minister of the Exchequer looked at Rubinstein for support, then, receiving a nod of encouragement, said: "Well . . . the money isn't exactly *real*, your Highness, in the sense of being piles of dirhams and gold dinars that you can handle. If it were, it wouldn't fit in this room. It's . . . ah . . . in the form of obligations which can be called in on demand. It's actually *information*, stored in bank computers. Oh, we could realize some of it in the form of currency if we wished, but if we called it all in at once, we'd cause a panic. The amount of physical currency actually in circulation represents only a fraction of this . . . web of mutual obligation. We mint and print only enough to grease the skids of commerce. But of course we don't have to actually transfer physical currency to carry out a financial transaction."

Bobo stared with incomprehension at the open folder that had been placed in front of him. "This piece of paper is my money?" he said doubtfully.

"Well—in a sense, yes, your Majesty."

"I don't understand any of this," Bobo wailed. He was definitely getting grumpy.

"The Minister is trying to explain about budgets," Rubinstein interposed smoothly. "Each of us is apportioned a certain amount of money to spend. The Department of Jihad has so much to spend on defense, the Charity Administration has so much to distribute in the form of *zakat*, and so forth. The Palace also has a budget. It takes in so much and spends so much, and when the money is gone there isn't any more to spend unless we take it from somewhere else, and that can cause difficulties with your subjects. The Chamberlain is in charge of administering your household expenses—that's why he attends these meetings and has cabinet status."

Ismail shot the Vizier a glance of pure hatred.

Rubinstein went on relentlessly. "But if we continue as at present, without any budget controls, the money will run out. For example, the orbital fireworks cost a billion dinars, and funds had to be diverted from Palace maintenance. That could be serious."

"They were pretty," Bobo said wistfully.

The assembled ministers exchanged glances. During the first few department reports, the Emir hadn't had much to say, and they hadn't thought much about his occasional capricious outbursts. Cabinet meetings with the Emir had always been a tightrope walk. But it was becoming increasingly obvious that something was amiss. The Emir had always shown a keen grasp of finances.

The awful possibility of brain damage must have occurred to several of them simultaneously. But none of them opened his mouth, and none ever would. You didn't rise to the level of department minister by being suicidal.

"Yes, of course they were pretty," Rubinstein agreed, "but some pretty things cost too much. The commission agents are cheating you. For example, the old Saudi royal palace that was dismantled, stone by stone, tile by tile, and packed in numbered crates and lofted into orbit for trans-Mars injection—and via the most expensive high-energy trajectory at that! Since they got here, the crates haven't even been unpacked—and probably never will be. They'll only remain in storage like most of the other things the Chamberlain's commission agents are sending you—things you don't want or need. If you wanted a historical memento like the Murabba Palace to be set up in the desert somewhere so you could go out and look at it sometimes, it would have been ten times cheaper to build a replica right here, from scratch. And in the meantime, the Chamberlain is neglecting to pay the soldiers and bribe the tribal sheiks whose loyalty you depend on."

The other ministers looked shiftily toward Ismail, trying to gauge which way the wind was blowing.

"Stop it, stop it, I'm getting dizzy!" Bobo quavered.

The Minister of the Exchequer, after assessing the situation, decided to align himself with Rubinstein. "The Vizier isn't suggesting that you be deprived of all your entertainments, your Majesty. Only that we rein in a bit, apply stricter spending controls." He carefully did not look at Ismail. "Perhaps with all his other duties, the Chamberlain finds bookkeeping too much of a chore. I could set up a budget overview department for the Palace within my own ministry. For example, perhaps the orbital fireworks *are* too expensive. We could substitute a fireworks display on the Palace wall."

Bobo's chin trembled. "I don't like him," he said, pointing at the Minister of the Exchequer. "Can't we cut off his head or something?"

The shocked and careful silence that followed was interrupted by Rubinstein's calm, humorous voice. The ministers relaxed; Rubinstein had deflected the Emir's outbursts a thousand times in the past.

"We don't want to do that, your Majesty. It's a good head, and we need it."

Bobo was on the point of subsiding when Ismail's vast bulk stirred and the drooping face came to life. "Doesn't your Majesty want to ask the Vizier where the money *goes*?" he said.

"Yes, yes," Bobo said, squirming. "Where does the money *go*?"

"We've been explaining that, your Majesty," Rubinstein said, giving the eunuch a dirty look. "It's all apportioned out to national defense, public works, charity, running the government—all the things that keep you in power."

"You see?" Ismail shrilled. "He *spends* it! That's where it goes!"

Around the crescent-shaped table, the ministers sat frozen, not wanting to call attention to themselves. The Minister of the Exchequer had gone white.

"Your Majesty—" Rubinstein began patiently.

Ismail lurched forward in his seat. "See, see!" he shouted. "He's always pretending to know best! He has no right to thwart his Majesty's wishes. To oppose the Emir is an act of treason!" His face was purple with synthetic fury. He turned to the ministers and demanded rhetorically, "Isn't that so?"

The ministers shrank within themselves. None dared raise their eyes.

Rubinstein gave Ismail a look of professional admiration. "Oh, the cunning of the serpent," he said dryly. He turned quickly to Bobo and even then might have saved the day, but Ismail was quicker.

"Traitor!" he shouted, slamming a meaty fist on the table. The table jumped and so did Bobo.

"Does that mean he's bad?" the clone said, sitting up straight and looking at Rubinstein with new interest.

"Yes, your Majesty," Ismail said. "Don't you want them to take the traitor away?"

Bobo nodded vigorously.

The soldiers ranged along the far wall in straightbacked chairs were quick to respond. Before anyone sitting at the table had time to react, they had Rubinstein's arms pinioned and were pulling him to his feet. The Vizier did not attempt to struggle. He permitted himself to be pulled and shoved toward the door without resisting, his face closed and a sere dignity wrapping him like a cloak.

Ismail grinned hugely, his teeth like a mouthful of dice. "We can put him in a cage till we think of a *really* funny way to execute him," he said. "If that's all right with you, your Majesty."

Bobo clapped his hands happily. "Yes, Auntie, put him in a cage!"

The soldiers dragged Rubinstein through the door. One of the eunuch palanquin bearers waiting in the anteroom snatched the elaborate turban from his head and booted him along with a kick.

Ismail turned and noticed the Minister of the Exchequer sitting paralyzed, trembling like a mesmerized rabbit.

"As for this one," Ismail said, "we can do him right now if you like."

Bobo nodded in assent. Ismail heaved himself ponderously out of his chair and waddled around behind the Minister of the Exchequer, the silken bowstring stretched between his hands.

The doors of the Hall of Ministers burst open and Hamid-Jones heard shouts and laughter from within. A moment later two soldiers emerged, dragging between them a disheveled creature who had been stripped to his underdrawers.

The soldiers on the steps began immediately to clear a path through the crowd, using the butts of their guns freely. People boiled out of the building after the untidy little spectacle, jeering and hooting at the unfortunate figure in the soldiers' grip—one or two of the more daring of them darting close enough to administer a kick or a blow. By their brocaded finery, Hamid-Jones recognized the taunters as the Chamberlain's octet of eunuch bearers.

It took him another moment or two to recognize the half-naked person being dragged along by the soldiers. It was someone bald and scrawny, resembling a plucked chicken with the bruises and discolorations that were already covering him. Dazed by the blows he had received, he had his head lowered.

Then Hamid-Jones saw one grinning eunuch displaying the Vizier's torn robes to the crowd. Another eunuch, prancing and strutting, wore the Vizier's distinctive conical turban atop his own head.

To Hamid-Jones it was like a punch in the stomach. It drove the breath right out of him. Rubinstein found the strength to raise his head just then, and it seemed to Hamid-Jones that the wizened face with its raisin eyes was staring directly at him.

He started forward without thinking, but the pressure of the crowd held him like a fly in honey. Perhaps it was fortunate that he wasn't able to make any headway, because one of Rubinstein's uniformed aides tried to approach the Vizier and was brained for his trouble.

"By Allah, I'm getting out of here," the man next to him said, and melted away into the crowd.

Others were doing the same. The great square began to bleed people around its edges as the more prudent among them slipped unobtrusively away from the focus of trouble.

But others in the crowd stayed to see the fun. Whispers had begun to spread through the crowd, and Hamid-Jones heard catcalls and cries of derision. A man standing near one of the animal cages scooped up a handful of muck and flung it at Rubinstein. It caught him on the bare shoulder, but he appeared not to notice. If Hamid-Jones had been able to reach the man, he would have struck him, but the crowd around the impromptu zoo was being compressed by the advance of the soldiers who were clearing a path for Rubinstein's captors, and the jam of people there was too thick.

A soldier shot out the lock of the monkey cage and ripped the door open. The monkeys, little green-furred things, swarmed out of the cage and escaped into the crowd. Bred for Earth gravity, they bounced off heads and shoulders in twenty and thirty foot swoops, too quick to get caught. A fat Earthman who looked as if he might be the proprietor of the traveling circus, darted about impotently, wringing his hands and shouting curses at the soldiers. The crowd found it all tremendously amusing, and some of the jeers that had been directed at Rubinstein turned into good-natured ridicule of the fat man.

Hamid-Jones found himself being pushed further back. The soldiers shoved Rubinstein roughly into the cage and slammed the door shut. Somebody produced a chain and padlock, probably from one of the other cages, and wrapped it around the door frame to lock Rubinstein in.

The cage was too small for Rubinstein to stand upright in. He sank to the floor, amidst straw and monkey droppings. The cage looked too small for him to stretch out full length in, either. There was a trough of dirty water and a tray of some kind of feeding pellets. A soldier rammed the butt of his gun through the bars to overturn the water trough and scatter the pellets. The crowd roared its approval. A clod of animal excrement taken from another cage by some foolhardy person struck Rubinstein on the side of the head. Hamid-Jones turned away, sickened.

"They should let him have water," a man near Hamid-Jones said disapprovingly.

Hamid-Jones half turned to give him a grimace of gratitude.

The man had a righteous, self-satisfied expression on a broad, well-fed face. "Otherwise," he said, "he might not live long enough to be executed."

Hamid-Jones struck him squarely in the face. The smug one went down, squealing like a pig and bleeding. Nobody paid much attention in a crowd that was beginning to churn with little acts of violence. The soldiers had pulled the wagon with the monkey cage a little forward to give it a place of prominence and were keeping people from getting too close to it.

Over on the steps of the Hall of Ministers, other soldiers made short work of Rubinstein's aides. They flung them to the ground one by one and riddled them with bullets where they lay, so as not to damage the intricate facade of the building. One body, impelled by the force of the fusillade, rolled halfway down the steps before coming to a stop. It was nothing but a tattered rag doll by then, but Hamid-Jones was able to identify it as Mashur, the sober young man who had been his seatmate on the dais at the ill-fated postoperative *majlis*.

More people began edging away at this new instance of violence. Once gunfire began, one never knew when it might stop. The crowd became thinner, leaving what would become a mob.

Hamid-Jones, with a last heart-wringing glance at the slight figure huddled in the monkey cage, slipped away before some patriotic bystander could recognize him as one of the Vizier's men.

"Get in quickly, master, before anyone sees you!" Aziz gasped, pulling him inside and closing the door behind him.

Hamid-Jones swayed, exhausted and ravenous. It had taken him more than seven hours to walk home through the mobs that were filling the streets. Public transportation had come to a halt, and the tricabs had disappeared, their drivers unwilling to venture out in the turmoil.

"You shouldn't have come home, master," Aziz blabbered on. "You took a terrible chance."

His eyes darted nervously toward the window, and Hamid-Jones saw that he had the shade drawn and the heavy curtains pulled over, though it was still light outside. A small table lamp had been placed on the floor to provide a feeble illumination.

"Has anyone been here to . . . to ask for me?" Hamid-Jones said.

"No—but it's only a matter of time. They're mopping up the Vizier's family and close associates—he has a brother and some nephews in Tharsis City. The mob's been given leave to plunder their properties. They're carrying off loot by the cartload: furniture, everything—even the plumbing. The Chamberlain's own deputies are stripping the Vizier's apartments in the Palace and carrying everything off to the Chamberlain's palace. They say there's a fortune in jewels and antiques. The whole staff, down to the kitchen help, has been arrested."

"What are they saying?"

"There's not much over the holovid. Just that the Vizier's been charged with treason. They haven't gotten an official statement out yet. But I've been out in the streets. Every story you can think of is going around."

"I can imagine," Hamid-Jones said with a grimace.

"They'll start with the Vizier's official staff. No one will think about you yet, if you're lucky. But eventually they'll get around to everybody who ever sent the Vizier so much as an *Iid al-Fitr* card. You can't stay here."

Hamid-Jones followed Aziz's glance to the bed. Two suitcases in the process of being packed lay there.

"Yes, I'm getting out, too. It's not going to be healthy here," Aziz said.

"You could get yourself off the hook by turning me in," Hamid-Jones suggested.

"Master, what do you take me for?" Aziz said, looking shocked. "I may be a miserable worm and—" He glanced ruefully at his regrown right hand, slightly larger and paler than the other one. "—maybe I haven't always followed the path of righteousness, but even the most miserable sneakthief and fingersmith can have his professional ethics. Give me credit for a little loyalty, at least!"

"I'm sorry," Hamid-Jones mumbled, abashed.

"I've found a hiding place for you. It may not offer all the comforts you're accustomed to, but it will keep you out of sight till I can buy you a false identity and get you off the planet."

Startled, Hamid-Jones said, "How are you going to manage that?"

Aziz gave him a snaggletoothed smile. "Trust me, master. I've stolen enough from you to pay for a ticket."

CHAPTER 13

The din through the window never stopped. It was compounded of haggling voices from the stalls below, family quarrels through other open windows, vendors' cries, the unending rumble of heavy traffic trundling toward the Bab al-Dahub, the periodic thunk of the great airlock itself. Background to it all was the ceaseless rattle and roar of the old-fashioned air ducts that served the quarter.

Hamid-Jones walked over to the window to shut it but changed his mind. The shabby little room was stifling enough; none of the miserable holes in this cheap warren carved into the rock face had its own air supply but depended on the public ventilation from above.

He stuck his head out the window, disregarding Aziz's advice to keep out of sight. He was too high up to be recognized easily from below, and the windows on the opposite side of the chasm were too far away, across a clogged river of commercial traffic, unless there were a dedicated bounty hunter with a telescope somewhere out there.

The whiff that assailed his nostrils went with the noise—uncollected garbage, industrial fumes, the acrid tang of burnt insulation from electric vehicle motors, the sour reek of a couple of centuries' worth of human sweat that had soaked into the very pores of the rock.

He couldn't complain. This grubby thieves' den that Aziz had found for him had kept him alive for a week. The bloodbath unleashed by the Chamberlain was still in full swing, from the hints he could gather from the censored holovid infocasts. The dungeons of the palace were full of Rubinstein's former allies, deputies, hangers-on, and relatives. The holding cells were overflowing; the overworked executioners were trying to catch up with the backlog.

"Better lie low till the first frenzy spends itself," Aziz had advised him. "Then you can chance your move." He had laughed unconvincingly. "Who knows, by then they may have forgotten about you."

Down below, Hamid-Jones picked out the white dot of a turban threading its way through the teeming crowds on the sidewalks. The ferretlike darting progress was distinctive. The turban paused, winked out to be replaced by the blink of a sallow speck of a face, then its owner continued his zigzag course toward Hamid-Jones's hideaway without looking up again.

Guiltily, Hamid-Jones drew back from the window and sat down on his cot to wait. It was another fifteen minutes before he heard a mouselike scratching at the door. He got up to open it, and Aziz slipped quickly in, puffing from the climb.

"You should stay away from the window," Aziz reprimanded him. "It's not as if the view were worth seeing."

"You worry too much."

"Your passport's not ready yet. You should have it in a few days. It's going to be a work of art—holo rotatable. It'll even have a valid serial number."

"What about the tickets?"

"I've got a fish lined up who'll let us use his credit card—too bad we can't use cash, but it would attract attention. It'll have to be a last-minute deal. I've also hired a reliable goon who'll baby-sit him to keep him from jumping the gun on reporting the card stolen. It'll cost us twice his credit limit, cash in advance."

"*Harami!*" Hamid-Jones spat.

"Be fair, master. The poor simp's in for it if they ever trace the ticket to you. It wouldn't matter if he produced witnesses to swear that the card was taken from him at gunpoint at high noon. Anyway, it's a bargain. I can bleed the card for *three* times its credit limit before we take off."

"We?"

Aziz put on a pious expression. "You don't think I'd desert you, master? Anyway, things are getting hot for me, too."

"Where are *we* going?"

Aziz grinned happily. "The Jovian Federation."

"*That* hellhole?"

"Luna has an extradition treaty with Mars, master. Things ought to quiet down in about a month. By that time it will be the season of the hajj. We can lose ourselves in the stream of pilgrims from all over the Solar system stopping off at Luna. I'll have a Jovian passport for you by then—good enough to get by. Immigration officials don't even try to cope with all the hajjis anyway. Then, on to the Venusian habitat. They're always in need of cloning technicians, and they don't ask a lot of questions.''

''Why not down to Earth?''

''That's all right for you, master, but think of my poor Mars bones. I'd be in cardiovascular cloning therapy and exercise programs for a year before I could walk around normally.''

''Well, *ya* Aziz, you seem to have pretty well decided the course of my life for me,'' Hamid-Jones said dryly.

''I do my best, master,'' Aziz said with restrained pride.

''All the same, *we* might decide to emigrate to Earth.''

''It's too early to worry about it—first we have to get off Mars. You're not technically a fugitive, as far as I could discover, but I wouldn't give a plugged piaster for your chances if you were caught.''

''What's happening out there? The infocasts don't give a great deal of information, and thanks to your unreasonable jitters I haven't dared leave this rathole to hear the coffeehouse gossip. I know that Bo— the Emir is making a lot of new government appointments, and that the announced executions have already passed the thousand mark. They've sautéed the Vizier's staff, but I gather that the Vizier himself is still alive and on display in his cage—just barely alive.'' Hamid-Jones felt his eyes sting and he blinked the hot tears away. ''I gather the Chamberlain's saving him for last. He can't bear to part with his old enemy yet.''

He remembered the unplugging of the Emir's head and prayed that the final end for Rubinstein, when it came, would come as swiftly.

''That wicked eunuch is turning things upside down,'' Aziz said with sudden venom. ''He's installed his fawning crew in every government department at every level—so much so that he's running out of manpower, if that's the expression. But there's no shortage of new volunteers for the gelding knife to replenish the ranks. Pickings are fat for Ismail's favorites—they're siphoning off billions. By the time they finish filling the Chamberlain's coffers, Mars will be plucked clean. But they're stupid. They'll kill the goose who lays the golden egg. They're squeezing the starships that dock at Phobos for so much *zakat* that Mars is losing the business to Luna.''

''Things can't be falling apart that quickly, surely!''

''Master, those eunuchs are draining the treasury to keep the Emir distracted! The latest extravaganza is a water pageant in Hellas! They're planning to lift a blue whale from Earth! It probably won't even get here alive!''

Hamid-Jones shook his head. ''What's happening at the Royal Stables?''

''There's a fat eunuch in charge. The laboratories have been put to work producing genetic novelties for the Emir—using human genetic material, which isn't allowed by the Koran. Two-headed dwarfs, a mule with a lady's head and a peacock's tail, a winged elephant that won't be able to fly. They've given your old title to that pink-faced toady, Rashid. He struts around acting important.''

Hamid-Jones was impressed. ''How did you manage to learn so much? You didn't go there?''

''Master, I'm not a fool. I made discreet inquiries.''

''The truth, *ya* Aziz.''

Aziz grew a little sulky. ''I bribed a bottle washer. He frequents a certain disreputable booth in the *suq* that I know of. Please don't ask me his name.''

''What are they saying about me there?''

''That Rashid is telling everybody that you're wanted for questioning for complicity in Rubinstein's plot against the Emir, but that *he* thinks you're innocent till it's proven otherwise.''

''Where are you staying?''

''Oh, here and there. Don't worry about me, master. Your rooms in the Street of the Well aren't being watched, by the way. They gave up on that after the first few days. But that thief of a landlord promised to notify the *shurtayeen* if you show up again. The other lodgers are no friends of yours, either.''

''You didn't . . .''

''Of course not, master. I fell into conversation with that little sneak of a servant, Saleh, while he was doing the marketing. I collected your mail, though.''

''You what?''

Aziz was pleased with himself. ''There was no risk, master. I was able to arrange a tap from outside the house.'' He held up a microwafer to show Hamid-Jones.

''Aziz, you're a wonder!'' Hamid-Jones said with heartfelt sincerity.

"Thank you, master." He frowned. "I wish there were some way to get at your belongings. They've been sequestered. I could sell that fancy hunting gear of yours for a good price. We could use the money."

"Don't even think about it."

"That rascally landlord of yours hasn't dared to put his hands on your things yet. He's waiting to see which way the wind blows. It's all still locked safely in your rooms. Nobody's willing to rent the place—they're still afraid of midnight visits from the *shurtayeen*. Even the rug merchant, Najib, who gave up the rooms to you, won't move back, though the landlord's offered them to him at half-rent."

"I said forget it."

Hamid-Jones took the microwafer from Aziz and was about to insert it in the secondhand terminal that was one of the cell's few articles of furnishings when Aziz grabbed him by the wrist to stop him.

"Master, master, you have much to learn," he chided. He unhooked the terminal from its socket and produced a self-contained power supply in the form of a flat plastic case the size of his palm. "There," he said, plugging it in. "Now no one can read over your shoulder."

"Aren't you being a little ridiculous?"

"Places like this live off the information they can tap from their tenants. You'd be surprised at what goes on in these rooms."

Hamid-Jones punched his mail up on the screen and watched it scroll. There were bills, second notices, threats to cut off services, junk advertisements. Three notes of increasing severity from the Department of Rectitude ordering him to appear at the nearest substation. A letter from the Royal Stables, stamped with Rashid's signature, requesting him to turn in all security keys and other property of the stables. And then a blank, requiring printout.

"Is there any paper in this thing?" he asked. His new landlord was short on amenities, including towels, blankets, and toilet paper. But Aziz had come prepared. He pulled a small pad of holosheets from an inside pocket and loaded the printer.

There was a click and a whir, and a printout emerged from the machine. The odor of cheap perfume hung in the air.

"An olifax," Aziz sniffed. "It's only some advertisement. I'll throw it away for you." He tried to take it from Hamid-Jones, but Hamid-Jones hung on.

"It's from Lalla!" he cried.

"Be careful, master! It's some trick!"

"She still cares for me!" Hamid-Jones exclaimed.

Aziz wrinkled his nose. "Smell that fake scent, master? Whatever you might say of the woman, she has expensive tastes. It's someone trying to flush you out."

"Don't be a fool! Of course it smells cheap. What can you expect of a computer-generated aroma? This is only a cheap machine. It couldn't handle the input, that's all. Look, the script is smudged, too."

"It's a trick," Aziz said stubbornly. "The woman doesn't want anything to do with someone in your shoes."

But Hamid-Jones was already eagerly scanning the missive. "She wants a rendezvous tonight. Thank Allah you picked up the mail today—it's been lying around for three days. She'll leave the delivery *bab* unlocked, and the servants will be out of the way."

"Master, this is madness!"

"I'm not leaving Mars without saying good-bye to her," Hamid-Jones said gruffly. "Don't worry, I'll be careful."

Aziz struck his scrawny chest with his cloned right hand. "Truly it's said that a feckless master is the servant's curse!" he cried in anguish. "Master, what good are all my efforts to pluck you from the frying pan when you undo all my work?"

"That's enough!" Hamid-Jones said sharply. Then, more softly, "Do you have any money on you? I'll have to pick up some gift at the *suq*."

The Street of the Peacock was emptier than usual, even for this late hour. People liked to stay at home during the bloodbath. Hamid-Jones got halfway down the block without attracting the attention of a night patrol, then slipped down a side alley in the vicinity of the Clonemaster's villa.

A cat yowled, almost underfoot, and streaked away. The humped shapes of refuse bins loomed in the darkness, lining the blank walls of the narrow passageway. There was furtive movement: a hungry bum trying the seal lock of one of the bins. The pickings were rich in neighborhoods like this, but it meant a three to five year loss of a right hand if caught. Hamid-Jones avoided looking at the bum, and the bum, after a skittish glance, avoided looking at him.

He reached the end of the alley and took a cautious peep around the corner before venturing further. A feeble phosphorescence shone from a mirror high above, reflecting the Martian night. The delivery lane was empty, and all the villa walls in the immediate vicinity were reassuringly dark.

The rear of the Clonemaster's house was blind except for a single barred slit above. The service door was set deeply within a shadowed arch. Hamid-Jones made for it, keeping close to the wall.

He pushed experimentally, and the heavy door was unlatched, just as Lalla had said it would be.

He stepped into a cool darkness. There was a stone floor underfoot and the bulky forms of kitchen equipment around him. He saw the dim outline of a door across the room and groped his way toward it. He stumbled into something, and there was a metallic clatter. The noise stopped him cold for a long moment of holding his breath and straining his ears, but there was no sound of anything stirring in the house. He made it to the doorway without further incident.

The big hall was empty, the stairs unguarded. Hamid-Jones picked his way through the semidarkness with growing confidence. His nerve almost failed him when he reached the harem entrance itself, but he told himself that it was only a set of rooms like any other. He took the fateful step through the archway and found himself in a wide marble corridor. A large common room opened at the left, and a row of alcoves, each with an inset door, branched off to the right. Lalla, the cherished daughter of the household, had her own apartment farther down the corridor, away from the common run of concubines and slave girls. Her father would have wished to preserve her from his nocturnal comings and goings, and the reverse side was, of course, that Lalla had her own privacy, too.

Lalla had figured it all out. She had explained it to Hamid-Jones in the note in case he should lack courage.

He counted doorways and came to one padded in gold-tooled leather, like a Morocco-bound book. There could be no mistake. He turned a gilt handle, and the door opened easily. Inside was a small foyer, just big enough for two spindly gilt chairs and a small table with a vase of flowers on it. An inner door looked just as heavy and soundproof as the outer one. He pushed his way through into a dim sitting room filled with Lalla's jasmine perfume.

His heart in his throat, he opened the final door. The smell of jasmine was overpowering here. A night light cast a pink glow. An oval brass bed with a headboard like a pipe organ stood under a frilly canopy that formed a sort of open pavilion.

A high-pitched gurgling sound came from a small basket at the foot of the bed. The bedclothes stirred, and a figure draped in white muslin sat up. "Who's there?" a woman's voice said.

"It's me, my beloved, your Abdul," Hamid-Jones said.

A small tangle of fur launched itself from the basket straight at Hamid-Jones's ankle. Two sets of miniature teeth buried themselves in his boot, but fortunately did not penetrate the leather. Hamid-Jones limped across the room, dragging the little two-headed mini-Peke with him.

"*Ya* Abdul, I never expected to see you again!" Lalla exclaimed, stuffing her fingers in her mouth.

"There was no need to worry, Little Candy," he said, touched by her concern. "I've been quite safe."

"You shouldn't have come here," she said. He could tell that she was rigid with tension.

"How could I stay away?" He thought of the note of invitation she had risked sending him. "It is you who are the courageous one."

"Shhh, *ya* Abdul. Keep your voice down."

He took another step toward her, with the tiny animal still fastened to his ankle. It was growling hysterically, sounding like a water-filled fife. "Bijou, be still!" she hissed urgently. The bantam Cerberus redoubled its shrill noises. She reached over the side of the bed and plucked it from his leg. Hamid-Jones could hear the click of little teeth closing on empty air. Lalla retreated to the heaped pillows at the headboard, sheets pulled up, hugging the twin-headed creature to her bosom.

Hamid-Jones felt a sudden gnawing of frustration. He had come so close to his heart's desire—close enough to smell the shampoo in her hair—and now the ill-tempered little brute had become a buffer, putting more distance between them. He had hoped she might have put it back in its basket. But he told himself he was being unreasonable; Lalla was only trying to keep it quiet. And it did seem to be subsiding somewhat.

Still, he reminded himself, settling down gingerly in a toothpick-legged bedside chair, he had attained the unattainable; he was with the ravishing object of his desire in her boudoir, and she was unveiled. He basked in the sight of her plump lips, the darling pudgy baby cheeks, the noble fleshy nose, like a charming version of her father's. But she remembered her breeding just then. To Hamid-Jones's disappointment, she reached out with one chubby arm and fixed a light veil over her lower face, pulling the elastic band high over the bridge of her nose. He consoled himself with her luminous eyes, the lids darkened with kohl, and with what he could make out of her features behind the gauzy fabric.

He fumbled in the pocket of his cloak and took out the little present he had brought her. "It's only a pair of earrings," he apologized. "It's all I could get at short notice at the *suq* in . . . near where I'm staying. I didn't dare go to any of the well-known shops. But they've been fashioned as *hiriz*—turquoise set in silver—so at least they ought to be good against the evil eye."

His little attempt at levity fell flat. Lalla took the small unwrapped box as if it were burning her fingertips and, with only the most cursory glance at its contents, set it down on a dressing table whose top was covered with a cascade of other jewelry.

"I know I have no right to ask anything of you," he rushed on, "with my . . . my prospects as they are. I'm leaving Mars. But . . . but things may change. There could even be a new Chamberlain one day. Who can know Allah's plans for us? And if that day comes, I'll be back. *Ya* Lalla . . . Little Sugarplum . . . could you wait for me just a little while?"

She drew back at his vehemence. "*Ya* Abdul, I can't talk about it now. You must go."

"I know you must care for me! Otherwise—"

"*Ya* Abdul, listen to me. There's something you must know."

". . . otherwise you would not have sent me that note."

"That was a foolish impulse, tossing that note to you through the window that day, *ya* Abdul. Things have changed—"

"No, not that first note. The note that—"

"Stop babbling and listen to me. I'm marrying Thamir. You must leave immediately. If the eunuchs find us together—"

"Thamir!" His face darkened with anger. "That cheap mobster! That codfish aristocrat! That—"

"Don't trifle with him anymore, *ya* Abdul. He's very angry with you."

"Angry with *me*?" he choked. "Him with his middle-of-the-night hirelings? He's nothing but an overpriced sneak!"

"He's going to be a very important man." Her eyes above the flimsy veil glowed. "He's doing business with the Palace now—contracting for the Emir's entertainments. He has influence with the Chamberlain . . ."

"Listen to me, Lalla," Hamid-Jones pleaded. "Don't get

mixed up with him. There are things you don't know. He's riding for a fall. Things can't go on as they are at the Palace . . .''

Lalla began weeping. "Why must you spoil things for me? You've got to leave before Thamir finds out you were here again." She paused and seemed to be listening for something. A moment later there was a click of a door and the shuffle of slippered feet in the room. And then, to Hamid-Jones's horror, Lalla sat bolt upright and screamed, "Oh! What's that! There's a man in my room! Help!"

Hamid-Jones whirled and saw Murad, the household's head eunuch, advancing with two more eunuchs behind him. Murad was dressed in his daytime mauve silks and towering corkscrew turban as if he hadn't gone to bed at all that night. He held his wicked little sickle-shaped castrating knife in his hand, and there was a nasty smile on his mud-colored face.

Lalla sobbed, "He must just have gotten in somehow. I was asleep."

Hamid-Jones backed away from the advancing trio. "Let's not be hasty, Murad," he said. "You know me. I've often been a guest in this house."

Murad made a swipe with the knife. Hamid-Jones leapt backward and found his further progress halted by the window grille pressing against his shoulderblades. The two assistant eunuchs moved to pinion his arms, and Murad prepared to lunge again with the knife.

Hamid-Jones scrabbled desperately at the window grille, and to his utter astonishment the whole thing came loose in his hands. There had been some kind of hanky-panky going on with the window some time in the recent past. He swung the heavy grille around and knocked one of the assistant eunuchs off his feet. There was a surprised squeal from the creature, and then Murad's knife was sliding past his ribs; Hamid-Jones's momentum and the sidewise profile he had presented had saved him. He dropped the grille on Murad's slipper-clad toes and heard a screech like a scalded cat. He grabbed Murad's wrist and kneed him in the groin before he remembered that there was nothing there to knee, but Murad, caught by surprise, dropped the knife anyway. Hamid-Jones grabbed the corkscrew turban with both hands and jammed it down on Murad's bulging neck. The knotted end caught like a noose around Murad's neck, and Hamid-Jones, without stopping to think, jumped out the window with the loose end of the turban in his convulsively closed hands. He plunged downward, while in the room above him the turban unwound like a ball of yarn and Murad spun like a top. The assistant eunuchs, quicker-thinking than Murad deserved, grasped frantically at the unraveling turban to keep Murad from being strangled when the material ran out, and as it slipped through their sweaty fingers, Hamid-Jones felt his fall being slowed.

He hit the pavement with his speed checked sufficiently for only a minor jolt, scrambled to his feet, and ran down the alley. Up above all was confusion as Murad and his two helpers got themselves untangled. To their shrill chittering was added the yelps of Bijou and the belated screams of Lalla. Squares of light began to go on in the dark walls of the adjoining villas, but by that time Hamid-Jones was around the corner and pounding down the alley.

The bum he had seen there earlier was long gone. Hamid-Jones waited expectantly for the beam of a police spotlight and a command to halt, but he was lucky. He emerged from the alley mouth at a walking pace, adjusting his cloak, and by incredible good fortune a tricab was at the curb, discharging two drunken gentlemen in expensive clothes. Hamid-Jones made himself wait, smiling, while one of them tipsily paid the driver off, then, feigning a nonchalance that he did not feel, he climbed onto the cab's passenger bench and lowered the bubble.

"Where to, *sidi*?" the driver asked, after sizing him up from his saddle and evidently deciding that the well-cut cloak and the dressy headcloth that Hamid-Jones had worn for his nocturnal call were satisfactory emblems of his right to be in the Street of the Peacock at this hour.

Hamid-Jones did not know how soon it would be before a public alarm would be out for him. He gave the only address he could think of where he might still be safe.

"Head toward the boulevard of the Bab," he said. "I'll direct you from there."

Traffic was relatively light on the boulevard at this hour—it wouldn't pick up again till the dawn rush—but the sidewalks and twisting alleys that gave off them were clogged with night-dwellers; every day was Ramadan for the denizens of this slum area.

"Where do I go from here?" the driver asked.

"Just keep going," Hamid-Jones said. "I'll tell you when to stop."

The cab proceeded at a crawl, working upstream against the

prevailing traffic. An urchin ran alongside with a rag, trying to wipe the bubble, but the driver ignored his cries of *"Bak-sheesh!"* and surged forward to leave him behind. *"Ya kan-zeer!"* the urchin yelled, shaking a grimy fist. "Your grandmother does it with dogs!"

The ground-level stalls lining the artificial canyon were awash with a dingy yellow light. Shabby people haggled over shoddy merchandise—some of it undoubtedly hot—or loitered outside the entrance of all-night coffeehouses, looking for action. A circle of furtive men huddled around some unseen focus of interest; money or something else was being passed from hand to hand. A swarm of small children buzzed through the throng; people in their wake felt for their purses. Above, unveiled women hung out of windows hacked in the rock and called out endearments to passersby.

As the tricab approached the leaning rookery where he dwelt, some instinct told Hamid-Jones not to tell the driver to slow down. There seemed to be a lot of idlers milling around the entrance, but keeping their distance. Then he saw the police cruiser pulled up on the sidewalk, a big armored floater with chain-mail skirts. Two large *shurtayeen* in patrolmen's robes bounded up to the stoop and into the building, guns drawn, as he watched. Around the entrance, another pair of Rectitude cops was keeping the crowd at bay with electric prods. One of them was absentmindedly kicking a shock victim who was lying, twitching, on the ground. The other had a large fist wrapped around the collar of a scurvy little fellow in work clothes, and was half lifting him off the ground.

The driver kept going, not wanting to get stuck in the mess, and as the tricab parted the crowd before it, Hamid-Jones got a closer look at the fellow in the cop's grip—and was immediately startled out of his wits.

It was Aziz.

The little man had shaved off his scraggly fringe of beard, and was dressed like a common laborer, but there was no mistake.

At the same moment, Aziz's eyes lit on Hamid-Jones through the bubble, and then rolled heavenward in some kind of signal or warning before the cop started shaking him like a terrier with a rat.

Hamid-Jones slumped in his seat, keeping his head down. Then the driver found a clear lane ahead and put on a burst of speed to get away from the trouble.

"Best not to get mixed up in that sort of thing," the driver remarked. "They pull in everybody who looks cross-eyed at them." He twisted around on his saddle. "You want to get out somewhere along here?"

"No," Hamid-Jones said.

He thought hard. There would be no getting off Mars now, not with Aziz in the hands of the *shurtayeen*. He could not go back to his room. If he stayed in Tharsis, it would be only a matter of time before he was picked up—he did not have Aziz's raffish talents for finding safe cover. He could think of only one answer.

"Take me to the Street of the Well," he said.

The driver sighed. "Make up your mind, *sidi*," he said. He spoke to his dispatcher through his handlebar mike, and turned off at the next side tunnel.

Ibrahim had left the gate unlocked. Hamid-Jones had hardly dared to imagine such luck! The old porter sometimes eased the strain on his creaky legs by leaving the gate ajar in the early evening, when the tenants trickled home, but he almost always remembered to lock it up again for the night.

He eased the gate carefully shut behind him and crept past the darkened window of the porter's lodge. All the lights in the building were out. He crossed the courtyard as silently as possible and by force of habit almost headed for the outside steps to his old room. He stopped himself with a bitter smile. He hadn't enjoyed his luxurious new quarters for very long, and now this would be the last time he'd see them.

He got out his key and stopped with a frown. The lock was broken. Somebody or other hadn't wasted time sniffing around after his fall from grace. It wouldn't have been the landlord; he had his own key. Perhaps it had simply been the police; they preferred to kick doors in rather than ask someone to unlock them.

But inside, he saw no signs of either a police search or a burglary. The furniture, the lamps, the small objects were more or less in the position in which he'd left them. Perhaps ibn Zayd had cleaned up the mess.

Glass crunched underfoot as he crossed the threshhold to his bedroom. He turned his wrist communicator to the prayer channel on "bright" with the sound off for the glow it gave him, and looked around. A lamp had been knocked over and the debris not swept up; ibn Zayd had not been all that thorough in his cleanup. Bearing the glow before him on his upraised wrist, he went to the closets. As far as he could see, nothing had been stolen; the expensive clothes and the custom hunting gear that Aziz had bought for him seemed undisturbed.

He made a parcel out of his pressure suit, heatcloak, respirator and two compact air tanks whose gauges showed them to be full. They were good for about twelve hours, but he'd only need them while on the move; the little portable air plant could pack up enough ambient oxygen to recharge them in about a six hour stop. He pocketed the inflatable walktent and the smartpistol, and after a moment's reflection added the sports Kalashnikov and a couple of magazines. It was a lot to carry, even in Martian gravity, but rolled up in a blanket and tied with a cord from the drapes, it made a bundle that perhaps wouldn't attract any particular attention.

He hefted it to the vertical to slip a loop of cord over his shoulder, and that was what saved his life. A small lead weight came whizzing around it, and as the wire to which the weight was attached wrapped itself around the bundle instead of around his neck, the weight rapped him painfully on the side of the head.

The hand that had been poised to catch the weight missed and scrabbled for it, and Hamid-Jones instinctively turned and blundered into the man behind him. Both of them went over in a tangle of arms and legs. The dark figure drew a knife from its sleeve, but the advantage of surprise was gone, and Hamid-Jones got a clamp on the wrist and started hammering the knife hand against the floor.

The figure, slippery as an eel, drew a second knife out of its trouser leg and slashed at Hamid-Jones with it. If it had been an edged weapon, that would have been the end of him, but it was a stiletto, meant for stabbing with like an icepick, and its point did no worse than to give Hamid-Jones a nasty scrape as it raked along his ribs.

He flung the Assassin from him like a hot potato. To Hamid-Jones, with his Earth-bred muscles, it was the equivalent of heaving a fifty-pound sack, and with the violence of fear lending impetus, his adversary went sailing through the air and hit the wall with a thud.

Both of them scrambled to their feet and faced each other, crouching. Though the Assassin was dazed, his training must have been superb, and his sequence of moves automatic. The next thing he did was to draw a small chain scimitar from a scabbard at his waist. The blade was an elongated oval, about a foot and a half long from haft to sprocket. He thumbed a switch and it started to buzz.

Hamid-Jones backed away. It wouldn't matter what part of the polycrystalline cutting edge touched him. The two counter-rotating belts, each razor-thin, could slice through stone, metal or bone with equal ease, and without kicking back in the operator's hand, even if he thrust with the end sprocket.

"This really isn't necessary," Hamid-Jones said, dismayed at the unworthy tremor in his voice. "The contract's pretty well moot now."

"Your death is paid for," the other said.

He waved the chain scimitar. Hamid-Jones ducked behind an overstuffed chair. As the Assassin advanced, he picked up the chair and threw it. The blade bit deep and a snowstorm of shred-ded stuffing exploded in the air. The composite chains grated on the metal and wood of the frame and the two halves of the chair fell apart. But the impact had knocked the Assassin back, and he barely missed severing his own foot as the whirring blade buried itself in the floor.

The Assassin pulled it free and raised it again. He was mad now. "You devil!" he growled, and prepared to lunge.

Hamid-Jones retreated and was stopped as the backs of his knees hit the edge of his bed. He dropped to the floor and rolled under the bed and out the other side. He leapt to his feet as the squealing blade cut his bed in half. While the Assassin tried to extricate the blade—which he had unintentionally twisted flat side down so that it was momentarily pinned under the wreckage of the bedframe—Hamid-Jones looked around wildly for some-thing else to throw.

At that moment there was the crash outside of a gate violently flung wide, and the bedroom windows lit up with blue flashing light.

"*Eftah, eftah*, open up!" an authoritative voice shouted, and there was a loud hammering on the landlord's door.

The Assassin dropped his motorized blade. "*Uzu billah!*" he swore, and touched forehead, shoulder, and chest in the sign of the Crescent. Like a flowing shadow, he oozed out the bedroom door toward the rear of the apartment.

Hamid-Jones did not pause to dither. He picked up his bundle of equipment and followed the Assassin toward the private courtyard in back. Out front, the police were wasting time by continuing to try to rouse ibn Zayd instead of coming directly to Hamid-Jones's door. Hamid-Jones reached his private court-yard just as the hammering stopped. The Assassin was nowhere in sight. Hamid-Jones tossed his bundle over the wall, made a fifteen-foot leap that no native-born Martian could have managed without a running start, and floated to the ground on the opposite side. He retrieved his bundle and high-tailed it down the alley, hoping that the *shurtayeen* had not posted a backup in the rear.

Fifteen minutes later he was sitting in a tube car full of night laborers and homeward-bound late carousers, the long bundle propped between his knees and his face buried in the collar of his cloak as if he were dozing. He got off at the Old Palace quarter with a mob of workmen and domestics from the night shift, and hung back until the last of them disappeared into the sprawling structure. Then, keeping an eye out for police and making wide detours around the guardhouse that jutted from the walls every quarter mile or so, he made his way to the Royal Stables annex.

He knew from experience that there would be only one dozing sentry on duty at this hour—the now almost disused annex rated low priority—and that the sentry box was on the side away from the horse barns. No one had ever been foolish enough to attempt to steal one of the Emir's horses: the penalties could not have been imagined by a Dante. And besides, it was only rarely that the more valuable animals were quartered here in the city.

He found the small, unguarded side door that he had used so often in the past—first in the company of the Clonemaster, and then, in his new eminence, alone—and dug into his pocket for the holographic passkey that he still illegally retained.

For one anxious moment he thought that the lock had been changed; then he realized that he had inserted the card the wrong way. He reversed it, heard bolts slide back, and let himself inside.

The entrance was through the tack room. The walls were hung with dusty saddles, bridles, feeding bags, electric horse blankets, goggle-eyed breathing masks. A rack held equine air tanks, with gauges reading variously from almost empty to almost full. The animals stabled here, unless they were ill or recovering from veterinary surgery, were exercised daily in the desert.

He passed through to the large barnlike structure that housed the stalls. Most were empty, but a few dozen horses and a hand-ful of camels were presently stabled here.

Animals whinnied at him from the gloom, unsettled by the

disturbance in their routine. He moved quietly down the first aisle of box stalls and stopped at the last one. A priceless oriental rug was spread on the floor in front of it; the hooves of al-Janah, the Winged One, could not be allowed to touch concrete like the hooves of ordinary horses while the straw in his stall was being changed. The Emir had doted on him, and with good reason.

Luck was still with Hamid-Jones. The Winged One was still here. With the Emir gone and the as-yet unhorsey Bobo taking his place, there was nobody around to care whether or not the project to clone an al-Janah variant went forward or not. Certainly Ismail had no interest in such things. It would be months—if ever—before the monstrous inventory that must be going on at this moment would get around to cataloguing a single horse in the Royal Stables annex, or before anyone uncovered the data on the cloning project.

He approached the great Marshorse from the front, speaking softly and soothingly all the while. "It's all right, boy, it's Abdul. You know me, don't you? We're going for a little ride."

High above his head there was an answering snort, and the dinnerplate hooves pawed the floor of the stall. The long neck descended and al-Janah nuzzled Hamid-Jones's shoulder wetly. He was a beauty, with the dished face and convex forehead of his *al-khamsa* ancestry—one of the five original Arabian strains that could be traced back to the time of Mohammed. Despite his spidery legs, the enormous barrel chest with its enhanced lungs, and the other genetic modifications, he was still, certifiably, *al-khamsa*.

He balked a little at the bridle but finally cooperated in letting it be put on. Hamid-Jones led him past the other stalls toward the tack room. His bundle was still leaning next to the door where he'd left it. He hitched the towering beast to a snubpost while he got a saddle and breathing gear, then mounted a tall stepladder to cinch the girth in place and buckle on the air tanks. Al-Janah whinnied with pleasure when Hamid-Jones slid the air mask over his muzzle; he knew he was going to have a run in the desert.

Finally Hamid-Jones climbed into his own gear, leaving the cowl thrown back and the mask hanging round his neck. He thrust the smartpistol inside his heatcloak and stowed the folded Kalashnikov and other equipment in the saddlebags.

He was just about to mount the Winged One, when a footstep

grated on concrete. He turned awkwardly and saw Yezid the Prod standing no more than a dozen feet from him.

"Stupid," Yezid said. "The police came by to ask me to open up the laboratory for them. They were checking every place you might have gone. After they left, I thought of the horse barn."

Hamid-Jones had difficulty swallowing. "There's a general alarm out for me, then?"

Yezid stepped forward, swinging his knout. He made a bulky figure in the dim light. The stiff leather of the metal-studded vest that enwrapped his thick torso might have been the carapace of some gigantic beetle. His lips parted in a jagged grin.

"Somebody wants you very badly, *mawali* pig, but they don't much care what condition you're in when you're delivered."

Hamid-Jones drew his smartpistol. The knotted cords of the knout flicked out, and the smartpistol spun away.

Hamid-Jones had a moment of horrid clarity as Yezid raised the knout again. Even in the dim light he could see little bits of wire embedded in the knots. He knew what the wire could do to flesh; once he had seen a slave almost flayed to death in the laboratory courtyard. More than twenty lashes was a death sentence. Yezid had a reputation for measuring out the number of lashes in miserly fashion, determining who would die, who would be permanently maimed, and who would merely spend a week or two in hospital.

As Yezid swung, an angry bellow came from above. The spindly legs of the Marshorse lashed out and knocked Yezid sprawling. Like some tottery construction of struts and poles, the tall stallion spun around and settled in the light gravity, and began kicking with his rear hooves, hysterically nickering all the while.

Hamid-Jones grabbed the dangling reins and got the huge beast under control. He stood trembling, foam bubbling at his lips. "All right, boy, calm down," Hamid-Jones said, patting a bony knee. There could be only one reason why the Winged One had gone crazy at the sight of a lash, and Hamid-Jones's lip curled in contempt at the thought of the sort of person who would mistreat a fine animal like al-Janah.

He turned to the broken shape lying at his feet. Yezid let out a groan. Three of his four limbs were smashed, and it looked as if his ribs were caved in.

"Someone will find you in the morning, *ya* Bent-Stick," he said without pity. "It shouldn't be more than a couple of hours."

He kicked the knout into the shadows so that the sight of it wouldn't upset al-Janah and retrieved the smartpistol. The Mars-horse highstepped carefully past Yezid as Hamid-Jones led him out.

It was a tight squeeze through the side gate, but the Winged One flattened his ears and stretched out his long serpentine neck, and got through in a kneeling position. Using a folded knee as a ladder, Hamid-Jones inelegantly scrambled up over the withers, hauling himself hand over hand by the straps of the air tanks. He was a bad rider, but his recent experience hunting on horseback had improved his seat, and after he got himself settled in the saddle, al-Janah decided to accept him.

The streets were pretty well empty, and the few pedestrians who saw him didn't seem to find the sight of a man on horseback and in desert gear unusual; the neighborhood must have been used to seeing the exercise boys taking animals out at a more reasonable hour. When he got clear of the Old Palace quarter, Hamid-Jones kept to the back alleys; even if he was unlucky enough to be reported, a police car answering the call would not be able to give effective chase here.

The broad boulevard of the Bab was another story. He intersected it at a point as close as possible to the airlocks and was lucky enough to encounter some early animal traffic—desert dwellers returning to their oasis villages at the first predawn light. There were two or three ragged groups of them, traveling more or less together for mutual safety and support, but not intermingling. There were a few dozen camels—both the primitive four-legged model and the six-legged improved version that had been the product of a later generation of bioengineering—some donkeys in much-patched pressure suits, piled high with now-empty produce baskets, and a few sorry-looking Mars-horses carrying the village elite. Hamid-Jones fell in behind them, hoping he didn't look too out of place with his thoroughbred horse and his tailored survival togs.

He crowded closer in among them as they approached the tollbooths. Al-Janah attracted a few envious glances. But the gatekeepers didn't appear to be paying any special attention to him; they were city-bred hacks who wouldn't know a good horse if they saw one.

The toll collector at the animal gate yawned as he gave Hamid-Jones his change. It was the end of the shift, and he was tired. Hamid-Jones kept his face averted, fidgeting until the transaction was completed, then followed a string of scruffy pack camels to the airlock.

Something prodded him out of his hunched rigidity and made him glance cautiously around. A transit cop in zebra-striped robes was approaching the tollbooth on foot, a holoslate in his hand. He was still talking into the portable phone into which the holoslate's modem was plugged. The toll collector peered at the holoslate, then craned his neck in the direction of the knot of men and animals logjammed outside the airlock. Hamid-Jones, sweating in his pressure suit, eased the Winged One in among the pack camels and got a lot of dirty looks.

"Wait your turn, brother," a gray-stubbled villager admonished him. "There'll be no jostling before the gates of Paradise."

"I'm sorry, brother," Hamid-Jones apologized, and squeezed in a little farther.

He sweated it out until the airlock closed behind him, but no challenge came from the booth. An inner safety lock had been wedged open to save time and trouble, and there was only the outer lock to get past. Hamid-Jones felt his ears pop, and the people around him began to don their ancient breathing equipment and see to their animals. Hamid-Jones did the same for himself and al-Janah.

The outer lock started to slide open. A thin breeze puffed past him and ruffled cloaks and headcloths—the gatekeeper, careless or impatient, hadn't waited to fully evacuate the chamber—and the mob of people and animals began to surge forward.

Then a red light began blinking, and Hamid-Jones heard the faint jangle of what would have been a strident alarm had the lock been fully pressurized. The door, unable to halt in midcycle, finished opening before it bounced back and started to slide shut again. By that time, Hamid-Jones had spurred his steed forward and was knocking people and camels aside in order to get up front. An angry man swung a camel stick at him, and he caught it on the point of the shoulder, but though his arm tingled with numbness, he was able to extract the Kalashnikov from his saddlebag and thumb the fire selector to full automatic. There was no time to unfold the stock. He held on to the jumping barrel with his left hand as he pumped a full clip into the doorjamb, hoping for the best.

He must have hit something delicate, because the door stopped in its tracks, leaving a narrow gap. Around him, panicky people had flung themselves aside at the sight of the spitting Kalashnikov. Other weapons had begun ominously to appear—venerable rifles and submachine guns that had been hidden under saddle blankets or suspended down villagers' backs under their robes to evade the rules about carrying weapons into the city. But nobody had made a hostile move—yet. They waited to see what he was up to. Desert people didn't commit themselves to a killing lightly.

Hamid-Jones ploughed through them to reach the exit. They cooperated, respecting his urgency. The Winged One pawed at the opening and pushed with his powerful chest. The door gave, just enough. He burst through into the first blush of a Martian dawn.

Behind Hamid-Jones, the desert folk were spilling out of the lock and dispersing as quickly as they could. Nobody wanted to be caught in the vicinity of a sabotaged airlock.

Hamid-Jones closed his mind to that line of thought. He didn't care to dwell on the penalties for endangering the city's air . . . or stealing a royal stallion . . . or breaking into a harem . . . or assaulting an overseer of the Royal Stables . . . or any of the other crimes he now could be charged with. There was no shortage of witnesses if his enemies wanted to observe the legalities— Yezid, Murad, Lalla. Even—he had no illusions—a frantically plea-bargaining Aziz.

If he hadn't been a fugitive before, he was now.

He turned up the Winged One's oxygen a notch and the tall stallion responded by increasing his pace. He was sailing over the desert in enormous leaps. Hamid-Jones could imagine the confusion on the other side of the lock. They wouldn't be able to open the inner door of the animal bab until the outer door was repaired and sealed shut. A patrol might be sent out after him through another lock, but it would take time to get it organized, and then they would find hoofprints going in all directions. By the time they got it sorted out and started tracking him and the others with sophisticated equipment, the chase would be dispersed over thousands of square kilometers of desert.

Even if they came after him, no civil service nag would ever catch up to al-Janah—they would need aircraft for that. And aircraft could not hover over every horseman and camel rider on the desert. A minor-league fugitive like himself was not worth the expense.

The thing now was to put as much distance between himself and Tharsis City as possible. He looked up at the brightening sky to get his bearings. The stars had disappeared, but there was a bright fleck overhead that had to be Phobos. He watched it a few minutes to establish the direction of its movement, then, still with no clear plan in mind, followed it eastward, toward the Valles Marineris.

The oxygen oasis was a patch of deeper green against the prevailing gray-green of the algae-furred rocks that littered the canyon floor. Hamid-Jones spurred the stumbling Marshorse forward. He was short of breath himself. They were down to the last bottle of air, and for the past fifty miles or so of this final approach, had been making do with the ambient atmosphere plus an occasional whiff of the bottled stuff. Here at the bottom of the Valles Marineris, the pressure was about three hundred millibars—about the same as at the top of Earth's Mount Everest—but the oxygen leakage from the oasis, trapped by the five-mile-deep canyon walls, provided an inspired partial pressure of oxygen of about seventy-two millimeters. A man could live, if he didn't move around very much, but Hamid-Jones's chest felt as though it was on fire.

He gave al-Janah another sip of air, and the horse perked up. Ahead, the patch of green was resolving itself into a huddle of half-buried domes, groves of bioengineered trees, and jumbles of ancient jerry-built equipment that was still, after centuries, mining the deep carbonate pockets, extracting oxygen from the CO_2 and condensing it. The tailored ecology had gained a real foothold and was doing its part, too. Someday all of Mars would be green—a world where human beings could walk unprotected under the open sky.

In the meantime, though his pressure suit wasn't strictly needed, Hamid-Jones kept it on, mainly for the extra warmth.

He raised his eyes to the canyon walls. This particular rift within the Valles Marineris system was about a hundred miles wide—broad enough so that he didn't feel as if he was at the bottom of a trench. The landscape became more fair and fertile as he proceeded—he could see little dusty-looking desert shrubs clawing at the sand with their roots, and once he crossed a small trickle of liquid water that the high air pressure was keeping from boiling away.

Al-Janah nickered with joy as he smelled the water and the greenery. Hamid-Jones paused to let him have a drink.

Hamid-Jones dismounted before entering the settlement, and led al-Janah through the cluster of sand-scoured hovels until he found an air dealer. The man was garrulous as he recharged Hamid-Jones's tanks.

"Traveling alone, are you? That's a hazardous thing to do,

even in the best of times. This has been a hungry year, and the *Bedu* are acting up. Oh, you're safe enough here—it's been a long time since this village suffered a raid. They need us for water, oxygen, a place to trade for their hides and other goods. None of the local tribes would tolerate a looting spree by any of the others. But once they catch you out on the desert alone— *ssst!*'' The man made a slashing motion across his throat with his forefinger.

"I'll have to take my chances," Hamid-Jones said stiffly.

"If I were you," the man persisted, "I'd join up with a party from one of the tamer local clans. Once you've crossed their palms with silver, they're honor-bound to deliver you safely. I'll be glad to put you in touch with some reliable *Bedu*. I won't even ask for anything but a nominal commission. Where did you say you were headed?''

"I didn't say." Hamid-Jones scowled.

Offended, the man finished filling the air tanks in silence. As Hamid-Jones started to leave, he made another try.

"You'll want a good inn to stay at. You look like a gentleman who's used to the comforts. Abad the Provisioner's is the best our little village has to offer. It's that triad of domes joined by a wall just beyond the watering hole. Tell him Omar the Airmaker sent you, and he'll treat you right."

Hamid-Jones didn't like the way Omar was eyeing al-Janah's expensive trappings. He gave a noncommittal grunt and started to walk away, leading the Marshorse by its long bridle.

"He'll take good care of your horse, too," the airmaker called after him. "His stable's used to fine animals—not like the ostler here."

There was a long wait at the wells. Bedouin herdsmen were leading through a herd of about two hundred camels, and a number of horsemen, muffled in heavy robes, were already waiting in line. A flock of shaggy goats, tended by cyanotic children and air-starved curs, stayed at a distance, sidelined until camels and horses were through. Only a few animals at a time could drink from the stone troughs. An antique submersible pump powered by an array of out-of-date solar cells fed the troughs, but Hamid-Jones noticed that leather buckets at the ends of pulleys stood ready in case of a breakdown.

He took his place at the end of the line and studied the no-mads. They were tough, stringy men, some of whom weren't bothering to wear their breathing masks. The animals were tough, too. The camels' masks hung loose around their necks while they waited for their drink, and none of them seemed inconvenienced by the three hundred–millibar atmosphere. Centuries of old-fashioned breeding and natural selection had improved the animals far beyond their original bioengineered stock; that was why desert-bred camels were at a premium at sportsmen's auctions. They could sniff out the minutest traces of water, subsist on hoarfrost, and go for a year without a real drink. They could convert ambient carbon dioxide to oxides and store it in their humps—and Hamid-Jones had even heard rumors that the remoter Bedouin tribes had bred a line of camels whose gut carried symbiotic air-producing algae that had saved the life of many a desert traveler in an emergency, though at the cost of sacrificing the animal.

When Hamid-Jones's turn came, the Bedouins stood aside and watched while al-Janah drank his fill; they knew fine horse-flesh, these fellows.

"Trade?" one of them asked hopefully in villainous Arabic, indicating by pantomime and an unintelligible flow of gutturals that he was willing to throw in a horse, a couple of camels, and—Hamid-Jones was not quite clear on this—a woman or two.

"No . . . *eh-sif* . . . sorry . . ." Hamid-Jones replied, stretching a smile beyond its natural boundaries.

The man kept trying. His eyes had sized up Hamid-Jones and the Winged One and somehow concluded that they did not go together; but if he thought that he could get round a city hick, he was disappointed. He stalked off at last with a scowl.

Hamid-Jones led al-Janah away without the appearance of undue haste. The Winged One had gotten him this far, but he could see now that he might be a liability.

The ostler's eyes, too, narrowed at the sight of the magnificent beast, but he said nothing and went about feeding him and wiping him down. He inspected al-Janah's hooves, pronounced them in good condition, and gave them some minor care with a hoof pick and dandy brush. "Do you want to stable him here to-night?" he asked.

"No," Hamid-Jones said, mentally counting his diminishing funds. "I'll keep him with me." He paid a silver riyal for a nosebag of oats for morning and left before the ostler could get too curious.

He camped a good distance away from the settlement, in someone's grove of anaerobic date palms. He tethered al-Janah to a stake, adjusting his nosebag to give him a trickle of oxygen, and set up his airtent. He valved enough air into it to turn it into a flaccid cone, and got the little portable air plant going. It would fill the tent to tautness in a few hours, and that was good enough; no need to waste the bought air in his tanks. He crawled inside and made a frugal supper out of a baggie of rice and beans he had stopped to buy from one of the impromptu vendors operating out of the scattering of half-buried dens that comprised the settlement; all the oasis inhabitants made their livings by extracting money from wayfarers. Finally he prostrated himself, belatedly mumbled the fifth prayer, and went to sleep under his heatcloak.

The gentle, reassuring chug-a-chug of the air plant lulled him into a profound and dreamless slumber. At first he didn't know where he was when the sound awakened him. Then he stiffened and became alert.

Someone was unzipping the outer flap of the airtent.

Every muscle in Hamid-Jones's body became taut. He could see the obscure shape of a man sandwiched between the two translucent layers of the entrance, outlined by starlight. The man was moving slowly, an inch at a time, to zip up the outer flap again. Then he turned with infinite care, so as not to shake the tent, and began unzipping the inner flap.

Hamid-Jones's first thought was that the police had caught up with him. Then he realized that the stealthy approach was not the *shurtayeen*'s style; they would have ripped the tent open and dragged him out, choking for breath.

He did not think it was one of the Bedouin. A Bedouin would not have coveted his meager possessions when al-Janah was staked outside; he would have quietly taken the Marshorse and disappeared into the desert. And it was not likely that it was an ordinary sneakthief from the settlement, either; they didn't last very long around an oasis.

That left the Assassins.

Hamid-Jones was careful to show no movement himself. His hand crept toward the pack where he kept the smartpistol, and he cursed himself for not keeping it closer to hand.

The figure came through the inner flap, and Hamid-Jones struck. He got the intruder by the throat and wrist and wrestled him to the ground. If there had been a knife or garrote in the man's right hand, he must have made him drop it; there was no disembowling stroke or slash across the throat, as Hamid-Jones had feared. The man thrashed feebly, no match for Hamid-Jones's Earth-bred muscles. Hamid-Jones let go with one hand and grabbed for the smartpistol.

"Please, master, don't shoot!" the figure gasped. "It's me!"

CHAPTER 14

Hamid-Jones found a handlight and turned it on. Aziz lay, teeth chattering, on the tent floor. A knife was scabbarded at his belt, but he was otherwise unarmed.

"What are you doing here? How did you find me?" Hamid-Jones demanded.

"Please, master, let me up." Aziz struggled to a sitting position. "It wasn't hard. Only a fool would have headed west toward the Tharsis Ridge and risked the New Palace desert patrols, and you're not a fool. I simply took the most obvious route east and followed the main channel of the Valles till I came to the first oasis."

"You had me bugged, you scoundrel! There's still a transponder planted somewhere in my clothing, isn't there?"

"That, too," Aziz admitted. "What could I do?" He spread his hands helplessly. "I couldn't leave it still transmitting. I came after you to inactivate it. Suppose the *shurtayeen* found the wavelength?"

With an apologetic grin, he turned Hamid-Jones's new headcloth inside out, ripped out a cleaning label and tore it into little pieces.

"Why did you bug me in the first place, you rascal? Who are you really working for?"

"That unworthy suspicion again, master?" Aziz said with a pained expression. "I thought we had that all settled."

"Answer me!"

With a long-suffering sigh, Aziz said, "I wired you for your own protection when you insisted on going out to see the woman.

226

It's hard to keep track of you, master. Who knows what trouble I might have had to bail you out of?''

"Are you sure you didn't wire me for the benefit of the Assassins? How did they find me?''

Aziz frowned convincingly. "The Assassins made an attempt?''

"One of them was waiting for me when I returned to my old lodgings. He would have finished me, too, if it hadn't been for a police raid.''

"You went back to your old lodgings?'' Aziz struck himself on the forehead with the heel of his hand. "*Wallah-i!* What did I ever do, oh God, to deserve this?''

"I *had* to go back, to get my gear,'' Hamid-Jones said defensively. "The police raided the hideout, and I saw you in their hands.''

"That's true,'' Aziz said, calming down. "Listen, master, the Assassins didn't *find* you. You handed yourself over to them. I *told* you the note from the woman was a decoy, but would you listen? Oh, no! They forged it to flush you out. I warned you about that computer-generated scent. It was fake before they digitized it! I don't care how cheap a computer is —stink in, stink out!'' He cocked his head. "Tell me, was that tricab you took waiting conveniently outside for you after that trouble at the harem?''

"Yes,'' Hamid-Jones admitted.

"He was an Assassin stoolie. He radioed ahead. The Assassins prefer an indoor kill.''

"How did you know I got into trouble at the harem?''

"I listened in on the police frequencies. Listen, master, do you know what the punishment is for violating a harem? They'll toast your *zib* and hand it to you on a bun. As for stealing the Emir's horse and assaulting Yezid, they'll peel you like an onion while the machines feed what's left of you stimulants and plasma intravenously.''

"Just a minute! Why did the police show up at the lodging house so opportunely?''

"Because of the complaint from Murad, that's all. It was only a routine check of your last known address.''

"Then why did they raid my hideout? Who told them I was there?''

"They weren't after you. They raid that thieves' den all the time. They were after one of your neighbors—a document forger named al-Alam. I was just doing some business with him, as a matter of fact. Thank heaven I was on my way downstairs. If they'd come five minutes sooner . . .''

He gave a weasel grin.

"You've got an explanation for everything. How did you get away from the police?"

"I talked my way out of it," Aziz said promptly. "Please, master, will you turn off the light? It shows through the tent. It's the only light for miles around. There's no need to attract undue attention."

Hamid-Jones switched off the torch. A velvet darkness enveloped them. "Why would you want to throw in your fortunes with a fugitive?"

"It's an honor to serve you, *ya* Abdul. Besides, things are getting hot for me, too, back in Tharsis City. There's an alert out to take me in for questioning. People like me need an employer. It keeps the police from looking at us too closely. You're a fine, educated gentleman with a profession you can practice anywhere in the Solar system. Eventually we'll make a connection for you somewhere. We'll lie low for a year or two and get off planet when things cool down. Till then, we can get by somehow in some small settlement where the Emirate's rule doesn't hold sway. Where there are people, there's always a way to separate them from their money." He yawned. "Can we get some sleep now, master? We'd better get moving at first light."

When Hamid-Jones woke up in the morning, Aziz was already up, making coffee outside in a small pressure vessel. He had a breakfast of flat bread and bean porridge heating over a small fire of animal dung enclosed by an overturned bucket fed by an oxygen bottle.

"I was going to bring you coffee inside," Aziz said cheerfully, lifting up his face mask. His voice sounded high and thin in the Valles air.

"This is fine," Hamid-Jones said, squatting down beside him. He raised an eyebrow at the low-slung animal tied to a date palm. It was a Martian sandipede, fully equipped with an eight-legged pressure suit, and loaded down with packs, desert gear, and jerricans of water. Sandipedes were derived genetically from donkeys, and the long ears in their transparent sheaths sticking up aft of the conical respirator showed it, but the stretched-out barrel torso with its multiple limbs gave the creature a caterpillar look. A leather bucket for collecting dung was suspended under the flap at the rear of the caboose.

"A fine animal, isn't it, master?" Aziz said. "Very handy in the desert, and it can carry a man and a full load at the same time.''

"How did you manage to acquire a traveling outfit like that, and all those supplies, on such short notice?''

"Oh, the prospector who was going to use them had a sudden change of plans," Aziz said glibly.

"How did you pay for it?"

"Better not ask, master."

Aziz had already fed and watered al-Janah, and packed everything but the tent itself. The Marshorse and the sandipede seemed to have made good friends despite the disparity in their heights. Hamid-Jones got in the saddle Bedouin style, with a running twelve-foot leap. Aziz mounted more sedately, climbing into the saddle on the sandipede's forward withers, with his feet dangling almost to the ground.

They stopped at the well on the way out to top off their jerricans. Omar the Airmaker was there, filling a tank truck with a hose.

"Leaving so soon?" Omar said, eyeing Aziz's gear as if adding up its worth. "Most travelers like to rest up a day or two before going on. The next oasis isn't till Crater Sixty-four."

Hamid-Jones started to open his mouth, but Aziz spoke first. "My master is in a hurry. He has to be in Melas Lacus for a kinsman's wedding."

"It's a long way to go overland," Omar said with a speculative pursing of his lips.

"Yes, it is," Aziz agreed equably.

Omar swung his attention back to Hamid-Jones. "Maybe you'll change your mind about taking my advice. I see your man caught up with you, but believe me, that's not enough protection—not in times like these. Word's just come in by radio about a Bedouin looting expedition at Noctis Labyrinthus, only a few hundred miles from here. Two men traveling alone are likely to get plucked clean. If you wait here a few more days, you can go out with a caravan."

"We'll take our chances," Hamid-Jones said.

They ran out of water on the fifth day. Al-Janah consumed twelve or fifteen gallons a day, and the sandipede scarcely less. Hamid-Jones and Aziz had tried to be frugal—performing their ablutions with sand, and drinking as little as possible—but the laboring condenser collected only a pint or two at best during their nightly stops, and the morning hoarfrost had yielded little more.

"There should be a well only a few hours away, master,"

Aziz said, peering at the red badlands ahead. "Look for a break in the escarpment. We leave this rift valley there and detour due north."

"Do you think you can find it?" Hamid-Jones asked sharply.

"Yes, *inch'allah*," Aziz replied.

"That's pretty good for a city boy."

"I took care to make inquiries and to procure good maps, master."

Hamid-Jones sighed. "All right. Lead on."

Another hour's riding took them to a fractured stretch of the canyon floor where the eye could readily discern the flow lines of ancient channels. Hamid-Jones kept his eyes peeled for the slump in the high cliffs that Aziz had mentioned. A plume of yellowish cloud in the distance caught his attention.

"Dust storm," he said. "It looks like it's headed our way."

Aziz eased back in the saddle and followed his pointing finger. After several moments of study he spoke.

"That's no dust storm, master. You're right, it's moving. But there's no wind."

"What is it, then?"

"Camels. A thousand camels at least, from the size of the cloud. It has to be one of the larger clans on the move."

"Let's get out of their way, then."

"Master, where shall we go?" Aziz said, smiling sadly. "This desert belongs to them. Even the Winged One cannot outrun their swiftest horses if they should decide to come after us." He leaned forward and scratched the sandipede's gloved ears. "And Jeroboam here couldn't even outrun one of their goats."

"What shall we do?"

"Keep going, don't run, and hope we don't attract their attention. We'll edge toward that crack in the terrain a couple of miles away. Even if they see us, they may not think two men worth plundering." He bit his lip. "Or they may invite us to coffee."

They were still a quarter mile from the cleft when a feather of dust detached itself from the main cloud and began to move across the desert toward them.

"They have keen eyes," Aziz said. "There's no way to hide from them. Sit tight and hope for the best."

He took a long weapon from a saddle holster, checked the clip, and kept it cradled in the crook of his arm, the strap hanging loose around his shoulder. Hamid-Jones followed his example, unshipping the Kalashnikov and unfolding the stock.

"That's right, master," Aziz approved. "Let them see that

we're men of self-respect, not oasis mud dwellers to be trifled with. But if we try to use these weapons, we're dead."

The sortie party caught up with them less than ten minutes later, covering the miles of desert with lightning speed. It was about a dozen men on camelback, black-robed, leather-masked, and bearing ancient slug-throwing submachine guns and long, thin metal tubes meant for firing finger-sized heat-seeking missiles. They swept around Hamid-Jones and Aziz in two encircling wings and reined to a halt, surrounding them.

"Let me do the talking," Aziz cautioned. He swung toward the tribesmen with a warm smile behind his face bubble. "*Salaum alaikum, beni am,*" he said. "It's an honor for two poor travelers like ourselves to pass through the *dirah* of a mighty tribe such as yours, whose reputation for justice and hospitality is such that wayfarers are safe as lambs."

The patois was not pure Arabic, but a dialect Hamid-Jones had never heard before. His respect for Aziz's talents grew.

The leader of the party, a powerful-shouldered man whose face—the exposed parts of it anyway—was as leathery as the mask he wore, answered in kind, and at length. The dialogue on both sides seemed to be very flowery. Hamid-Jones could follow it word by word, except for a few unfamiliar expressions, but there seemed to be very little information content in it. After several exchanges, Aziz turned to Hamid-Jones.

"Their tribe's the Beni al-Rub—the Children of Emptiness. This isn't their *dirah*. They're way off their range. Hard times, poor pasturage. They're the terror of the local Valles tribes—raiding some, getting paid protection by the weaker ones. They're on their way back to their home range now."

"Lucky you could talk their lingo," Hamid-Jones said. "I'm relieved that you could make friends with them."

"Make friends with them?" Aziz gave a short bark. "They're taking us prisoner."

All at once a dozen submachine guns and missile tubes were pointing at Hamid-Jones and Aziz. A couple of the Bedouins leaned over and confiscated their weapons. A few prods and gestures sufficed to get Hamid-Jones and Aziz moving toward the pillar of cloud. It seemed to be hovering over one place now, and the dust in its wake was imperceptibly settling in Mars's low gravity.

After fifteen or twenty minutes at the eight-legged trot favored by Jeroboam, the horizon peeled back enough to reveal the source of the cloud. A tremendous throng of animals rose suddenly above the skyline, peppering the red landscape from side to side of the great valley rift. Thousands of camels, horses, and goats milled around, as men racing back and forth on camelback herded them into cohesive groups. Long black tents were going up with incredible speed in areas staked off by fabric fences strung on ropes.

They rode past a tarpaulin corral containing some of the finest Marshorses Hamid-Jones had ever seen—animals that rivaled and even surpassed the best specimens in the Emir's stables. Al-Janah was among his peers here. One of the horses startled Hamid-Jones—a six-legged mare that was kneeling on its rearward knees to allow a magnificent six-legged foal to suckle. It had to be a natural mutation—the Bedouins had no facilities for genetic engineering—and if it bred true, as the foal indicated, the sheik of this desert tribe was about to found a great line.

"*Wallah il azim!*" Aziz exclaimed, lifting his faceplate to speak to Hamid-Jones. "The sheik of this tribe is someone to be reckoned with! It takes twenty camels to carry his house of hair!"

One of their escorts heard him and lifted his own rustic mask to show a grin.

A half-dozen women were still working to set up additional sections of the tent, erecting ridgepoles and pounding stakes into the sand, but there was already fifty feet of it, making a long swaybacked structure of hairy goat hide. The airlocks were ingenious pockets of skin, sealed with gaskets of what looked like inflated lengths of camel gut. A distended translucent bag the size of a small shed showed a greenish tinge inside; Hamid-Jones took this to be an organic airmaking plant, probably filled with the oxygen-concentrating thallophytes with which the Martian desert had been sown by the early terraformers. The pack camels that had carried the whole arrangement were still being unloaded, and Aziz had been right—there were twenty of them.

"They're taking us round the back way," Aziz informed him. "So we can't be considered guests. If we were guests, he couldn't touch us, even if we had murdered one of his sons."

The inside of the unfinished tent was splendid, the floor covered with thick, richly-colored carpets. Brass utensils hung on thongs from the poles. Curtains of goat and camel hair, woven in intricate abstract patterns, screened off the rest of the tent.

The man sitting cross-legged on a pile of rugs by a hearth of hammered metal looked like a tough old bird. He had a face of carved hickory stained dark by ultraviolet, a great arched hook of a nose, and an iron-gray beard standing out stiffly from his chin. The headcloth, given an extra lap round his chin and tucked up under his *agal*, added a dashing touch. A flowing, wide-sleeved topshirt of royal blue hung open over his robes. He was armed to the teeth with a series of leather belts and crossed straps over his chest holding sword, dagger, microrocket launcher, and submachine pistol. A Kalashnikov leaned against the post behind him.

The men of the raiding party were busy dumping Hamid-Jones's and Aziz's possessions at the sheik's feet. The sheik's face lit up at the sight of all the expensive camping equipment. The band's leader dropped to one knee to kiss the sheik's hand, then leaned forward to whisper in his ear.

"Who are you men, and what are you doing in the Emptiness?" the sheik asked at last. His voice was low, thick, unhurried. He glanced at the embossed royal seal of the saddle that had been taken from al-Janah and added: "And how do you come to be riding a horse from the stables of the Usurper?"

There was an angry muttering from the other men in the tent. The desert tribes, except those who were bound to the Emir by kinship, were not fond of the man whose father had seized the throne of Mars by force. Even after a couple of centuries of despotism, they were still attached to the memory of the deposed king, Ahmar bin Naji bin Abad al-Habbibi, called the Righteous, who had been known as a friend to the Bedouin.

"We are no friends of the false Emir," Aziz said quickly, overriding Hamid-Jones's attempted reply. "We are his sworn enemies, fleeing for our lives."

"So says many a traveler. A jackal fallen among wolves may try to howl. How do you explain the horse?"

Again Aziz interrupted Hamid-Jones. "This is Abdul ben Arthur, a man of consequence, knowledgeable in the breeding of fine horseflesh. He served a prince of the old royal blood, who was betrayed and treacherously murdered by the false Emir. Abdul ben Arthur is a brave man of mighty deeds. He boldly broke into the false Emir's stables in the dark of the night and took what was his due." He gave a sly grin. "Al-Janah was the false Emir's favorite, his darling, the light of his life. He hoped to breed a mighty line from him. It must have been a terrible blow to lose him."

There was more muttering, this time friendlier. Hamid-Jones heard an appreciative chuckle. Aziz had hit all the right chords. Horse stealing—and failing that, semen stealing to artificially impregnate a mare waiting out of sight in the desert—was a 3,000-year-old Bedouin tradition. Records on Arabian bloodlines had been kept since before the time of Mohammed.

"Blessed be the horse breeders," the sheik grunted. Hamid-

Jones could see the glint of avarice in his eyes. One way or another, al-Janah was going to improve the bloodlines in this desert tribe's herd.

"It was necessary for Abdul ben Arthur to flee," Aziz went on. "He is the possessor of a great secret—the secret for which the prince he served was killed. His own life is in danger because of it. It is information which will be of great value to al-Sharq, the Shining."

That brought the sheik up short. "What do you know of *al-Rogui*?" he asked sharply. The word he used meant the Pretender. From his lips it was not a pejorative.

"I know that the blood of the desert people flows in his veins," Aziz said, unintimidated. "I know that one day he will topple the corrupt den of sycophants and eunuchs who lord it over this planet."

"What is this information?"

"It is not to be bandied about lightly. It is information of great power—if it is used right. It is useless if it is dissipated."

"What is the information?" the sheik repeated with dangerous patience.

Hamid-Jones spoke up. "The false Emir is dead. I saw it myself. Now there is a *false* false Emir. He is made out of two of the Emir's sprouts, and though he is as much the Emir as the Emir's own finger, he has not a brain in his head. Given time, he will grow crafty. Al-Sharq cannot afford to give him that time. The Palace is in disarray. The moment to strike is at hand."

The sheik pondered for a while. He raised his impressive head and said to his followers, "No one will speak of this." Then he fixed an eagle's sharp gaze on Hamid-Jones. "What you say may be true. Or it may be some tall story to save your skins. We will go to al-Sharq and let *him* decide. And then we will see what will be done with you."

Atop the swaying camel, Hamid-Jones clung grimly to the saddle pommel and wished for the hundredth time that day that camel saddles had stirrups. The view from his high perch was dizzying, but the muscles of his legs screamed with pain, and his bottom, after a week of nonstop riding, was rubbed raw.

The camel chose that moment to swing her long neck around and stare malevolently at him from a foot away. He was glad she was wearing her respirator. Without it, she had shown a tendency to nip at him, or failing that, to spit. The Bedouins derisively called her al-Af'a—the Snake—and she deserved the name. They had taken away al-Janah, who was spending all the rest stops servicing the sheik's mares, and given him this *naga*—a female of uncertain age, in their parlance—who was beyond doubt the most ill-tempered, mange-ridden beast in the herd.

"We're turning west, master, have you noticed?" Aziz said from a point about twelve feet below him.

Hamid-Jones looked sourly down to where Aziz rode at ease on the broad back of the plodding sandipede. Aziz had moved the saddle back to the middle withers and was lounging indolently with his legs stretched out and his feet up, as if he were resting on a divan. The nomads often rode with their legs crossed tailor-fashion beneath them, as if sitting on a hassock, but Aziz was positively sybaritic by comparison. His captors had tried to give him a camel, but he had kicked up such a fuss that they had let him keep Jeroboam. He had also managed somehow to persuade them to let him provisionally keep his gear, except for the weapons, and a towering pile of bundles rested on the sandipede's rearmost withers, providing a cushion for Aziz's head whenever he wanted one.

"Yes. I thought so this morning, but I wasn't sure till now."

He raised his eyes to where Phobos floated overhead like a glowing potato in the twilight. Its twice-daily passage had helped him keep track of their course; until now they had kept going due north toward Candor. Now they were well above the equator, beyond Mars's inhabited latitudes. Ahead of them lay only a volcanic plain.

The thumbnail-size moon, moving as slowly as a watch's minute hand, passed over the line of camels and shrank into the distance behind them. This morning it had crossed their path at an angle. The caravan's wide turn was complete.

"There can't be many oasis craters or airholes in that wilderness," Hamid-Jones worried.

"If there are, they'll find them," Aziz said confidently. "You can be sure they know every inch of ground."

"We're stopping," Hamid-Jones said. "Praise Allah. I thought they meant to keep me in this saddle all night."

Aziz pounded the last tent stake into lava and got the little compressor working on the thin Martian air. "There," he said. "By the time I finish unpacking, you'll be able to get inside, get out of that suit and mask and get some linament on those muscles. Don't worry, master, you'll toughen up in another week or two. Me, I'm all gristle. After the first few days it wasn't so bad."

Bruised and aching, Hamid-Jones sat with his back propped against a saddle. The Snake was tethered nearby, rummaging with her bulbous nose in the volcanic earth for ice crystals or oxides, or snuffling up the microbial lichens that Marscamels seemed to be able to sniff out anywhere.

The life of the huge encampment was unfurling with astonishing speed. All around Hamid-Jones, tents were going up with an efficiency that rivaled that of his lanyard-triggered sports model, the vast herd was being turned out to its cyanophytic pasture, and women whose leather respirators served as their veils milked camels and goats. The Bedouin women seemed freer than their city counterparts, wearing colorful dress and working outdoors alongside the men of their families, but each tent had its *raba'a* section for men and its *mahram* section for women, divided by a curtain. The slaughtering was done by the women, out behind the *mahram*, and as he surveyed the scene, Hamid-Jones heard the terminal bleat of some unfortunate animal.

Aziz had unloaded Jeroboam and had all their possessions spread out in front of the tent. Now he began dragging everything inside—saddles, utensils, clothing, supplies. "Why don't you leave it piled where it is?" Hamid-Jones said. "There won't be enough room left for us."

"Master, even if we were the sheik's guests, there would be those who stole from us. And we're not his guests."

The accuracy of the remark was brought home a while later when a scurvy-looking fellow in a camel-gut pressure suit brought them a tray of covered dishes. "From the sheik's feast," he announced brusquely, setting out the dishes.

"A nice distinction," Aziz said to Hamid-Jones. "We can't be invited to the shiek's blowout along with the slaves and hangers-on, because that would put us under his protection. But it's all right to give us our fodder alfresco, like the animals. And yet he invites us to the *es-shigg*, the visitors' section of the tent, every night to spin yarns with us and pump us for any gossip we can dredge up."

"Prisoners or not, I guess we're a break in the monotony," Hamid-Jones said. "The sheik has a radiophone, and he could watch satellite television on that little set he has hanging from the tent pole, but I suppose primitive folk prefer their entertainment live."

"Primitive!" Aziz choked on a gobbet of meat he had poked under his respirator. "Master, these *Bedu* have a high technology! How long do you suppose a city man could survive out here, even if he emptied out the sporting goods store?''

The fellow who had been serving the food could not have been paying attention to their conversation, but he chose that moment to point to the tent and say, with more pity than contempt, ''*Sugay-yar*. Small. Why don't you live in a *beit sha'ar* like regular people?''

''It's just for camping,'' Hamid-Jones said, trying not to be condescending. ''*Mukay-yam*. With a small volume, you don't need to make so much air to fill it.''

To underscore the point, he waved at the valiantly laboring condenser with its sealed fiber composite flywheel that could be charged up by solar cells, any heat source, an electric plug, or— in a pinch—could be cranked up manually or by the axle of any spinning wheel.

''*Kindusah*,'' the Bedouin said, to show that he knew very well what it was and wasn't impressed by it. ''What happens if it breaks down or needs a new part, and you're all alone in the middle of the desert and don't know how to fix it?''

''It comes with a warranty, brother,'' Aziz said dryly.

''A camel is better,'' the Bedouin said. ''You can always get air from a camel.''

''We can't dispute that,'' Aziz said. ''Cut out a camel's lungs and intestines, and the symbiotic plants that extract oxygen from ambient carbon dioxide can keep a man alive for days.''

''And the *gamal* gives us its milk and its meat, its hide and hair. Its urine for woolmaking and its dung for fuel. It leads us to water. And it seals us off from the great Outside.''

He placed a leather-gloved hand over the translucent silvery pressure suit made of camel gut, then tapped the camel-leather respirator hanging carelessly around his neck and the attached greenish airbag fashioned, Hamid-Jones had learned, from a camel's stomach.

''Still,'' Hamid-Jones said mildly, ''I've seen other tribes that'll use a water truck and other conveniences.''

The man spat—an astonishing expenditure of moisture that expressed the deepest contempt. ''Those tame sheep that hang around the towns and oases for their scraps! They're no better than *fellahin*!''

Hamid-Jones remembered some of the fierce tribesmen he had seen in the desert surrounding Tharsis City and made a note not to underestimate the kind of Bedouin who would consider them effete.

"What good is a truck?" the man went on. "Can it forage for its own fuel? Can it go where a camel goes? Can it repair its own wounds? Can it sire more trucks? Machines are no good here in the Emptiness!"

He spat again for emphasis.

"Peace, brother," Aziz said.

"Peace," the Bedouin replied. He nodded at them and then departed in an easy, air-conserving series of bouncing lopes.

"No mask," Hamid-Jones said wonderingly. "Showing off, I guess. These people are as tough as their camels."

"Tougher," Aziz said. "Camels don't eat Bedouins."

The sheik's messenger arrived a couple of hours later. He was a Memnonian slave who had been captured as a child on some southern raid, a pasty-faced, good-natured man of mixed Russian and American ancestry. "Sheik wants to see you now." He grinned at Hamid-Jones. "Not him." He gave a grin of equal width to Aziz.

Hamid-Jones got to his feet. "Tell him I'm coming." The sheik's slave replaced the mask over his grin and slipped away through the field of tents. "He wants to see me alone this time," Hamid-Jones said to Aziz. "I wonder what that means."

"It means he's graded us for status and decided which one of us is the retainer. Better get going. You don't keep a sheik waiting."

"You don't seem awfully put out."

"I have a limited interest in hobnobbing with sheiks. I'd rather spend the time exploring the camp. Have you noticed some of these *Bedu* girls, master? Harem or not, there are bold and wandering eyes above those masks. I think one of them's trying to encourage me. I bet she's had past experience in slipping out from under the *muharram* section after dark for a rendezvous behind some boulder in the desert."

"Don't you go getting involved in any hanky-panky. Our position here is precarious enough."

"You'd better worry about your own hanky-panky. The sheik's daughter is making sheep's eyes at you. Don't think I haven't seen it."

"I haven't done anything to encourage her," Hamid-Jones said indignantly.

"That could be just as delicate a situation. You don't want to make her mad at you. She's the apple of her father's eye."

Hamid-Jones writhed inwardly. He had in fact noticed that

one of the sheik's daughters seemed to have found an inordinate number of chores and errands to do in the vicinity of the *es-shigg* section of the tent when he and Aziz had been summoned for an after-dinner chat. She always contrived to be fetching water from a camelbag or carrying a bucket to the goat corral just as he entered or left, or poking her head through the curtain into the *es-shigg* and feigning surprise to find male visitors still there. Above the draped veil, he could see sloe eyes shaded with kohl, a pimply forehead shiny with the camel grease used as a sealant, a vee of thick blue-black hair showing low under the head shawl. It seemed, now that Aziz had mentioned it, that her gaze had been intense, and longer-lingering than necessary.

"Perhaps the sheik wishes to offer you her hand." Aziz laughed. Then, more soberly, he added, "Or if al-Sharq doesn't give us a clean bill of health, he may give you to her as a slave instead of slitting your throat."

"That's enough nonsense," Hamid-Jones said. An image of the girl's hands as they milked a goat came to him. They were square, chapped from going without gloves for outdoor chores, decorated with tattoolike designs drawn in henna.

"Just be careful not to get caught with the girl. For punishing fornicators, the Bedouin have a charming custom of—"

"I don't want to hear it," Hamid-Jones interrupted. "Try to stay out of trouble while I'm gone."

Women were still clearing away the remains of the feast to which he and Aziz had not been invited when Hamid-Jones arrived at the sheik's tent. A huge copper guest dish, easily six feet in diameter, was being levered onto its edge to be rolled away for a scrubbing with sand, and the leg bones of a camel, longer than a man, lay picked clean beside it. Other women were scraping leftover sand-rice into jars for their own supper, and rolling up the uneaten bread. One of them paused in her labors to look up soulfully at Hamid-Jones; it was the sheik's daughter. He hurried past and stooped through the airtight envelope that provided ingress to the *es-shigg*.

"*Salaam aleikum*," the sheik said, motioning him to sit down on a pile of rugs.

"*Wa aleikum asalaam*," Hamid-Jones replied, contorting himself into a cross-legged position. His abused leg muscles protested, and he shifted surreptitiously for more comfort.

"You are well, *ya Abdul*?" the sheik inquired, fondling one of his half-dozen weapons, an innocent-looking popgun that fired explosive pellets.

"Yes," Hamid-Jones replied. "And you are well, *ya* Majid bin Auda?" He noticed that all the brass coffeepots, the emblems of the sheik's hospitality, had been removed from the visitors' section. The sheik was running no risk of being misinterpreted; Hamid-Jones was not yet his enemy, but he was not a guest.

"I am well."

There followed a long conversation about horse breeding and the intricacies of the bloodlines of the five great breeds of Arabians that had come down from the time of the prophet Mohammed, during the course of which Hamid-Jones realized that the sheik was trying to draw him out about the ancestry of al-Janah. "*Al-khamsa*, is he?" the sheik probed. "That fine arched neck and the high set of the croup. With perhaps a touch of the *Kuhailan* in the angle of the gaskin and hock."

"You're very astute," Hamid-Jones said. "His genes will be a fine addition to your herd."

This led into a conversation about the Royal Stables, which led into a discussion of the cloning department and its relationship to the Palace cloning department, followed by a chat about Palace politics and the infighting between Rubinstein and Ismail. The sheik followed up every opening. Hamid-Jones realized that the sheik was, in fact, skillfully establishing his bona fides as someone who could claim to have been part of those events and personally witnessed the pulling of the plug on the Emir's head.

"So," the sheik said finally, "your friend Aziz"—he would not use the word "servant"—"came to you through the Palace, but you cannot be sure whether he came to you through the Jew or the eunuch?"

"He must have come through the Vizier," Hamid-Jones said, "or he would not be so loyal to me, and he would not be fleeing for his life."

"Or he may have come through a third party," the sheik said, fingering the handle of his microrocket launcher.

Hamid-Jones didn't like where the conversation was heading. "I'll vouch for Aziz," he said. "He's risked his skin for me. He may have had a somewhat checkered past"—Hamid-Jones was sure the sheik had noticed Aziz's regrown right hand; a thief was about the worst thing to be among Bedouins—"but when he gives his loyalty, he's a man of honor. It doesn't matter who hired him originally. He was sent to me as one of my perquisites, that's all, and the Vizier's personnel department may have scraped him up anywhere, but I've been paying him ever since.'' He looked the sheik full in the face. ''And now that I can't pay him anymore, he's *still* loyal.''

At that moment, the sheik's daughter poked her head through the dividing curtain. She was unveiled, and her round face wore an expression of spurious surprise. Her father gave her a furious look, and she withdrew hastily, knocking over something inside that rattled metallically.

''I'm a simple man of the desert,'' the sheik said. ''I know nothing of palace intrigues and the infidel science that puts one man's head on another man's body. All that's for al-Sharq, the rightful prince, to judge.''

The camp was quiet when Hamid-Jones traced his way back through the tents and improvised corrals of rope and fabric. It was early to bed and early to rise in a Bedouin encampment, unless you were a sheik, staying up half the night to enjoy a talkfest with an outsider whom Allah has sent your way.

Aziz was not in the tent. Hamid-Jones cursed him, struggled out of his pressure suit, and fell asleep. Aziz crawled in an hour or two later, waking Hamid-Jones up.

''Where were you, you scoundrel? You could get us both killed.''

Aziz protested unconvincingly. ''I hung around the tent all night in the cold, master. I was sure she would come out, but she didn't. Finally a woman's hand came out from under the flap of the *muharram* section and made the gesture of intercourse. I was trying to work up my courage to accept the invitation when one of the men of the tent came out the other side to relieve himself. So I made myself very flat until I was out of sight, and came back here.''

Hamid-Jones was too tired to pursue it further. He burrowed down into his thermal blanket and tried to go back to sleep. But Aziz's snoring kept him awake for the next two hours, and then it was dawn.

The next day was a bleary-eyed horror. He clung dizzily to the saddle pommel, trying not to doze and fall off, while al-Af'a loped across the desert, listing from side to side; all the time trying to contain his irritation at the sight of Aziz blissfully napping in the saddle as the sandipede undulated sedately along.

A tremendous saddlebacked hump rose above the littered horizon, dwarfing the nearer landscape. Behind it, a shroud of white clouds rose into the stratosphere. There was only one feature on Mars tall enough to be seen at that great a distance past the sharp curve of the Martian horizon. They had been riding toward it for days, and there was no longer any doubt that it was their destination.

"Olympus," Aziz said, squinting at the enormous volcano. "We're not going to go around it, so that's where al-Sharq's headquarters must be."

"Impossible," Hamid-Jones said. "The spy satellites would notice any kind of permanent encampment. When they didn't move with the seasons like the other nomads, it would give them away."

"Not if they were hidden in the caldera, master."

Hamid-Jones was startled by the idea. "Mount Olympus is over sixteen miles high. Its top is in the fringes of space. How could men and animals on foot reach it?"

"Excuse me, master. You spent your first childhood years growing up on Earth. You must have absorbed your attitudes about planetary atmospheres in the elementary grades at mosque school. You're thinking of mountain climbers gasping for breath at the top of Mount Everest—at one-third the height of Olympus Mons—or balloonists in pressurized gondolas at fifteen or twenty miles up. But the pressure *gradient* of the Martian atmosphere is less than Earth's. It goes with lower gravity, less air to start with. To folk like these—who don't bother with pressure suits half the time anyway—the fringes of outer space aren't all that different than the Martian surface. They just button up a little tighter, that's all."

"Aziz, sometimes you amaze me. How did you acquire all that lore?"

"You never know what's going to come in handy, master."

By noon next day, all of Olympus was above the horizon, and Hamid-Jones could see the next problem. The base of the volcano, three hundred miles across, formed a solid wall of cliffs that had to be at least two miles high. The cliffs were the hardened edge of the lava flow that had created the great sprawling shield of the mountain itself.

"How are we going to climb that?" he said. "Al-Sharq must be hidden away somewhere in a crack at the bottom."

"You'll see, master," Aziz said smugly.

"What makes you so sure?"

"I'm guessing, master. There'll be all sorts of flow channels, terraces, old lava spills. You can trust the *Bedu* to find them all."

Aziz proved to be right. The cliffs, that had looked so formidable from a distance, proved to be climbable after all. The caravan skirted the base of the shield for about fifty miles and found a ramplike slope that must have been formed by a secondary lava flow, since it had fewer pits and craters than the main spread of Olympus. The camels picked their way through a network of intricate channels, climbing steadily upward. Hamid-Jones was surprised at the relative ease of the climb. The slope would have been a fairly gentle one, even on Earth, and in the lighter gravity of Mars, it seemed to bother the animals hardly at all.

But there was an awful lot of it. To climb sixteen miles, they were going to have to travel more than sixty.

They broke twice to make camp. The Bedouins were wearing pressure suits all the time now, even for brief excursions between tents.

"Blood boils at the top, master," Aziz said. "The sheik's servant, Mishaal, warned me. Even camels are stretched to the limit."

On the third day, all the goats and horses were zipped into pressure suits equipped with double-ended dung collection bags. There was a short delay while an elderly camel was sacrificed to make a suit for al-Janah, the only horse that didn't already have one. None of the old spares from deceased Marshorses would have fit his long legs and heroic barrel. Hamid-Jones was amazed at the speed with which a suit was tailored; the women disappeared into a tent with lengths of freshly-washed camel gut and emerged with a completed suit only a couple of hours later.

Aziz used the interval to get Jeroboam back into his factory-made pressure suit, which had been removed some weeks earlier because the patching kit that came with the outfit was running out of patches; sandipedes ordinarily got along fine in their genetically engineered skin, but Aziz had acquired all the optional equipment along with his secondhand beast and had used it in the interests of saving on fodder.

"Eight legs, and all of them kick!" Aziz grumbled as a crowd of grinning Bedouins hooted derisive advice and watched him struggle to get one pair of legs into the suit while another pair popped out. "Isn't there anyone here who'll give me a hand?"

Only the camels were exempt. They wore respirators but no suits. The original stock had been bioengineered back in the days when Mars's atmospheric pressure had not been raised much past about fifty millibars—the level at which the body fluids of an unaltered mammal would boil away. Even so, the Bedouins smeared the more exposed parts of the camels' face and undersides liberally with grease.

Hamid-Jones cooed to the Snake to soothe her as he rubbed

a layer of grease into the sensitive skin around her muzzle. "*Ala mahlik, aziz.* Hold still, darling. This will make you feel better." The camel responded with a patient sigh, and lowered her head cooperatively. Al-Af'a had become gentle. As Hamid-Jones had become a better rider, her behavior had improved; the Bedouins no longer jeered at the two of them. In fact, Hamid-Jones had come to feel some affection for the ungainly creature.

The months on the trail had toughened him. While he still rode without particular grace, his seat was confident and less punishing. The blisters had gone away. With his lean, savage features burnt almost black by ultraviolet, he looked almost like a Bedouin himself now, if it had not been for the sportsman's pressure suit that peeped from under his borrowed robes and the modern respirator with its gold-plated valves.

"Are you calling me, master?" Aziz asked, popping up at his side.

"I was speaking to the camel. Why your mother ever gave a rogue like you 'Darling' for a name, I'll never know."

"I was a lovable baby, master," Aziz said cheerfully. His eyes narrowed professionally. "Better use plenty of that stuff around the nostrils and eyes. She really needs a headbag. I don't think she's taking this too well."

"What do you know about camels, *habibi*? You're a city boy."

"True, master. But I keep my eyes open."

On the fifth day, camels started to die. It was the older ones, mostly. They would start groaning, slow down, and finally give up. They would lie down on the trail and refuse to get up. It could be seen that they had developed tiny hemorrhages around the mucous membranes. A couple of them had more spectacular blowouts—a sudden explosion of blood from an ear or other orifice. By the end of the day, a dozen camels had been lost.

"We can't go on much longer," Hamid-Jones said. "Look at us, we're moving like zombies—even the sheik."

"Patience, master, we're almost there."

Al-Af'a moaned and collapsed under him. Hamid-Jones leapt clear in time to keep from being pinned under her falling bulk. Tumbling like a snowflake, he managed to land on his hands and feet.

The stricken beast raised her serpentine neck and stared reproachfully at him. Then, with a final sob of complaint, she rested her chin deliberately on the ground and died. Hamid-Jones couldn't find a mark anywhere on her.

The sheik appeared at his side. "Too old," he said. "No

more *naga* for you. We'll give you a *hagga* this time, a good strong one.''

Great, thought Hamid-Jones. The Bedouin had two hundred words for camel, and he had been promoted to halfway down the list. He knelt to look into al-Af'a's large, liquid eyes. They were rapidly glazing over, a thin film of ice forming as he watched. He felt an inexplicable sense of loss. *Naga* or not, he had come to depend on the crotchety old creature.

''Come,'' the sheik said. ''We've got to reach the top before nightfall.''

The nearness of their goal seemed to give men and animals a new lease on life. No more camels died that afternoon. The pace quickened, and there were still hours of daylight left when the caravan reached the peak of the vast volcano.

It was a complex caldera. Hamid-Jones found himself standing on the rim of a gigantic bowl, fifty miles across, with smaller craters opening up in its depths. Wisps of white cloud edged the rim; there was plenty of water vapor rising from below.

He looked down into the multiple hollows. He thought he saw a microscopic hint of movement, a flash of bright metal miles below.

''So close to Tharsis,'' Aziz said at his side. ''Who would think of looking for al-Sharq here?''

The caravan moved in its thousands through a great notch in the rim. A series of ledges formed by the collapse of inner rings provided a meandering descent. It was hard to tell with a pressure suit on, but it seemed to Hamid-Jones that he was already moving through thicker air.

''The camels are eager,'' Aziz said. ''They can smell the air and water at the bottom.''

Hamid-Jones let his new camel have her head. She needed no guidance from him. He perched on the teetering hump, legs folded under him like a proper Bedouin, and descended into the abyss.

CHAPTER 15

The smell of roasting sheep came wafting through the night, several billion molecules at a time, seeping into the tent through the slit of the airlock through which Aziz had just thrust his head. They were expending a lot of oxygen out there to keep the fires going.

"We're not invited to the festivities, I guess, master," Aziz said, withdrawing his head and zipping the flap up again. It was a regulation vacuum zipper. This was no Bedouin tent of hairy hide with camel-gut gaskets, but military equipment, probably captured. A line of what might have been bullet holes in the plasticized canvas had a neat row of new patches stitched across it.

"What's going on out there?" Hamid-Jones asked.

"The *Bedu* are mingling with al-Sharq's men, socializing and having a high old time. They're trading tall tales, holding hurdling contests, wrestling, racing camels, and generally whooping it up. There'll be some bruised heads by morning. The *Bedu*'ve bivouacked for the night on the edge of al-Sharq's camp—I guess they're planning to move on to their own traditional stamping ground in the big crater on the other side of the caldera tomorrow. In the meantime, the *Bedu* and the Pretender's forces are trying to outdo one another in slaughtering sheep, goats, and camels for tonight's blowout. Who's going to win the hospitality war is anyone's guess."

"Is there still a guard outside the tent?"

"Yes. He's not all that gung-ho—he'd rather be at the feast. There's no place we could go."

The sheik had turned them over to al-Sharq's forces immediately after he had paid his respects to al-Sharq himself. He had smothered them in long, flowery good-byes and kissed them both on the cheeks before leaving them to their new captors; he didn't have to worry about crossing the line into hospitality anymore—they were no longer his responsibility. Al-Sharq would interview them personally in due course.

In the meantime, Hamid-Jones and Aziz had been led off under guard and put in a square tent with a couple of hours' worth of air. They could live outside, crawling and gasping for air—there was about three hundred millibars of pressure at the bottom of the caldera—but they wouldn't get very far. The sandipede and the new camel had not gone with them, but they had been allowed to keep their basic survival equipment. Any luxuries that Aziz had packed in Jeroboam's saddlebags were presumably the property of the sheik now.

Al-Sharq's freedom fighters were tough, disciplined, and dedicated, from what Hamid-Jones had managed to see so far. They were well-equipped, too. They did not share the Bedouins' prejudice against motor vehicles and other mechanical aids. There was an extensive parking lot under an overhanging ledge of rock. It contained big ten-wheel-drive Bobtail sand trucks, hoverjeeps, a half-dozen late-model tanks—even a small air force of jethoppers, sailplanes, and a black-painted orbital vehicle. There was a power plant that ran on methane, to judge by the pile of animal dung heaped next to it, and a great big metal doughnut, still sitting in half of the crate it had come in, that looked like the makings of a small fusion generator.

"They seem to have forgotten about us," Hamid-Jones fretted. He started to pace, then remembered the half-empty condition of the air tank they'd been given and sat down again.

"Relax, master. I wouldn't be in a hurry to see al-Sharq if I were you. Enjoy life while you can."

"What's that supposed to mean?"

"Nothing. Just that the Shining has to worry about spies all the time. I imagine there've been other odd characters that got this far. These rebels don't take chances. When in doubt, drop them down a vent."

"Half the desert must know that al-Sharq's here."

"Yes, but they're his brothers. The blood of the desert people flows in al-Sharq's veins. A traitor wouldn't last long out here."

"We're no danger to him. We've come with valuable information."

"Ah, but can he trust you? A Palace official, confidant of the Vizier!"

"For God's sake, al-Sharq must know that Rubinstein was put in a cage to rot to death! They'll get satellite television, even on Mount Olympus!"

"Then why didn't you rot to death along with him? The bloodbath swept through his whole staff, his family—everybody who didn't jump fast enough to switch sides."

"Are you trying to talk me into a grave?"

"I'm only trying to show you how it must look from al-Sharq's point of view, master," Aziz whined.

"Well, don't! We're in enough trouble without borrowing any."

The air gauge was almost on empty when the inner flap unzipped and an armed guard came through, not bothering to zip it up again behind him. He was a young, wiry man in desert-pink khakis and army-issue respirator with a bubble faceplate.

"Come," he said, motioning with his submachine gun at Hamid-Jones. "The Shining will see you now."

"What about him?" Hamid-Jones said, gesturing at Aziz.

"Him later. Just you now."

Following the guard's example, Hamid-Jones donned only his mask, not bothering with the pressure suit. The guard held the flap open for him.

"Wait a minute!" Aziz yelped. "What about my air?"

"Not my department," the guard shrugged. "Whether or not you get another tank depends."

"Talk with a silver tongue, master," Aziz implored Hamid-Jones.

There was enough oxygen in Hamid-Jones's backpack to take him across the encampment to al-Sharq's tent. If the interview didn't go off all right, he wouldn't have to worry about getting back.

In the shadow of the caldera rim he saw a great crescent of dappled movement punctuated by hundreds of tiny winking fires where whole spitted camels and sheep were roasting. The sentry close behind him, he made his way through the tent city that housed al-Sharq's forces. The black tents of the nomads, shrouded in shadow, were too far away to be seen clearly, but the greater part of both groups seemed to have gathered around the fires. He could hear the whoops and shouts of impromptu sporting contests carried on the thin air, and once a troop of Marscamels thundered by, perilously close to an avenue of tents, their riders tossing what looked like the headless body of a goat back and forth.

His guard took him down a path, sandbagged on both sides

to a height of four or five feet, that zigzagged to a modest tent about forty feet long that was designed like a Bedouin *beit sha'ar*—house of hair—with swaybacked caterpillar sections, but that was made of plasticized canvas. A couple of sentries stood alertly at the entrance but let them through without too much fuss. The wiry guard took Hamid-Jones through an audience section where about a dozen men—Bedouin chiefs and rebel staff officers in desert pinks—sat drinking coffee and conversing with one another, and deposited him in a small section that was partitioned off by khaki tarpaulins.

The man who was seated at a low folding desk, working at a small lap-top computer, snapped the screen shut when he came in and swiveled around to have a look at him.

Hamid-Jones stared back with unabashed curiosity. So this was the famous al-Sharq, the Pretender, who claimed to be a royal prince of the blood, and who distinguished himself from other fedayeen leaders by asserting his right to the throne of Mars itself. His followers called him "the Shining" after the sun that rose in the east, but he was denounced as a murderer, a common terrorist, and a traitor by the government organs of propaganda.

Al-Sharq looked the part of a prince. He was a tall, well-knit, imposing man, burly-shouldered for a Martian, with a neatly clipped beard and mustache. His hazel eyes were clear and forthright. They radiated authority—no one would think of questioning this man. He wore a plain uniform, open at the neck. He was about forty. There was a controlled strength of movement about him that contributed to the striking impression he made.

"So you're the chap who claims to have helped to paste together a new Emir?" he said with a questioning lift of an eyebrow. "Hamid-Jones, is it?"

The language he had chosen was English—the distinct, unaccented English of the Protectorate rather than one of the American dialects. He had not waited to confirm Hamid-Jones's background, so his information must have been good—not limited to what the sheik had told him. The lap-top was plugged into a small FM modem that probably led to a data bank containing Hamid-Jones's intelligence file.

But al-Sharq had not chosen to address him that way out of simple courtesy, or even a desire to show off, Hamid-Jones realized with a growing respect. There were other men all around them, separated only by canvas curtains—he could hear the polite murmur of voices in the visitors' section; al-Sharq wanted to keep this interview as restricted as possible until he could assess Hamid-Jones's information. A few of his staff officers almost certainly spoke English as their second tongue, but the Bedouins, despite their Greater Arabian ancestry, had forgotten it generations ago.

"Yes, that's right," Hamid-Jones replied.

"And you say that you personally saw the old Emir's head die, but that it happened some time after the freedom fighters' courageous attack in the operating theater."

"Yes."

"Could you be mistaken?"

Hamid-Jones shuddered. "No."

Al-Sharq became pensive. "We couldn't be sure. The video was cut off before we could confirm it. We had reports that the head had died right there on the operating table, but then there were other reports that it had survived. And then, of course, there was all the Palace propaganda, showing what was presumably a recovering Emir, and then the press conference about his possessing his wife in front of witnesses, and his various appearances at all the bloody *majlis*es that followed. Our analysts pretty much came to the conclusion that the so-called reconstituted Emir was another pair of clones—but we had no independent confirmation. But you say you were actually present at the second—secret—operation?"

"You can give me a lie detector test if you want," Hamid-Jones said, getting a little surly and instantly regretting it.

Al-Sharq only looked amused. "My dear chap, *I'm* your lie detector."

Hamid-Jones said nothing.

"All right," the rebel leader said with a sigh. "You'd better tell me all about it."

Hamid-Jones went through the whole story. Al-Sharq drew him out skillfully and incisively. He made Hamid-Jones repeat several minor observations about Bobo's behavior and his relationship to Ismail. Hamid-Jones finished with a description of his last sight of Rubinstein in the monkey cage.

"Rubinstein was a very great man," the Pretender said soberly. "He was the only restraint on that despicable tyrant. It's too bad he was my enemy. I would have liked him as an ally."

He made Hamid-Jones describe his escape in minute detail and slapped his thigh and laughed when Hamid-Jones got to the part about stealing the Winged One right out of the Royal Stables. "And now the sheik has him, the old fox! He didn't say anything about that to me. Ah, well, *ya* Abdul, easy come, easy go."

Behind al-Sharq's easy affability, Hamid-Jones knew, was a grimmer purpose. He was judging the plausibility of Hamid-Jones's escape from Tharsis City and deciding how genuine was his story of fleeing for his life. The rebel leader followed with an expert probe of Hamid-Jones's feelings about being a condemned fugitive with no place to go.

"You can't go back to Tharsis City or any other settlement on Mars, you know. Not even the most remote oasis village on the other side of the planet. There's a price on your head."

"I wasn't sure."

"Yes indeed." Al-Sharq tapped the lap-top with a thumbnail. "It's in your file. You've been condemned in absentia. Nothing remains but to carry out the sentence. I believe it's a slow flensing by the eunuchs. There are people in every town who make a profitable hobby of scrolling through the daily proscription lists and studying the mug shots. You'd be fortunate to escape detection for a few hours. No, I'm afraid you're a pariah until the Emir is overthrown."

He uttered the last phrase so casually and with such conviction that Hamid-Jones was taken aback. Al-Sharq seemed to take it for granted that it was only a matter of time until he deposed the Emir—or the imitation who posed as the Emir—and that it was not going to be a very long time, either.

"I'll just have to do my best," Hamid-Jones said gruffly.

"How does the Bedouin life appeal to you? There are worse ways to survive outside the Emirate's so-called civilization. It's a hard life, but it offers a kind of freedom that city folk never know."

Hamid-Jones thought it over. "I wouldn't mind it. They're grand folk."

"The sheik likes you, you know. He admired your pluck in staying aboard that old nag he gave you. He says you have that quality the *Bedu* call *qalb*—heart. He thinks you'd make a good fighting man. I'll put in a word for you."

"You'd do that?"

Al-Sharq laughed. "My dear Abdul, you've done me a favor. Now I know where things stand at the Palace. I couldn't have gotten a spy into Ismail's bedroom in a thousand years—though I do have a few loyal followers who'd be willing to give up their sporting goods on the promise of having them recloned afterward." He waved a hand in a large gesture. "Now I can get the propaganda mill rolling, stir up the desert tribes, make my strategic plans. Your information will give me leverage with other fedayeen groups—pave the way to coordinating an offensive with them.''

''I'm glad I could be of use.''

Al-Sharq was sensitive to the bitterness in Hamid-Jones's tone. ''My dear chap, you used to be a very solid citizen, I know. Very commendable. It's all in your file. It's hard to change your values overnight. But surely you must realize now that your loyalties were misplaced. We're going to make a better Mars, people like you and me. And believe me, you can do your part as one of the sheik's fighting men. The *Bedu* are going to help me put the pressure on. So far their raids have been probing ones—testing the Emirate's outlying defenses, keeping them off balance. Now they'll go for the lifeline—step up their raids on the Emir's caravans.''

''I thought they were raiding because they were hungry.''

''That, too. How do you think revolutions start?''

''I'm not a freedom fighter,'' Hamid-Jones said stiffly. ''I haven't joined your cause. But if I'm going to be adopted by a desert tribe, I'll live their life—including joining their forays.''

''Excellent fellow! That's all I expect. I know you haven't identified yourself *with* our cause—you're just *against* the Emirate. That's good enough for now. In time your own common sense will bring you around. You see, I'm the only alternative.''

''Is that why the Alpha Centaurans bankroll you?''

As soon as the words had left his mouth, he was appalled at his boldness. He was still at the mercy of this brigand, whatever al-Sharq's civilities toward him.

But al-Sharq took no offense. ''The Centaurans have an important stake in events here. Our two systems may be living four years in each other's pasts, but they're still the only star close enough to Sol to be affected by political events here—albeit in slow motion. Tell me, will your patchwork Emir press his claim to the Caliphate for the upcoming congress?''

Hamid-Jones thought it over. ''No. There's too much on their plate. Ismail won't risk greater exposure for Bobo so soon after the switch—and he certainly won't dare to let him out of his sight to go on the hajj this time. And Bobo himself hasn't caught the Caliphate bug yet.'' He thought it through a little further. ''But he *will*. He's as greedy as his nucleotides. In time he'll want it all. I'd say he'll go after the Caliphate by the *next* congress. Or the congress after that, at most.''

''Then that's five years, maybe ten, after next year's summit.

That will buy the Centaurans a breathing space. They'll be glad to hear that."

Al-Sharq turned back to his desk and became busy.

Hamid-Jones hung around a while, then said, "Am I free to go?"

Al-Sharq did not glance up. "What?" he said absently. "Oh, yes. Why don't you join the feast. Be my guest."

A subaltern lent him a bottle of air to get back to his tent with; somehow word had spread by the time he emerged through the inner flap that he was now in al-Sharq's good books.

The sentry who had fidgeted at being kept from the feast was no longer guarding the entrance of his tent when he got there. The ridge of the tent sagged a little, as if pressure had been allowed to get low inside. He pushed through the double flap, unzipping and zipping up as he went, and opened his mouth to give Aziz the good news.

But Aziz wasn't there. A shiny new air tank leaned against a tent pole. His own pressure suit sat propped up in a corner like a headless stocking-doll where he had left it, but Aziz's suit was gone.

He walked over to the air tank. Its gauge read three-quarters full. If it had been full when it had been delivered, then Aziz must have used it to recharge his own suit bottles. But why had he bothered with a full suit? He couldn't have gotten very far in an armed camp, and no one in the caldera bothered to suit up for brief exposure outside. Despite the height of Olympus, the six or seven miles-high walls that surrounded them and the continual upwelling from the vents kept pressure comfortably above two hundred millibars. And it was warm—as warm as the equator at noon.

He shrugged. Aziz could take care of himself. If he got into trouble he'd have to talk himself out of it. Probably, Hamid-Jones told himself, he'd see Aziz at the feast.

But how had Aziz managed it? The guard's disappearance in the time it had taken to walk from al-Sharq's tent might be explained by radio gossip from a buddy at headquarters. But for Aziz to be gone by the time Hamid-Jones arrived, he would have had to have started suiting up and recharging his tanks while Hamid-Jones was still closeted with the rebel leader, his fate as yet undecided.

He poked his head outside the tent. In the firelight several hundred yards away, thirty men staggered under the weight of a whole roasted camel that was being borne along on a sheet-metal tray the size of a whaleboat. The six arched legs rising high overhead might have been ship oars. It looked as if the camel had been stuffed with a whole roasted sheep; four more stiff legs rose like the points of a crown from the camel's belly. What the sheep might have been stuffed with, he couldn't tell at this distance.

He clapped his respirator back over his nose and sauntered over to get his share.

Aziz was still missing when he returned to the tent some hours later, full of mutton, frostrice, camel giblets, and gravy. The celebration was beginning to break up, though diehards still lingered around the force-fed campfires, swapping tales and urging a few more songs and dances out of the tired amateur performers among them. Hamid-Jones stumbled inside, weighted down by fatigue and too much food.

Aziz had not been anywhere in evidence at the feast, though Hamid-Jones had gone from campfire to campfire looking for him. At one point he had started toward a slight figure in a pressure suit, but it turned out to be a messenger just arrived from outside.

He could not be bothered worrying about it further. He set the air on low, rolled himself up in an army blanket and went to sleep.

A zipping noise and furtive movement inside the tent awakened him. "Shhh, master, it's me," Aziz whispered. "Go back to sleep."

Hamid-Jones struggled to sit up. He tapped his wrist screen for the time and found that it was halfway to morning. "Where have you been?" he demanded.

Aziz had his back to him as he unsuited. "Oh, master, I've been in paradise," he said.

"Speak more plainly, you liar. What have you been up to?"

Aziz turned around, a dark bulk in the tiny light from Hamid-Jones's wrist. "I've been sampling the wares of one of the rebel women," he said, audibly smacking his lips. "Would you believe it, master, they are not under restriction, but are as free as men."

"Don't tell me any more stories. You didn't put on a pressure suit to go tomcatting. Have you been out of this crater?"

"I had to meet the woman far from camp, master. They may

not be under restriction, but their men are correspondingly jealous."

"And this woman?" Hamid-Jones said with heavy sarcasm. "Was she wearing a pressure suit, too?"

"She was, master. It made a nice problem."

Hamid-Jones gave up. "Go get some sleep. We're becoming Bedouins in the morning."

"I know, master."

"You know? How?"

"I found out from the woman, master. You can't keep secrets in a camp like this."

"You're my son," the sheik said.

"Thank you, *ya* Majid," Hamid-Jones replied.

"You're my kinsman, the hand of my right arm."

Hamid-Jones lowered his eyes modestly.

"You're my brother, my eye!" the sheik insisted, working up steam.

They were standing in front of the remains of the sheik's tent— the last humped segment of the guest section, reduced now to a symbolic canopy with its sides taken down. Women were taking the rest of the tent apart, seam by seam, and packing it up for the waiting camels. One of the wrapped figures, Hamid-Jones saw with some discomfort, was the sheik's daughter; she kept peering through the folds of the face shawl that covered her respirator and making moon eyes at him.

A crowd of Bedouin had paused in their camp-striking labors to watch the little ceremony. A large brass coffeepot sat on the sand, its spout still issuing steam. The sheik had ground the beans with his own hands and poured out the first cups for Hamid-Jones and Aziz, knocking the cups against the spout and placing a hand over his heart.

"To my son I give a camel," the sheik went on.

Hamid-Jones made the ritual protests, but the sheik could not be stopped.

"And not just any camel. A *mehari*."

He had been promoted again. A *mehari* was a fine racing camel, and the meharists were the elite of the Bedouin cavalry. One of the sheik's biological sons led the great spindle-legged beast over and handed the reins to him with a scowl.

"And not just any *mehari*," the sheik continued relentlessly. "An *umaniyah*."

Hamid-Jones stepped up his protests, but the sheik brushed them aside.

"And not just an ordinary *umaniyah*," the sheik persisted. "A *batiniyah*—the finest breed for speed and riding!"

Hamid-Jones showed that he was suitably dazzled with an incoherent outpouring of protests. The sheik smiled magnanimously.

He was fully equipped with a *thop*—a riding robe that fit over his pressure suit, a Bedouin heatcloak impregnated with little heat-producing organisms, an old-fashioned slug-throwing Kalashnikov, and a *khanjar*—a wicked curved knife from the sheik's own arsenal. The sheik had retained Hamid-Jones's sports model Kalashnikov and its store of microflechette magazines for his own use, along with the laser smartpistol and the fragmentation grenades. He also had kept al-Janah.

"It's nothing," the sheik said. "A son of the desert deserves a steed worthy of his prowess."

Another of the sheik's biological sons was heading their way with a Marscamel in tow. Hamid-Jones was no expert, but he had learned a thing or two during his sojourn with the tribe, and he could see that the camel was no *batiniyah*, or even an *umaniyah*. He rated it at about a *raba*—a pretty good camel, four years old.

"And to you, *ya* Aziz," the sheik was saying, "I also give a camel."

The huge beast stared superciliously from its lofty heights and hissed. Aziz jumped back and almost tripped over the coffeepot.

"I can't ride a camel, *ya* Majid," Aziz protested. "I'm just a city boy."

"You'll learn, *ya* Aziz," the sheik said. "It isn't seemly for a fighting man to ride a donkey, even an eight-legged one."

"Where's Jeroboam?" Aziz said, looking trapped.

The sheik gave a deep booming laugh. "Why, we ate him last night, *ya* Aziz. He was your contribution to the feast. Very tender, and he provided eight drumsticks."

Aziz gave a moan. The sheik's son was pressing the camel's reins on him, and reluctantly he took them.

"We usually winter over in the volcano," the sheik said. "This time we stay only a few weeks to let the animals graze. Then we return to the desert and plunder the false Emir's caravans."

CHAPTER 16

Down below, the caravan was a great dappled snake crawling sinuously through the passes and gullies, its scales catching glints of copper sunlight. No, Hamid-Jones thought—more like a river of beads, spilling out to widen where the landscape allowed, narrowing again when constricted.

"Keep your head down," the sheik said. "Don't let it show above the ridge."

He handed Hamid-Jones the monocular. Hamid-Jones adjusted it for glare and bent it into an approximate Z shape to form a rough periscope. He put his eye to the little fiber-optics screen and turned up the magnification.

It was rich pickings. This was no procession of flea-bitten pack camels, merchants banding together for mutual protection, carting goods from one oasis to another. It was a convoy of the great desert trucks that carried the heavy overland traffic between the major population centers. It stretched for miles—a bumper to bumper parade of immense, multiwheeled flatbed vehicles rolling on twelve-foot mesh tires, their enclosed cabs like the bridges of ships.

Camels there were, too, but they were only an escort—some Bedouin tribe loyal to the Emir that had been hired as outriders. They rode back and forth along the line of traffic, more mobile than the lumbering behemoths they were guarding. Hamid-Jones focused on one of them. He was a tatty-looking fellow in striped robes, riding with one leg hooked around the saddle pommel. Some kind of a carbine with an oxygen feed at the breech was slung across his back—probably an Earth import that wasn't

257

adapted to use Mars-style ammunition with its own oxidizer. His camel wore a cheap mass-produced plastic respirator.

"Beni Akhdar," the sheik said with a wolf's grin. "Equator Arabs, sons of the soft life. They'll run as soon as they see who they're up against."

There had been remarkably little killing during the raids on caravans—Hamid-Jones was a veteran of a half-dozen of them so far. There was a sort of law of the *rahzoo*—the looting expedition—that both sides observed. When a tribesman saw that he was outnumbered or outmatched, he gave up or ran—and the winners weren't anxious to spill unnecessary blood, either. It was the damn city men—the security guards or the occasional army squad—who were the problem. They were not sensible men. The sheik's desert fighters had regretfully left such belligerent fellows with their throats cut, when they would have been glad to look the other way while they escaped into the desert.

"Looks like easy booty," Aziz said. "Too easy."

The sheik looked him over with good-natured contempt. "What are you afraid of, *ya* Aziz? Perhaps we're not city dwellers with marvelous devices, but we're not ignorant. We have our own methods of intelligence. And we can use technology when we want to, as well. Al-Sharq launched a stealth satellite several days ago, a little thing the size of a melon, and it hasn't been detected yet. I checked with him by radio only an hour ago. There are no troop concentrations nearby, and there's nothing in the Emir's air force that's ready to scramble. By the time they could get a flight of sailjets into the air from Candor base, we'll have long since scattered."

"Forgive me, *ya* Majid, I'm a naturally cautious man," Aziz said meekly. He peered up at the sky. "What's that?"

Hamid-Jones saw a fleck of light, almost drowned out by glare. He consulted the little astronomical brain in his wrist communicator. "It's only Deimos. According to my *zij*, it should be almost at zenith about now."

The sheik had a hearty laugh at Aziz's expense. "Did you think the Emir was going to drop a moon on us, *ya* Aziz? Or perhaps one of the starships that are docked there?"

"We'd do better to worry about Phobos," Hamid-Jones said. "It's less than four thousand miles overhead—the Emirate uses it as a natural surveillance satellite. But even if some spy camera had noticed us the last time Phobos zipped by, there's nothing they could do about it. You heard the sheik say there were no troop concentrations in the area."

"That's right, master, you make fun of me, too," Aziz sulked. "I'm only trying to look out for you."

One of the sheik's sons, the quiet one named Bachir, slid a clip into his automatic weapon. The click as it snapped into place seemed emphatically loud, even in the thin air of the desert. The others took it as a signal and began backing down the lee side of the slope on all fours, not standing up until their heads could not be seen above the ridge. The sheik gave a paternal smile and gathered up his robes. Hamid-Jones and Aziz followed him at a backward crouch, then hurried to catch up as he headed in long strides to where the animals were waiting.

A restless throng of mounted men filled the depression behind the ridge, wearing out the sand with a thousand milling hooves. Every able-bodied man in the tribe between the ages of sixteen and sixty was here; it would have been unthinkable to miss out on a share of the loot. Most rode Marscamels—the primitive four-legged kind favored by desert warriors; though a few of the very young boys, out for their first *rahzou*, had shamefacedly had to make do with the family's pack hexapod. The minor chieftains rode horses for the actual attack, though they had brought along camels for their transportation; these were tethered to stakes and would be retrieved later.

The sheik made a flying leap and swung himself aboard al-Janah. Mounted atop the lofty, long-shanked steed, he was scarcely lower in altitude than the camel riders. The noble Marshorse snorted through its silver-chased respirator and pawed the earth in its eagerness to go.

Hamid-Jones scrambled inelegantly but efficiently onto his high perch and settled himself firmly in the saddle, hooking one knee correctly around the forward pommel and tucking that foot under his other leg. Riding a Marscamel was no more difficult than riding a horse, once you got the hang of it, and he had had plenty of practice.

To his left, Aziz was still trying fruitlessly to get his camel to kneel for him. Finally he gave up and climbed the dangling thongs like a sailor ascending the rigging.

"*Yallah!*" the sheik cried, and the thick mass of knobby creatures began to move forward, slowly at first, then gaining speed as they scrabbled up the loose shale of the slope.

They spilled over the top of the ridge in an extended line that was nowhere more than a few beasts deep; no one wanted to be last in the headlong race toward their prize. They charged down the steep bank in a spray of sand and gravel, the animals sliding and plunging, but managing to stay on their feet.

Below, the caravan outriders hadn't seen them yet. The string of squarish vehicles crawled slowly by, small as matchboxes, the toy men on their toy camels like red spiders beside them. Then the spiders became agitated, colliding and bunching together, and a couple of micromissiles came soaring toward the raiders, trailing gray smoke.

The missiles were dumb; they buried themselves in the sand and made little snapping explosions without hitting anything alive. The raiding party set up a great yell and streaked flat out for the caravan, the camels' long necks stretched low and straight. At the head of the truck convoy, Hamid-Jones saw a bright flash, and a second later came the crack of plastic explosives; Bachir, riding at the extreme end of the Bedouins' left pincer, had gotten off his prepared satchel. The lead vehicle went up in smoke, and the long line of trucks ground to a halt. Several failed to stop in time—monsters that size carried a lot of inertia—and collided in several rear-end collisions. Hamid-Jones saw one enormous wheel come rolling loose to crush a man and camel who were in the way.

A spray of bullets and microflechettes came zinging toward them, and Hamid-Jones saw riders around him fall. The Bedouins returned the fire, leaning outward from the saddle to avoid shooting their own beasts in the head, and the defending outriders started to tumble from the saddle themselves.

The return fire was definitely halfhearted after that first exchange. Before the desert raiders had covered a third of the distance, the tribesmen in the striped robes began to scatter. By the time Hamid-Jones reined to a skidding halt in front of the stalled line of flatbeds, the Equator Arabs were hightailing it in the distance.

The drivers, by and large, stayed in their deckhouses and looked down sourly at the proceedings. One overzealous fellow, thinking that it was up to him to protect company property, emerged from his cab waving a small scattergun—a seven-barrel Thursday Night Special—and promptly got himself shot in the center of his forehead. That damped any enthusiasm of other possible heroes.

Jubilant men on camels were cutting ropes and cargo nets, and peeling back the tarpaulins that covered the flatbeds. Others had dismounted to clamber aboard the sandtrucks and shoot open locked containers. Gleefully, working like stevedores, they pitched cargo into the sand—cartons of small appliances, bales of fabric, furniture, cryocontainers of liquid oxygen, luxury foodstuffs. Eager hands were waiting below to paw through the revealed treasures.

"Stay in your saddle, master," Aziz said, pulling up beside him.

"What's troubling you?" Hamid-Jones said with some surprise. "I'd have thought you'd be first in line to grab your share."

"Just wait a while. There'll be plenty left, if all is well. In the meantime, it would be prudent to stay mounted and be prepared for a quick getaway."

"What do you mean, if all is well?"

Before Aziz could reply, there was a thunderclap in the sky above. The camels shied and bellowed with fear. A huge shadow swooped along the sands.

Hamid-Jones jerked his head up and saw an enormous nacelle dropping from the sky, a flattened, streamlined pod the size of a carbarn. It hit the sands with jarring impact, as if it were being dragged along, and skidded to a stop.

In a flash, Hamid-Jones realized what it was. It was the Deimos skyhook, and the nacelle was one of the starport terminals that hauled passengers and cargo up to the little potato moon, 12,500 miles overhead. Deimos moved at only about a hundred miles an hour relative to the Martian surface, and the 12,500-mile-long superfilament cable—the equivalent in terms of strain to a mere 4,750-mile line in Earth gravity—had enough elasticity to minimize the risk of sudden acceleration and possible whiplash injury to passengers when the trailing hook caught up the pod's harness. A careful operator could skid the nacelle to a fairly gentle stop, too. But this operator wasn't being gentle.

The front of the pod dropped open with a clang, making a wide ramp, and men and vehicles poured out—armored Hovercraft and floating, shallow-bowled personnel carriers stuffed with soldiers. They emptied the pod in about half a minute flat and fanned out to both sides to get out of its way. The lid snapped shut and the invisible line yanked the pod back into the sky.

It was like some kind of magic trick. Where there had been only empty sands a few minutes before, a formidable fighting force was now arrayed against the Bedouins. It moved without pause in a broad front, the Hovercraft kicking up clouds of thick dust.

The Bedouins were caught completely off guard. Only a few dozen were still mounted, and these tried bravely to rally. The others, scrambling about in the sand or exposed to view on top of the truckbeds, were cut down as they tried to reach their animals. They were no match for the armored Hovercraft skimming toward them, guns spitting.

Horses screamed, camels bawled in terror. Confused shouts filled the air. There was a *pop pop pop* of little explosions and the crack of heavy weapons. The choking clouds of dust made the scene a washed-out, brownish watercolor in which dim blurred shapes could be seen stumbling about. Hamid-Jones's camel was shot out from under him, and he ejected from the saddle with a push of his boot heels. He hit the sand rolling and scrambled on his hands and knees for the shelter of a sandtruck's undercarriage. He tripped over a corpse and dived behind one of the enormous basket wheels.

It was over in minutes. Soldiers prowled among the fallen, finishing off the hopelessly wounded and those among the still living who showed fight. With brutal efficiency they rounded up those who could still walk and herded them to a collection point on a patch of flat sand where officers with sidearms waited.

A gun was poked in Hamid-Jones's face. *"Yalla bina!"* a harsh voice commanded.

"Don't shoot." He had lost his weapon in the tumble from the camel and being unarmed saved him. Soldiers hauled him roughly to his feet. One of them gave him a gratuitous smack in the faceplate that cracked it and started his nose bleeding. Hands clamped around his neck and elbow and dragged him to the collection point.

About thirty survivors were there, kneeling with their hands locked behind their necks if they were able, sprawled in the sand if they were not. No one talked, no one looked at anyone else. Shame and fear were palpable in the air. A young boy of about sixteen with a couple of fingers shot off and blood welling from the opened stubs on his pressure glove, suppressed a whimper and tried to look stoic. Hardly any of the camel-gut pressure suits were intact—they hung deflated on the survivors' frames—but most still had their respirators. A couple who didn't sucked in great lungfuls of thin air, wheezing.

The sheik was not among the prisoners, nor were any of his sons. They had stayed on horseback to the last. Over at the scene of the carnage, al-Janah lay jumbled in the sand, his beanstalk legs sticking out at the wrong angles.

Aziz was not among the kneeling men, either, nor could

Hamid-Jones recognize his camel among the slaughtered beasts lying on this side of the train.

Soldiers pushed him to his knees and left him kneeling with the others. Officers in short belted robes over their pressure suits were questioning some of the captives at random, not hesitating to employ a measure of desultory rough stuff when they didn't like the answers—yanking off respirators or clubbing a head or a kidney with the butt of a machine pistol.

"We'll get nothing out of these fellows," said one with a captain's badge pinned to the *agal* of his headcloth. His superior was a major—the highest visible rank Hamid-Jones had seen so far, and probably the officer in command of the mobile force.

"It doesn't matter," said the major, a thin man with a Sandhurst mustache. "They're all desert scum anyway They won't know anything important."

"Al-Sharq is too smart to walk into a trap," the captain said. "I have to give him that."

Hamid-Jones stiffened. So it had been a trap, with the caravan as bait. Had Aziz known that, or had he only been guessing?

"It worked, at any rate," the major replied. "One less band of desert rabble for us to worry about. If the tip we got was good, then Force Beta should be mopping up the women and children about now."

Hamid-Jones writhed in impotent rage. They had been betrayed! But by whom? Some desert Judas who would shortly be collecting his thirteen silver shekels? An infiltrator in al-Sharq's camp?

The Equator Arabs who had been the caravan's outriders were drifting back, now that the fighting was over. They were brave now, shouting taunts at the kneeling prisoners. The soldiers watched with incurious eyes, shooing them back halfheartedly when they got too close.

"Give them to us, *sidi*," pleaded a suety chap in salmonstriped robes, leaning over from an adjustable-back camel saddle to talk to one of the junior officers. "We know what to do with their sort. We're decent men—not like these Emptiness tribes who stop up their ears from the word of Allah."

Some of his companions were edging their stringy beasts closer to the rows of kneeling men. One of them suddenly reversed his fifteen-foot lance and swung it like a polo club, catching a prisoner on the jaw with the butt. The man fell over sideways, his respirator knocked off, and lay there twitching feebly. The Equator Arabs laughed and shouted congratulations at the fellow who'd done it.

"I can't hold my men back much longer," the suety one argued. "They're righteously angry. We don't want trouble between us and your soldiers, Allah forbid."

Not all of the outriders were feeling that righteous; some of them were casting covetous glances at all the merchandise scattered in the sand and getting warned off by the soldiers for edging over to it.

The suety one had taken his case to the major. "They're no good to you anymore. They're no good to God. You can't take prisoners all the way back to Tharsis City. Let us do the job for you."

At that, the one who had swung his lance now spurred his camel into the huddled group, bowling prisoners over. A soldier stepped forward and grabbed the reins of the camel, looking toward the major for guidance. With a bored expression, the major moved back out of the way. Taking their cue from him, the soldiers withdrew a short distance, and the mounted tribesmen began to have their sport.

At first they contented themselves with poking at a victim or two with their long lances and having the camels trample them a little. Then a sword flashed and a head bounced to the ground, the black leather snout of the respirator still attached. That caused laughter and excited babble. The Equatorial Arabs slid from their saddles then and began hacking away at the helpless men in earnest.

Hamid-Jones bunched his Earth-bred muscles for a last hopeless act of resistance. He knew he was dead, but he thought he might be able to crash into one of the butchers—knock him off his feet and get his hands around a scrawny Martian throat for a convulsive squeeze before all the blades descended on him.

The boy next to Hamid-Jones shrank, afraid to make a run for it—runners were caught and cut down right away. Three grinning Equatorial tribesmen finished their bloody work a short distance away and looked around for a new victim.

The major with the Sandhurst mustache was staring at Hamid-Jones's custom-tailored pressure suit where it showed through the borrowed Bedouin robes. He raised a palm at the three approaching executioners and they paused, looking annoyed.

"You, fellow, you're not *Bedu*. What were you doing with this rabble?"

"I . . ." His tongue was too thick. He clenched and unclenched his fists and tried to estimate his chances of reaching the major.

"By George, what's this?" The major had noticed the Royal Stables seal on the auxiliary air bottle Hamid-Jones wore. It had been part of al-Janah's stolen kit. "Was that your horse?"

His subordinate was at his side, whispering. Part of al-Janah's breathing rig was dangling from his hand, and he showed the stamped royal crest to the major.

"What's your name?" the major asked sharply.

Hamid-Jones found his voice. He said coldly, "I'm Abdul ben Arthur Hamid-Jones, acting Clonemaster of the Royal Stables."

The major peered at him. It was obvious the name meant nothing to him; he was a professional military man, a field officer who did as he was told no matter who was in power. He wouldn't necessarily be familiar with all the names on the proscription lists.

"Hmm, what do you think, Gammal?"

"It could be. I think I recognize his face from the holovid — wasn't he in one of the Palace news conferences?"

The major scowled at his new problem. Suddenly he whirled and barked at the cowering Bedouin youth: "You, boy! Did your people capture this man? Were you holding him for ransom?"

The boy was too scared to speak. "Let me, *sidi*!" one of the grinning Equatorials said, and pounced on him with a rotary knife.

The boy screamed. Hamid-Jones blundered toward him, but soldiers pinioned his arms.

"You don't want to get in the way of these chaps," the major said softly. "You might get hurt."

"Yes, yes!" the boy bleated. "We captured him!"

There were about fifteen seconds' worth of horrible sounds that stopped abruptly in midshriek; the Equatorial tribesman had been too eager.

Hamid-Jones struggled impotently in the soldiers' grip. His head was reeling; delayed shock had caught up with him. The major watched his efforts through narrowed eyes, then turned to his subordinate.

"I don't know," he sighed. "We'd better take him back with us. The politicals can sort it out when we get to Tharsis City."

There was no chance to escape. They'd left him unfettered, but there was someone close by to watch him all the way. The first thing they did was to take away his pressure suit and breathing apparatus, telling him he'd be more comfortable. He rode in the enclosed bubble of an armored Hovercraft as far as the Pavonis forward base, then was transferred to a staff car that was headed toward Tharsis City with a load of dispatches.

His personal watchdog was an earnest young lieutenant named Arnab, who kept trying to reassure him. "It'll be all right, *ya* Abdul," he said, offering him some salted poprice from a snackbag. "As soon as they can verify your DNA print, they'll turn you loose."

Hamid-Jones sat glumly, not caring about the distress his uncommunicativeness was causing Arnab. A part of his mind was trying to make plans. He wondered if he'd have a chance to slip away before they delivered him to whoever was going to decide about him, or if there'd be an interval at the other end when his custody would be loose or careless enough for him to make a break for it. At the moment, such thoughts were not very productive; he was hemmed in between Arnab and an ill-smelling soldier fingering a palmgun loaded with mushroom slugs, and facing him on the jumpseats were two more large fellows armed with fixed bayonets over their minicarbines.

"Say, what was it like, living with *Bedu*?" Arnab asked. "Is it true that their women go around with bare faces?"

"I don't know. Not usually." Hamid-Jones wondered what had happened to the sheik's amorous daughter. She had been getting to be a problem during these last weeks, careless about her veil and rubbing against him when she served the men in the guest section. It hadn't seemed to bother the sheik; he had been getting fond of Hamid-Jones. The only problem about having him for a son-in-law was his utter destitution in Bedouin terms. But his share of the loot from the caravan raids was supposed to take care of that. The sheik used to wax rhapsodic about the flocks that Hamid-Jones would one day acquire, the gold and the slaves and the portable household appurtenances.

"The guys from Force Beta have all the luck," Arnab said, licking his lips.

Hamid-Jones restrained himself. There was no point in reacting anymore. There was no point in anything.

"Ah, there's a signpost," Arnab said, peering through the side curtains. "Twelve kilos to the Bab al-Dahub. It won't be long now."

* * *

At the army barracks they left him in a bare room with a guard at the door. After a half-hour or so, Arnab came in and said in an embarrassed tone, "They're sending someone to pick you up."

"Have they checked my DNA print?"

"Er, I wouldn't know about that."

"I guess I'll say so long now, then. Take care of yourself, *ya* Arnab."

"Er, you, too," Arnab said, looking more embarrassed. He left hastily, and Hamid-Jones did not see him again.

Two members of the civil police arrived a quarter-hour later, armed with shrapnel guns and electric truncheons. "This the one?" one of them asked the sergeant who had shown them the way.

"You got to sign for him," the sergeant said, holding out a clipboard.

The policeman scribbled a signature and the sergeant left. The two policemen did not speak to Hamid-Jones. They forced his wrists up behind his back and wrapped monofilament cuffs around them. Another monofilament drawloop went around each ankle, giving him about a foot of play for hobbling along. Arnab was nowhere in evidence as they led him out the main entrance. A large police van was parked out front, its motors humming, with another cop waiting at the rear hatch.

"Got another one for the Palace," said one of Hamid-Jones's captors, shoving him forward.

CHAPTER 17

The soldiers came again at about three in the morning for another prisoner, the fifth since midnight. There was a rattle of locks at the end of the dank corridor, followed by the hollow ring of footsteps on stone. The prisoners in the crammed cells fell silent as they waited to see where they would stop.

"Doesn't the Emir ever sleep?" grumbled one of Hamid-Jones's cellmates, a once-portly man named ibn Nuri who had been an official in the Department of Paradise Maintenance; he had been arrested for sabotage, Hamid-Jones had learned, when some of the caged nightingales confiscated from the Vizier's gardens had failed to sing.

"The Emir has insomnia," said the human skeleton chained at Hamid-Jones's left. His name was Asad, and he had been here longer than any of them. He knew the prison routine better than anyone. "It soothes him to watch the executioner," Asad said. "It looks like an all-night session tonight."

The footsteps stopped outside the cell door and conversation ceased. Hamid-Jones's cellmates avoided looking at one another. A key grated in the lock and the dim light from the corridor threw the shadows of the soldiers over the cement floor. The warder followed them in, a squat toad of a man who kept well away from the men chained to the walls, though none of them could have reached him.

"Mustapha al-Sif," the warder said.

Mustapha stood up unwillingly. "Not me," he said. "It's a mistake."

"No mistake, brother. Be brave."

The soldiers grasped Mustapha's arms firmly while the warder unlocked his leg chains and cinched a plastic hobble in place. Then the warder, consulting a list, chalked a symbol on the man's forehead.

Mustapha went white. "What was it?" he whispered. "For the love of God, somebody tell me what he wrote."

Asad lifted an emaciated face. "It was only a simple X, brother. Have courage. One stroke of the axe and it will all be over."

Asad was lying. Hamid-Jones saw that the chalk mark was more complicated—a sort of chevron with a line through it.

"There were too many strokes for an X," Mustapha said, growing agitated.

"It often feels like that, brother," Asad said calmly. "The mind plays tricks. You must have moved before he completed the stroke."

"Yes, that must have been it," Mustapha said, still pale. He hobbled after the soldiers as best he could. The door clanged shut and the footsteps retreated down the corridor.

"Why did you tell him that?" Hamid-Jones said.

"To make the walk easier for him," Asad replied. "Let him have a few extra minutes before he realizes what they're going to do to him."

"What was the mark?"

"He'll be beheaded. But the executioner will draw him first. It could be worse. He may be lucky and faint."

Hamid-Jones shuddered.

"They say the warders can sometimes be bribed," ibn Nuri said. "One hundred dinars for an X. But you've got to have connections on the outside."

"None of us has connections anymore, brother," Asad said. "When you're on the Chamberlain's list, no one dares to help."

"We're all still alive," ibn Nuri said. "They've only taken four men from this cell in the last week."

"It's just a matter of time, brother," Asad said. "They'll get around to all of us sooner or later. They've mostly been working the east cells the last few days—they've got a lot of civil offenders there. The Emir must be on a dismemberment jag. When he gets tired of that, the Chamberlain will throw in a few more unusual sentences for variety's sake." He turned his wasted face toward Hamid-Jones. "What are you in for, brother?" he asked.

"I was one of the Vizier's assistants," Hamid-Jones said.

Asad turned his face away and did not ask any more questions. All around Hamid-Jones there was a discreet scraping of chains on stone as people tried subconsciously to put an extra inch or two of distance between him and them.

It was only about ten minutes later when the outer door rattled again and the sound of footsteps was heard in the corridor. "That was fast," Asad said. "The executioner must have bungled it."

"Allah is merciful," ibn Nuri said.

The footsteps stopped outside and the cell door swung open.

"It isn't fair," a prisoner whimpered. "Two, one right after the other from the same cell."

They had changed shifts. It was a different warder and another set of soldiers. But they moved just as purposefully, and the warder had the same list in his hand.

"Abdul ben Arthur Hamid-Jones," he said.

Hamid-Jones rose slowly to his feet, the chains dragging at him. The soldiers held him firmly while the warder exchanged his chains for plastic cuffs and hobble. Then, with the frown of a man doing serious work, the warder drew a design on Hamid-Jones's forehead. Hamid-Jones did not need a mirror to tell that the symbol was rather more intricate even than the one that had been chalked on Mustapha.

Asad did not try to soothe him. His cellmates drew aside as the soldiers marched him past their chained ranks to the door.

"Take it easy," Hamid-Jones said. "I can't walk fast in these things."

No one answered him. They passed into the outer corridor and through a series of twisting passageways that climbed steadily upward. The way seemed longer to Hamid-Jones than the way in had been, but he supposed that they were heading toward the throne room above. A wash of ice water went through his veins as he remembered what was waiting for him there—the black leather Carpet of Blood, the scarred chopping block, the pegboard display hung with various ingenious hooks, screws, winches, pulleys, and electrically heated pincers.

The soldiers hustled Hamid-Jones along, supporting him when he stumbled. At the end of one branching corridor was a dogged door, old and rusted. The warder turned a spoked wheel with some effort and fastened the door behind them. A second door was beyond it. The warder wrestled with a toggle, and when the door popped open the soldiers propelled Hamid-Jones through it.

A slap of cold air hit him in the face. It was too thin to be much good for breathing. He took a great labored breath and it seared his lungs. Someone clapped a respirator over his face.

He looked up and saw stars, huge and brilliant. A chill Martian night started to freeze him to the bone.

His captors, still bare-faced, shoved him into a waiting ground car and piled in after him. A driver was hunched over the control yoke, and as soon as the door spun shut he gunned the vehicle forward with a weaving movement that told Hamid-Jones he was in a ground effect machine, one whose compressors and fans were powerful enough to lift it from zero and set it going in seconds.

The floater picked up speed fast, heading toward the corner of a wall in what seemed to be a blind courtyard. At the last moment, when a collision seemed imminent, there was the jolt of a silent explosion underneath and the floater popped up like a cork in water, cleared the top of the wall and plumped down on the other side. It rocked for a moment, then spurted across the desert.

"No alarm from the palace," the warder said, looking backward. "I guess we got away with it."

"There's a blind spot in the monitor board," one of the soldiers said, shucking off his robes to show civilian clothes underneath. "Mrabet got a worm into the camera for that courtyard. It shows a looped image of the wall over and over again."

All four men were busily removing their disguises. They left their heads impiously uncovered. The two had spoken with foreign accents, one that Hamid-Jones could not quite place for the moment.

"Who are you people?" he demanded.

"Friends, *ya* Abdul," said the one who had posed as a warder. "You're too valuable to be ground up into fertilizer for the Chamberlain's gardens."

"What do you want with me?"

"It will all be explained. You're going to help to change the universe."

It was a pleasant room with an attractive view, though there were no windows. The landscape outside was only a holographic projection behind the window frames. It had been explained to Hamid-Jones that the walls, ceiling, and floor were a complex sandwich, baffled against microwave, laser pickup of sound vibrations, muon scanners, and anything else the security busters could think of. The entire room itself, he had been given to understand, floated on huge coiled springs resting in a bed of liquid nitrogen through which randomized ultrasonic waves were propagated.

"Diplomatic privileges are not always respected as they should be," the ambassador had remarked dryly. "We have the satan of a time with our diplomatic pouches as well. For the really sensitive ones we supply laser mirrors and other defenses that burn out the more obnoxious peeper devices."

Hamid-Jones glanced at the scenery showing through the false windows. The landscape was as green and lush as Earth's, but there were two suns in the clear azure sky. The second sun was only an orange point of light, but it was very bright, casting its own long shadows.

"Is that the view from Alpha Centauri?" Hamid-Jones asked.

"Alpha Centauri Alif," the ambassador said. "From its third planet, the seat of the Sultan's empire. There are also thriving populations on the planets of Alpha Centauri Baa' and Proxima. It all makes for a tidy domain—a whole clutch of inhabited worlds at little more than planetary distances. Of course that's because we had a fresh start. Here at Sol, even Earth itself is fragmented among rival potentates."

"That must make the Sultan a very powerful ruler."

"The scale of his dominions has never before been seen in human history. Your little Martian Emirate can't begin to compare." The ambassador stroked the corkscrew curls of his square-cut beard. "Of course the obstacle to his exercising that power as it should be exercised is distance. Distance makes each little frog the sovereign of his own pond."

"And the Sultan wants to rule all the ponds?"

The ambassador shook his fine head. "The Sultan is not a tyrant. Far from it, no matter what nonsense your Solarian image makers try to fill people's heads with. He believes that he governs best who governs least. He doesn't want to strip friendly and reasonable rulers of their thrones—only to exercise a benign influence."

"I'm grateful to you for saving my life, of course," Hamid-Jones said stiffly.

"Ah, ya Abdul, al-Sharq warned me that you were a difficult young man. He said you refused to swear allegiance to him, but that you fought bravely with the Bedouins all the same."

Hamid-Jones kept his lips shut.

The ambassador sighed. "It was a mistake to try to bribe you that time—but I'll tell you frankly that I think the better of you for refusing me. Even though you were in the service of a corrupt master. Now you must decide. Do you intend to transfer your stubborn loyalty to the bloodthirsty wart who pretends to be the Emir and his eunuch familiar? If so, you might as well go back to the condemned cell.''

"No," Hamid-Jones said tightly. "Let's get on with the debriefing."

"Good," the ambassador said. "You're our only available firsthand source of knowledge about the new clone. In a sense, you helped to create him. Al-Sharq's given me the highlights of your evaluation, but I want to hear it from your own lips."

Hamid-Jones hesitated. "Please, before we start . . . can you tell me anything about Rubinstein? I never heard how he finally died."

Pity showed in the ambassador's patrician features. "He was still alive a month ago, though he might have preferred not to be. They put him on display in the major population centers, for anyone to abuse. The idea being, of course, to demolish any vestiges of his remembered power. Then, when they'd squeezed all possible public relations value out of it, he was returned to the Palace. His cage—" The ambassador made a grimace of distaste. "—was taken to the Chamberlain's bedroom. As another gruesome memento, I gather. Nobody's seen him since."

Hamid-Jones squeezed his eyes shut, but he could not blot out the memory of Ismail pulling the plug on the Emir's head.

"One would hope that the eunuch did not keep him around too long," the ambassador went on. "Perhaps he would have found it difficult to tolerate the smell, if nothing else. Don't fret, ya Abdul. It would have been a kindness."

"What is it you want to know?" Hamid-Jones said roughly.

To his surprise, the ambassador did not begin with questions to verify the operation that had turned Bobo into a second Emir, or even ask him to confirm the demise of the original head. Instead, he asked about al-Sharq.

"You had the opportunity to talk to al-Sharq personally. What did you think about him?"

"He's an impressive figure," Hamid-Jones said without hesitation. "He inspires loyalty."

The ambassador's eyes bored into his. "Give me your best opinion. Would he make a good ruler of Mars?"

It took about four hours to squeeze Hamid-Jones dry.

The first hour was simply a rather informal conversation with the ambassador over tea and cakes. The ambassador asked a lot of probing, intelligent questions—and a few that seemed pointless to Hamid-Jones, though the ambassador was very particular about getting precise answers to them. After that, the ambassador brought in a parade of technical experts on the embassy staff—quick, feral young men who interrogated him on subjects that ranged from Bobo's medical records before and after the head transplant to the kind of weaponry carried by the eunuch security guards in Ismail's suite. Last of all was an intelligence ministry psychologist, who hooked him up to a lot of complicated monitors and used deep-recall techniques on him. He must have been unconscious for the last part of it, because he found himself sitting in the ambassador's armchair with the sensors and needles detached, and the two suns in the holographic landscape outside the false windows considerably higher in the alien sky.

The ambassador rang for more tea, and thanked Hamid-Jones for his cooperation.

"Invaluable detail," he said. "It makes all the difference. Our intelligence analysts are very good—they can spin whole universes from a sneeze. But there's nothing like an inside man. It was worth all the risk we took to rescue you. We'll encode the transcript and send it off to Charon right away."

"Charon?"

"Yes. One of our secure radio links. We have a rather large communications facility in the Oort Cloud that handles interstellar traffic for all the Centauran embassies in the Solar system. We've planted our own system of radio relay buoys all the way to the Centauran cometary cloud." He gave a frank smile. "Only the harmless stuff gets sent through the regular interstellar beacons—and we encode it all to make our Martian and Terran hosts work for it."

Hamid-Jones tried not to show his surprise. He was beginning to realize dimly the extent to which the Sultan of Alpha Centauri had his fingers in the Solar system's pies. He'd known, of course, that the Sultan was financing al-Sharq's revolutionary movement, and he'd just had a graphic demonstration that the Centaurans had even infiltrated the Emir's dungeons. But now he was starting to wonder just how big a game the Sultan was really playing—here and among the other inhabited stars.

"We'll have hard copy aboard the next starship to Alpha Centauri, of course," the ambassador went on. "It leaves this week. But the radio transmission will beat it there by a year—fortunately we don't have to boost radio waves up to lightspeed at a paltry one G, the way we do with ships carrying human beings. And that year will make a difference in our planning."

"Planning?" Hamid-Jones repeated stupidly. It was hard to conceive of planning on that cosmic a scale.

"Oh, yes," said the ambassador. "Time is of the essence. I think you're correct in assuming that this bogus Emir of yours will want to skip the upcoming Caliphate Congress. And the rest of a fragmented Solar system won't be able to agree on another candidate. They'll squabble among themselves, as usual, and you can be sure that our agents here will do their best to keep things hot. The congress will dissolve without agreement, as congresses have been doing for the last thousand years, and there'll be another congress ten years hence. Ten years is all we need."

Ten years, Hamid-Jones realized, was just about the amount of time required for a round trip to Alpha Centauri, including the sliding scale for boosting and deboosting. The figure could not be a coincidence.

The Sultan had something up his sleeve. Something specific.

"The Sultan," Hamid-Jones ventured, "will be faced with the same irreducible problem ten years from now. He can't come to Mecca to campaign. He daren't leave his kingdom for ten years even to undertake the hajj. And even if some miracle were to make him Caliph of Islam despite that handicap, he couldn't exercise real power from afar. He'd have a bunch of heads of state paying lip service to his piety, and doing pretty much as they pleased."

"An excellent analysis, ya Abdul. But the situation may change."

"How? You can't change the laws of nature."

A small, secret smile played about the ambassador's lips. "What if you didn't have to change the laws of nature, ya Abdul?"

"Forgive me, your Excellency. Every so often someone announces that he's found a way to trisect the angle or square the circle or has discovered the secret of perpetual motion, but it always turns out that there's a flaw in the reasoning. If you're suggesting that it's somehow possible to travel faster than the speed of light . . ."

"No, I'm not suggesting that, ya Abdul. I'm only asking, what if a solution could be found to the problem of interstellar empire which did not violate Allah's rules?"

"Then Allah would indeed be magnanimous," Hamid-Jones said with raised eyebrows.

The ambassador's eyes twinkled. "Indeed He would, *ya* Abdul. And as in so many other things, perhaps His prophet has already given us a hint as to His way. As the parable goes, 'If the mountain will not come to Mohammed, then Mohammed must go to the mountain.' In other words, one must look at the problem differently. The problem of star travel is that of great distance and a limiting velocity. If one can't do anything about the limiting velocity, perhaps one can do something about the distance."

To Hamid-Jones it sounded very much as if some scientific charlatan had been trying to sell the Sultan of Alpha Centauri a bill of goods. Like some new form of the old, discredited "hyperspace" notion, where one got a free ride to one's destination through a medium whose scale of distances was much smaller than that of the real universe. Or the mythical "worm holes" supposedly bored through space by black holes, through which a space ship could skylark without being torn to pieces.

The late Emir, too, had succumbed to the scientists and mullahs who told him what he wanted to hear. Hamid-Jones's estimate of the Sultan went down a notch.

"Well, physics is best left to the physicists," he said in an attempt at breeziness. "I can't offer any opinions there. I can only be of help, possibly, in the political picture."

"Quite so, *ya* Abdul, quite so," the ambassador said gravely. "The Sultan owes you a debt, and he always pays his debts. You can't remain on Mars, that's for certain. Besides, the Sultan will want to thank you in person."

"I don't understand, your Excellency."

"There's only one remedy for your current plight. We'll have to smuggle you to Alpha Centauri."

Hamid-Jones sat there, stunned. "Alpha Centauri?" he said slowly.

"Don't look so surprised, *ya* Abdul. You didn't think we were going to hide you in the embassy forever?"

"N-no, but I thought . . ."

"You thought that somehow you'd evade the thousands of police and security forces who are combing Tharsis for you, get past the army and out into the desert, outwit the paid informers who've been alerted at every oxygen oasis, and join up with al-Sharq's forces again. If he'd have you."

"Something like that," Hamid-Jones said sullenly. He resented the ambassador's condescending tone.

"My dear young man, you're of no value to anybody, including yourself, here on Mars. We didn't snatch you from the dungeons only to give you back to the Emir's thugs, you know."

"That's my problem." Hamid-Jones realized he was being rude, and added grudgingly, "I know you've gone to a lot of trouble over me, and all that, but Mars is my home and it's in the grip of a tyrant that *I* helped to create. I'm not running away from the fight."

"Al-Sharq has plenty of fedayeen fighting for him. You'll be more valuable to him as a lobbyist."

"A *what*?"

"The game is larger than you think, *ya* Abdul. So far you've been only a minor piece on the board. But now you're going to get a chance to play a larger part."

Hamid-Jones thought of all the people who had died to overthrow the Emir and his grafted reincarnation. The Clonemaster. Rubinstein, who'd worse than died. The sheik and all the desert tribesmen who'd been betrayed in the Mesogaean skyhook ambush. Even Aziz—assuming he'd been one of the betrayed and not the betrayer, and whom in any case he'd never see again.

He shook his head stubbornly. "I don't know about your grand design. I've lost too many friends. I'm not running out on them."

The ambassador sighed. "You won't be running out on anybody. Al-Sharq won't take you back anyway. He'd rather have you on Alpha Centauri."

"He would?"

"He *needs* someone to politic for him there—somebody who knows first hand what kind of a war he's fighting. There are Palace factions who want to cut off his funds and throw their support to fedayeen groups with whom he's at odds. There are other factions that favor backing him but don't have the slightest notion of what kind of supplies he needs to be effective. I believe that on one occasion he actually received a shipment of watercraft instead of the mechanical sandwalkers he'd requested eight years earlier. Military intelligence is no good at four light years—what's needed is someone on the spot with intuition." He paused balefully. "And while *you* don't care about our grand design, as you call it, al-Sharq does. He wants to fit into the Sultan's big picture. It's the only way he can be sure of getting what *he* wants out of it when all the political dust settles."

"I don't know anything about such things," Hamid-Jones protested.

"You'll learn, *ya* Abdul," the ambassador laughed. "After all, you learned to ride a camel."

Hamid-Jones lay in darkness, feeling every cushioned jolt transmitted through his hermetically sealed coffin. Despite the little heater they'd given him, he could feel the chill from the layer of liquid nitrogen that surrounded his supposedly insulated shell; it was small comfort to know that if the shell sprang a leak he'd be instantly frozen into a human popsicle. If he'd understood the ambassador correctly, randomized waves of ultrasound were traveling through the fluid to thwart any possible spy devices at customs, and a clever little computer program built into his cocoon made him look like a mailbag to any prying muon probes.

"How are you going to get me out of here?" he'd asked the ambassador when he'd finally given in, and the ambassador had replied, "Why, we'll mail you in a diplomatic pouch."

He could feel movement now—the first since the bumpy ride across the desert had ended with a toboggan ride down a chute into a depot. Probably a forklift was manhandling him, wheeling him into one of the parked nacelles that was waiting for the Deimos skyhook.

He remembered the last time he'd seen the skyhook in action—unreeling itself from Mars' not-quite-synchronous moon thousands of miles above and slamming into the ground at a hundred miles an hour, then being yanked up into the sky again on its superfilament cable after it had disgorged its load of soldiers.

It made a vivid picture.

The forklift dropped him unceremoniously. He found himself upended, sprawling to brace himself.

No damage seemed to have been done. At least he had not turned into sherbet. He hoped rather impersonally that his air supply would hold out until he got past the Emir's customs and Centauran officials in the Deimos spaceport could pry him out of his tomb.

But he wasn't at all worried about it. They'd given him some sort of tranquilizer to hold any possible panic reaction at bay— other smuggled refugees in the past had sometimes reacted to confinement and sensory deprivation with hysteria, injuring themselves. But the tranquilizer acted only on the primitive portion of his brain, evidently. He was thinking as clearly as ever—able to worry about abstractions, like the fate of Mars, but with a profound disinterest in his own physical situation.

The force-grown false whiskers, cloned from his own DNA and spliced to his stubble by nanomachines, itched. They were beautifully curled and ribboned. The ambassador had assured him that he looked like a real Centauran now. He had a false identity to match, and a backtracked biography in all the appropriate data banks. It only had to get him across a few acres of spaceport and into the starship, which was Centauran territory. A ringer would switch places with him at the terminal, a bona fide Centauran junior attaché who had already been passed through Mars-side customs and spaceport security.

Hamid-Jones's tranquilized but marvelously lucid consciousness returned to his parting conversation with the ambassador.

"So far you've seen only a corrupt dictatorship on Mars, and a tired and fragmented Earth still groaning under the burdens of its past, *ya* Abdul," the ambassador had said as the technicians prepared to seal the lid of the diplomatic pouch. "We started fresh on Alpha Centauri. Now you're going to have a chance to see what a benign and brilliant Islamic society can be like."

"I just want to help al-Sharq and his freedom fighters kick that damned clone off the throne," Hamid-Jones had replied. It had just occurred to him with renewed poignance that if the revolution were won while he was on Alpha Centauri, he wouldn't hear the news for another four years, and that it would take him another five years to get back home.

"Oh, you'll certainly do that, and it's a fine and noble aim," the ambassador had said with a wave of the hand. "But I hope you'll eventually come to realize that it's not a final goal in itself. There's more at stake than the overthrow of one petty tyrant on one planet. The game's played with stars, and it's nothing less than the transformation of the universe—a gathering of all the inhabited stars under a wise and compassionate Caliph who will outshine the splendors of previous caliphs as a sun outshines a moon."

The tranquilizer was beginning to take hold by then. Hamid-Jones, with the clarity it brought, thought to himself that the ambassador was laying it on a bit thick. A gathering of stars seemed a rather grandiose way to describe what could only be an attenuated association of isolated stellar systems under the purely symbolic hegemony of a Caliph. At best, there could be some kind of slow motion commerce and cultural exchange between Alpha Centauri and Sol themselves, with perhaps one or two nearby stars like Tau Ceti and Epsilon Eridani thrown in for good measure.

"You're to be envied, *ya* Abdul," the ambassador went on. "You'll take part in the flowering of a great, benign empire, where the arts and sciences flourish under a tolerant shepherd, and all people—believers and unbelievers alike—have a chance at a decent life. An Islamic civilization as Islam should be—not brother against brother."

Perhaps things *would* be better on Alpha Centauri, Hamid-Jones thought as the cryogenic coffin lid clanged down on him. They couldn't be worse.

He was still thinking about the new world he had indentured himself to when he felt a shudder rock his dark confines. That could only be the muffled blow of the skyhook, latching into the static line assembly of the mail pallet at a hundred miles an hour. There was a long wait as the rushing bulk of the Martian moon high above stretched twelve thousand miles of elastic line taut.

Then there was a tremendous yank and a rising sensation, as Hamid-Jones was hoisted to the stars.

The Mechanical Sky
concludes in Book Two
A Gathering of Stars
Published by Del Rey Books

About the Author

Donald Moffitt was born in Boston and now lives in rural Maine with his wife, Ann, a native of Connecticut. A former public relations executive, industrial filmmaker, and ghost-writer, he has been writing fiction on and off for more than twenty years under an assortment of pen names, including his own, chiefly espionage novels and adventure stories in international settings. His first full-length science-fiction novel and the first book of any genre to be published under his own name was *The Jupiter Theft* (Del Rey, 1977). "One of the rewards of being a public relations man specializing in the technical end of large corporate accounts," he says, "was being allowed to hang around on the fringes of research being done in such widely disparate fields as computer technology, high-energy physics, the manned space program, polymer chemistry, parasitology, and virology—even, on a number of happy occasions, being pressed into service as an unpaid lab assistant." He became an enthusiastic addict of science fiction during the Golden Era, when Martians were red, Venusians green, Mercurians yellow, and "Jovian Dawn Men" always blue. He survived to see the medium become respectable and is cheered by recent signs that the fun is coming back to sf.

DONALD MOFFITT'S
SCIENCE FICTION

IS OUT OF THIS
WORLD